DON'T BELIEVE IT

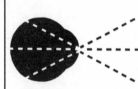

DON'T BELIEVE IT

CHARLIE DONLEA

THORNDIKE PRESS
A part of Gale, a Cengage Company

Farmington Hills, Mich • San Francisco • New York • Waterville, Maine
Meriden, Conn • Mason, Ohio • Chicago

Copyright © 2018 by Charlie Donlea.
Thorndike Press, a part of Gale, a Cengage Company.

LIBRARY OF CONGRESS CIP DATA ON FILE.
CATALOGUING IN PUBLICATION FOR THIS BOOK
IS AVAILABLE FROM THE LIBRARY OF CONGRESS

ISBN-13: 978-1-4328-5171-2 (hardcover)

Published in 2018 by arrangement with Kensington Books, an imprint
of Kensington Publishing Corp.

Printed in the United States of America
1 2 3 4 5 6 7 22 21 20 19 18

To Red,
Fisherman, father, friend

ACKNOWLEDGMENTS

As always, I'm indebted to the great folks at Kensington Publishing. Thanks to my editor, John Scognamiglio, whose mind, I've discovered, never stops working to fine-tune the details of a story he loves. I'm lucky enough to have written this manuscript under his watchful eye, and it's a much better book because of it. Thanks to the amazing sales force, who manages to get my books everywhere and gives me the thrill of seeing my novels next to authors who have inspired my career. And thanks to Jackie Dinas and the sub-rights division, who work hard to sell my books around the world!

Thanks again to my agent, Marlene Stringer, who has become one of my greatest cheerleaders. Foresight and composure are great talents, and she has both.

I tip my hat to Bev Cousins, my editor at

Random House Australia, for her insights into this story, which helped polish the final version.

Thanks to my first readers – Amy, Mary, and this time around, Chris. Your observations and suggestions made *Don't Believe It* much stronger than when I first handed you the manuscript.

Running a household is difficult, and doing it nearly solo while your husband hides in the den and disappears before sunrise is even harder. Thanks to my remarkable wife, Amy, for keeping our lives on track while I chase my dream. To Abby and Nolan for giving up the computer when I needed to beat a deadline, and for decorating my office with every piece of promotional material they could find for *Don't Believe It* in order to cheer me over the finish line. It worked!

I know nothing about television production or international law, and leaned heavily on many people to help me. Thanks to the producers at NBC who took my calls and answered my questions. Nothing about my fictional documentary is true, or even possible, but it worked for my story.

Thanks to my old friend, Michael Chmelar,

Assistant U.S. Attorney, who took my calls and answered my emails for nothing more than my meager payment of a couple of beers at an outdoor patio in the heat of summer. You are a much smarter man than I am, and your smarts helped me navigate the world of international law. I used my literary license when I needed the law to work for my story, so anything "illegal" that occurs in this book is my doing, not Mike's.

Finally, thanks to my niece, Sidney Ella, for allowing me to borrow her name for my protagonist.

DOCUMENTARY: A movie or television program based on or re-creating an actual event, era, or life story that purports to be factually accurate and contains no fictional elements.

— *Cambridge English Dictionary*

In feature films the director is God; in documentary films God is the director.
— Alfred Hitchcock

■ ■ ■ ■

SUGAR BEACH:
ST. LUCIA,
EASTERN CARIBBEAN

■ ■ ■ ■

Gros Piton
Jalousie Plantation
March 29, 2007

The blood was a problem.

I knew it as soon as I felt it spit across my face. It streamed from his hairline and ran along his jaw until it dribbled onto the granite bluff, first in sporadic red blots, like the leading raindrops of a coming storm, and then in a continuous stream, as though a spigot had been plugged into the spot on his head where I had struck him and had opened wide. It was an error in judgment and strategy, which was a shame because up to now I had been perfect.

A moment earlier, the soft soles of my shoes had squished through the mud on the final turn of my arduous hike up the Piton. My system was rich with adrenaline, which made my journey nearly effortless. The endorphins would serve me well. I would need their analgesic and energy-producing powers to get back down the mountain as quickly as I'd made it up. To kill someone required perfection, timing, and luck. I hoped all three were with me this evening.

He came into view. As he stared out over the bluff, the setting sun cast his shadow toward me like a black panther painted over the ground. He stood next to the blanket he had laid over the granite, a bottle of champagne and two flutes waiting. In the backdrop the sun was approaching the horizon, casting its glow across the calm Caribbean waters and interrupted only by a sailboat whose bright spinnaker was bloated with the evening breeze.

It was one hundred feet to the water. A straight drop, and shallow at the base of the mountain. No way for the sea to substantially break his fall. I'd confirmed this the day before. I had put much thought into this evening. Besides the depth of the water, I calculated the time it would take for me to reach the bluff and return to my cottage. I plotted my route back through the resort. I factored in the unexpected, a necessity to any proper strategy. And, most important, I considered the amount of time I would spend with him on the bluff. It wouldn't be long.

From my spot in the foliage, I took a few silent steps forward until he was accessible, close enough to touch. But physical touch would be limited this evening. Physical touch would leave clues and fibers and forensics. My weapon allowed me to stay at a safe distance. I lifted it, pausing slightly at the peak of the arc when my hand was raised high above my head, then brought it down in a sharp rap against his skull. The connection was solid. A direct strike that he didn't anticipate and likely never felt. Besides a quick synapse that radiated through the neurons of his central nervous system, he likely felt nothing at all. No pain, no suffering. Unless, of course, he was still conscious when he went over the edge. I try not to dwell on that.

I knew immediately that I had been too aggressive with my assault. My goal was to stun him and render him incapable of defending himself. Instead, my strike nearly killed him. He reflexively reached for the back of his head and fell to his knees. I waited and watched, unsure how things would progress. He seemed to recognize the blood as it poured onto the granite, and gained enough wherewithal to stagger back to his feet. Before he could turn around, my shoe met the back of his pants and he was gone. I didn't hear him land, never heard a splash. I dared not venture to the edge of the bluff for fear that someone had spotted his body tumbling toward the ocean, like a skydiver whose chute had failed, and would subsequently look to the source of the fall and see me peering over the ledge.

I assessed the bluff now and worked to figure out the best way to fix my blunder. The blood would tell a different story than I had hoped to draw tonight. It took only a fraction of a second to make my decision. The carnage on the bluff was impossible to hide. The splatter across my face, however, needed to be addressed. On closer inspection, the spray of blood streaked down my chest and onto my left hand. Another collection of red, I noticed, had speckled my weapon. It was an unfortunate error — unforced and brought on entirely by my eagerness. There was no way to solve all of these problems. I chose the most pressing — the blood that was covering me — and settled on a solution. I turned from the setting sun and the blood-covered bluff and ran down the Piton, stomping over dirt and through brush and down the man-made staircase of boulders and bamboo on a beeline to the cottage.

Gros Piton
The Bluff
March 29, 2007

Julian Crist made the hike up Gros Piton in
St. Lucia's southwestern point in just under
thirty minutes. Summiting the Piton was a
popular tourist excursion, and he and his
group had made the trek the day before.
This evening, though, Julian ascended only
to the Soufriere Bluff, a spot he had found
yesterday and determined to be a perfect
place to watch the sunset. A simple hike, it
required little more than following the trail
that spun its way around the base of the
mountain. The most strenuous part of the
journey was a steep climb up a series of fifty
steps built into the side of the cliff by native
St. Lucians who used boulders and bamboo
to create a navigable staircase across the
steep lower gorge.

Once a hiker was past the only spirited

challenge on the way up to Soufriere Bluff, the rest of the climb was a tranquil waltz along a dirt path that offered occasional glimpses of the Caribbean Sea and the Jalousie Plantation. It was a picturesque hike, but when he made it to the clearing, Julian knew he'd picked a flawless location for what he had planned. He pulled his backpack off his shoulders and laid the blanket across the smooth granite of the bluff. Below him was a pristine view of the Pitons Bay, where, in about forty minutes, the sun would descend from the cloudless blue sky and sink into the horizon.

He checked his watch. To make up for his foolishness, the setting needed to be perfect before she arrived. He had nearly ruined everything earlier today. He'd been wrong to accuse her, especially when it was he who was hiding things. But he'd make it up to her tonight. He pulled two champagne flutes from his bag and popped the top on a bottle of Veuve Clicquot Yellow Label, the cork rocketing into the air in a high arc until it fell out of sight over the edge of the bluff. His stomach dropped as he watched the cork's flight. For the twentieth time since starting up Gros Piton, Julian checked his pocket, rubbing his fingers over the edges to make sure he hadn't lost it.

With everything prepared, Julian stood to the side of the blanket as he looked out at the falling sun. A sailboat, with its colorful sail full of wind, angled across Pitons Bay. Down to his right, he could see Sugar Beach and the small group gathering to watch the sunset. If there were a more beautiful place on earth, he'd never seen it.

He heard a twig snap behind him, and wondered briefly how she had reached the bluff without him sensing her approach. Before this thought could trigger his muscles to react, a jolt coursed through his body. It started in his head, a quick shock that stalled time and congested his movements, like swimming through oil. Only the trickle of blood through his hair and over his ear caused his mind to catch up with the present. He touched the spot on his head where the shock wave had originated, managing to get his hands back out in front of himself as he fell forward onto his knees. On all fours, he watched as blood fell onto the granite as he leaned forward, like an artist dribbling paint onto a canvas. The sun highlighted his right hand, the fingers of which were shiny red prongs that felt as though they belonged to someone else.

He staggered back to his feet and took unsteady steps, two forward and one to the side in an attempt to turn around. A firm jerk — a shoe planted in the small of his back — snapped his neck backward and sent him careening toward the edge of the bluff. He felt his stomach rise again, as if he were rewatching the arc of the champagne cork. A twisted image of the mountain face, lush with green foliage, filled his vision for three full seconds before the ocean came up and grabbed him.

High on Soufriere Bluff, the setting sun highlighted the spilled blood and cast shadows of the champagne bottle and two flutes across the granite. They stretched to their full length, three inanimate objects pulling all the contradictory darkness of their shadows from the brightness of the sun, until an hour later when they faded and melted into the night.

Grand Courtroom
St. Lucia High Court
Nine Months Later

The NBC reporter stood in front of the camera, microphone in hand and the high court of St. Lucia framed behind her. The cameraman counted down, "Three, two, one." He pointed at her.

"We've just received word that the jury is back in the Grace Sebold case. It's been a long nine months for Julian Crist's family as they've sought justice for their son, who was killed here in St. Lucia back in March. A fourth-year student at New York Medical College, Julian Crist's body was found on the morning of March thirtieth having washed up on the famed Sugar Beach, where he and classmates had gathered over spring break to celebrate a friend's wedding. Originally believing it to be an accidental fall from one of St. Lucia's legendary Twin

Pitons, detectives quickly began to suspect foul play. Just two days into the investigation, Crist's fellow medical student and girlfriend, Grace Sebold, was taken into St. Lucian custody and charged with Julian's murder. An intense, and sometimes wild, trial followed in St. Lucia's High Court. Today, Grace Sebold's fate will be determined by a group of twelve jurors."

The reporter put her finger to her ear. "The jury, I'm being told, is returning. We're going to take you inside the courthouse for the verdict."

The production crew cut to the inside of the courthouse, which was crowded with spectators lining the pews like a busy Sunday church service. Reporters and cameramen from CNN, the BBC, and FOX News crowded along the back wall. The jury members shuffled into their spots, and the chamber buzzed with a silent trepidation that was broken occasionally by the snapping of cameras, their shutters opening and closing as photographers attempted to capture every gesture and facial expression. Through the stillness, a side door rattled open and a constable led Grace Sebold into the courtroom. The press was frenzied as they jockeyed for position to steal the best photo of the enigmatic Grace Sebold, described over the past three months as a combination of a brilliant future physician and ruthless murderer.

The constable led Grace to her counsel, who was seated at a table in front of the judge. The lawyer stood when Grace arrived and whispered into her ear. Grace gave a subtle nod. The magistrate brought the high court to order with three booming raps of his gavel.

"This is St. Lucia's High Court, Southern District, presiding over the case of St. Lucia versus Grace Sebold." He looked to the jury. "Foreman, have you come to a unanimous decision in this case?"

"Yes, Your Honor," the middle-aged man said, holding a thin folder.

The constable took the folder from the foreman and handed it to the judge, who placed it on the surface in front of him. His facial expression gave nothing away as he opened the file and silently read the verdict, then looked out at the crowded room.

"I would ask all who are present this morning to respect the high court by refraining from emotional reactions after I've read this verdict. I further ask the press to remain in the media section and to please cross none of the barriers that have been constructed."

The judge looked down at the verdict, paused briefly before setting his gaze on Grace Sebold.

"Ms. Sebold, please stand."

Grace stood, her chair piercing the silence of the courtroom with an awful screech as it slid across the tiled floor.

"In the case of St. Lucia versus Grace Sebold," the judge said, "on the count of first-degree homicide, the jury finds the defendant . . . guilty." A murmur went through the courthouse, a combination of applause from Julian Crist's family and supporters to weeping and gasps from Grace Sebold's parents.

"By order of the high court, Grace Janice Sebold, you have been found guilty of murder in the first degree and will be held at the Bordelais Correctional Facility to await sentencing. Ms. Sebold, do you fully understand the charges levied against you and the potential penalties for being held accountable for said charges?"

Grace mumbled a nearly inaudible *yes.*

"Would you like to address the court or the jurors, as is your right?"

Grace shook her head and mumbled again. *No.*

The judge rapped the gavel three more times as Grace Sebold's attorney tried to support her. The weight of her limp body overwhelmed him, and he settled her onto the hard wooden chair that had broken the silence of the courtroom moments before. The constable was quickly at her side, lifting her under her arm to usher her back to jail.

Despite the judge's continual gavel banging, reporters shouted questions as Grace left the courtroom.

"Did you do it, Grace?"

"Are you guilty?"

"Will you appeal this decision, Grace?"

"Are you remorseful for what you've done?"

"Do you want to say anything to Julian's family?"

One particularly adamant reporter made his way to the front of the barrier, leaned over the mahogany railing to get as close to the side door as was possible. The constable shuffled Grace toward the open doorway.

"Grace!" the reporter said in an urgency that caught her attention and made Grace glance at him. When their eyes met, the reporter shoved his microphone over the barrier, cutting the distance between him and Grace to an impressive twelve inches.

"Why did you kill Julian?"

Grace blinked at the bluntness of the

reporter's question. The constable swatted the microphone away and pushed Grace through the side door, leaving the shouting reporters and their clicking cameras behind.

■ ■ ■ ■

PART I
THE DOCUMENTARY

■ ■ ■ ■

CHAPTER 1

Hewanorra International Airport
St. Lucia
March 2017
Ten Years Later

Sidney Ryan finished tapping on her computer, saved her file, and folded the laptop closed. She reached under the seat and slipped it into her carry-on. The popping in her ears told her they had started their descent. She pulled a thick folder from her bag, opened it, and removed the maiden letter that had started her journey.

Dear Sidney,

It's been a while. Fifteen years? Congratulations on all your success. I've followed your career, as you can imagine, quite closely. You are a champion for those who cannot help themselves. As I'm sure you are aware, your accomplishments have echoed far beyond those who have directly benefited. For those like myself, whose fates have long ago been determined, you give hope that somehow things can still change.

I'll assume you know my story. And I hope this letter makes it into your hands. You are, quite literally, my last chance. I've exhausted the appeals process. It is different here than in the States. I've learned the St. Lucian justice system well over the last decade. There are no more loopholes to find, and no more formalities to follow. From this point forward, I can count on only one thing to help me — a re-examination of the evidence. Without it, I will spend my life here. And with each year that passes, it feels as though fewer and fewer people are looking at my case. Lately it seems that no one remembers me besides my family.

I'm writing you, Sidney, to ask you to consider helping an old friend. Of course, I understand no promises can be made. And I'm able to offer nothing in the way of compensation. Yet, I still find myself writing to you. I have no one else to ask.

My attorney and I can provide you with every bit of information about my case. Perhaps, if you look through it all, you will see what so many others have missed.

Thank you, Sidney, for anything you can do for an old friend.

Yours Sincerely,
Grace Sebold

Sidney folded the letter and looked out the window. The plane was on a gentle glide and ready to set down in the ocean when a runway reached out and grabbed the Airbus A330 to pull it safely onto dry land. A five-minute taxi settled the plane on the tarmac just outside the terminal doors. Everyone onboard opened overhead compartments and gathered bags. Sidney walked through the plane's exit door and stepped onto the landing of the staircase, where the humid Caribbean air quickly worked her skin to a glistening shine. She took the stairs to the tarmac and felt the heat of the pavement rise in invisible flames around her. The camera crew sorted their equipment as she headed into the terminal. Through customs thirty minutes later, she bounced in the backseat of the taxi van as the driver navigated the rolling mountains of St. Lucia and the twisting roads that cut through their slopes.

Hills lush with rain forest filled the windows of the taxi for most of the sixty-minute ride. Eventually the driver shifted to a lower gear and the van strained to climb a steep bank. As they crested the precipice on the outskirts of the Jalousie Plantation, the ocean came into view across the valley. In the middle of the afternoon, the water carried an emerald brilliance, and from such an elevated vantage point looked almost cartoonish as it smoldered bright cobalt in the area near shore, melting to a deeper navy farther out to sea.

The driver began the descent into the valley toward Sugar Beach Resort. Contrasting the journey to this point, which had been defined by a series of steep inclines barely conquered by the taxi van's straining engine, the ride down into the valley came with the constant squeak of brakes and slow turns around hairpins. The deeper they ventured into the basin, the higher the twin volcanic plugs of Gros Piton and Petit Piton rose on either side of them. The prehistoric nature of the precipitous mountains gave Sidney the sense of heading into Jurassic Park.

Finally the van made the last turn and tall iron gates parted as they approached the entrance to the resort. The humidity again mugged her when the door slid open and

Sidney climbed from the van.

"Ms. Ryan," a staff member said, extending a basket of ice-cold hand towels. "Welcome to Sugar Beach."

Sidney draped the towel across the back of her neck.

"The staff will manage your bags," the woman said in a pleasant Caribbean accent. "Your firm has already arranged check-in, so your room is waiting."

Sidney nodded and followed the woman onto a path lined by Lansan trees, the shade of which offered a reprieve from the heat. The staffer pointed out landmarks as they walked.

"The spa is that way," she said, pointing. "It's world renowned and highly recommended. Built directly into the rain forest."

Sidney smiled and nodded, surveying the tree-house–like structures built within the forest and the wooden staircases that twirled down to the ground.

The woman pointed in the other direction. "This path will take you to the beach."

Overhanging branches of palm trees cocooned the long cobblestone walkway. Their heavy fronds rustled in the ocean breeze toward the far end of the path, where a spot of bright sunshine and surf was just visible from where Sidney stood.

They made one more turn. "And here is your cottage."

The woman keyed the door and allowed Sidney to enter the posh room, the furniture of which was white and immaculate. Dark cherrywood floors shone brightly with afternoon sunlight that spilled through the windows and French doors.

"The bar is stocked with anything you might like — water, juice, and soda. Spirits as well. Your bags should arrive shortly."

"Thank you," Sidney said. She glanced at the placard outside the door: *306.*

"Yes," the woman said, recognizing the question in Sidney's eyes. "This was the room she stayed in."

Sidney nodded.

"Please call if you need anything," the woman said.

"Thank you."

Sidney closed the cottage door and allowed the air-conditioned interior to cool her body and unstick her shirt from her skin. She looked around the room, moving her gaze from the shining wooden floors to the lush bathroom accommodations, to the sun-drenched patio, and finally to the plush four-poster bed, with its brilliant white comforter. She ran her hand over the thick blanket before sitting on the edge.

Ten years earlier, Grace Sebold had slept in this very room the night Julian Crist was killed.

CHAPTER 2

The tropical gardens were plush and green as Sidney and her crew walked along the resort's serpentine paths that wound toward the beach. Once past the pool, her tennis shoes sank into the sand of Sugar Beach. Around her, the twin peaks sprouted into the sky. On her right and to the north, Petit Piton; on her left and to the south, Gros Piton. Laid between the summits was a two-hundred-yard stretch of sugar-white sand that glistened under the hot sun. Closer toward the water, the sand was darker, where the surf washed over it and bathed it into wet caramel.

"Ms. Ryan?" a young Caribbean man asked as he approached.

"Sidney." She reached out and shook his hand.

"Darnell. I'll be guiding you and your crew today. Are you ready?"

Sidney nodded. She looked back to her

camera guys and pointed to the Pitons. "Get these," she said to her crew. "A few stills from the base to the peak, with a clouded sky above. Maybe time-lapse it to get a tropical storm moving through. Might be a good promo, beautiful scenery one minute and a ferocious storm the next. Aerials would work well, if we can budget it." She looked back to Darnell. "Is the hike difficult?"

"To the summit?" He smiled. His teeth were broad and white. "Yeh, man. To the Soufriere Bluff? Easy."

"Easy?" Sidney asked.

"No problem." Darnell pointed to Sidney's bicep, then flexed his own and let out a jovial laugh. "Trust me. No problem."

Thirty minutes later, they had completed the necessary paperwork and signed the waivers required to partake in a guided hike up Gros Piton. The trip to the summit was an all-day excursion taking more than four hours. To the bluff where Julian Crist was killed required thirty minutes of walking along a narrow path flanked by heavy foliage, with occasional views of Pitons Bay to the north and the Jalousie Plantation to the east.

Sidney and her crew were halfway to the bluff when they came to a staircase made from boulders and flanked by a makeshift bamboo railing. The structure had been reinforced over the years with additional balustrades and a few odd rocks. The man-made arrangement tackled a steep gorge that would otherwise be too challenging to traverse.

"Darnell," Sidney said as they approached the Stone Age staircase. "Has this portion of the hike changed over the years?"

"No. Same now as it's always been."

"So, ten years ago, this was the same staircase?"

"Yeh, man. Same is same."

Sidney directed her crew. "Get this from bottom to top, and then top to bottom. Capture a first-person account of climbing up the staircase, no one else in the frame. And time me on the way up. Take a few more runs and get an average of how long it takes to walk it, jog it, and sprint it."

Sidney followed Darnell up the boulders, the first vigorous portion of the day's hike. With temperatures in the low nineties and 100 percent humidity, her tank top was soaked by the time she was halfway up the staircase.

A healthy thirty-six-year-old woman in good physical shape, Sidney considered that she was ten years older now than Grace had been when she supposedly made this journey. Sidney needed the aid of the bamboo railing to make it to the top. The steep incline toward the peak required her to grab the bamboo with both hands, one on each side, to hoist herself to the top. Once there, she surveyed the landing and then headed back down. At the foot of the stairs, she grabbed a tripod from one of the crewmembers and extended it to its full length, placed it over her shoulder, and repeated her climb up the boulders with only one hand available to grab the bamboo.

When Sidney was satisfied with her test runs, she found Darnell sitting in the shade of a Lansan. "How much farther?"

"Not much," Darnell said, pushing himself away from the tree's trunk. "A few switchbacks."

She followed Darnell along the narrow dirt path until they made one last turn. Then the foliage cleared and a bluff came into view — smooth beige granite that mirrored the afternoon sun. Sidney walked over to it, already visualizing how she could present this majestic and tragic scene.

"Is this it?" she asked as she walked carefully onto the bluff.

"Yeh, man." Darnell was more daring, walking fearlessly to the edge. "He went over right here. All the way down to the water." He pointed over the ledge, then smacked his palms together.

Sidney stopped a few feet from the edge, bent at the waist, and took a hesitant glance over the threshold. Her stomach rose into her throat. It was a long way down. She looked behind her. The camera crew was just now arriving after capturing the staircase from the angles she requested. Sidney walked over to Leslie Martin, her producing partner, turned back to look at the clearing and the bluff and the pristine view of Pitons Bay sparkling with afternoon sun. She put her arms out wide.

"I need a full shot of this view. A first-person perspective, coming around the bend and witnessing the bluff and the clearing and the bay. We'll need to get a shot at sunset as well, with the sun in the backdrop and long shadows creeping toward the camera. That's about the time he was killed."

"I can see the promo," Leslie said. "Gorgeous, but eerie."

Sidney nodded. "Get a blanket up here, too. With a bottle of champagne and two glasses. Low shot, okay? Ground level, with the glasses in the foreground and the setting sun behind them."

"You're a genius. I love it," Leslie said.

"It was a long time ago," Darnell interrupted. "When that boy went over the edge. What is the interest so many years later?"

"Research."

"For a book?"

"No, a film."

Darnell's bright smile appeared again. "A movie?"

"Documentary."

Sidney walked back onto the bluff as her camera crew prepared to film the area where Julian Crist was killed. She enjoyed a moment of solitude as she looked out over the ocean, and then down to Sugar Beach, where vacationers strolled hand in hand, their footsteps melting in the sand.

"Okay, St. Lucia. Tell me your story."

THE GIRL OF SUGAR BEACH
"Pilot" Episode
**Based on the interview with eyewitnesses
from the scene*

They were celebrating in St. Lucia and had chosen this morning, the day of their twentieth wedding anniversary, to watch the sunrise. With dark outlines of the twin Pitons rising on either side of Sugar Beach, like broad-shouldered guards on night watch, the couple strapped into their kayaks in the predawn hours. The sky was still dark and the moon was the only light that guided them as its charcoaled brightness fell softly across Pitons Bay. Sugar Beach, situated on the west side of the island, offered the perfect locale for sunsets. To witness the sunrise, vacationers needed to navigate across twelve miles of mountainous terrain to reach the eastern side of St. Lucia. The other option was to take to the ocean. A five-mile paddle over calm water brought kayakers to the southern tip of the island, just past Vieux Fort, and presented an unfettered view to the eastern horizon.

They clicked on their headlamps as they took off through the darkness, hugging the shoreline around Gros Piton. They stayed fifty yards off the coastline, keeping a good pace of nearly three knots. It was a strenuous workout they had undertaken many times before. They maintained a tandem formation, him in front of her so she could utilize his draft. After an hour of paddling, the black inkiness of night melted as a cerulean glow took to the sky. After three miles, he fell back and allowed her to take the lead until the southern portion of the island jetted away from them to the southeast. Here they kept a straight tack that took them farther offshore, a more direct line that eventually rendered a clear sight line to the horizon.

When they made it past Vieux Fort, floating in the middle of the Caribbean Sea, they pulled their kayaks together and drank from their water bottles. Their breathing came under control just as the sun emerged from the ocean. A magnificent sight, the tip of the sun pierced the horizon and the couple leaned over the edges of their kayaks and kissed.

After ten minutes, the sun was bright and its reflection spread from the horizon to capture their kayaks in its glow. They turned and started their journey back to Sugar Beach. The twin peaks in the distance acted as their navigational tool. With a steady northwest current, it took just over an hour to make it back to the base of Gros Piton, where they clung to its structure and paddled around its base. One final turn and Sugar Beach came into view. Still too early for resort life, the beach was empty but for a few early-morning walkers. The huts were vacant, and the bungalows void of activity. A few staff members prepared lounge chairs and hustled dishes and glassware to the beach bar.

She glided the kayak paddle through the water on the left side, then dipped the paddle into the water to her right. She'd repeated the same process for the past three hours. This time, however, her paddle didn't glide smoothly through the water, but instead struck a solid object. She jerked, scaring herself that a sea animal was ready to capsize the kayak. But when she looked into the water, she saw immediately that it was no animal.

Her scream was nearly enough to topple her husband, who was a few yards ahead and preparing to exit his kayak and step into the shallow waters off Sugar Beach. He pivoted in a quick U-turn as his wife continued in hysterics, slapping her paddle at the water in an effort to get away.

When he came up beside her, his stomach turned. The body floated on its stomach, arms and legs outstretched like a skydiver in midflight. A cloudy swirl of blood muddied the crystal-clear waters.

CHAPTER 3

"What's the interest, Ms. Ryan?" Inspector Claude Pierre asked.

A tall, thin man with hair so short his scalp was visible, Pierre had run the investigation division of the St. Lucian police force for the past two decades. A native St. Lucian, born and raised, he was a product of the island and the school system, and was an example of how hard work and determination could bring you to the top of your occupation. It was the same here on a small island as in any large city in the United States. Sidney had done her research on Inspector Pierre, and knew him to be a terribly proud man of his homeland and his role within it.

"I'm filming a documentary about Julian Crist, and looking for anyone who had knowledge about the case. Anyone who might be able to offer details."

"What is the nature of the documentary?"

"To tell the truth about what happened to Julian Crist. It will air in the States. I'm in St. Lucia on a fact-finding mission to gather details about the case and take some footage. My studio floated me a slim budget to get my crew down here to see if there's enough to run with."

"Enough what, Ms. Ryan? The Julian Crist case was closed many years ago. The truth has already been told."

"Enough intrigue," Sidney said.

Inspector Pierre smiled. "I'm not sure I'd call a young man's tragic death 'intriguing.' I'll presume you're looking for *disturbing* more than anything else."

Sidney was looking for much more than a disturbing story. She was looking for holes in the case. For things that might have been missed by Inspector Pierre and his associates. She was looking for clues that would confirm the story she'd read in the hundreds of letters Grace Sebold had sent her over the past two years in which the woman clung to her innocence and offered many examples of how the case had been mishandled. So, was she looking for disturbing? Sidney would never argue that unsettling stories didn't sell, but what she was really after was anything she could take back to her bosses at the network that might con-

51

vince them a grave injustice had taken place.

Sidney was tasked with putting together the pilot episode of her proposed documentary about Grace Sebold. The network would then decide if they'd give the project a summer run after they viewed the first few cuts. The documentary — assuming she could get it off the ground — would be Sidney's fourth. Her first two films had been online-only events streamed through a subscription service, and her third was an add-on to the prime-time news program *Events,* Sidney's first foray into television. She had done all the work — filming, writing, producing the hour-long special — only to play a secondary role to Luke Barrington, the face of the network's prime-time lineup, who insisted on narrating the special edition and ultimately received most of the credit for the documentary's success. Still, the network liked Sidney's work, and contracted her for another film. Her pitch was a biopic that broadly covered Grace Sebold's life, including the girl's love story with Julian Crist, her conviction for his murder, and the ten years she's spent in a St. Lucian prison, claiming innocence of the grisly crime. But to get such a project green-lit, Sidney needed proof that Grace Sebold's case had been mishandled. Proof that the St. Lucian government had pinned on her a crime she did not commit. That they'd made assumptions and mistakes ten years ago that had cost an innocent woman her freedom.

Sidney would share none of this with the man who was responsible for putting Grace Sebold behind bars. In order to keep her true motives hidden from Claude Pierre, she would focus her questions today on Julian Crist.

"Disturbing or otherwise, Inspector Pierre, I'm looking for facts," Sidney finally said. "It's been ten years since this boy was killed. Sadly, America has forgotten about him."

This statement was mostly true. America *had* forgotten about Julian Crist, but not about his death. American popular culture remembered only that a young medical student had been killed in St. Lucia, and that his girlfriend was convicted of his murder. Julian Crist was a footnote in Grace Sebold's story. She had stolen the headlines over the last decade. Her appeals and cries of injustice had been loud. America knew her as the girl stuck in a foreign land, accused of a murder she claimed not to commit.

A convict claiming innocence was nothing

53

new. Many convicted felons ran the gamut of the appeals process. But only a select few found a voice. Those who follow news about the wrongfully convicted knew Grace Sebold well. Indeed, entire websites had been created to prove her innocence. Donations had been collected to help mount a fight in her defense. Grace had been fortunate enough to fall under the eye of the Innocence Project, a watchdog group that worked to overturn convictions of those they feel were wrongfully accused and unfairly sentenced. This group had taken Grace Sebold under their wings years ago and had staged more than one assault on the St. Lucian judiciary system, which the group claimed used illegal interrogation techniques and false testimony from expert witnesses to gain a conviction. The St. Lucian government was motivated, the group argued, by the desire to solve Julian Crist's death quickly so that the island did not endure a drop in tourism. But despite spirited assaults, all previous attempts to free Grace had failed.

"Well," the inspector said, "I have not forgotten about Mr. Crist, nor has St. Lucia. I am aware, however, of America's true-crime documentary obsession. I've watched many of them myself. The police and the prosecution are not typically presented in a brilliant light, but rather cast as irresponsible in our search for justice."

Despite his easy Caribbean vibe, Sidney sensed that Inspector Pierre was not only proud, but fierce in his convictions. He was responsible for putting Grace Sebold behind bars, and much scrutiny had fallen on his shoulders over the last decade. He'd managed so far to keep the weight from crushing him.

"Of course, you haven't," Sidney said. "That's why I've come to speak with you. American citizens only know the story of Grace Sebold. They only know her claims."

"That's a travesty. But that is not how it is here. In St. Lucia, people know the boy who was killed. And people know the one who killed him has been brought to justice."

"So help me, will you?" Sidney said. "Tell me about your investigation. About what you discovered and your path to find justice."

Inspector Pierre thought on this a moment. "I've gotten a lot of pressure from the group in America that thinks this girl is innocent."

"The Innocence Project. Yes, I know."

"Will your documentary show the truth, or what *they believe* the truth to be? Because the truth about Ms. Sebold, I assure you, is overwhelming."

"That's what I'm after," Sidney said. "The truth. Will you help me find it?"

A void of silence stretched between them. Sidney could see that Inspector Pierre not only wanted to talk, but after so many years *needed* to tell his story. He needed to defend his decisions and his actions. The thought of doing so in a documentary that could potentially reach a large audience outside of his tiny island was appealing.

Pierre nodded slowly. "I'll help you."

THE GIRL OF SUGAR BEACH
"Pilot" Episode
Based on the interview with Claude Pierre

St. Lucian police from the Southern Division station were first on the scene and quickly roped off the area, which included not only Sugar Beach but also the base of Gros Piton. Instructed by the medical examiner in Castries not to disturb the body, one officer was tasked with the dismal job of standing in waist-high water clouded by blood and holding with gloved hands the heel of the dead man's shoe to prevent the tide from carrying him out to sea. Eventually, around 9:00 a.m., Claude Pierre arrived and took control of the scene.

"Sir," the manager said when Pierre had asked to speak with him. "When do you suppose the beach will be back up and running?"

Pierre looked at him with dark eyes slightly squinted with disbelief. "A dead body was just discovered floating off its shores. It will be some time. Now I'll need a list of everyone at the resort. And I'll need to know if any guests are missing or unaccounted for."

"Yes, sir. I'll pull a register off the computer. It is still early, so many of our guests are not awake."

"Start knocking on doors, man! You are the only resort on this beach and it is quite likely one of your guests is dead. Do it now, please."

"Sir," another officer said. "Dr. Mundi has arrived."

"Show him down," Inspector Pierre said.

Moments later, Emmanuel Mundi stood on Sugar Beach and peered out into the water. He waved at the officer in the water who was holding the dead man's heel. "Bring it here."

"I hope not to disturb anything," the officer said as he floated the body over toward shore.

Dr. Mundi looked around the beach. "The scene has already been terribly disturbed." He turned and waved again, this time to his crew who waited farther up the beach toward the resort. "We'll need photographs," he said as his crew made their way down to the shore.

The crime scene unit snapped photos of the dead man who floated facedown in the ocean. A combination of death and salt water bleached the skin on the dead man's arms and legs as they poked through his shirtsleeves and shorts. Distended and waterlogged, the pallid wedge of skin between his shirt collar and hairline looked like soft bread dough ready to go in the oven. Dr. Mundi's crew carefully rotated the body onto its back, exposing the face and chest. More photos followed until they secured the body in a black vinyl bag. The technicians carried it across the beach and up to the pool area, where a gurney waited on solid ground. They loaded the gurney onto the back of a tuk-tuk and transported the dead man up the steep hills of the resort and into the parking lot, where Dr. Mundi's van waited. By now, a few guests had caught wind of the police activity and noticed the crime scene tape near the beach. They gathered in small groups and whispered to one another about what might have happened.

"Inspector."

Pierre looked up from the beach and saw a young officer standing on a bluff high up on Gros Piton. His hands were around his mouth to act as a megaphone.

"Better come up and check this out."

Inspector Pierre stood atop the bluff on Gros Piton and looked down at the Caribbean Sea, where two divers floated on the surface and stared into the shallow waters looking for anything that seemed out of the ordinary. The crime scene unit was combing the sand of Sugar Beach searching for evidence. On the bluff, Pierre ordered his deputies to bag the blanket that covered the granite, along with the champagne bottle and two flutes, which were standing eerily alone.

He had already placed twelve inverted V-shaped placards around the bluff, labeled by number. The first stood by a blood splatter on the granite; another by a larger collection of blood that had pooled farther down the bluff from the original splatter. A shoeprint in the dirt just off the bluff was also labeled. Pierre stood by while an officer took photos of each of the areas marked by yellow placards. Another officer meticulously videotaped the entire scene, sweeping the bluff from one side to the other, capturing the blanket and the champagne and the blood. The video was for the detectives, so they could later revisit the crime scene to unearth clues they had missed initially. They had no idea that a decade later this footage would play across American televisions during a true-crime documentary.

Dr. Mundi came to the bluff and took a spot next to Pierre, also peering down into the water where the body had been discovered.

"You don't suppose it was a simple accident? Perhaps too much alcohol and poor balance?" Mundi asked.

"Not unless he spat blood before he fell." Pierre pointed to the blood splattered across the granite.

Dr. Mundi surveyed the dozen yellow markers, which suggested signs of foul play. He nodded. "Very well. I will have a look at the body back at my mortuary."

"Maybe suicide," Pierre said. "But that doesn't account for the blood."

"I'll know soon enough," Dr. Mundi said.

"Keep me on top of things."

"Same." Dr. Mundi left the bluff and headed down to the beach.

"Inspector," the young officer said again as he approached. "It appears one of the guests at the resort is missing."

"Name?"

"Julian Crist. An American."

CHAPTER 4

"Yes," Inspector Pierre said after they had settled at the conference table, cups of coffee in front of them.

For a country with an average daily temperature in the mid-eighties, coffee was an oddly popular drink in St. Lucia. Sidney had the interview recorded from multiple angles. The first was a shot over Sidney's shoulder that captured the inspector's responses straight on, with an occasional glance of the back of Sidney's head. Other viewpoints came from a second cameraman, who moved from side to side, recording for a few minutes before moving to a new location, which occasionally framed Sidney's face as she asked her questions, but which mostly concentrated on Claude Pierre.

"After Julian's body was discovered, we were called onto the scene," Pierre said. "The beach was cleared and taped off, and the medical examiner was brought in to handle the body. Our forensic team as well."

Sidney had notes on her lap that the cameraman was careful to leave out of the shot. The goal, when Sidney was in the scene, was to give the appearance of a neutral journalist curiously asking questions about the case.

"What do you remember about Julian Crist's body from that morning?"

"When I arrived, the body was floating in shallow waters off the beach. I remember the way he was inverted, even to this day. His feet came in first and his torso and head were still underwater, like the sea was trying to take him, but the beach wouldn't allow it."

"Do you remember anything specific about Julian's body?"

"I remember most vividly the head trauma. It was nearly all I could notice when the medical examiner's crew pulled him onto land."

"It was determined Julian had died from a blow to the back of the head. Is that correct?"

"Ultimately, yes. But at the scene that morning, it was assumed he had fallen from Gros Piton."

"And why was that assumption made?"

"He was a guest at the resort, and Gros

Piton is a popular attraction. It was a reasonable assumption to begin with, assuming the tranquil and isolated nature of the resort."

"And when did your assumptions change from an accident to homicide?"

"My first clue was a blood splatter that we discovered on the bluff."

"The blood you found," Sidney said, imagining the crime scene photos that would run over the audio of her interview, "made you suspect foul play?"

"Of course. If the original assumption was that Julian had fallen accidentally, then there was no way to explain the blood splatter."

"With the discovery of blood, you figured someone had struck him."

"That's correct."

Sidney paused for a moment before asking her next question.

"More than one hundred guests stayed at the resort on the night Julian Crist was killed. How did you so quickly settle on Grace Sebold as the one who killed him?"

THE GIRL OF SUGAR BEACH
"Pilot" Episode
Based on the interview with Claude Pierre

Grace Sebold sat in a small meeting room behind the lobby's reception desk where the St. Lucian police had set up an impromptu interview area. A small rectangular table sat with three chairs: two on one side for Pierre and his assistant, and a lone chair across from them, where the subject of their interview would sit. Grace was first up, with a long list of others to follow as the day wore on.

"How did you know Mr. Crist?" Pierre started in a flat affect, all business. He sat with his hands folded on the table, his long, thin fingers interlaced. His assistant scribbled furious notes onto a legal pad. A recorder sat in the middle of the table to capture the interview.

"He was my boyfriend."

"And what was the nature of your visit to the island of St. Lucia?"

The thick Caribbean accent, along with her nerves, made it difficult for Grace to understand the detective.

"The nature of what?" Grace asked in a strained voice that was on the verge of tears again. She'd been crying all morning, and had become hysterical when the tuk-tuk that transported the gurney pulled past her group. Word had spread by then that Julian was missing and a body had been discovered in the water.

"Why are you here, Ms. Sebold?" Inspector Pierre asked in a stronger tone. "Vacationing?"

"No. Yes, my friend was married a couple of days ago. We are here for the wedding."

"Who is *we*?"

"Uh . . . Julian and I came together. But we met my parents and brother here as well. And all my friends."

"What is the name of the friend who was married?"

"Charlotte."

"Surname?"

Grace shook her head. "I'm sorry, I didn't understand what you asked."

"Surname?" Pierre said in a booming voice.

The charming Caribbean accent that Grace had so enjoyed from the resort staff had now turned into an ugly obstacle she had trouble hurdling.

"Your friend's last name," the assistant said in a calm voice less deluged by impatience.

"Oh, Brooks. Charlotte Brooks."

"How did you know each other? You and the bride?"

"Charlotte and I have been friends since high school. I guess, what? Ten years or so? I was her maid of honor."

"As the maid of honor," Pierre said, "I can assume you and Ms. Brooks are best of friends?"

"She's a friend," Grace said. "Yes, of course. A dear friend."

"Your closest friend?"

Grace hesitated. "She is a close friend, yes."

"Why are your parents and brother traveling with you?"

"Our parents are friends," Grace said. "Mine and Charlotte's. My parents were invited to the wedding."

"Where were you last night, Ms. Sebold?"

"Here at the resort."

"Where, exactly? Tell me your day."

Grace wetted her lips and ran a finger under her right eye to capture the last of her tears. "We were at the pool in the afternoon."

"Again, Ms. Sebold. Who is *we*?"

"All of us. Julian and me, and all our friends. Then I had a late lunch with my parents and brother. Maybe three o'clock.

After that, I went to my cottage to shower."

"Did Mr. Crist join you for lunch?"

"No. He had something planned for last night. So he asked to skip lunch with my parents to get ready for it."

"What was he planning, Ms. Sebold?"

"I'm not sure. Dinner, I think. He asked me to meet him up on the Piton."

Inspector Pierre straightened in his chair. "On Gros Piton?"

"Yes."

"Did you meet him?"

Grace shook her head. "No."

"Mr. Crist asked you to meet him, and you said *no*?"

Grace shook her head again. "No, I planned to meet him, but . . . Marshall became ill and I had to stay with him."

"Who is Marshall?"

"My younger brother."

"How much younger?"

"Just a year. He's twenty-five."

"Your brother, who is an adult, became ill and you were required to tend to him? What was the nature of his illness?"

"He had a seizure. I had to stay with him until it passed."

Pierre wrinkled his forehead. *"A sei- zure?"*

"Yes," Grace said. "He has a . . ." Grace

tapped her fingers on the table to help her thoughts. "He has a medical condition. Seizures are common for him, but when they come, he needs help. So I stayed with him."

"Surely, there will be a record of you calling for medical assistance? An ambulance or the resort nurse?"

"No. I know how to manage Marshall's seizures," Grace said. "He's had them for many years, ever since . . . the accident."

"Where did this seizure take place?"

"In my cottage."

"What time?"

"I'm not sure. I was getting ready. So, about six, I guess."

"Guessing does not help me, Ms. Sebold."

Grace took a deep breath and looked up to the ceiling. "I would say it was just before six o'clock. I was just out of the shower, putting on makeup and drying my hair, when I heard him start to seizure in the other room."

"Does your twenty-five-year-old brother often spend time with you while you're dressing to meet your boyfriend? Your room seems like an odd place for your brother to be while you were showering."

"Marshall has a condition that makes

69

him . . . He spends a lot of time with me, yes. It makes him comfortable."

The scribbler took furious notes. When he was finished, he nodded at Pierre, who then continued his questions.

"Your brother had a seizure. What happened next?"

"His seizures last only a few minutes, but it takes a while for him to recover afterward. Maybe thirty or forty minutes. It took some time to clean him up and get him back to his room and into bed."

"Clean him up?"

"He had vomited," Grace said, the first strain of annoyance coming to her voice. "And urinated on himself. I got him new clothes and waited while he took a shower."

"How long did the process take?"

"An hour, maybe. It was probably seven o'clock by the time I got him back to my parents' cottage."

"Your vagueness is not at all useful, Ms. Sebold."

"I'm not trying to be vague. I didn't record the time, sir. I'm telling you what I remember, the best that I remember it."

"You had plans to meet Mr. Crist, though. You must have had a sense of the time since you were now running late."

70

"Yes, a sense. I just can't tell you the exact time."

"Your brother is now in bed and with your parents. According to you, it is seven in the evening. Did you stay with him?"

"No. I mean, for a while, yes. To make sure he was okay. My parents took over from there. Then I went to meet Julian, but by the time I got out to the beach, it was getting dark. I knew the hike up to the bluff would take too long, and I was scared to try it in the dark. So I waited on the beach."

"For Mr. Crist?"

"Yes."

"And when Mr. Crist did not appear on the beach, as I'm sure he did not, you surely attempted to contact him, no? Call him or text-message him?"

"Our phones don't work here. There's no service down in this valley."

"Fair enough. But you must have mentioned his absence to someone of authority, no? Your parents? Or perhaps resort security?"

Grace curled her bottom lip inward and shook her head. "No. Not to anyone at the resort. I told my friend Ellie Reiser. Ellie came to my cottage and stayed all night."

"Your boyfriend is missing, and this is of

no concern to you?"

"No. I mean, it was. I was concerned, but not that he was *missing.* Not that anything bad had happened to him."

"If you weren't worried that he was missing, what exactly was the source of your concern?"

"We had gotten into an argument that day. When I couldn't make it to the bluff on time, I figured Julian assumed I blew him off. I waited on the beach until it was dark, then I checked his room. When I couldn't find him, I figured he was angry and avoiding me."

"You and Mr. Crist had gotten into an argument? About what? Why was he angry with you?"

Grace took a deep breath. She held open her palms. "He was my boyfriend. Occasionally we got into fights."

"But this particular argument, which occurred on the day that he was killed. What, exactly, were you fighting about, Ms. Sebold?"

Grace took a deep breath. "Do we really have to get into all this?"

"I'm afraid we do."

Grace looked to the ceiling and wiped her tears again. "Julian was mad about . . . another guy. He was jealous, I guess."

"Jealous about what?"

"I don't know. Julian thought Daniel and I were . . . He thought we had feelings for each other."

"Daniel?"

Grace shook her head, moved her gaze to the side, and stared helplessly at the notepad, where the scribbler was slashing away.

"Daniel Greaves," she said. "Daniel and I dated a long time ago, just briefly in college. Julian found out about it that afternoon and thought something was going on between us."

"Between you and Daniel Greaves?" Inspector Pierre asked.

"Yes. There wasn't, by the way. It was just a stupid misunderstanding." Grace shook her head, tears starting to well again on her lower lids.

"Who, exactly, is Daniel Greaves, and why was he at Sugar Beach Resort?"

Grace looked once again at the recorder, which sat on the table, and at the messy shorthand, which Inspector Pierre's assistant was jotting onto the legal pad. Grace eventually closed her eyes.

"He was the groom. Charlotte's boy—" Grace stopped herself. "I guess, at that point, he was Charlotte's husband."

CHAPTER 5

Sidney looked at Inspector Pierre.

"So this argument," she said, "between Grace and Julian. I understand that many resort guests witnessed it, since it occurred near the pool. And it happened in the afternoon of the day Julian was killed. But is an argument between two young lovers so uncommon that it made you immediately suspect Grace? I don't know any young couples who don't have a spat every so often."

"The argument alone was not what raised my suspicion, it was the *cause* of the argument," Pierre said.

"Grace admitted that it had to do with her past relationship with Daniel Greaves."

"That's what she suggested," Pierre said. "It was a convenient way to explain the fight, and clearly implied that Julian was angry with *her.* That *he* was the jealous one."

"But you didn't believe this?"

"No. We pulled the phone record from Julian's room. It showed three calls to a New York extension during his stay. When we tracked down the recipient of the calls, we discovered that it was Julian's past girlfriend. What you called, a *lover.* The final call to New York was made on the afternoon before Julian was killed, and immediately preceded the witnessed argument between Julian and Ms. Sebold. And when we pulled Ms. Sebold's phone log, we found an outgoing call to the same New York extension. So it was my logical conclusion that Ms. Sebold discovered that Julian had been phoning his ex-lover, and that she called the number to confirm her suspicion. *This* is what caused the argument between them. And despite how Ms. Sebold would like things perceived, *she* was the one who was angry that day, not Julian Crist."

"This ex-girlfriend of Julian's," Sidney said. "Does she have a name?"

"Ms. Allison Harbor."

"You spoke with her during your investigation?"

"Of course. And she confirmed that her and Julian's relationship was still ongoing."

"Ongoing in what way?"

"In an intimate way, Ms. Ryan."

Sidney took a moment to collect her thoughts. The idea of Grace discovering Julian's continued relationship with a past girlfriend had caught her off guard. Finally, she looked back at the inspector.

"I can understand how this omission on Grace's part could be considered deceptive."

"I would classify it as a lie," Pierre said.

"Understood. But this single misrepresentation of an argument, given by a young girl under tremendous stress — remember, her boyfriend had just been found dead, and she was now being interrogated by the police — that was enough to cause you to focus your investigation so tightly on her, and her alone?"

Inspector Pierre shook his head. "No, Ms. Ryan. You asked how Ms. Sebold originally came under my suspicion when more than one hundred guests were registered at the hotel. Her lie about the argument was the origin of my distrust. But it was the blood that caused me to suspect Ms. Sebold above anyone else."

"The blood?" Sidney said.

"Yes."

Sidney had seen the photos of the splatter on the bluff many times. "The blood was so minor, though. I'm confused."

"I would argue that the blood was minor in no way. There was a great deal of it."

"A great deal?" Sidney asked. "Four drops of blood, isn't that correct? The splatter pattern on the bluff contained four drops of blood?"

"That's correct. Plus another collection of blood from a second location on the bluff."

"So a single splatter of four drops and a second collection is considered *a great deal of blood,* by the St. Lucian Police Force? And how, exactly, did the blood up on Gros Piton raise your suspicion that Grace was involved?"

Pierre narrowed his eyes and slowly shook his head. "You are considering only the blood found on the bluff, Ms. Ryan. When taken with the other blood we discovered in Ms. Sebold's room, it can be described as a great deal."

THE GIRL OF SUGAR BEACH
"Pilot" Episode
Based on the interview with Claude Pierre

"That man has a serious authority problem," Ellie Reiser said as she stormed into Grace's cottage. "It's abuse of power and intimidation."

Detectives had interviewed all the members from their group, shuffling them one by one into the small conference room near the front lobby of the resort. Soon after Grace was allowed to leave, they had summoned Ellie Reiser.

"What happened?" Grace asked, her eyes still red-rimmed from her time with Inspector Pierre.

"He's an asshole. He can't treat us like that."

"Ellie! What happened?"

"He asked me the same question a hundred times while his little minion scribbled everything I said into a notebook. I asked why he was transcribing my words if they were recording the interview. No answer. They're trying to intimidate us."

"God, Ellie. Just tell me what you said. It was the same detective, right? Pierre?"

"Yes. He asked if I saw you last night."

"You stayed in my room. Please tell me

you said this to him."

"Yes, Grace. I thought it might be important to mention that I was in your room overnight."

Ellie looked to the corner of the room where Grace's younger brother, Marshall, sat at the table with his chessboard laid out in front of him, the pieces perfectly arranged. Her face took on the expression of smelling a foul odor.

"Does he ever stop with the chess thing?" Ellie lowered her voice. "I swear, I love him Grace, but does he even know what's going on?"

"He hasn't fully . . . recovered. From the seizure last night."

"I'm not deaf," Marshall said in a calm voice while he surveyed the chessboard in front of him. "And, Ellie, yes, I'm well aware of what's happening. Thanks for the air of superiority, though. It's always charming."

"Marshall," Grace said, shaking her head subtly when her brother made eye contact with her. It was all she needed to do to keep Marshall at bay. Just sixteen months separated them in age, and the brother-sister relationship between Grace and Marshall Sebold was strong. Sometimes even overwhelming to those around them.

It was something only the two of them understood fully. Since Marshall's accident, they had only grown closer.

Marshall returned his attention to his chessboard. Grace looked back at Ellie. "What did Pierre say when you told him you were with me?"

"He wanted to know what time I came to your room, and how much I had had to drink. His partner scribbled everything I said in his notepad."

Grace ran a hand over her cheek and to the back of her neck. "They think I did it. God, Ellie! They think I did this."

"Stop being hysterical. That's what they want. *Hysterics.* Instead of looking for who actually killed him, they're wasting time trying to scare us."

Grace startled at the loud knock on the door. Two loud smacks followed by the once-rhythmic, but now jarring, Caribbean lilt from the other side.

"Ms. Sebold. It's Inspector Pierre, with the Royal St. Lucia Police. Please open the door."

Grace's lips separated in a frozen pose as her eyes went wide while she stared at Ellie. In the corner, Marshall quickly collected his chess pieces and folded his set closed.

"Ms. Sebold!" More knocking came from the door.

"Go!" Ellie said, pointing at the door.

Grace wiped her eyes with the back of her hand as she walked across the cottage and pulled open the door. Inspector Pierre stood in the door frame, a huddle of police officers behind him.

"Ms. Sebold," Pierre said, handing Grace an envelope. "We have a warrant to survey your room."

The cottages were isolated by the lush grounds of the resort and speckled within the rain forest at the foothills of the Jalousie Plantation. Despite being small in its capacity — only eighty-eight cottages, villas, and bungalows made up Sugar Beach Resort — the resort grounds were expansive. Tuk-tuk carts transported guests throughout the property, both because the walk from the cottages to the beach was long, but also because the terrain was hilly and difficult to manage on foot.

After the Sebold girl was ushered from the room, Pierre and his team entered through the front door, greeted by a large bedroom of cherrywood floors and an expansive four-post bed draped in brilliant white sheets. A matching sofa and overstuffed chair sat in the corner and faced a flat-screen television. A private bar was stocked with Chairman's Reserve rum and Piton beer, the countertop covered with coffee and tea paraphernalia.

Off the bedroom was a walk-in closet, which led to the luxurious bathroom. Lining the closet walls were built-in shelves for clothes, suitcases, and hanging garments. The bottom row of cubbies held an assortment of Grace Sebold's shoes, to which Pierre pointed. The technicians approached with gloved hands and retrieved each pair of shoes, dropping them into clear plastic evidence bags, which they quickly sealed. Grace's dresses and blouses, which hung in the closet, were placed in clear plastic bags, too.

Pierre took thirty minutes to inspect the room, disturbing as little as possible as he surveyed and sifted through Grace's belongings. He eventually made his way into the bathroom. The wooden shutter blinds were operated by a middle-panel lever, which he pulled down until the room was dark.

"I can smell it before we even look," Pierre said.

"Me too," the technician said.

As Pierre stood in the corner, the technician squirted luminol from a plastic spray bottle. Methodically he covered in a grid formation the sink and countertop, the mirror and wall, the armoire, and finally the floor in front of the sink. When he was finished, he backed away. Inspector Pierre clicked on the handheld black light. The mirror and wall were blank, but the sink and floor glowed with a fluorescent blue, bright and eerie in the darkened room.

The second technician removed several vials from his pack, unscrewed the top to one of them, and withdrew the cotton swab, which had been soaking in the vial's solution. He methodically swabbed each area that glowed under the spell of the black light. He used four vials to swab the floor, and another six to capture the evidence on the countertop and sink.

Finally he unscrewed the drain from under the sink, emerging with the U-shaped PVC fitting in his hand. Pierre opened the blinds and clicked on the bathroom light. The technician dipped another swab into the black shadow of the drainpipe, momentarily losing sight of the white tip as he brushed against the top of the fitting. When he pulled it out, the once-white cotton tip was muddy red.

CHAPTER 6

On the windward coast of St. Lucia, in the town of Dennery, the white buildings of the Bordelais Correctional Facility spread across a flat plane as hills jetted up in the distance and palm trees swayed in the ocean breeze. Sidney's crew consisted of two cameramen, a sound engineer, and a lighting tech, all of whom had piled into the van for the long journey from Sugar Beach, out of the Jalousie Plantation, and through the mountains of St. Lucia to the island's only jail. One of the cameramen opened the sliding door of the van as they crested the hill. The Bordelais Correctional Facility came into view in the basin below; with the camera on his shoulder, he leaned out the open door to capture the footage. Tall chainlink fences topped with spiraled barbed wire surrounded the entire complex. After the twelve-foot brick interior wall and four guard towers, the chain link was the last line of defense to separate an inmate from the rest of the island. Long rectangles of two-story white brick buildings, four in total, made up the cell blocks. An arid dirt soccer field represented the prisoners' only relief from confinement; and from their place up on the hill, Sidney and her crew witnessed two teams of felons running through the dusty haze. This was where Grace Sebold had spent the last ten years.

The scores of letters, written by Grace Sebold over the years, had come as Sidney climbed to some semblance of fame for her previous documentaries and the exonerations that followed. The first letter had arrived after Sidney's documentary featuring Neve Blackmore, a middle-aged woman who had spent eighteen years in a Florida jail for the murder of her ten-year-old son. As a young and inexperienced producer, Sidney poked around the case until she became certain of the woman's innocence. Some great investigational journalism, along with dumb luck, and the discovery of a scathing piece of DNA evidence had been enough for Florida's newly elected state's attorney to reopen the case. Nearly two decades after her son was savaged, Neve Blackmore was exonerated. Sidney Ryan documented Ms. Blackmore's journey, the unearthing of new evidence, and Neve's eventual release from jail, and put it all together in a two-hour film.

Although that first documentary was hailed as a symbol of justice, Sidney looked at it as just the opposite. In the wake of her son's death, a mother was accused of his murder and forced to mourn in prison. Neve Blackmore fought for most of her adult life to clear her name. Yes, she was ultimately vindicated, but she had paid a hell of a price for the mistakes of those too eager to convict. And eighteen agonizing years later, still no one had been held accountable for her son's murder. Neve Blackmore had spent nearly two decades, not tracking down her son's killer, but simply working to prove her innocence. It seemed to Sidney much less an image of justice than a pitiful waste of two lives.

When that first documentary gained critical praise and a moderate audience, letters trickled in from inmates around the country hoping for Sidney to conjure the same magic that had freed Neve Blackmore. Sidney paged through each letter, researching the convictions and the evidence that produced them. Back then the mail was manageable. She handled every envelope herself and settled on the case of Byron Williams, a young African-American man accused of shooting and killing two plainclothes police officers who were on surveillance duty. With alibis from five different sources and forensics that suggested the shooter to be female, Sidney attacked the case with zeal. With her camera crew in tow, she led a yearlong investigation that finally caught the attention of a U.S. senator and the local district attorney. This time, after eight years in prison, Byron Williams was released and cleared of all charges.

Sidney organized her journey into a four-part documentary and shopped it around. Netflix purchased it, created an aggressive marketing plan, and released it to subscribers to be streamed over the Internet. It became the most downloaded true-crime documentary of the year, putting Sidney Ryan's name on the radar of every convict in the country who believed he or she was innocent. Her in-box flooded with requests from felons requesting her assistance with their appeals. Family members of the accused also penned letters, begging Sidney to help their loved ones who rotted in jail for crimes they didn't commit. In a given week, she'd receive a stack of envelopes six inches thick. Inside the packages were shoddy investigational work, lists of appeals, and makeshift interviews with "witnesses" that would surely crack each case. The mail became too much to handle, and much of it sadly piled up, unopened and ignored, in the corner of her office.

Suddenly a sought-after producer and filmmaker, she fielded a host of offers before finally taking a producing spot on the primetime show *Events,* which was tied to the popular magazine of the same name. There she began work on her third documentary, entering into the ruthless world of television network hierarchy. Sidney was naive to the backstabbing and conniving that dominated the industry, and had been eaten alive and overshadowed by Luke Barrington during her first year as his producer. Still, Sidney's style and strong filmmaking skills won many accolades and spawned many lookalikes, including podcasts and YouTube documentaries of little-known crimes. It was about that time that she opened the first letter from Grace Sebold.

Sidney knew the case well, and not simply because she and Grace had attended Syracuse University together. The story had made national headlines a decade earlier and the American media were frenzied about the sordid details. GRUESOME GRACE

SEBOLD and GRISLY GRACE were the chosen headlines of the day used to describe the fourth-year medical student who had bludgeoned her boyfriend before pushing him off a cliff in the Caribbean. Although they never ran in the same circles, Sidney remembered Grace well enough at the time the news broke, four or five years after Syracuse, to be shocked by the story. Sidney didn't, however, have a good enough connection with her to know if the accusations were true or false. A decade later, Sidney was getting an opportunity to find out.

She spent hours reading the more than one hundred letters Grace had sent over a twenty-six-month span. Sidney noted as she carefully paged through each of them that none was repetitive. Other than asking for Sidney's help at the end, each letter tackled a different subject. Many were powerful attestations about the inconsistencies in the case against her, the rules of good investigational work that were violated, the physical evidence that was engineered, the DNA findings that were misinterpreted, and the complete lack of motivation for Grace to have killed the man she loved. Others were about Grace's life before the conviction, the family that desperately grieved for her, the brother who was ill and required more care

89

than her parents could offer, and the life she was missing as the years passed by in jail. Some were nothing more than congratulations on Sidney's success and her rise in the ranks of television journalism, praising her hard work and the difference she made in the lives of those she helped exonerate. Through the letters, Sidney felt a sense of charisma emanating from Grace, a trait she could neither explain nor remember from her time with Grace at Syracuse. There was something alluring about Grace Sebold. And if Sidney could sense it through letters, she was certain viewers would see it in a documentary.

Grace's attorney had provided Sidney with a thumb drive of all relevant information about the case. From Julian Crist's autopsy report and photos, to toxicology findings, to evidence collected during the investigation, to high-res crime scene photos, to recorded interviews and court transcripts, Sidney knew everything about Grace Sebold's case, her trial, and her conviction.

At least, this was her belief before interviewing Claude Pierre.

CHAPTER 7

The guard unlocked the door to the interview room and Sidney walked through the
threshold. Grace Sebold sat at the table.
With the only references being decade-old
photographs, television video from the trial,
and dusty images in her mind from their
time together in college, Sidney tried hard
to suppress her surprise when she laid eyes
on Grace.

The beautiful, young college girl was
gone, replaced now by a rough-looking
woman much closer to middle age. Convicted of Julian Crist's murder at age
twenty-six, Grace Sebold was now closer to
forty. A decade in a foreign prison had not
aged her well. She carried edematous bags
under her eyes, which suggested years
without a peaceful night's sleep. Her hair,
once long and sandy blond, was now
cropped inmate-style short and had retreated back to its original brunette color

besides the few random streaks of gray that snaked through it. Without makeup, her lips were pale and chapped, and her complexion carried the pallor of a decade without the company of sunshine.

Sidney's cameramen captured the two women meeting for the first time in more than fifteen years. Grace pursed her lips and worked hard to prevent the welling tears from spilling down her cheeks.

"Wow," Grace said in a shaky voice as she tried to smile. "It's been a while."

"Hi, Grace."

They embraced in a gentle hug. Sidney sensed that it was both a welcome relief, as well as an awkward display of physical emotion, which Grace had been without for the past ten years.

When they parted, Sidney dropped a stack of envelopes onto the table, a thick rubber band holding the heap together.

Grace looked at her years of work. "I wasn't sure you were reading them."

"I read every one. They're why I'm here."

They sat down across from each other. Grace looked at the cameras, which were pointed at her and filming from each side.

"This will take a little getting used to."

"We only have an hour," Sidney said. "So get used to them quickly, okay?"

Grace nodded.

"For this to work, for there to be any chance that I can help you, you have to be honest with me."

Grace nodded again. "Of course."

"One hundred percent. No exaggeration. No bending the truth."

Another nod.

"I've spent the last couple of days speaking with the detective who ran your case. I also read the medical examiner's report who performed the autopsy on Julian and testified against you at your trial."

"Okay," Grace said.

"There are several issues that stand against your claims in these letters."

"Start with any of them," Grace said, with an unflinching look to her eyes. "I'll tell you why they are incorrect."

Sidney leaned closer. "I want to start with your relationship with Julian. For the audience to believe that you didn't kill him, they have to believe you loved him."

"I did love him."

"I believe that," Sidney said. "But while talking with Inspector Pierre, and reading through the trial transcripts, a lot of things were revealed about your relationship with Julian. That, perhaps, your relationship wasn't as perfect as you suggest in your letters to me."

"We were twenty-something. I don't know if any relationship is perfect at that age. But I did love him. Some part of me still does. The part that's not angry with him." Grace shook her head. "I've spent countless hours and more than a few sleepless nights trying to figure out this emotion, but on some hard-to-explain level, I'm mad at Julian. I don't have access to a psychiatrist in here, so I've had to figure these emotions out on my own. But what I've settled on is that I'm angry with Julian because he left me here. Because his death has brought me so much pain and heartache. His death cost me my own life. And yet, all these years later, I still love him. I know none of it is his fault. I just have nowhere else to place the blame. So poor Julian takes much of it."

Sidney nodded. "I want to find a way to show the audience how much you loved Julian. Because when I read about your love story, as you presented it in your letters, it touched me. I want to do the same to my audience."

Grace looked over at the guard who stood out of camera shot. She pointed at the small table next to her, and the guard nodded. Grace reached over and retrieved an item, placed it on the table in front of Sidney.

"Have you ever seen one of these?" Grace asked.

Sidney looked down at an old-fashioned padlock. It was large, the size of her open palm. Antique bronze, the lock had a medieval look, with smooth edges that offered the resemblance of a miniature rustic kettle-bell.

"It's a lock?" Sidney said.

"A love lock," Grace said. "My grandfather gave it to me when I was ten. He told me it was for my heart. To lock it away and only open it when I found the right man. When I found Julian, I finally understood my grandfather's gesture."

Sidney picked up the heavy lock and ran her thumb over it. Engraved into the smooth surface were two names: *Grace & Julian.*

"It seems silly to me now," Grace said. "But back when Julian and I were dating, these love locks were trendy. They still are, in France and some other countries. Pont des Arts Bridge in Paris is, perhaps, the most famous love lock location in the world. When you find the person you will spend your life with, you engrave your names on the lock, secure it to the bridge, and throw away the key. I always thought Julian and I would go to Paris someday, to the Pont des Arts Bridge to secure our lock and throw the key into the Seine. Or maybe we'd go back to Delhi, where we met, and find a place there." Grace smiled. "I had a lot of crazy plans back then."

"What was Julian's plan?"

"He never knew about this lock. I put his name on it but never got the chance to show it to him."

Sidney noticed that Grace was becoming emotional, so she steered the conversation in another direction. She held up the lock. "You were allowed to keep this? During your incarceration?"

"No," Grace said, taking the lock from Sidney and staring at it. "Not at first. Only last year did the prison allow me the privilege of personal items, because of good behavior. My friend Ellie Reiser kept this for me all these years. When the warden allowed me to have a few comfort items from home, I chose my love lock as one of them. Ellie brought it during a visit."

Grace forced a smile and again worked to stop the tears from spilling over her lids before she let out an awkward laugh. "I'm sorry." She took a deep breath. "A lot has changed between Julian and me over the years that I've been here. He was everything to me. Now, he's this . . . *thing.* This voice in my head that gets me through tough days.

He's a dark shadow in my mind that cries with me. I scream at that shadow sometimes, too, because I'm still angry. It's odd to consider, but I've known this spirit of Julian longer than I knew the man."

Grace held up the love lock.

"I've kept this all these years, because I loved Julian back then, and I still do today."

Sidney looked down at her notes.

"Allison Harbor, Julian's ex-girlfriend, came up during my interview with Claude Pierre."

Grace let out an annoyed laugh. "Claude Pierre was obsessed with her."

"Do you think Julian was still involved with her?"

"No."

"Do you think he still loved her?"

"No," Grace said. "Julian loved me."

"You are so confident of this fact," Sidney said. "Both in your letters to me, and now. But when I dig into your past, and Julian's, will I find a different story?"

Grace took a deep breath. "Julian was going to propose to me. That's why he asked me to meet him on Soufriere Bluff. He was going to ask me to marry him. Why would he do that if he was in love with someone else?"

THE GIRL OF SUGAR BEACH
"Pilot" Episode
Based on the interview with Claude Pierre

It was approaching 6:00 p.m. when Pierre left Sugar Beach. It was another hour before he reached Victoria Hospital in Castries, where he entered the mortuary and found Dr. Mundi standing next to the autopsy table that held Julian Crist.

"How far have you gotten?" Pierre asked from the doorway.

"Finishing up now. Sorry to call you over so late, but I thought you'd want to have a look," Dr. Mundi said as he pulled a long thread through the incision to close Julian Crist's chest. He tied it off quickly and cut the excess.

Pierre approached the table. He could see that Julian Crist's body had been recently tugged back together after Dr. Mundi's examination. The sight of a tormented body, limp and helpless to protest the search for clues it left behind, was always disturbing to Pierre. He was no stranger to autopsies. He stomached them because they were part of his job, but he much preferred to read reports than to see the results in person. In this case, though, he could not wait for Mundi's written summary. The American girl was lying to him, and he wanted to know as soon as possible what had killed Mr. Crist.

"What have you found?"

"Typical injuries seen in a long-distance fall," Dr. Mundi said. "From the bluff to the water is nearly thirty meters. Broken bones — tibia and fibula, humerus and two ribs. All on the right side. There was damage to the spleen as the result of one of the broken ribs lacerating it. No other internal organ injuries. No severing or shearing of vessels that would lead me to believe the patient bled to death internally. And no collections of blood other than from the spleen."

"So the fall didn't kill him?"

"No."

"What did?"

With a bit of effort, Dr. Mundi turned Julian's body over so that he rested face-down on the stainless steel. He pointed to the back of Julian's head.

"I discovered a large, deep skull fracture here." Dr. Mundi ran his gloved finger in a circle around the upper-right portion of Julian's freshly shaved scalp. "Excuse me, I know you consider such things unpleasant."

Dr. Mundi placed his fingertips in the

crowning incision at the top of Julian's hairline and peeled back the scalp to expose the naked bone of his skull. Pierre swallowed hard at the crude procedure.

"*This* is what killed him," Dr. Mundi said, pointing to the undressed cranium. "This fracture was the result of blunt-force trauma caused by an object swung at medium speed. Other fractures," Dr. Mundi said, tracing the break lines in the bone, "were suffered during the fall, but this was the primary insult."

"How can you tell that?" Pierre asked, studying the jagged spiderweb of fractured bone, which looked to his untrained eyes like a mess of total destruction.

"The secondary fractures produced during the fall approach this initial fissure, but do not, and cannot, cross it. They all stop at the outer edge of this principal fracture. From the nucleus of this break, I can map radiation lines through all the other fault lines. Once the bone is broken, a second fracture cannot bridge the original breach. This is why I'm still here so late, Inspector. Mapping the fracture took me hours. But it is with certainty that this injury is what killed him. It caused a large subdural hematoma that spread around the skull and likely concussed the brain to render him unconscious, or possibly semiconscious but not functionally alert. He was not dead when he fell from the bluff. Based on salt water in his lungs, he was still breathing when he hit the ocean."

Dr. Mundi pulled Julian Crist's scalp back over his skull and began to sew shut the crowning incision.

"And this." Dr. Mundi pointed to the back of Julian's skull, where he had shaved away the hair to leave a circular patch of bare skin that looked like a burnt-out spot on a grassy knoll. Within the clearing was a gaping wound. Devoid of blood this long after death, the gash reminded Pierre of a split in a leather sofa. "This scalp laceration is the source of the blood splattering you found on the bluff."

"How can we be sure he didn't suffer this fracture and laceration when he fell? Perhaps he struck a rock on the side of the cliff."

Dr. Mundi shook his head. "Because of the location. Essentially on the top, back side of the head, it is impossible that this fracture was caused from the fall. For that to be the case, the victim would have had to land headfirst on a hard, blunt object. And for this to be true, from an estimated height of thirty meters, there would certainly be neck and spinal cord trauma, which there is not. And such a fall would certainly have caused a much more substantial fracture than this localized one. Finally my forensic team found no blood anywhere on the face of the Piton, or its base."

Pierre nodded at the explanation while he watched Dr. Mundi pierce the scalp with the suture and pull the thread.

"I believe," Dr. Mundi continued, "the patient was struck in the back of the head from a downward angle with a blunt object. The object caused a seven-centimeter stellate fracture, three centimeters deep."

"Any idea what this object was?" Pierre asked.

"Impossible to tell from the examination. But it was likely something with some weight to it."

Dr. Mundi finished suturing Julian Crist's scalp, clipped the excess, and snapped off his glove.

"The blow to his head sent him off the bluff, where he sustained the right-sided injuries when he hit the water. Either the initial trauma to his head, or the impact from the landing, rendered him unconscious, but still breathing, which filled his lungs with water and asphyxiated him."

Pierre studied the body for a moment. "Someone struck him in the head, he fell into the water, and then he drowned. Do I have your hypothesis correct?"

"That's correct, Inspector. Cause of death — blunt-force trauma leading to asphyxiation. The manner of death will be listed as homicide. I suspect this is no surprise to you?"

"It is not."

"Any idea who killed this young man?"

"A good one, yes."

The morning after Julian Crist's autopsy, Inspector Pierre entered the laboratory in Castries, where the crime scene technicians had worked late into the previous night. Because the victim was American, and Pierre's lead suspect was from the States, too, time was short.

"Anything?" Pierre asked.

"Much," the lead tech said as he peered into a microscope. He swiveled his chair and brought his computer to life by shaking the mouse. A split-screen photo came into view. On the left was the shoeprint impression taken from the dirt just off the bluff on Gros Piton. Next to it was the sole of Grace Sebold's running shoe, which they had bagged the previous day during the sweep of her room.

"It's an exact match," the technician said. "Visually it looks the same. Microscopically it's identical. Database matched the tread in the impression to Nike Crosstrainers. TR 3 Flyknit. Women's size seven. It's the same shoe taken from the American's room."

"So our girl was on the bluff?"

"No doubt, sir. Also," the tech said, swiveling his chair again. He grabbed a sheet of paper as it came off the printer and handed it to Pierre. "The analysis came back from the swabs collected in the American's bathroom. What we smelled was correct. It's positive for chlorine bleach. But she was sloppy. Must've been in a hurry, because there were traces of blood, too, mixed in with the bleach."

"And the drain?" Pierre asked.

The tech nodded. "It was blood."

"No bleach in the drain?"

"No, sir. She only bleached what she could see. The floor and the countertop. The rest of the blood went down the drain, and . . . what is the saying? Away from the eyes . . ."

"Out of sight, out of mind. Does the blood match Mr. Crist?"

"We're testing it now. The lab is rushing

the DNA analysis."

"Her clothes?"

The technician shook his head. "No blood on her clothing. I tested them myself."

Pierre shook his head, thinking of all he needed to do in a short window. The local media were already, just two days into his investigation, a heavy presence at the resort. Their calls to headquarters demanding updates had been incessant. And the American media, Pierre was sure, were on the way. He needed to get ahead of the wave. The only thing more spectacular than a dead tourist was an American accused of killing him.

"Good work. Let me know when the DNA comes back." Pierre turned to leave.

"One more thing, sir."

Pierre turned back and followed the technician over to the corner of the laboratory, where the evidence cabinets stood. All relevant materials were stored in secured lockers during the analysis portion of an investigation before police took formal custody. The technician opened one of the cabinets.

"Dr. Mundi delivered the victim's clothes to us yesterday. We didn't get to them until late. The blood on the shirt collar belonged to Mr. Crist, no other blood found."

"Preserve the rest for DNA analysis."

"Yes, sir. We have already done so. We'll just need a sample to compare it against eventually."

"I'm working on it," Pierre said. He'd already spoken to the judge who rendered the search warrant. Fingerprints and mouth swabs would come only after an arrest. "Anything else?"

"Yes, sir." The technician removed a sealed plastic bag from the locker and handed it to the inspector. "In the victim's pocket, we found this."

Pierre took the evidence bag and held it up. A small box was preserved inside. Gray felt covered the exterior.

"What is it?" Pierre said, holding the evidence bag higher, as if this would make its contents more easily recognizable. "A box?"

"Yes, sir."

"What's in it?"

"A ring."

"A ring?" Pierre asked. "What sort of ring?"

"It appears to be an engagement ring, sir."

CHAPTER 8

"You never saw it, though, correct?"

"The ring? No," Grace said. "Julian's belongings were returned to his parents, who have not talked with me since then."

"Inspector Pierre's theory was that the ring found on Julian's body was meant for Allison Harbor, and that this discovery sent you into a jealous rage."

"I've heard his arguments. He presented them to me during the many hours when he interrogated me, much of which was done without a lawyer present, despite me asking for one. I never knew about the ring, or Julian's intention to propose to me. I had to put it together while everything was happening. Pierre taunted me with the ring, and all his theories about it. It's nonsensical that Julian would bring a ring to St. Lucia for anyone but me."

"How do you know Julian's intention was to propose on Gros Piton? He never told you this."

"He told my friend, Ellie. He wanted her help to make sure everything went smoothly."

Sidney consulted her notes again. "You mentioned your friend Ellie Reiser."

Grace smiled. "Yes. Dear friend."

"In the past ten years here at the Bordelais Correctional Facility, besides your family, two friends have made regular visits. Ellie Reiser and Daniel Greaves."

Grace nodded. "Prison is lonely, and being so far from home makes it difficult to visit. I understand this. But I'm grateful for Ellie and Daniel, who have come faithfully over the years. Their visits have helped me get through this."

"You and Ellie Reiser have been friends since childhood. Ellie, too, has sent me letters over the years asking me to look into your case."

"She's a good friend."

"Tell me about Daniel Greaves."

"Daniel is a special person. He and I have a strong friendship. One that has changed a lot since we first met, but it's a friendship that means a great deal to me."

"Daniel was a big part of your trial."

Grace nodded her head. "Yes."

"The prosecution suggested you two were

in a relationship."

"They suggested a lot of things. It doesn't mean any of it is true. Daniel and I had a relationship in the past. It ended. That's the whole story in a few words. Anything else is false."

"The prosecution suggested that your relationship with Daniel was active, and that Julian discovered this."

"Yes. It's all lies."

Sidney glanced down at her notes. "You were in St. Lucia to celebrate the wedding of Daniel and Charlotte."

"Correct."

"You said your relationship with Daniel has changed over the years. How so? You two used to date. How did you remain friends?"

Grace smiled slightly. "Daniel and I dated briefly in college. It was a fling. We had both just gone through breakups and we were there for each other. That's the end of the story."

"He had broken up with Charlotte?"

"Briefly, yes," Grace said. "We were together for about a month before we realized we were too good of friends to get involved romantically. And that was the end of it."

"Daniel has visited you eighteen times in ten years. Twice a year, essentially."

"Yes," Grace said.

"You can understand how someone might analyze your visitor log and get the impression that you and Daniel were more than friends?"

"If you believe Pierre, and are looking for something nefarious. Otherwise, to me, it looks like one friend visiting another."

"Okay," Sidney said. "But Daniel has visited you eighteen times over the years. Charlotte? Zero."

Grace stared at Sidney. She offered no reply.

"Why would Daniel make such an effort to keep in touch with you, but his wife — a friend who asked you to be her maid of honor — hasn't seen you in more than a decade?"

"I guess you'd have to ask Charlotte that question." Grace shook her head and ran a hand through the back of her hair. "This is not how I imagined our conversation would go."

"I'm just struggling with some of your history," Sidney said, "because I'm learning things that you didn't mention in your letters."

THE GIRL OF SUGAR BEACH
"Pilot" Episode
Based on the interview with Claude Pierre

Through the winding roads of St. Lucia, Pierre drove back to Sugar Beach Resort. The journey provided time to think. A complicated issue had fallen into his lap: an American killing another American on his island. It would not be long, once he made his findings public and his accusations apparent, that the Sebold girl would seek help from the American embassy. Authorities from the United States would surely want to become involved and updated. Their Federal Bureau of Investigation would offer their assistance. Pierre knew he had to act quickly, and keep his cards close until it was time to show his hand. The expedited search warrant for the American's room had surely put her on notice. Already he'd caught her in more than one lie — the cause of her argument with Julian had been the first, and now the shoeprint, which put her on the bluff despite her denial of this fact. And the discovery of the bleach cleanup and Mr. Crist's blood in her room would be paramount during the immediate chaos after her arrest. Indeed he'd need to act swiftly when the time came, but calmly until then.

The motorcade of four police vehicles pulled to the front entrance of the resort. Pierre stood from the backseat of the lead car and walked with his crew into the welcome atrium. The general manager hurried from behind the front desk to greet him.

"Inspector, good morning."

"I'm going to need your office again," Pierre said. "For another round of interviews. With my crew, I'd like you to contact the guests and organize the times."

A police officer handed the GM a list of names.

"Very well, sir. Anything we can do. I must ask, though, some of our guests are quite upset that the beach is still under survey. It is the main attraction of the resort and it is still roped off."

"I'm afraid the needs of sunbathers have been overshadowed by the dead man found on the shores of your resort. If any guest has an issue, please add their names to the interview list and I'd be happy to speak with them. As far as the yellow tape securing the beach, it will remain in place for the foreseeable future."

■ ■ ■ ■

Grace Sebold sat once more in the small office.

It was two-on-one again, with Grace sitting across from Pierre and the man who scribbled in his notebook. Pierre pressed the recorder that sat in the middle of the table.

"My parents told me to ask for an attorney," Grace said.

"Are you asking for one, Ms. Sebold?"

"Am I in trouble?"

"You would be best equipped to answer that question," Pierre said. "Your boyfriend was found dead just over forty-eight hours ago. We are trying to figure out who killed him. If you would like to go to Castries for formal questioning, that can be arranged. We could offer local counsel once you are settled there. However, it will take some time to organize such an event, and we'd have to hold you in a jail cell while we made the arrangements. It would likely be late tomorrow or perhaps the following day before we could secure counsel for you. There is, of course, no problem with this method, but I'd just assume we keep things moving as quickly as possible and avoid the delay."

Grace shook her head. "Fine. What do you want to know?"

"There is evidence to suggest that Mr. Crist was settled up on the bluff on Gros Piton for some time. Perhaps an hour or so. We suspect he was waiting for someone. I'd like to ask you again, did you see Mr. Crist on Wednesday night?"

"I saw Julian on Wednesday, during the day. We all hung out at the pool. But not Wednesday night. I thought we went through this the other day."

"You were on vacation together, Ms. Sebold. Was it common for Mr. Crist to spend an evening by himself, apart from the woman he was traveling with?"

Grace stared at the inspector. "I . . . No, it was unusual."

"Did he tell you where he was going? Did he tell you why he would hike up Gros Piton at evening time?"

Grace shook her head. "He invited me to watch the sunset. Same thing I told you two days ago."

"But you did not go? Your younger brother fell ill?"

"That's right."

"How long had you and Mr. Crist been dating?"

"A year and a half."

"So you would categorize your relationship as serious?"

Grace struggled again with the Caribbean inflection and the blending of words and oddly placed syllabic emphasis.

"Yes," she said.

"Were you in love?"

Grace's eyes teared over. "Is it really necessary to ask these questions?"

"I'm afraid it is, Ms. Sebold."

Grace wiped her lower lid with the back of her finger. "Yes, we were in love."

"Was Mr. Crist in love with anyone else, besides yourself?"

"What?" Grace asked with a confused look.

"Was there anyone else that Mr. Crist also loved?"

Grace shook her head. "No."

"No?" Pierre asked while keeping his eyes focused on her.

Pierre's assistant slid papers across the table until they rested in front of Grace.

"This is a list of calls made from Mr. Crist's room phone. Three calls were made to New York. The phone number is listed to Ms. Allison Harbor, who we've learned was a friend of Mr. Crist."

Grace swallowed hard. "She's his ex-girlfriend."

"Is that so? When I spoke with her, she suggested their relationship was still active."

"They go to school together, so I'm sure they still see each other on campus."

"Isn't it true that they were still *intimate,* Ms. Sebold, and not merely acquaintances, as you suggest?"

"No. That's not true."

"And you were not concerned about this?"

"No."

"But isn't it true that *you* also called Allison Harbor during your stay at the resort? Why make such a call if there is no concern?"

Grace looked down at the list of phone calls in front of her. She did not answer.

"So let me organize my thoughts," Pierre continued. "Mr. Crist, who was in love with you and only you, climbed up Gros Piton, spread a blanket out over a bluff, opened a bottle of champagne, poured two flutes, but never told you about this rendezvous?"

Grace shook her head again. "No, he *did* tell me. Not about a . . . rendezvous. He just asked me to meet him on the bluff. I didn't go, though."

Pierre's voice was rising. "But you and

Mr. Crist had an argument that day, is that correct?"

Grace shook her head and opened her palms. "Yes."

"You claim this argument was about Daniel Greaves, your friend's new husband."

"Yes, it was."

"Perhaps Mr. Crist found out about your relationship with the groom?"

Grace squinted her eyes at the detective. "There was no relationship."

"Is it not true that you and Mr. Greaves once dated?"

Grace took a deep breath. "Years ago. Yes."

"Perhaps you still had feelings for him."

"No, I did not."

"Perhaps being in such a romantic setting brought those feelings back to you? Perhaps you started to doubt your relationship with Mr. Crist."

Grace did not answer.

"No?"

"No," Grace said.

Inspector Pierre consulted his notepad. "A few nights ago, you and Charlotte Brooks also engaged in an argument at the Bayside Bar. Other guests of the resort witnessed this argument. Is this not true?"

Grace again remained silent.

"Without your input, Ms. Sebold, I can only assume your argument with the bride, understanding now your romantic history, had to do with your relationship with Daniel Greaves. Am I correct, Ms. Sebold?"

"Yes. But it was just a misunderstanding."

"A misunderstanding? Surveillance video of the resort shows Mr. Greaves visiting your cottage the day before his wedding. Are you certain you want to go on the record as denying a relationship between you and Daniel Greaves?"

"We are friends. That's all."

"You can see my confusion, though, Ms. Sebold. And how one might look at all of this and assume you were balancing many men at one time?"

"Many men? What are you saying?"

"And that, perhaps, after discovering the phone calls made between Julian and his lover in New York, you were angry and jealous. Perhaps, you were not thinking clearly? Perhaps, you did something out of rage?"

Grace shook her head. "No."

"Were you on Gros Piton on Wednesday evening, Ms. Sebold?"

Grace looked back and forth at the

recording device and the scribbling man, confused by the quick change in topics.

"Ms. Sebold! Were you on Gros Piton on Wed—"

"No."

"No?" Pierre asked, standing from his seat and hovering over her. "Then can you explain why your shoeprint was found there?"

Grace shook her head, then put her palms to her temples, as if trying to corral an impending migraine.

"No, I suppose that is unexplainable," Pierre said. "Can you tell me why you so thoroughly bleached your room?"

Pierre waited.

"No? Can you explain why Mr. Crist's blood was found in the drain of your sink?" Pierre waited. *"No?* You have no answers to any of this?"

"I'd like to speak to an attorney," Grace said.

Pierre continued to hover. After his outburst, the only noise in the room came from the hum of the air conditioner. The silence was broken when the door swung open.

"Sir," an officer said as he poked his head into the room. "We need you down on the beach. We've found something."

CHAPTER 9

"Fifteen minutes," the guard said.

Sidney nodded and looked back to Grace. "If I can frame it correctly, and explain away the doubts and misinformation about Allison Harbor and Daniel Greaves, I can imagine your love story with Julian making up the early narrative of the documentary. I can see this pulling the audience onto your side. But eventually the guts of the film will delve into Julian's murder. I'll have to present the case against you, Grace. Before I can refute the claims or highlight any inconsistencies, I'll need to show the audience everything that convicted you. All the evidence."

"I understand," Grace said.

"The problem is, there's a helluva lot to show. The print that puts you on the bluff, the blood in your room, the cleanup."

Grace exhaled and shook her head in defeat. "I just want the opportunity to tell my side. When viewed only through the lens the detectives offer, even I wonder how so much evidence could exist against me. But please remember that everything about this investigation was tainted, from the collection of evidence to the analysis. From the physical evidence to the DNA evidence to the proposed motives and methods . . . Sidney, it's all contrived. It was wrong then and it's still wrong today, ten years later. The detectives did exactly what they're trained *not* to do. They picked a suspect first, and then looked for evidence that supported their theory. And the problem with investigating a crime in that manner is that any evidence they came across that didn't support their theory was ignored or discarded."

Sidney nodded. She paused before she spoke again.

"But the murder weapon, Grace. It's a sticking point for me, and likely will be for the audience."

THE GIRL OF SUGAR BEACH
"Pilot" Episode
*Based on the interview with Claude Pierre

Pierre placed Grace Sebold under arrest. Two officers led her, hands cuffed behind her back, through the atrium and placed her in the back of a police car. Pierre headed with another officer in the opposite direction, through the lobby and toward Sugar Beach. He walked past the pool, where vacationers elbowed themselves up on deck chairs at the sight of Inspector Pierre and the officer hurrying by. Pierre stepped onto the soft sand of Sugar Beach and made his way past the open-dining restaurant, where breakfast was being enjoyed amid a cacophony of chiming plates and silverware. Those on holiday seemed oblivious to the fact that a guest had washed up on shore two days before.

"We roped it off as soon as we found it, sir," the officer said as they walked.

Pierre followed the officer down the beach until they reached the water-sport hut. Yellow tape blocked the entrance of the free-standing structure, which consisted of a palm-thatched roof that sat atop four stucco walls. Beige tile surrounded the shack, offering a break from the sand. It was here that guests rented all sorts of water-sport equipment: snorkels and fins, boogie boards and volleyballs. Because of the calm waters off Sugar Beach, and the protected location of Pitons Bay, stand-up paddleboarding was a popular attraction. A long row of yellow paddleboards stood in the sand to the side of the hut.

"What did you find?" Pierre asked.

The young officer offered a pair of latex gloves, which Pierre slipped over his hands as he entered the hut. The beige tile led him inside, and the interior of the shack was as meticulously maintained as the rest of the resort. Snorkel masks and scuba gear hung neatly from the walls: fins and vests and wet suits and regulators. Scuba tanks stood in organized fashion along an adjacent wall.

"Here, sir," the officer said as they walked to the back wall, which was covered with kayak and paddleboard oars. The officer pointed a flashlight into the back corner of the hut. A long, wooden oar stood haphazardly in the corner, resting sidelong with the handle on the tile floor and the blade wedged into the corner.

"It looked out of place because it was not hanging with the rest of the oars.

When I took a closer look, I noticed this," the officer said as he placed the beam of his flashlight close to the paddle.

Pierre leaned down. Without taking his eyes off the paddle, he waved his index finger at the officer and took the flashlight, placing it inches from the wooden blade. He ran the light down the shaft, then back up.

"Has anyone touched this oar?"

"No, sir. The activities hut has been vacant since Thursday morning when the beach was cordoned off. As soon as I noticed the paddle, I roped off the hut and put a call in for you."

"Well done. Get the crime scene men back down here."

As the officer hurried from the hut, Pierre continued to stare at the speckles of blood that covered the blade of the paddle.

A clear plastic tube preserved the wooden paddleboard oar as if it were on display at a museum. It rested next to Dr. Mundi as he stood at the autopsy table. He was finishing the postmortem of a St. Lucian man killed the night before during a drug deal gone awry.

"Is it possible?" Pierre said.

"Possible?" Dr. Mundi said as he mo-

mentarily stopped his work to stare at the preserved oar.

"Yes. It matches the nature of the fracture. A blunt, heavy object that could be swung at low-to-medium velocity. But I'd need to take measurements to see if the blade matches the size and shape of the skull fracture."

"Emmanuel," Pierre said, getting the doctor's attention by addressing him by his first name. "I understand the methodology you must use to confirm my suspicion. I also know that will take some time, of which I'm very short. What I'm asking you today is if you think this paddleboard oar could have been, not if it was for certain, but if it *could have been used* to strike Julian Crist and cause his head trauma."

"Perhaps," Dr. Mundi said, still scrutinizing the plastic tube while his hands were frozen midsuture above the body in front of him. "But from here, the size of the blade doesn't match what I remember about the fracture."

"His blood is on the blade, Emmanuel. DNA will prove that it is a match," Pierre said.

"You've made me aware of that fact, Claude."

Pierre looked across the mortuary at the

doorway, then back to Dr. Mundi. "I need this, Emmanuel," he said in a controlled voice. "I have pressure on me to get this under control quickly. I need you to tell me this oar caused the skull fracture."

"You're asking me, while I have a different body on my table, to confirm that this oar caused the skull fracture in the Crist case. My initial instinct is only that it's possible. I need to run the tests and perform my analysis. I'll need to pull the body from the cooler and have a closer look."

"When?"

"I'll be done here in an hour."

Pierre nodded, rested his hand on top of the plastic tube. "I'll wait."

CHAPTER 10

"Time's up," the guard said.

"Listen, Grace," Sidney said. "I'll be honest with you. Exonerations are terribly rare. They don't happen often, and never without new evidence turning up. I want you to know that I will be pitching this documentary to my network as a spotlight on you and your story. I can't promise anything will change for you because of this film. I can promise, however, that if we get the project off the ground, you and your case will gain mainstream attention from a major network in America. You'll have the haters and the cynics, those who will never believe you are anything but Julian Crist's killer. But if we present your case correctly, we may also capture the attention of others who believe you. And none of us know who those people might be, or where that attention will lead."

"I'll take attention right now," Grace said. "Because I've got nothing else. I've exhausted my appeals, so legally there is nothing left for me to pursue. This documentary is all I have. So I'm on board with you telling my story. A story the world has never heard because the real Grace Sebold was overshadowed ten years ago by the spectacular headlines of blood and cover-ups and shoeprints and skull fractures. 'Grisly Grace' with all her lovers who flew into a jealous rage. All that crap that had so little to do with who I am and what Julian meant to me. So, please, tell the world who Grace Sebold is. For that, I'll be forever grateful. But I'm begging you, Sidney. Look into my case. Look at the evidence that was used to convict me. Show how wrong it was. Show how inconsistent it was. Promise me you'll look."

Sidney opened her mouth to speak, then put her lips together to consider her words. "Listen, Grace, you've been through a lot in your life. Things I'll never understand and will never be able to relate to. I'm not going to be another person who delivers disillusionment to you. I'm going to make a documentary about *you*. About your history. About who Grace Sebold was when she came to Sugar Beach back in 2007, about how her boyfriend was killed, and about how she was accused and convicted of his murder. I'm going to highlight the way you've clung to your innocence for the past ten years. I'm going to present the idea that a police force, eager to avoid a drawn-out murder investigation that would hurt tourism, too quickly jumped to conclusions, utilized illegal interrogation techniques, and assigned you an incompetent defense attorney. I'll highlight the discrepancies of your case, and I'll cover everything you've told me in your letters. Will that be enough to find an audience? I think so. Will it be enough to prove your innocence? I doubt it."

"I *am* innocent, Sidney."

"I understand your conviction, Grace, but I can't promise that my documentary will prove this. Again, my intention is to tell your story. If, in doing so, we cast everything that stands against you into doubt, I'll consider it a victory."

Grace sat back in her chair, folded her arms across her chest.

"You don't believe me, do you?"

Sidney blinked a few times as she considered the question and all the evidence that had convicted Grace Sebold years ago. Her mind was clouded by everything she had learned from Claude Pierre. She glanced quickly at the camera filming from the corner of the room, and then looked back to Grace. "I'm not sure what I believe."

JURY DELIBERATION
DAY 1

As the twelve jury members sat around the conference table, it took thirty minutes of introductions until it was decided that Harold Anthony would act as foreman. Harold was one of four men on the jury; the other eight were women. Five were business professionals, two were retired, and one was a stay-at-home mom.

Harold Anthony was a local businessman with a calm demeanor and clear ability to lead. He was an easy choice to head a group discussion that would determine a woman's fate, and decide if she was guilty or innocent of murder.

"Okay," Harold said from the head of the conference table. "The entire case, offered from both sides, has been presented to us. The judge has made it clear that the world is watching and waiting for the twelve of us to make a decision. The media scrutiny will be intense and, perhaps, overwhelming. The judge has made clear that after a thorough and complete deliberation, we need to stand together as one on our decision. So I think the first thing we should do is discuss our initial thoughts and clarify any areas we do not fully understand."

"Her fingerprints were found on the murder weapon," one of the retired women said. "I'm not fully understanding what there is to debate."

"Well," Harold said. "Since our initial vote was not unanimous, we've been burdened with the task of debate until such time that we all agree. But you bring up a good jumping-off point. The murder weapon, and her fingerprints on it, is as good a place to start that debate as any."

■ ■ ■ ■ ■

PART II
THE PITCH

■ ■ ■ ■ ■

CHAPTER 11

Monday, March 20, 2017

The network's headquarters building was located in midtown. Sidney took a cab across Forty-second Street until traffic choked her progress. She dropped the fare over the seat, thanked the driver, and stepped into the spring morning. Weaving between cars until she reached the curb, she blended into the steady current of Monday-morning commuters flowing through the streets of Manhattan. She bumped shoulders for four blocks until she pushed through the revolving doors and into the lobby. The elevator took her to the forty-fourth floor. She showed her ID card to get past reception, then swiped it again to gain access to the executive offices. Her meeting was at 9:00 a.m. and traffic had slowed her down. The plan had been to sip coffee in the lobby's café and peacefully collect her thoughts before her pitch. Instead, she was rushing to make it on time.

The office was a cacophony of glass walls that offered little in the way of privacy for the executives running the network. The architectural design allowed Sidney, as she exited the elevator, to see that the media room was already full. She took a deep breath and hurried across the office. When she pulled open the door, she was relieved to hear the quiet murmur of several overlapping conversations. A dozen rows of chairs lined the room, all facing the north wall, where a DVD projector lit up a floor-to-ceiling screen with the title:

The Girl of Sugar Beach,
Producer: Sidney Ryan

She squeezed into the only vacant seat, which was in the front row and reserved for her. She believed for a moment that her last-minute arrival went unnoticed.

"The Great Sidney Ryan has finally joined us for her own screening," Luke Barrington announced in his deep, obnoxious voice.

Sidney closed her eyes and exhaled. She had mistakenly believed Luke only used the insufferable voice during the recording of his prime-time news program. However, over the last year, she learned the rhythmic churning of hop-along syllables and cavern-ous inflection came with everything he ut-tered, from the detailing of a young wom-an's death on his top-rated news show, to the retelling of his weekend over Monday-morning coffee. Sidney wanted to claim that the sonorous voice, which had privately earned him a nickname of "the Bear," was plastic-banana fake, but since Luke had never once faltered from this tone, she could only argue that it was annoying.

"Now that we're all behind schedule," the Bear continued, "let's rush things along, shall we?"

This was directed at Graham Cromwell, who ran the news division at the network.

Graham walked to the front of the screen-ing room and stood in the glow of the DVD projector. "Thanks, Luke. Sorry to keep you from your morning round of golf. But perhaps you should put in a few hours of work this week. Your ratings are flat."

This brought a chorus of chuckles.

"Flat," Luke said. "And still the highest ratings of the network. And on all of prime-time news."

Graham opened his mouth in mock amazement. "Highest ratings of prime time? Really? No one in this room has heard this breaking news."

This brought more chuckles. Luke Barrington was a self-promoter of epic proportions, and modesty had never been a strong suit.

"My ratings are flat, incidentally, because I was on vacation for ten days. And, as we all know, the network has yet to find a guest host that can hold my audience."

"It was a joke, Luke. We're trying to set Sidney up here in prime time as well, since her previous documentaries have been so well received. We think there is opportunity here with this latest pitch. She has clearly generated a following."

"So let's see it then," Luke said. "The suspense is killing us."

Spoken, Sidney thought, *like a true asshole.*

"Sidney?" Graham said.

Sidney stood and took her place at the front of the media room. In addition to the packed audience inside the room, she noticed other staffers congregating in the hallway to get a sneak peek of her much-buzzed-about documentary.

"True crime is popular," Sidney said. "We all know this. And it's getting hotter. We don't have to look further than *Making a Murderer* and *The Jinx* to see the huge ratings potential for the networks. *48 Hours* is a perennial ratings winner. *Serial* was one of the most downloaded podcasts in history. The public has an appetite for true-life crimes broken down into real-life thrillers told through documentaries.

"As Graham pointed out, my previous three documentaries took unknown cases and unknown prisoners and brought to light their stories of wrongful conviction. We grew a larger audience with each doc, and we've developed a bit of a niche here — finding victims of wrongful conviction and bringing their stories of injustice to light. My pitch today for my new documentary is different in two ways from my previous films. It's an ambitious pitch that is filled with potential. I hope you all agree."

Sidney noticed that additional network staff had filed into the back of the media room, making it a standing-room-only crowd. She also noticed that Graham Cromwell had given up his seat when Dante Campbell, the cohost of the network's top-rated morning show, *Wake Up America,* snuck in. Sidney faltered for just a moment when she recognized all of the power that had assembled in the room: the queen of morning television, Luke Barrington, the suits in the front row. She was suddenly glad she had been running late so that the enormity of the moment hadn't had a chance to crush her.

"First," Sidney continued, "instead of an unknown case, this time I'll be highlighting a well-known individual."

"Who is it?" Luke Barrington asked in a bored voice.

Sidney smiled, a veneer that suggested to all in the room that she was thrilled to be conversing with such an esteemed legend of prime time. In her own mind, though, her curved lips were the equivalent of raising her middle finger.

"Grace Sebold."

There were some murmurs in the crowd, a quiet buzz of excitement at such a high-profile case.

"That's an old story," Luke said.

"Which is why it's interesting," Sidney said. "She's been in jail for ten years and has clung to her innocence without falter."

"Let me interview a hundred inmates at Otisville and I'd hear the same thing a hundred times. All sob stories from felons who are guilty as sin."

"You run current-event stories, Luke," Graham Cromwell said. "You've cornered the market on opinion news. This is a true-crime documentary. It won't pull from your audience."

Now Luke was the one who offered a fake smile. "You think I'm worried about her taking my audience?"

"Are you?" Sidney asked.

Many in the room turned to stare at the Bear.

He offered a small chuckle. Even this sound came with an annoying echo. "Certainly not."

"Then stop interrupting and listen to her pitch," Graham said.

Sidney glanced at Graham, then back to her audience. She caught a quick wink and a subtle head nod from Dante Campbell.

"Grace Sebold is well-known, so I anticipate an early surge of interest to piggyback on my base viewership. My other docs started slowly and built a larger audience over time as the episodes got closer to the conclusion. Here, I'm hoping for a bigger initial audience."

Sidney cleared her throat. "The other difference is that *The Girl of Sugar Beach* will be produced as a real-time documentary. I'll produce episodes as I investigate. I've cut the pilot and roughs of the opening couple of episodes, a summary of which we will screen this morning. It includes my interview with Inspector Pierre from St. Lucia, the evidence that convicted Grace

Sebold, and the early love affair between Grace and Julian Crist. The episodes will be a retelling of events, as I understand them. A mix of reenactments as well as live footage of my investigation. The audience will discover what I discover as I discover it."

"There's a lot of risk there," Luke said.

"I tend to agree with Luke on this," Ray Sandberg said from the front row. Sandberg was the president of the network. He would have the final say in green-lighting Sidney's project, or cutting its throat. "A problem with *Serial* was a very unsatisfying ending that left more questions than answers."

"So let's learn from that," Graham said. "We'll build the suspense, and give them a satisfying ending. The payoff could be huge. We're going to bring back Grace Sebold and Julian Crist. We're not only going to dive into their love story and find out who they are, but we're also going to find the truth. *That* will capture an audience."

"Capturing an audience is not what concerns me," Ray said. "It's capturing them with a grand promise and not delivering. Then we lose their trust. Has anyone seen the numbers for the second season of *Serial*? We don't know the whole story about Grace Sebold. What happens if you come up with nothing revealing other than a young medical-school student who killed her boyfriend?"

"That's the lure," Sidney said. "I don't know what I'm going to find when I start digging, and neither does the audience. But there's more to the Grace Sebold story than any of us know."

"Based on what?"

"My trip to St. Lucia, where Grace Sebold has spent ten years in jail. I spoke with the detective who ran the case. The investigational capabilities down there are not the same as here in the States. Their economy hinges on tourism, and the entire police force was under pressure to solve this case. Wrap it up and make it go away so potential tourists weren't deterred from visiting the island. I think, in order to close the investigation as quickly as possible, they made the evidence fit the narrative. I also spoke with Grace Sebold, as you're about to see. We had a long discussion about her case and about the evidence that got her convicted a decade ago. She can convincingly poke holes in every bit of it."

"If she can so convincingly convey her innocence to you," Luke Barrington said, "why could her attorney not convince a jury?"

"She was forced to use local counsel. It's

law in St. Lucia that a local attorney needed to be part of her team. He was not a skilled defense attorney and made crucial errors during the trial. Of course, in the heat of the battle and after the shock of losing her boyfriend and being accused of his murder, Grace was unaware of these mistakes. Only with time did her attorney's inadequacies become so glaring. And we all know that juries can be persuaded by theatrics as much as they are by facts. The day she walked into court, Grace Sebold was practically convicted by the news media and by the Internet."

"How many episodes?" Ray Sandberg asked.

"I'll need to map out my production plan and get a grip on the arc of the story. But my current proposal is for ten, with some leeway, obviously, based on my investigation. I've cut the pilot and have outlines for what I want to do for the first four installments."

"Timing?"

"Summer," Graham said. "Three months in summer. June through August. Ten weeks to let Grace Sebold's story unfold."

"Not just *tell* her story," Dante Campbell said from the front row. "Sidney wants to give the audience the truth, which she thinks is different from what has been told to the world up to this point. I'm already a fan."

Sidney smiled at Dante, pinched her brows together in a silent nod of gratitude. The woman trumped even the great Luke Barrington in the network's power rankings, her morning show bringing in hundreds of millions in yearly revenue.

Without delay, and as Dante's backing still hung in the air, Graham dimmed the lights and Sidney stepped to the side of the screen as the first cut of her pilot episode began to play.

THE GIRL OF SUGAR BEACH
"Match Day" Part of Episode 1
Based on the interview with Grace Sebold

On the third Friday of March, Grace Sebold joined 158 of her classmates as they all gathered in Hiebert Lounge on the campus of Boston University Medical College. Besides the occasional students who wore jeans and sport coats, or casual blouses and skirts, formal spring dresses and suits were the common attire. Coffee and breakfast pastries covered a long table, where students filled plates and talked the hour away. Grace woke with an upset stomach and couldn't muster the thought of a jelly-filled doughnut, let alone the acidic burn of coffee. Instead, she paced the hallways in isolation, not interested in mingling with her classmates. She had this way about her, taking joyous moments and turning them into angst-clouded misery.

There was a palpable buzz in the air. Today, every fourth year medical student would learn which residency program they had matched to. The ceiling of Hiebert Lounge was netted with balloons that would fall through the air and cascade off students as they opened their Match Day envelopes. The university had taken, during the last few years, to documenting the morning's event through a professional videographer service that set up cameras in strategic positions to capture everything. Cameramen strolled the crowd of students and their families taking testimonials and ready for close-up shots when envelopes were opened.

Grace had participated in the early-morning group photo as the fourth years gathered on the front steps of the medical-school building and made "Oh, my God" facial expressions so the university could upload the whole day onto their websites and attract future applicants. But now, after the initial photo shoot and as the envelope opening was nearing, she had no interest in making small talk as the cameras rolled. All she wanted was to open her letter and see if she matched to New York.

She stood in front of the window and stared at the buildings of downtown Boston. She pulled her phone out and her thumbs moved like lightning as she texted Julian:

Five more minutes.
Yes! Everyone is nuts here.

This is so stupid. Just let us open the cards. Such a stupid production.
Relax! Have fun and stop stressing.

A clinking and some whistling drew Grace's attention.

Gotta go. About to open our envelopes! Us too. Call you in a minute.

Grace looked up from her phone and took a deep breath. She walked down the long flight of stairs, pushed through the glass doors and into the lounge.

"We are very pleased to welcome all fourth-year students and their loved ones to Match Day at Boston University!" the program director said into a booming microphone. "We are proud of our students and the dedication they have shown in the past four years. We wish you the best of luck. And now, without further ado, we present your Match Day envelopes!"

Placed neatly on a table were 159 white envelopes containing the names of each fourth-year student. Inside was a single piece of paper that told each where they had matched. Grace thought she heard a countdown, people around her chanting numbers in reverse. But the noise and voices were in the background. She was concentrating only on the table. She estimated where her envelope would be located in alphabetical order. The crowd began to cheer, the singsong countdown ended, and the herd moved toward the table. Grace moved with everyone else, weaving past students, and finally came to the table. The envelopes had been picked over, and the once-pristinely-organized rows of white rectangles were now scattered at odd angles. She found the *S*'s and scrolled down until she spotted her name. She snatched the envelope.

Already students around her were cheering as they read their letters. She walked calmly through the crowd with her unopened envelope and exited Hiebert Lounge, took the elevator to the ground floor, and pushed through the front doors of the building and into the cool March morning. She stuck her finger into the flap of her envelope and tore it open, pulling the page from within and letting the remnants of the torn envelope drop to the ground. She skimmed past her name and ID number until she came to the middle of the page:

Congratulations, you have matched!

Program: Neurosurgery
Location: The Hospital for Special Surgery
Cornell University, New York

Without allowing the feat to register, she dialed her phone.

"Where?" Julian asked before the first ring had ended.

"Cornell."

Silence.

"Julian? Did you open your envelope?"

There was a long pause.

"Tell me!" she said.

"Same."

Sidney's face came onto the screen in the media room on the forty-fourth floor of the network's headquarters building as she stared into the camera with Cornell University in the background. It was a bright morning and the rising sun highlighted the hospital's glass lobby behind her.

"On Match Day — March 17, 2007 — Grace Sebold and Julian Crist, an all-American couple that had met during a medical-student program in Delhi, discovered their futures. They both placed into the highly competitive specialty of neurosurgery, and matched together at the same residency program at Cornell University. By any measure, these two accomplished and ambitious young adults were on their way to a storied future. But saving lives was not what waited for them. Tragically, less than two weeks after they opened their Match Day envelopes, Julian Crist was dead and Grace Sebold was on trial for his murder."

Sidney moved slowly down the campus walkway, never taking her gaze from the camera. "Over this summer, and through the next ten episodes, we will become intimate with this once-promising couple. We will learn the sad events that led to Julian Crist's death on St. Lucia's famed Sugar Beach, and we will meet the girl who loved him. We will work to understand her, to show you the events that molded Grace Sebold's life and sent her on a quest to become a surgeon. We will also delve into the last decade of her life, which she has spent in a foreign correctional facility alongside other convicted murderers. We will learn her story. A story rife with baffling twists and bizarre revelations. A story told both from Grace's perspective and from those responsible for convicting her. We will examine the evidence that put Grace behind bars, and determine if it was based on science or fiction. This summer, we will look into the soul of Grace Sebold and finally discover the truth."

Sidney stopped walking, the hospital and its brilliant glass façade shining in the background.

"I'm Sidney Ryan, and this is *The Girl of Sugar Beach.*"

The DVD projector died and the lights in the media room came back on. There were more murmurs from the audience, and Sidney noticed that a larger crowd had gathered in the hallway during the screening.

"I love it!" Dante Campbell said. "It makes me want to know Grace's story. Absolutely love it."

"Thanks, Dante," Sidney said. She shared a moment of eye contact with the network's biggest star.

"Ray?" Graham said.

Ray Sandberg stood from the front row. "Helluva pitch." He looked at Sidney. "Let's talk logistics this afternoon."

"Absolutely," Sidney said.

The crowd thinned out as the audience shuffled for the doors.

"I don't think Luke is a fan," Sidney said

when she and Graham were alone. "Luke doesn't sign the checks."

CHAPTER 12

Tuesday, March 28, 2017

A week later, after scores of meetings with network executives, Sidney had her project green-lit for summer. She sat at her desk and edited a clip from the opening episode. Over the past seven days, the pilot episode was polished and pitched to the suits who made programming decisions, and to sales managers who decided on potential advertisers. In house, there was a general sense of excitement about the documentary and for the real-time format. Sidney had screened and outlined the guts of the first few installments, and as those began to air, she would work to put together new episodes from revelations she hoped to discover as she dug into Grace Sebold, Julian Crist, their pasts, and the events at Sugar Beach.

The anticipation over what she might turn up was the genesis of the buzz within the network, and the source of angst Sidney felt in her stomach. As she sat at her desk, she reminded herself again, as her heart rate began to rise and the voice in the back of her head whispered its doubts, she didn't have to show the audience *who* killed Julian Crist. She just needed to present coherently the possibility that it wasn't Grace Sebold.

The edit suggestions Sidney was working on came from Ray Sandberg, who didn't have a creative bone in his body, but who felt the need to tweak the pilot before he wrote a check. Before Sidney could disagree with Ray's suggestions, Graham Cromwell had given Sidney a discouraging headshake during the meeting that told her everything she needed to know.

Say yes to the edits in order to get the documentary off the ground.

Graham's subtle gesture was a reminder that Sidney was not creating a documentary to be optioned for distribution, but was instead kowtowing to network executives to get her project approved. If she could hurdle this initial obstacle, Graham promised she'd have more creative control going forward. And so, with a broad smile, Sidney had spent the morning with the administrators, sales managers, and general bureaucrats of the network's news division, listening to the suggested edits to the pilot episode of *The*

Girl of Sugar Beach. And now, after these final tweaks, the documentary's maiden episode was slated to air in the beginning of June.

The summary she had screened in the media room a week before had enough content for four one-hour episodes. Sidney's goal over the next couple of weeks was to find enough material, and new and relevant evidence, for the next four installments. And then, somehow, create a conclusion that would span the final two episodes and turn up enough proof to show that Grace Sebold is not as guilty as the world believes.

It was a tall task, and not for the first time, Sidney considered that she had bitten off more than she could chew. And there lay the dilemma of trying to break into an industry: When your pitch is so strong that people like Dante Campbell start to believe in you, along with their confidence comes the pressure to deliver. Today, after a year of reviewing Grace Sebold's case and reading the hundreds of letters she and Ellie Reiser had written to her, after researching, interviewing, and creating the rough cuts of the opening episodes, and after her official pitch, Sidney was no longer chasing this project. The documentary was a go. Now she was chasing relevance. Now it was time to deliver. Her first deadline felt like a tightening noose around her neck, which was why, when she looked up from her computer to see Luke Barrington strolling into her office, she let out a long sigh.

"What do you need, Luke?"

"It looks like you need more than I do. You need a story, and I'm not sure you have one." The Bear's voice echoed off the walls of her office.

"Thanks for your concern. I'll manage."

"Do you?"

"Do I what?"

"Have a story?"

"Yes, Luke. I have a story. And work to do, so . . ."

"You know," Luke said.

Sidney heard his deep, fake voice begin, as if he were imparting some piece of wisdom to his audience.

"This thing of yours. This crusade to help victims of wrongful conviction . . . it's noble. It's quite a niche, but is it sustainable?"

"Is it *what*?"

"*Sustainable.* Can you make a career out of it? You see, my career is the news. Politics, which has forever been and will forever be."

"I guess you're covered then. But I don't like politics."

"I'm not worried about my career."

Sidney smiled. "Don't worry about mine, either, Luke. I might be just a feeble woman, but I can manage just fine. And I don't like being harassed."

He offered a condescending laugh. "I'm not harassing you. I'm trying to help you. Are there actually that many wrongfully convicted people out there? Are you going to save them all? One after another?"

"Right now, I'm only worried about one of them. And I'm under deadline, Luke, so give me some privacy."

"Where does it come from? This crusade of yours?"

"It comes from three successful documentaries. I know you're not going to acknowledge anyone's success besides your own, but my interest comes from the fact that I've done this three other times with great success."

Luke puckered his lower lip and tilted his head to the side like a dog that heard a high-pitched whistle. "I'd classify the success as moderate more than great, but that's neither here nor there. And I was only asking to discover your influence. Many people ask me mine."

Sidney went back to her edits without taking the bait.

"You seem like you're busy, I'll let you get

back to work."

"Perfect," Sidney said.

"If you need any advice, let me know."

This caused Sidney to smile. "Luke, you've never made a documentary series in your life, even though you slapped your name on the one I created for the network last year. Why would I ask you for advice?"

Now Luke smiled. "Not on how to make your documentary, sweetheart. But perhaps you'd like advice on how to find an audience. I'm quite versed at that."

Sidney rolled her eyes and went back to her computer as the Bear mercifully left her office. Even after he was gone, she could hear his plangent voice reverberating in the hollows of her office.

"Where does it come from? This crusade of yours?"

She went back to her editing, but forgot what she was attempting to accomplish in the current clip.

"Damn it," she said as she pushed the laptop aside.

She glanced to the edge of her desk, where a lone envelope rested. She had been avoiding it since it arrived two days before. Finally she reached for it and tore it open, pulling out the letter, which was creased sharply in thirds. When she unfolded the page, a small square of tissue paper rested inside, also folded neatly.

Sidney paused at the discovery, examining the pouch before carefully pulling apart the tissue. When she did, several crescent-shaped fingernail clippings fell onto her desk. She dropped the tissue and let out a long, defeated breath.

"For Christ's sake."

CHAPTER 13

Friday, March 31, 2017

Baldwin State Prison was located in Milledgeville, Georgia. Some of the worst offenders of Georgia's most grievous crimes end up at Baldwin, a male-only prison. Over the years, Sidney had made her share of visits. She had gotten to know a few of the guards, who joked about which convict she was going to set loose. It had been six months since her last journey to Georgia, and she wasn't sure why she chose this weekend to visit Baldwin. She blamed Luke Barrington. The voice that whispered from the dark corners of her mind, telling her that *The Girl of Sugar Beach* was too difficult a project to pull off, also played a part. And like a ten-year-old running from the playground, Sidney ignored the thought that she was seeking condolence on this trip to Baldwin. It was too pitiful to consider, so she pretended it wasn't true.

She went through the now-habitual routine of signing forms, showing ID, walking through metal detectors, standing crucifix-like while a guard ran a wand up and down her body, and allowing a polite female guard to pat her down to check for drugs and weapons. After thirty minutes, she was allowed to sit in a waiting room with a half-dozen other visitors. Leslie Martin, her coproducer, had sent video footage she was hoping to include in the pilot, and Sidney spent her time watching the clips on her phone and making notes. Eventually a staff member slid the glass partition open.

"Sidney Ryan."

Sidney looked up from her phone and raised her hand.

"You're up, darlin'," the woman said.

Sidney walked to the door next to the glass partition and pulled it open after the woman buzzed it unlocked.

"No camera crew?" the woman asked.

Sidney smiled. "Not today."

The woman pointed down a row of booths, where glass barriers separated visitors from inmates.

"Number six."

"Thanks," Sidney said as she headed down the row. She was always careful to pay no attention to the other visitors sharing this intimate time with those that were locked away. She kept her eyes down and stared at her feet until she was seated in her booth. Only then did she look up at the glass divider. Sometimes he was seated there, waiting. At other times, he appeared from a side door as a guard walked him to the booth.

Today she waited nearly five minutes for him to materialize. The orange suit he wore looked far too big. His skinny, pale arms leaked from the sleeves like wilting vines. He offered a subtle smile as he sat down. She knew inmates learned only that they had a visitor, not the identity. He picked up the phone and placed it to his ear. Sidney did the same.

They stared at each other without saying a word. Sidney blinked a few times and finally spoke.

"Hi, Dad."

CHAPTER 14

Thursday, June 1, 2017

On the first Thursday in June, as temperatures in Manhattan began to surge and humidity hung heavy in the air, the hospital room was cool. Too cool, in fact, for the nurses, but kept at the frigid temperature by the room's sole resident for two simple reasons. One: He despised being hot, and his body overheated in a flash. Always had, since the age of fifteen. And considering he wasn't able to bathe himself yet, the last thing he needed was to wallow in sweaty sheets and a foul-smelling T-shirt. And two: He knew the thermostat set at sixty-one degrees pissed the nurses off. And, well, to hell with them.

The blinds were closed and the last he remembered was the final remnants of the summer evening spilling through the boxed edges of the window. Physical therapy wiped him out by seven o'clock each evening,

164

causing him to doze the nights away, only to wake alert and restless at three each morning. This was something else that angered the nurses, since he pressed the call button as soon as he woke to ask for assistance to the bathroom. He didn't piss in bed, he'd told the nurses more than once. And the other act was completely out of the question.

They didn't like his defiance, his contempt, or his generally curmudgeonly attitude, and the nurses had let him know.

"I'll add you to the long list of folks in my life who feel the same way," he had told the head nurse who staged an intervention-type sit-down with him two days after his arrival. "I'll even do it today if you'd just help me to the john."

What pissed him off most about being in this place was that he had no control over his environment. Helplessness had never been part of his character. He simply didn't buy into the premise. He had lived his life by taking control of situations, and lying in this hospital bed had stolen not just his dignity, but his authority as well. To ram this reality home, the nurses played the game of making him wait for half an hour before they appeared each morning. He was sure most chumps in this place soiled themselves during the wait, or filled the clear plastic container that stood on the breakfast table and then lingered like cattle for their keepers to come and congratulate them on such a fine accomplishment before dumping their waste in the toilet.

But he was new to this place, having just been delivered after surgery a little more than a week before, and the nurses hadn't quite figured out that he wasn't like most chumps. Once he recognized the purpose of the waiting game, which he took as a non-verbal way for the nurses to explain to him how things worked, he turned the predawn hours into a real treat for everyone yesterday when he purposely capsized the breakfast table in his attempt to make his own way to the toilet. The chaos sent nurses sprinting into his room to find him sitting on the edge of the bed.

"Lil' help would be nice," he had said.

They were not amused.

That was yesterday morning and the witches had adapted their strategy this morning. He noticed now as he opened his eyes in the darkened room that they'd moved the breakfast table to the other side of the room; and while he slept, the plastic receptacle had been tucked between his good hip and the side rail of the bed. They may as well have attached a sticky note: *Up yours.* He almost appreciated their tactics.

The glowing windows were dark now, the first clue that he'd been asleep for at least a few hours. The next was the pressure in his bladder. When his eyes adjusted to the dark, the wall clock told him it was just past 3:00 a.m.

He pressed the call button and waited. He took a deep breath, adjusted in bed to take the stress off his bladder, and considered that he might have no choice this morning but to use the plastic receptacle. He watched the clock tick along until the minute hand crept past the nine. He knew that's what they wanted — to walk into his room and discover that they had broken him. A broken man he was, there was little doubt of that. But beaten? Not a chance. He didn't piss in bed, simple as that.

The IV and port came out first with a surge of pain up his arm. The tubes in his nose next, and the sticky buttons on his chest after that. One of them — he couldn't tell which, since he'd ripped them all in such quick succession — created a hell of a racket with alarms beeping and blasting. The nurses were there in a blink, two of them bolting through his door.

When they saw him alert and awake, they

started their scolding.

"What are you doing, Mr. Morelli?"

"I'm not playing your game," he told them. "I pressed that button forty minutes ago."

"We have other patients to take care of," the nurse said as she assessed the damage, picking up the loose IV. "You could've hurt yourself pulling this out."

"At three in the morning? You're not so busy in the middle of the night that you can't at least check on me. I have to take a leak. I'm not asking you to fluff my pillow. If I could make it to the bathroom on my own, trust me I'd do it."

"There is a urinal right here," the nurse said, holding up the plastic container.

"And I told you I'm not using that. It'll take five minutes out of your shift to help me to the john. Have some goddamn compassion!"

The nurse pulled the wheelchair over, while the other grabbed him under the armpit. "It's such a joy to have you here, Mr. Morelli."

He grunted as they lowered him into the chair. "The pleasure's all mine," he said.

The following evening, Friday, was the start of the weekend staff. Although he hadn't seen any of them yet, he knew they had arrived for the 7:00 p.m. to 11:00 a.m. shift. He would never admit it, but the regulars were making his life miserable. He hoped for a better crew this weekend. Even made a quick vow to be more tolerable.

His hip was on fire from physical therapy, and the pain was preventing him from dozing off to sleep like he normally did at this time of evening to escape the pain. He pressed the call button and was surprised when a nurse appeared a minute later.

"What do you need, Mr. Morelli?"

Gus opened his eyes. "Oh, I didn't expect you so soon."

"I'm Riki. I'll be your nurse tonight. And again on Sunday. What's up?"

"My leg hurts from therapy."

She checked the log next to his bed. "Where's the pain? One to ten?"

"Eight."

"Your last morphine was six hours ago. I'll give you another dose. Your doctor approved it every four to six hours for the first week post-op."

"Thank you."

Riki returned a minute later, pushing a tray draped with white sterile paper. A syringe and vial rested on top. She peeled open the syringe and speared the needle through the top of the vial, drawing out the morphine. As she adjusted the port on his arm, he twitched lightly at the pain.

"Sorry, sweetie," Riki said, looking at Gus's arm. "You're all bruised. What've they been doing to you? Beating you up?"

Off to such a good start, Gus felt it unnecessary to explain that his tantrum the previous morning was the cause of his purple arm.

"Nah," he said. "I had a new gal. She did the best she could."

Riki shook her head as she examined the port. "I'll take care of you."

Never great with needles, he looked up at the television screen to keep his eyes occupied. He saw a woman's face filling the screen.

"See," Riki said. "You didn't feel a thing."

A direct avenue into his blood supply, the morphine had an immediate effect. Though he stared straight at the television, Gus struggled to hear as the morphine pulled him away.

Riki drew the needle from the port and dropped it back onto the cart. She looked up at the television as she peeled off her latex gloves. "Oh, I'm excited to watch this. It's about that girl who killed her boyfriend in St. Lucia. Remember that?"

Gus blinked his eyes. He heard the nurse's voice, but her words didn't fully register.

The nurse finished cleaning up, keeping her gaze on the television. When she looked back at Gus, his eyes were in a stoic haze, unblinking as he stared straight ahead.

"She was convicted years ago," Riki said, pointing at the television. "Now she says she's innocent. The documentary is supposed to be good. Supposed to show that maybe she didn't do it. At least, that's what a few of the spoiler websites are saying. Tonight's the first episode."

The nurse looked down at her patient. He was staring at his hand, like it belonged to someone else, opening and closing his fingers into a tight fist.

"Yep," Riki said. "That's the morphine. Makes you numb. How's the pain?"

"Gone," Gus said in a far-away voice.

"Good."

Riki picked up the remote and changed the channel to the Yankees game.

"Here, this seems like it's more up your alley."

Gus leaned back into the pillow and stared up at the game. The Yankees were winning in the bottom of the eighth. "You're a sweetheart."

CHAPTER 15

Monday, June 5, 2017

The conference room was full by nine o'clock on Monday morning. Steam spiraled from ceramic mugs resting in front of each of the twenty-two people seated around the table, filling the air with the smell of hazelnut. Morning sunlight spilled through the forty-fourth-floor windows and shone off the mahogany. Graham Cromwell brought the meeting to order. He talked about the coming weeks of programming.

"Luke has two specials planned for this summer. The first will begin next month, covering the history of the White House. We've confirmed the president's participation with one prerecorded interview, as well as a personal walk-through of the Oval Office. This, obviously, is a huge honor and speaks to Luke's influence."

"It's not just the current president, Graham. Over the weekend, my producer confirmed that the previous two presidents have also agreed to participate in the special. We'll interview them at their private residences. I'm off to Texas later in the week to conduct the first interview." Luke smiled. "I mean, why stop at one if they're all on board?"

"Really?" Graham said. "How did you pull that off?"

"It's amazing," Luke said as he glanced quickly at Sidney. "I hired a producer that actually gets his calls returned. . . ."

Graham nodded. There was little doubt the network had a solid star in Luke Barrington. He had been at the top of the prime-time ratings for more than a decade, and this summer's Fourth of July special with exclusive access to the White House was sure to keep him there. As pompous and demanding as Luke could be to his staff and producers, Graham knew he was hands-on with this White House project. Graham had seen the content summary of the proposed special. Along with the White House tour — staged currently to show viewers the president's first-person journey and morning routine, from waking in the East Wing to sitting in the Oval Office — Luke had a fascinating history of the White House planned, showcasing secret tunnels, safe rooms, and vaults. It was sure to draw a large audience. And now, with interviews confirmed with two former presidents, it was sure to be a ratings giant.

"Impressive. We're all looking forward to it," Graham said. "Marketing and promotion have already started and will pick up this month. The four-episode special, *Inside the White House,* is due to premiere just ahead of the Fourth of July. Anything else to add?"

Luke smiled and looked around the conference table. "Tune in."

"Okay," Graham said. "Onto *The Girl of Sugar Beach.* Episode one aired this past Friday and drew one-point-two million viewers. Excellent start, Sidney. America is still interested in Grace Sebold."

"Are we classifying this as an excellent start?" the Bear asked. "My evening news program pulls in eight million viewers each night, and she didn't even retain a quarter of my audience. I was her lead-in because we thought my viewers would make the jump."

"We knew there would be falloff," Graham said. "The demographics of the two programs don't match perfectly, so we may rethink the timing."

"Old people watch your show," Sidney

said. "We're working to generate a larger audience in the eighteen-to–forty-four demographic."

"I'd suggest you work harder then," Luke said. He looked back to Graham. "And she's not finished with the investigation . . . so will the million viewers she managed still be interested at the end?"

"My investigation is ongoing, which is why it's called a real-time documentary, Luke. The excitement comes from discovering things as you go along. Since it's not scripted and you can't read it off a teleprompter, I don't expect you to fully grasp the concept."

This brought a few chuckles.

"We don't have a lot of history to go on, since this is a new format," Graham said. "But what history we have from other programs tells us that viewers enjoy this type of journalism, since they learn about new findings at the same time, or close to it, as the program itself."

"What if, God forbid, no new findings are discovered?" Luke asked in an overly dramatic tone.

"We have faith that Sidney knows what she's doing."

"Maybe so," Luke said. "But a million viewers for the debut?"

"They're summer numbers. The comps are not against the most-watched prime-time dramas from spring. Comps are from this time slot last June, and *The Girl of Sugar Beach* did well. The network has backed this project, Luke. It's a new concept for us, and we're all pleased with the opening numbers."

Luke shrugged. "It's safe to say that you can only go up."

"Luke, what's the problem? You're being a bit of an ass, frankly," Graham said.

"She left my show for this pet project. She carries at least an air of my reputation with her." The Bear looked at Sidney. "So excuse me if I'm concerned about your ratings. Someone around here has to be."

Sidney offered him an ugly smile. "Thanks, Luke. Your concern is touching."

Sidney wheeled her small case into the elevator a few minutes later.

"He's a serial misogynist and a complete asshole," Leslie Martin said as soon as the doors closed. She was producing *The Girl of Sugar Beach* with Sidney.

"I've got too much to do to worry about Luke Barrington," Sidney said, pressing the button for the lobby too many times and much harder than necessary. "But goddamn, that man can smell blood in the water. We should call him 'the Shark' instead of 'the Bear.' He knows we were expecting higher numbers for the debut, even though Graham swore that only the production heads knew the projections."

"One-point-two is great for a premiere. And we pulled in a decent share of the eighteen-to–twenty-four demo."

"They wanted two million, as a conservative number. I'm woefully short. And they projected two million so that we could all jump for joy when the numbers came back higher than that."

"These things build with the story. *Making a Murderer* had three times the audience for the final episodes than it had for the early ones. Same thing with *Serial*."

"This is prime time, not a subscription service and not a podcast. All that matters are the ratings. They drive advertising. Advertising drives revenue. Revenue pays the bills and keeps the suits in their cushy jobs." Sidney looked up briefly and watched the elevator numbers decline. *An omen?*

She blinked away and shook her head. "Christ, Leslie, what if he's right? Do we even have a story to build on?"

"Of course, we do. We're going to show inconsistencies. Raise doubt. Offer alternative theories. All of that will build suspense and intrigue. Did *Making a Murderer* prove Steven Avery's innocence? Did *Serial* prove Adnan Syed's? It's not about guilt or innocence. That's the hook, but the guts will be about Grace Sebold's story. Who was she? How did this happen? People are still interested in her — we just have to tap into that interest. Forget about the Bear. The network is behind you and heavily promoting it. You've got Dante Campbell on your side and ads are running on *Wake Up America.* Previous episodes can be viewed online, so our audience will grow. Don't wig out on me now. I need this job."

The elevator *pinged* as it reached the ground floor. "You've got a job, don't worry about that."

The doors opened and they walked into the lobby, where the tinted glass of the façade blunted the morning sunlight. Herds of Monday-morning commuters crisscrossed on the sidewalk outside.

"You know he's working like a son of bitch just to score massive ratings with his damn White House special so he can bury us," Sidney said. "Probably cashed in on a bunch of favors to secure those interviews."

"Why do we care?"

"Because the goddamn Bear is trying to

devour us, Leslie. He's trying to put together a ratings tsunami that wipes *The Girl of Sugar Beach* off the map, so by the end of summer, no one has ever heard of it. Or me. And then he can show everyone on his staff that when they leave to do something on their own, you end up like Sidney Ryan."

"Well, let's prove the blowhard wrong then."

Sidney shook her head. "Have you pulled the old high-school footage of Grace?"

"Yeah. Her parents turned over everything they had. Hours of family videos, so we should be able to pull plenty of cuts from them."

"Good. Did you manage to find any material on Julian?"

Leslie shook her head. "His parents wouldn't return my calls, so all we've got are stock photos. Yearbook and limited Facebook content from 2007."

"Get me what you can. We'll meet back here tonight to cut the draft of the next episode. Seven work for you?"

"Perfect. The suits will be gone by then. I'll bring the wine." Leslie tapped Sidney's Starbucks cup with her own. "Cheers. This thing's going to be a hit, Sid. Screw Luke Barrington."

Sidney forced a smile and lifted her coffee, then wheeled her files to the curb to catch a cab.

CHAPTER 16

Monday, June 5, 2017

She slammed the cab's door and walked to the corner restaurant in Midtown. Inside, she spotted a tall, athletic woman tapping on her laptop and knew from photos — and recent television interviews, including one with Dante Campbell — that she was looking at Dr. Livia Cutty, from the prestigious North Carolina Office of the Chief Medical Examiner. Dr. Cutty was finishing a fellowship in Raleigh, and had come to Sidney's attention, and most of America's, during a high-profile missing person's case involving Dr. Cutty's sister.

Needing forensic help with Grace's case, Sidney could think of no one better than Livia Cutty. Coming off such a notorious case, Dr. Cutty's involvement in the documentary could only attract attention. Cutty was still in the spotlight and Sidney, quite simply and selfishly, was hoping to share some of the warmth. It didn't hurt that Livia Cutty was striking to look at and would play nicely on television. Sidney nearly retched at her last thought. Luke Barrington was rubbing off on her.

She walked over. "Dr. Cutty?"

The doctor looked up and smiled. "Yes. Sidney?"

"Sidney Ryan, yes."

They shook hands.

"Livia Cutty."

"Thanks for meeting with me."

"Of course. The timing worked out perfectly. I'm in the city until tomorrow, trying to get things organized for next month."

Sidney knew that Dr. Cutty had recently accepted a position at the famed New York Medical Examiner's Office, which would start later this summer.

"Raleigh to New York will be quite a change for you."

"It will. But I'm really enjoying the city. This is my fourth time visiting."

"Find an apartment?"

"I'm signing the lease later this morning. One more meeting with my soon-to-be boss tomorrow, and then I head back to Raleigh to finish my last three weeks of fellowship."

"And you start at your new position here . . . when?"

"Officially September first. But I'll have privileges, so I will be slowly getting my feet wet during the summer. Full-time in September."

"Allow me to welcome you officially to New York," Sidney said. "I'll try not to take too much of your time."

"I've got an hour." Livia gestured to the table and they both sat down. A waitress appeared and they ordered breakfast and coffee.

"So here's my pitch," Sidney said. "I'm making a documentary about Grace Sebold. Remember her story?"

"I do. She was the medical-school student who killed her boyfriend in Jamaica?"

"St. Lucia, but yes. That's the one."

"I was a junior in college when that happened. My entire sorority watched it unfold. The indictment, the trial, the conviction. We had viewing parties. It was like the O.J. Simpson trial in the '90s, but instead of a famous athlete, it was a student just like us. It was, sadly, fascinating."

"It certainly captured the headlines back then. Grace has maintained her innocence for the past decade, and has also retained a cult following, even if she has fallen out of the mainstream. My documentary is a reexamination of the evidence that convicted her. I need an expert in forensics to help me root through the details."

"With the idea that she's innocent?"

"With the idea that there are many unanswered questions. Forensic evidence played a major role in Grace's conviction. The prosecution argued that a boat oar, actually a paddleboard oar, was used to strike Julian Crist in the head, causing a skull fracture that rendered him unconscious and led to his drowning. Grace insists the oar in question weighed five pounds, perhaps more. And it was seventy-four inches in length, which is longer than she is tall. This was back a decade ago, before the resort upgraded their equipment to graphite and composite plastic. Grace claims it would have been impossible for her to lug that long, weighty oar up the Piton, where Julian was killed, retain the strength and coordination to swing it with enough force to cause Julian's head injury, then transport it back down the rugged terrain and return it to the sports shed, where it was later discovered by detectives. At trial, there was some back-and-forth about whether the blade of the oar was a forensic match to Julian's skull fracture, but the defense's expert — a coroner with little homicide experience — was shredded on cross-examination."

Livia shrugged. "Sounds interesting. Where do I come in?"

"Would you be willing to review the autopsy findings and discuss your opinions? On camera, of course, as I'll need footage for the documentary. It's airing during the prime-time lineup and currently follows *Events,* Luke Barrington's news program, so you can expect decent exposure. If that's something that interests you."

Livia nodded. "I'm certainly curious. Especially if you're suggesting the forensics don't match the crime."

"Well, I'm not sure. That's why I need your help. I can pay you for your time. One hundred fifty an hour. I'm sure you're worth much more than that, but that's what I'm budgeted for. Log the hours, and you'll be paid as an independent contractor." Sidney pulled a thick file from her bag and pushed it across the table. "I'm gathering more each day, but this is what I have so far. Much of this is public record. Some, what's on the thumb drive, came from Grace's defense attorney here in the U.S., who kept not only everything from the trial, but also new information that has come along over the years. Crime scene photos, interviews, trial transcript, and everything from Julian Crist's autopsy, which is what I'm mostly interested in getting your opinion on. And I wish I could tell you to take all the time you need, but, unfortunately, I'm under a tight deadline. How soon could you look at this?"

Dr. Cutty flipped through the file. "I'll take a look on my flight. My fellowship in Raleigh is just about finished, so I'll have time to dig in when I get home. Can I call you next week?"

Sidney nodded. "That would be perfect."

"When is the documentary set to air?" Dr. Cutty asked.

Sidney smiled. Apparently, Dr. Cutty was not among the slightly more than (and disappointing) 1 million viewers who tuned in for episode one.

CHAPTER 17

Monday, June 5, 2017

The Sebolds lived in a two-story Colonial in Fayetteville, New York, just outside of Syracuse. Sidney pulled her car into the driveway as Derrick, her cameraman, grabbed his backpack from the rear seat. Sidney popped the trunk and surveyed the house while Derrick removed his lighting equipment. She noticed a ramp that ran up the front stairs and another that paralleled the steps leading to the back of the house. An obvious addition had been added to the home's north side, where the aged brick gave way to newer cedar in a single-story supplement.

The front door opened and Mrs. Sebold waved from the doorway.

"You good, Derrick?" Sidney asked.

Derrick gave a thumbs-up as he assembled his Ikegami and lighting props. Sidney walked to the front stairs.

"It's so nice to meet you finally," Mrs. Sebold said as she embraced Sidney in a tight hug.

"Nice to meet you, too," Sidney said as she returned the greeting.

"You've got to help our little girl," Mrs. Sebold said softly into Sidney's ear. "You've just got to help her."

Sidney escaped from Mrs. Sebold's clutch. "I'm going to do everything I can."

"It's more than anyone else will do for us. Our own damn government won't help us. Please come inside."

Sidney followed Grace's mother into the house. The entrance doorway was badly scuffed, and what looked like bicycle treads marred the hardwood in the entry foyer. Mrs. Sebold noticed Sidney's wondering eyes.

"This is from Marshall," she said. "Our son. He was just fitted for a new wheelchair and is not happy about it. He doesn't like change. This is his way of showing us."

Sidney noticed scuff marks along the walls — deep, sideswipe gouges in the drywall.

"Only in the last couple of years has he succumbed to a wheelchair. We knew the day would come, and we avoided it as long as possible. His mobility was simply too compromised, so we took the therapist's suggestion and had him fitted. He hates it, of course. The worry is that if he relies on the chair, he'll lose his ability to walk entirely. Again, the situation is inevitable and change is always hard. We had him read *Who Moved My Cheese.* Didn't help. So, please, excuse our home." Mrs. Sebold pointed down the hall. "We can tape in the living room, if that works."

Sidney followed Mrs. Sebold into the room. "Yes," Sidney said. "This will be perfect. You and Mr. Sebold can sit on the couch here. Derrick will set up the lighting and record from over here. Your son could join us, too."

Mrs. Sebold shrugged. "Maybe. It will depend on what type of mood Marshall is in. And please call me Gretchen."

Mr. Sebold walked down the stairs and into the living room.

"Sidney, this is my husband, Glenn."

"Hi, Sidney. Thanks so much for what you've done for Grace," Glenn Sebold said as he walked into the room. He shook Sidney's hand.

"I haven't done much at all, I'm afraid."

"You've done more than you think. Since you agreed to shoot this documentary, Grace's spirits have lifted considerably. I can hear it every time we talk, which is once a week. And I went down to Bordelais last month for a visit. It was the first time in quite a while that I saw a glimmer of my daughter, and not the stranger that place has turned her into."

Sidney was reluctant to accept the premise that agreeing to shoot a documentary could have such a profound effect on Grace's well-being. She was reluctant, perhaps, because Sidney knew if it were true, it was because she had given Grace hope. And the problem with evoking hope was that it led one of two places: salvation or damnation.

"I'm glad she's doing better," Sidney finally said. "I hope something positive comes of this."

Derrick had set up two umbrella pads on either side of the couch that would cast the Sebolds in the proper light. A camera perched on a tripod was positioned in front of Grace's parents, who sat close together to show their united front. He held the Ikegami on his shoulder to get dynamic shots as he moved from side to side during the interview.

"Why didn't you hire a personal attorney?" Sidney asked as the interview began. "From the U.S., to represent Grace?"

"We did," Glenn Sebold said. "As soon as they formally charged Grace, we started making calls back home. But acquiring a U.S. attorney took time, at least a couple of days. Longer for someone to actually fly down to St. Lucia and help us. We couldn't stand the thought of Gracie in jail, so we also hired a local attorney so we could attempt to post bond as soon as possible. What choice did we have? We were trying to get our daughter out of jail. Plus, the St. Lucian courts require local counsel to lead the defense in capital-murder cases. During the trial, the local counsel — Samuel James — was not only ineffective, but incompetent. He and Grace's American attorney never gelled well together, never agreed on the same strategy. The result, if you watched any of the trial back then, was a circus. If Scott and his team had been allowed to take over the defense, I believe Grace would be home with us today."

"Scott Simpson?" Sidney said in way of clarification. "Grace's U.S. defense attorney."

"Correct," Glenn said. "Real sharp guy. He's kept working the case even all these years later."

"Scott Simpson is not sharp," said a voice from the hallway. "He's actually a fool who is just as responsible for Grace's situation as the backward Caribbean attorney."

191

Sidney looked over to see a man in a wheelchair.

Glenn smiled at Sidney. "Sorry. I hope you can edit that out."

Sidney shook her head. "It's no problem."

"Why edit it? It's the truth."

"This is Marshall, Grace's brother."

"Scott Simpson was a pawn," Marshall said. "Expendable in every way, and used by the prosecution to strategically set up their case."

"Okay, Marshall," Glenn said in a practiced tone a parent might use on a teenager. "That's enough."

"Are you going to help my sister?"

Sidney hesitated. "Am I going to help . . . I'm going to try, yes."

"These two are going to send me away if Grace doesn't come back."

"All right," Glenn said as he stood. "Excuse me." He walked over to his son and took the handles of the wheelchair. "Come on. Let's go back to your room."

When Marshall and Glenn were gone, Sidney looked at Mrs. Sebold with an awkward smile.

"Sorry," Gretchen said. "Marshall is upset lately. We're looking into a facility to help him out, and he's not happy about it."

Sidney smiled and nodded her head as

though her words made perfect sense.

Gretchen hesitated. "Did Gracie fill you in on Marshall? About what happened?"

"No. We've only really talked about her case. I was hoping today's conversation might shed light on Grace's past, though. Before Sugar Beach. It will be important to show the viewers who Grace really is, get them past the headlines many of them remember her for. Was she close with Marshall?"

"Very. Still is." Gretchen Sebold gave a far-off stare, then looked back at Sidney. "Marshall used to be quite an athlete. Football was his sport. During his freshman year of high school, he was on the varsity squad as the backup quarterback. By the third game, he was starting. Led the Wildcats to two state championships his freshman and sophomore years, and was being seriously recruited by some big universities. It was a big deal around this town."

The ramp up the front steps and around the corner flashed in Sidney's mind, as did the first-floor addition on the side of the house.

"What happened?"

"I'm surprised Gracie never told you. It's the reason Gracie decided to go into neurology. I mean, that grand idea she had about neurosurgery instead of delivering babies, like she always wanted to do."

Sidney noticed Derrick as he positioned himself across the room to capture Mrs. Sebold's impending confession. The next episode flashed in Sidney's mind. The world had never heard anything about Grace Sebold's family life.

"Can you tell me what happened?"

*"The Accident" Part of Episode 2
*Based on the interview with
Gretchen Sebold*

With the parents out of town, the party raged well past midnight. Predictably, the small gathering originally planned had bloated to include most of the junior and senior class. Sarah Cayling frantically tried to clear her house and stop the destruction that was occurring, from spilled beer to sex in her parents' bed. She was ready to call the police, but instead recruited two guy friends from the football team to empty the house. The jocks gathered their friends and started shoving. At first, small scuffles broke out in the foyer. Then more kids joined in. Sucker punches were thrown, and before long, the fighting turned into a riot that spilled onto the front yard.

The smart kids ran. The drunken kids stayed to watch.

"We're leaving," Grace said to Marshall.

"No way," he said. "Somebody threw a sucker punch. I'm not leaving my teammates."

"The hell you're not. The cops are coming, you idiot. You want to get thrown into a paddy wagon with a bunch of meatheads? Mom and Dad will kill us."

Marshall tried to walk back toward the house and the riot. Grace grabbed him by the back of the shirt. "Let's go." She cocked her head sideways and gave him a look when their eyes met. Her lips moved, but her voice stayed silent. *Come on.*

"Your recruiting days will be over if you get arrested," Ellie Reiser said.

A far-off police siren screamed through the night. When they heard it, all three ran.

"Gimme the keys," Marshall said. "You're shitty drunk."

"Screw you," Grace said. "You were just doing shots."

"You can't even run straight," he said as Grace veered off the sidewalk.

"Let me drive," Ellie said. She had never had a sip of alcohol in her young life.

They found their car on a side street two blocks over from Sarah Cayling's house, where they had been instructed to park to avoid detection by the neighbors. Ellie sat behind the wheel and stuck the key in the ignition.

"Let's go!" Marshall said, climbing into the passenger seat.

Grace slammed the door as she sat in the backseat behind Ellie, who put the car into gear and hit the accelerator. A police car streaked past on a crossroad ahead of them, causing Ellie to take a sharp right turn down a side street. Marshall veered with Ellie's sudden jerk of the wheel.

"No one's chasing us, Ellie," Marshall said. "The cops are going to break up a party. Just drive like a normal human being."

Ellie took a deep breath to calm her nerves, closing her eyes momentarily.

"Stop," Marshall said. "Stop! Ellie, there's a goddamn stop sign!"

Ellie opened her eyes in time to see the red hexagon, but it registered a second too late. The sign was already past her, and the nose of the car was well into the four-lane highway before she lifted her foot from the accelerator and slammed it onto the brake pedal. It was in that moment that Ellie looked to her left to see the car speeding toward her. She flipped her foot back to the gas and punched the engine, hoping to squeeze past the oncoming car in just enough time to make the left turn. Her hopes came true. The car, screeching and veering, narrowly missed her, coming within an inch of the rear bumper as Ellie skidded across the lanes, pulling the car hard into a left turn.

She never saw the U-Haul truck speeding from her right. The impact of the truck's front grille was square to the right passenger-side, where Marshall was sitting. His head connected with the side window, producing a sickening impact that rose above the screeching tires and crunching metal like a gunshot fired into the night.

When the cars stopped spinning, nothing was left but the bleached aftereffect of a collision: ringing ears, blurred vision, and the smell of rubber burned across the pavement. Grace looked from the backseat at Marshall, who was slumped and unconscious in the passenger seat. A spiderweb pattern clouded the glass to his right.

CHAPTER 18

Monday, June 5, 2017

After her interview with Mr. and Mrs. Sebold, Sidney asked to visit with Marshall. It was agreed that Derrick would not record, as the Sebolds worried that sensory overload would cause Marshall to shut down. Maybe after Marshall got to know her, the Sebolds suggested, he'd be open to a documented interview. Sidney was looking for ways to show the audience who Grace was before Sugar Beach, and meeting her brother would only help her efforts. If it led to a recorded interview later, all the better.

"He's going to ask you to play a game of chess," Glenn Sebold told Sidney before she entered Marshall's room.

"Chess?"

"It relaxes his brain and takes the edge off his anxiety. All he's known since he was a little kid was how to compete. He can't do that on the football field anymore. Hasn't touched a football since the accident. But somehow with chess, it makes him a normal kid again. Hell, he's not a kid anymore, but when he plays chess, it reminds me of the old Marshall."

"Is that how you two connect with him?" Sidney asked.

Glenn shook his head. "Gretchen and I haven't played chess with him for some time. He's thirty-five years old, but having to rely so heavily on us has caused a teenage-type rebellion in him. I told him you'd play, if that's okay."

Sidney nodded. "Of course. If it helps him answer a few questions."

"He'll talk your ear off during a game of chess. If you need anything, let me know. I'll be in the living room."

"I'll let you know when we're done."

She knocked softly and then opened the bedroom door. Marshall sat in his wheelchair staring at his computer screen.

"Can I come in?" Sidney asked.

Marshall shrugged, so Sidney walked into his bedroom and closed the door.

"I was hoping to talk with you a little bit about Grace. No cameras."

"They said you'd play chess," Marshall said.

"Yeah, I'd love to play."

Marshall maneuvered his chair away from his desk and pointed to his closet.

"You'll have to get my chess set down."

Sidney pointed to the closet. "In here?"

"On top," Marshall said.

Sidney opened the closet door and stood on her tiptoes to peer at the top shelf. Next to shadowed football trophies, she found Marshall's chess set stashed away in a satchel. She pulled it off the shelf.

"Your parents told me you haven't played for a while," Sidney said as she handed the chess set to Marshall.

"Not with them," he said.

He turned to the table in the corner and slid his chess set out of the sack, which consisted of two pinewood cases that each held the competing black and white chess pieces. Opening the first case, Marshall revealed elaborately sculpted figures. The characters were seated in thick protective foam inside of the chess case. Eight white pawns ran in a circle around the perimeter. The rooks, bishops and knights made up an inner ring, and in the center sat the king and queen. Marshall removed each piece and studied it before placing it on the board. Sidney sat in the chair across from him amazed by the transformation. Marshall seemed to have an easier time with his motor skills when he handled the chess pieces. He sat taller in his chair and his articulation when he spoke was more precise and direct.

"This is quite a chess set," Sidney said, opening the second case, which held the black pieces. "I've never seen one quite like this before."

"It's a Lladró. The pieces are porcelain and handcrafted."

Sidney removed a figurine and studied the design. She was never much of a chess player, but even to her untrained eye, she knew this was a unique set. Medieval themed, the figures each carried long, stoic facial expressions. The king was decorated with a tall crown and elongated beard. The pawns carried blank stares under their head-dresses.

"These pieces are amazing," Sidney said.

"Grace gave it to me," Marshall said. "After the accident. It was a way to pass time while I was laid up. I haven't played with it much since she's been gone." He pointed to the board once the assembly was complete. "You can open."

Sidney moved a porcelain pawn forward. Marshall did the same.

"It seems a shame to keep this chess set stored in the closet. Why haven't you played lately?"

"I play online."

"Your dad says you won't play with him."

"He's said that for ten years. But the truth is that since Grace has been gone, I haven't played with anyone on this board."

"Why?"

Marshall was quiet while he studied the board.

"Your dad thinks it's because you're angry with him," Sidney said as she moved another pawn forward.

Marshall shook his head. "No. It's because Grace asked me to put my set away after she went to jail, so I did. Today is the first time I've had it out since."

Sidney smiled. "You two played a lot? You and Grace?"

"Used to," Marshall said, still scrutinizing the board.

"Your mom said you and Grace are close."

"As close as you can get when you never see each other. But Grace and I don't need to see each other. We have something that connects us."

"What connects you two?"

Marshall pointed to the bedroom door. "They didn't tell you?"

"Your parents? No."

"Grace was born with a rare type of leukemia. The only thing that would save her was a bone marrow transplant. My parents couldn't find a matching donor. So they had another child — me. I was a perfect match. Grace likes to say that part of me is inside her, so we'll always be connected. And we each understand that neither of us would be around if the other didn't exist. If I didn't come around, Grace would have died. And if Grace hadn't gotten sick, I wouldn't have been conceived."

"That's an amazing story, Marshall."

"They say they were always planning to have another child, regardless." Marshall shrugged. "Grace and I talk about this invisible string that connects us. We always feel it, even now when she's so far away."

Marshall advanced his pawn. Sidney imagined the story of Grace's younger brother saving her life would play strongly into her intention of changing the way America saw Grace Sebold.

"But you've still visited her, yes?" Sidney asked. "While she's been in St. Lucia?"

"Whenever they decide to go. They claim they can't afford to visit more than a few times a year."

Sidney made another move. "It's a long way, for sure. And expensive."

"It's their daughter," Marshall said, moving another piece.

"Your mom told me a little about your accident."

Marshall shrugged, keeping his focus on the board.

"Would you mind if I included your story in the documentary? Not just about the accident, but also about what you did for Grace to save her life?"

"Why?"

"Because it shows Grace in a different light than how she's been portrayed for many years. I heard she decided to go into neurology so she could help people who had similar injuries as yours."

"She changed to neurology because she felt guilty."

"About the accident?" Sidney asked.

Marshall nodded. "It's the same reason she bought me this chess set. Just another way to try to fix something that's unfixable."

"I'm sure everyone involved has regrets. Ellie Reiser, I'm sure," Sidney said. "She was driving."

Marshall remained silent as he continued to stare at the chessboard.

"I was hoping to ask you about Grace's friends. You two are close in age. Did you hang out in the same circles?"

Marshall shrugged. "Before. Not so much after."

"Before the accident?"

Marshall nodded.

"Can you talk about Grace's friends?"

"Like who?"

"Ellie Reiser. Or Grace's friendship with Daniel Greaves. They are the only two friends who have stayed in touch with Grace while she's been in jail."

Marshall let out a laugh. "I can tell you anything you want about those two."

"Really? Anything? You know them that well?"

Marshall looked up at Sidney, finally taking his gaze off the chessboard. "Ever since the accident, people assume that I'm unaware of what goes on around me. That I don't listen. Just because I don't drool over their every word doesn't mean I don't hear their conversations. I listened a lot while I was in St. Lucia."

"Listened to who?"

"Grace and her friends."

"Can you tell me about any of it?"

"Sure," Marshall said, pointing at the board. "It's your move, though."

THE GIRL OF SUGAR BEACH
"Friends" Part of Episode 2
*Based on the interview with
Marshall Sebold

They sat in Grace's cottage sipping rum and Diet Cokes. Ellie lay on the bed, legs crossed and with her back against the headboard as she stared at the television. Marshall sat at the table in the corner and arranged his chess set.

"We should probably get going," Grace said. "Charlotte will freak out if we're late. She's already acting weird today."

"Do you think she knows?" Ellie asked.

Grace paused as she ran a mascara brush over her lashes. She was standing in front of the full-length mirror and glanced at Ellie's reflection, then at Marshall in the corner, before quickly shifting her gaze back to her lashes.

"Knows what?"

Ellie made an unpleasant face. "That George Bush is president."

Grace smiled. "Probably. It's common knowledge."

"Do you think Charlotte knows or not?"

Grace turned from the mirror. "I don't know, E. How would she know?"

"Maybe Daniel told her."

"Why would he do that?"

"To be honest. To start their marriage off on the right foot."

"Telling your fiancée that you slept with her maid of honor is not getting off on the right foot. It's self-sabotage, and Daniel is too smart for that."

"He's not that smart," Ellie said. "He came to your cottage to pledge his love to you two days before his wedding."

"He did not pledge his love to me."

"Then why did he come to your room?"

Grace turned back to the mirror. "I'm not talking about this anymore."

Ellie took a sip of rum. She glanced quickly at Marshall, who was lost in his chessboard. "I thought this was supposed to be Daniel's." She held up a long pouch that had been resting on the bed.

Grace walked over and took the pouch from Ellie. She untied the tassels and stared down at the lock that was inside, an ancient-looking thing given to her by her grandfather. Turning the bag over, she allowed the heavy lock to fall into her palm. Engraved on it were the names: *Grace & Julian.*

She studied the lock now, thankful to have only fallen once to the urge of engraving the name of a high-school boyfriend onto it. One mistake was plenty. Any more and she would have ruined the lock.

"No," Grace finally said. "This lock is meant for Julian. I brought it to St. Lucia to show him how much he means to me. Daniel's name was never meant to be on the lock. That whole thing was a mistake. A big, shitty mistake that's thankfully in the past."

"Let's hope it stays there. You know he still loves you."

Grace faked a laugh, glancing quickly again at Marshall. "Daniel does not love me."

"Have you seen how he looks at you? He could barely make eye contact at the pool yesterday. He's still shy like he's in high school trying to work up the courage to ask you to prom."

"That's because Charlotte was around and he still feels guilty."

Grace took the lock and dropped it back into the satchel, cinching the cords and tying them off, before placing it on the dresser.

"Sleeping with the groom and being the maid of honor is a delicate balancing act," Ellie said.

Grace smiled at Ellie. "Why are you being a bitch?"

"I'm trying to protect you."

"Thank you. But it's only a balancing act if Daniel and I were still involved." Grace turned to the mirror and went back to her lashes. "And the subject is only delicate if someone starts talking. And I'm certainly finished discussing it."

Grace looked into the mirror and locked eyes with Ellie.

"Just be careful, Gracie. I don't want to see you get hurt."

"Hurt happened a long time ago. Everyone's over it. Now get dressed, we've gotta go."

CHAPTER 19

Tuesday, June 6, 2017

On Tuesday morning, the day after Sidney visited the Sebolds in Fayetteville, she and Derrick left the network headquarters in Midtown and cabbed to Bellevue Hospital. Inside, directions came from the information desk, and after two elevator rides and a quarter mile of fluorescent-lit hallways, they found the OB-GYN ward.

"Sidney Ryan to see Dr. Reiser," she said to the receptionist.

"Through the doors and to your left."

Derrick lifted his camera and set it on his shoulder. He peered through the viewfinder and adjusted for the bright lighting on the obstetrics ward. After a moment, he put his thumb and index finger together to give Sidney the *okay* sign as the automatic glass doors opened.

A brief perusing of Grace's visitors over the years showed only a couple of nonrelatives that had consistently made the trip to Bordelais Correctional Facility in St. Lucia: Ellie Reiser was one of them. As Sidney knocked on the door frame, Dr. Reiser was already moving across the office to greet her. With a broad smile, she shook hands with Sidney as Derrick backed into the corner of the office to capture the meeting. Heels pushed her to nearly six feet tall. Dressed in a chic, slim-fitted dress, Ellie Reiser looked more like a model than a surgeon. But Sidney knew well the preparation people took when they were about to be recorded.

"Thanks for meeting with me," Sidney said.

"Of course. When Grace told me you finally contacted her, we were elated."

"I received your letters," Sidney said. "I read all of them."

Over the years, Ellie Reiser had been nearly as persistent as Grace with letters and e-mails asking for Sidney's help.

"I'm sure you're swamped with requests," Ellie said. "I'm just grateful Grace's story will finally be told. So much of what's out there was distorted during her trial."

"We're going to work to clear that up," Sidney said. "Derrick will record while we talk. You'll get used to the camera. Just ignore it the best you can."

Ellie pointed to the desk and they both sat down. Derrick moved into position.

"How much of what we discuss will be used?"

"As much as is relevant," Sidney said. "But I'll let you know what I think we'll use before I cut the episode. All I need is for you to answer the questions honestly. I know we're talking about events from ten years ago, and longer, so do the best you can. Like you said, the public knows only Grace Sebold, the convicted murderer. In the next episode, we're going to show them who Grace was before Sugar Beach. I spoke with the Sebolds yesterday and understand a lot about Grace that I didn't know before. I'm hoping to expand on that history today. Are you ready?"

Ellie Reiser nodded.

"Tell me how you know Grace."

Ellie offered a small laugh. "Grace and I have been friends since grade school. Gosh, third or fourth grade, I suppose. We've been inseparable since then, all the way through high school. We stayed close through college and medical school. I was at SUNY and Grace was at Boston University."

"And you were with Grace in St. Lucia at Sugar Beach?"

"Yes. Charlotte Brooks, one of our best friends from high school, invited us to her wedding. She was marrying Daniel Greaves, another friend of ours. We all gathered at Sugar Beach, like it was a high-school reunion. Julian was Grace's plus one."

"And for the last ten years, you've practiced medicine?"

"Yes, obstetrics."

Over the years when Ellie Reiser had learned to survive the rigors of surgical residency and the demands of hospital life as a busy physician, Grace Sebold had learned to survive in a foreign penitentiary. Sidney would make sure that point came through clearly in the next episode.

"Did you know Julian Crist?"

"Not well," Ellie said. "But, yes, I knew him. I knew Grace was crazy about him. They met in India during the summer after second year of medical school when Grace volunteered for a couple of weeks with a Doctors Without Borders program. Julian was at NYU, so I had only met him a couple of times before Sugar Beach."

"During the trip to Sugar Beach, Grace and Julian broke the news that they were accepted to the same residency program in neurosurgery. But Grace's interest was not always neurology, am I correct?"

"That's right," Ellie said. "She had wanted to go into obstetrics, same as myself. For most of our childhoods, we both wanted to deliver babies. Grace was born with —" Ellie stopped. "I'm not sure how much Grace told you, but she was born with a rare form of leukemia."

"Yes," Sidney said. "Marshall was a matching bone marrow donor."

"That's right," Ellie said. "It made Grace want to deliver babies. She said she wanted to protect them." Ellie smiled. "That was our thing, sort of our childhood dream that we shared."

"What changed her mind about obstetrics?"

There was a short pause as Ellie searched for the correct wording. "Marshall's accident. Did Grace's parents tell you about that?"

"They did."

"He's . . . Marshall has had a lot of trouble since then. He's not . . . TBI can change a person's personality, and cause a number of physical ailments as well."

"TBI, traumatic brain injury," Sidney said to clarify.

"Correct. Marshall was never the same after the accident, and it broke Grace's heart. Marshall's condition is what caused

Grace to go into neurology." Ellie blinked a few times. "That was the plan. She obviously never got the chance."

"The accident," Sidney said. "I understand the driver of the U-Haul truck was charged with DUI."

"Yes."

"I still sensed, though, that Marshall Sebold holds you in contempt. He had a roundabout way of telling me about you."

Ellie nodded slowly. "I'm afraid that will likely never change."

Sidney pulled a stack of papers from her bag. "I counted sixty-two letters that you've sent me over the last three years asking for help," Sidney said. "What makes you so certain Grace is innocent?"

"Oh . . . so many things," Ellie said. "She's my best friend, first of all, and I know she could never kill anyone. But that's a subjective answer, and I understand it doesn't stand up to scrutiny. That's just what's in my heart. The better answer is that I was with Grace the night Julian died. Slept in her cottage at the resort. Simply stated, I'm her alibi. You can run the timeline anyway you'd like — and I have many times over the years. There is no way Grace could have killed Julian that night."

"How did the investigators and detectives

in St. Lucia respond when you told them this?"

"They didn't. They interviewed me once, and never asked me another question."

"During that lone interview, though, did you tell them you were with Grace the night Julian was killed?"

"Of course. But they weren't interested in details that didn't support their narrative. I eventually told my story to Grace's attorney, but my testimony was not allowed during the trial."

"Why?"

Ellie offered a dejected expression.

"The prosecutor argued that I'd been drinking that day, and that by evening, I was intoxicated. He argued that although I slept in Grace's room, I was too drunk to know if she left after I . . . what they suggested, passed out. At trial, the prosecution petitioned the magistrate to keep my testimony out of the courtroom. The request was granted."

"*Had* you been drinking?"

Ellie nodded. "We were twenty-five years old and on spring break. We were *all* drinking."

"Were you drunk?"

"Not to the point that I don't remember being with Grace that night."

"Did you pass out?"

Ellie shrugged her shoulders. "I've never been a big drinker. I didn't even taste alcohol until my twenty-first birthday. So I was not intoxicated to the point that the prosecution was suggesting. I . . . fell asleep at some point. But did I fall-on-my-face pass out? No. I went to sleep."

"In Grace's cottage?"

"Yes."

"Why did you sleep in Grace's room that night?"

"She was upset. She and Julian had gotten into an argument. Grace asked me to come to her cottage, so I did. I was being a good friend."

"The fight about Daniel?"

Ellie nodded. "It was probably my fault, the fight they had."

"How so?"

"I wasn't keen on how fast things were moving between them. I felt like Grace might be getting in over her head."

"In what way?"

Ellie shrugged. "Julian was planning to propose. I thought it was a bad idea."

"How do you know this?" Sidney asked.

"Because he told me. I mentioned that I thought it was too soon to ask her." Ellie shook her head. "It didn't matter, he never got the chance."

Ellie's eyes glassed over as though she might cry.

"He was gone the next day."

THE GIRL OF SUGAR BEACH
"The Proposal" Part of Episode 2
Based on the interview with Ellie Reiser

The members of the wedding party lay on loungers around the pool and soaked up the Caribbean sun. The guys drank Piton beer and the girls sipped rum runners and mojitos. Charlotte Brooks, the bride, had invited five of her girlfriends as brides-maids, including Grace and Ellie. In their midtwenties now, they were all at different stages of life. Charlotte was an elementary-school teacher about to marry her high-school sweetheart, whom she had dated since they had all met in Fay-etteville, New York. Grace and Ellie were now in medical school. One other brides-maid was finishing law school, and the oth-ers were scattered in marketing and event planning.

Daniel Greaves was the groom. He, too, had invited a host of friends from high school as his groomsmen. Since the group had known each other for years, many of their parents were invited to the wedding, and a few — including the Sebolds — had made the long trip to St. Lucia.

"Ellie," Charlotte said. "Where did you place?"

"Duke."

"To deliver babies?"

Ellie smiled. "Yes. OB-GYN."

"So, if Daniel and I get pregnant, you can deliver my baby?" Charlotte laughed. Too many mojitos.

"Give me a few years to figure out what I'm doing first."

"Don't worry," Charlotte said, leaning back in her lounge chair and crossing her legs. Her Bottega Veneta crocodile flip-flops were covering her feet. "We'll need some practice before we have a baby."

"Wear those eight-hundred-dollar flip-flops to bed," Ellie said, "and I'm sure Daniel will want to practice often."

This brought laughs from the other intoxicated friends who sat around the pool. The peaks of the Pitons, draped with green foliage and rain forest, rose up on either side of the resort. Petit Piton to the north, and Gros Piton to the south. Massive twin volcanic structures that held Sugar Beach Resort between them.

"Are you guys ever going to stop making fun of my shoes?"

"I could finance medical school with what you spend on footwear," Ellie said.

"But they're so pretty. Anyway, Daniel and I have been together since high school, so we're not going to wait too long. We know we're right together."

"You guys broke up for a while, didn't you?" Ellie asked. "In college?"

Grace put a stare on Ellie, and squinted her eyes. *What the hell,* she mouthed as she brought her mojito to her lips.

"Yeah," Charlotte said. "But just for a couple of months. Besides that, we've been together for close to ten years now."

"Of course," Ellie said. "That's my point." She glanced briefly at Grace with a suppressed grin. "You guys took a break to see other people and then decided you were right for each other. It's the best way to do it. Make sure, you know."

"I was a mess for two months. Never left my house that summer. Daniel was the same way. Neither of us dated anyone, just took a break and then ran back to each other."

"Well," Ellie said, "you two did it the right way. Took a break, got into other things." Another quick smirk at Grace. "And then found each other again."

"Yes," Grace said. "You're great together. You, Daniel, and your outrageously overpriced shoes. Cheers to you guys. Really, Char. We're so happy for you."

They touched glasses.

"So Ellie will be at Duke. And where did you end up?" Charlotte asked.

"Cornell. In New York," Grace said.

"Neurology, right?"

"Neurosurgery."

"Wow!" Charlotte said. "That sounds so . . . I don't know. *Serious.*"

Grace looked back at Ellie. "OB-GYN is serious, too. And seriously difficult. But, yes, I'm expecting it to be a challenge."

"And Julian?" Charlotte asked.

"Julian and I placed together."

"Aww," Charlotte said. "That's the sweetest thing I've ever heard. So when are we all coming back here for *your* wedding?"

Grace smiled. "Who knows? Maybe after residency."

Ellie Reiser had met Julian Crist a handful of times over the last year and a half since he and Grace started dating. The first time Julian had caught Grace's eye, Ellie knew, was during the summer after second year when Grace went off to do volunteer work in India. She met Julian on that trip, both spending a three-week stint aiding in a general-surgery clinic in Delhi. Despite that Julian was at NYU and Grace was in Boston, the miles didn't seem to hurt their relationship. Grace and Ellie had discussed the pros and cons of a serious relationship during medical school and what sort of distractions it might cause. And about how difficult long-distance relationships were to maintain. Ellie had gently warned her friend to be careful going into the crucial third year of medical school. Eighteen months later, Grace and Julian were going strong, were damn near inseparable, and were both heading off to a highly competitive surgical residency, where they would be pitted against one another.

Ellie stirred her mojito at the thatched-roof beach bar, sitting on a stool and looking out toward Pitons Bay and the sun waltzing over the calm water. Julian walked up next to her.

"Hey," he said.

Ellie smiled. "Hi, Julian."

"I've hardly had a chance to talk with you this trip."

"I know. This is the first afternoon the bridesmaids haven't been ordered around. I think Charlotte saw that we were all stressed out and pissed off that we came to this beautiful resort and haven't had the chance to enjoy it."

"You guys are good friends," Julian said. "I don't even talk with anyone from high school anymore."

"Really? We're like a cult."

"No kidding. I'm feeling a little like an outsider."

"Don't be silly. Everyone loves you. Grace loves you, so that's good enough for me."

Julian smiled. "Thanks. That's why I wanted to talk with you." He looked back over his shoulder to make sure Grace was occupied. She lay on a pool lounger and soaked up the sun.

"About what?"

Julian placed a small jewelry box onto the granite bar and looked at Ellie.

Ellie stared at the box for a moment, then slowly asked, "What is that?"

"I'm going to ask Grace to marry me. I need your help to pull it off."

Ellie also looked back toward Grace. She put her hand over the box and glanced around. The other patrons of the beach bar sucked piña coladas through straws and tilted bottles of Piton beer up to the sky.

"You're kidding me, right?" Ellie asked.

"*Kidding?* No, I'm dead serious."

"You guys just met."

Julian laughed in his casual manner, flashing his perfect teeth and sharp-angled jaw. "We met a year and a half ago, Ellie. We've been inseparable since."

Ellie leaned closer. "You go to school in New York, and she's in Boston. That's the opposite of inseparable. You're actually separated almost all the time."

"We've been very good Amtrak customers."

Ellie rolled her eyes.

"Every weekend we have free, one of us travels. It works for us. And next year, we'll both be in New York. And then, during residency, yes, that will be a new form of *inseparable.*"

"Listen, Julian, I'm happy for you guys. But why don't you wait to see how things go before you jump into an engagement. I mean, what's the rush?"

Julian reached for the engagement ring. Ellie relinquished her hold on it and he slipped it back into his pocket.

"Forget I asked," he said.

"No, that's not what I meant. I just want to make sure no one gets hurt."

"How will proposing hurt Grace?"

"I don't know, Julian. A lot has changed lately. Up until Match Day, Grace was looking at UNC and Duke for her residency. Then she matches with you in New York. She never told me any of this, and that's fine. It's her business. But for nearly four years, her plan was to go to North Carolina, and now suddenly she'll be in New York for the next seven years. When you make these huge decisions without putting a lot of thought into them, you sometimes regret them later. I don't want the same thing to happen with a proposal."

Julian nodded his head. He tipped his Piton back and drank the last third in one swallow. "We've actually put a lot of thought into this. All of it. Our residency and getting married. You see, Ellie, Grace and I talk a lot when you're not present. I know it's hard for you to imagine, but Grace does things in her life that don't include you." He put his empty beer bottle down.

"No kidding. More and more, lately."

"At least, act surprised when she tells you."

Julian turned to leave. Ellie grabbed his wrist.

"Wait, Julian."

He turned back. "What?"

"I'm her best friend, so I'm only bringing this up to prove a point."

"Bringing what up?"

Ellie took a deep breath, looked back over at Grace lying by the pool. "Has

Grace told you about Daniel?"

"Told me what?"

"See. Maybe you guys don't know each other as well as you think."

Chapter 20

Friday, June 9, 2017

The past week had been a productive one. He learned how to control the bed and lower it to the correct height so he could gingerly slide his leg over the side and touch the ground without too much pain. Then, with his foot flat on the floor and his ass on the edge of the mattress, he pressed the control again to raise the bed back up to its original height, effectively placing him in a standing position. From here, and with the use of crutches, he could make it to the bathroom. Of course, venturing off on his own was strictly prohibited this soon after surgery, so his stealth operations always took place in the middle of the night when his bladder woke him at 3:00 a.m.

Calling the nurses and playing the waiting game was no longer an option. And the tantrums he had staged for the past two weeks were quickly depleting his energy, which he needed for his physical therapy sessions. Having made it through the post-operative fog of narcotics and pain, he now had his eye on the end game: walking his ass out of this hellhole. With that goal in mind, he stopped fighting with the nurses. In fact, he stopped talking to them entirely. He made it through most days with grunts and head nods and waited for Friday afternoons when the weekend crew showed up. They were kinder and gentler than the Nazis that ran this place during the week. Riki, his overnight nurse, was his savior.

The middle-of-the-night mission to the Promised Land, which took the better part of an hour to complete, combined with a double physical therapy session on Friday afternoon, had left him depleted. He crashed as soon as they settled him in bed. When he opened his eyes Friday evening, for a moment he believed it was again the middle of the night. His bladder was screaming and he wasn't sure he'd have the energy to get himself to the bathroom.

"Hey, there he is," Riki said in her pleasant voice. "You've been sleeping ever since I clocked in. Howya feelin'? Jason told me you had a heck of a therapy session today."

He nodded. "That kid's the second coming of R. Lee Ermey."

"Who?"

"*Full Metal Jacket.* You've never seen it?"

"No, what is it?"

"Never mind," Gus said. "Listen, I'm very sorry to greet you like this, but I need to get to the bathroom right away or I'm going to make a damn mess of myself."

"No problem. Do you need help with the urinal?" She held up the plastic bottle he loathed.

"That thing and I don't get along. It steals my dignity, and I've barely got any left, as it is."

Riki smiled. "Let's get you out of bed, then."

He closed his eyes. *Thank God for Fridays.*

"Crutches or walker? I can help you attach your prosthesis, but it'll take a few minutes."

"I don't have a few minutes, and I haven't put that thing on yet. Let's go with the crutches."

With Riki's help, the round-trip from his bed to the bathroom and back again took nearly thirty minutes. But the layover, during which he stood and enjoyed the easily forgotten luxury of urinating while standing on his own, was worth the effort.

When he was settled back in bed, the nurse asked how his pain level was.

"Eight-ish."

She scrolled through the computer at the side of his bed. "You haven't had morphine today. Actually, you haven't had it all week."

"I'm trying to get away from it. It screws up my mind."

"The pain will slow you down. I'm all for tapering off the pain meds, and there's a plan in place for that. Cold turkey is too hard on your recovery. Let me give you a dose that will help you through the night."

He shook his head. "I can't think straight with that stuff. My body's for shit, excuse my French. All I've got left is my mind, and when they dope me up with that stuff, my mind goes to shit as well. And between you and me, I think the weekday nurses are too liberal with the morphine and use it as a way to shut me up. The regular crew and I don't . . . see eye-to-eye. Let's leave it at that."

"Fair enough. How about we go with half your typical dose. It'll take the edge off. It'll make you loopy just after the dose is administered, but you'll come around faster. Sleeping will be easy tonight, and by morning, you and I will be having coffee together."

"You buying?"

"No, sir. Coffee is on you, but I'll deliver it."

"Deal," Gus said, grimacing at the burn in his hip.

Riki disappeared and returned a few minutes later with the sterile-dressed cart. She clicked on the television. "Here, watch this. I know you don't like needles."

He looked up at the television. On it, a woman stood in front of a hospital in New York and spoke into the camera.

"Julian Crist had just two days to live," the woman said. "St. Lucian police argued that during her entire stay at Sugar Beach, Grace was ruthlessly planning to kill her lover on the very night he was to propose to her."

Riki adjusted the port in his arm and emptied the syringe of morphine into his bloodstream. The smoldering in his hip melted away like ice water poured over the orange coals of a campfire. Gus kept his eyes on the screen.

The woman took a few steps along the sidewalk with the glass façade of Bellevue Hospital behind her.

"Why?" she said. "Because Grace was actually in love with another man? Because her relationship with Julian was moving too fast? Because Grace discovered that Julian

233

was involved with another woman? The prosecution made all these arguments during the trial, but the alleged motive was not what brought a conviction. Hard forensic evidence is what convinced the jury to hand down their sentence. We'll dive into that next time, taking a closer look at the forensics that played such a crucial role in the trial." The woman stopped walking. "That's next time on *The Girl of Sugar Beach.*"

"Are you keeping up with this?" Gus heard the nurse ask. "It's addictive."

Gus strained his eyes against the dozing effect of the morphine and tried to bring the television into focus. A promo flashed on the screen, and he watched a woman climb up a heavily wooded path that reminded him of a rain forest. She came to a bluff, which overlooked the ocean. The voice-over faded and Gus wasn't able to understand the words. But he saw the ocean and the sun and dreamed about being on a beach, able to walk freely through the sand and dive into the surf. He closed his eyes. The water was cool against his skin; the salt stung his eyes, but felt wonderful at the same time. He turned in the ocean and floated on his back with no effort at all.

"I don't think she did it," he thought he heard the nurse say.

Gus grumbled something in reply, but stayed comfortably in his morphine-induced oasis, which had placed him in the warm Caribbean sun, floating weightlessly through the ocean and kicking through the current with both his legs and no pain.

CHAPTER 21

Tuesday, June 13, 2017

It was the following week and Sidney and Derrick took a cab to the Lower East Side. A light mist fell, just enough to crystalize the lights of New York and cause the driver to flash his wipers every few seconds. Brake lights and stoplights smeared across the roads in red streaks. It was Tuesday, close to 10:00 p.m., and Derrick was not happy to be running around so late.

"Why can't he meet us during the day?"

"He just got off work, said this was the only time he had. Take it or leave it. I took it, because I need his testimony for Friday's episode. If you can frame it and Leslie can cut it before our deadline."

"Who is he? There are hundreds of cops we could ask."

"Don Markus. He did some work for my first documentary. I trust him. Plus, he has no issues being filmed. Signed everything."

Derrick looked at his watch. "I'm coming in late tomorrow, just letting you know."

"No, you're not. We've got to get this to production by noon to make the deadline." Sidney leaned forward in the cab. "Up there on the left," she said to the driver.

The cabbie pulled to a stop outside the bar. Sidney dropped money over the seat and stepped into the misty Manhattan night. They found Detective Markus inside with a sweating highball of scotch resting on a wrinkled napkin in front of him.

"Hey, Sid," he said when she entered.

"Hi, Don. Thanks for meeting me. This is Derrick, he'll record for me."

"Drink?"

"Sure. Casamigos on the rocks."

Don pointed at Derrick, who shook his head. He ordered Sidney's tequila and another scotch for himself.

"Probably better to do this in a back booth," Sidney said.

They took their drinks to the back of the bar. Derrick turned on the light of the Ike-gami and the back corner of the bar came to life under the brightness. A few patrons turned to look, but quickly lost interest.

"You've read through the case," Sidney said. "What are your thoughts on the way the investigation was handled?"

Don smiled. "It was handled like a bunch of rookies who didn't know their asses from a hole in the ground."

Sidney pouted her bottom lip. "Thank you, but I probably can't use that on prime time. Try again."

Don paused, took a sip of scotch. "In my twenty-five years on the force, and thirteen years in Homicide, I've never seen a case mishandled as badly as this one."

"Much better. Why? Expand on what you read, and how you would do it differently."

"Let's start with the interviews. Not only were they conducted incorrectly, but possibly fraudulently. If you compare the list of people interviewed to the hotel's registered guests, you'll see right away many guests were never interviewed at all. So people who were present at the hotel the night Julian Crist died were never asked basic questions about what they saw or what they heard, or about their own whereabouts that night. Out of one hundred eighty-eight guests, only one hundred four were interviewed. What happened to the other eighty-four?

"Plus, the staff at the hotel were interviewed in groups. This is gross mismanagement. All potential witnesses and suspects should be interviewed separately. This is done for many reasons, but the most common is to confirm individual accounts of the night in question corroborate with each other. Interviewing witnesses and suspects individually also helps create a timeline of events. Many members of the staff were interviewed in groups of two and three, which allows their stories to change based on what each interviewee is hearing during the course of questioning. Gross, gross incompetence."

"Have you read through the interview of a guest named Ellie Reiser?"

"No, I have not. To the best of my knowledge, this person was never interviewed by the St. Lucian investigators."

"Ellie states, in letters to me and in a recent interview, that police *did* question her on the day Julian's body was discovered."

"If so," Detective Markus said, "there's no record of it."

"Ellie claims she was in Grace Sebold's room the night Julian Crist was killed. She says her testimony was not allowed at Grace's trial because she was intoxicated during the day and her accounts of the evening could not be relied upon to be accurate."

"I don't know if she was drunk or not," Markus said. "But if she provided a clear alibi, and if this had happened in the States, the judge would have allowed her to testify and allowed the defense to cross-examine her. Then a jury would decide if she was a reliable witness. However, with her interview never being formally logged by the investigators, it disappeared from existence. This shows me that the detectives were looking for information that matched their suspicions, not allowing the information they found to lead them to their suspicions. A very backward way of running an investigation. From what I read, they decided early on that Grace Sebold was guilty, and then set out to prove it. Tried to make everything fit that narrative."

Sidney referred to her notes.

"A shoeprint was found near the bluff where Julian fell to his death. Forensics matched the print to a shoe found in Grace Sebold's room. Soil analysis shows that the shoe held dirt that came from this location. How accurate is the forensics, in your opinion?"

"Very. It means Grace Sebold, or someone wearing that shoe, was on the bluff at some point in time. What I find interesting is that there were six other prints found at the bluff, but investigators never bothered to look into them or find out who they belonged to. And it was documented that the day before Julian Crist was killed, the entire wedding party had hiked together to the summit of Gros Piton. So there you go. The shoeprint could have been created during that hike and *not* when Grace Sebold supposedly went back to the bluff to commit a murder. What's worse is that the detectives sequestered twelve pairs of shoes from hotel guests. Photographed the tread and ran ID analysis on them to come up with the make and manufacturer. But once they got a hit on Grace Sebold's shoe, they stopped there. They didn't bother to see if any of the other prints on the bluff matched the shoes they collected. This is called *selectively* investigating. They didn't want it formally recorded that any other matches were discovered on the bluff, because the defense would have used it at trial."

Sidney referred to her notes again and took a sip of tequila.

"Julian's blood was found in Grace Sebold's cottage at Sugar Beach," she said. "As was bleach. The suggestion was that the bleach was used to clean away the blood. How accurate again is the method by which this evidence was collected."

"Very," he said again. "Basic swab testing after luminol application. Squirt the luminol, turn on the black light. Bleach and blood, invisible to the naked eye, glow blue. The DNA results of the blood discovered matched to Julian Crist. It's accurate."

Detective Markus looked over at Derrick. "Turn that off a minute."

Derrick took the camera off his shoulder.

"Listen," Markus said to Sidney. "I think they targeted her. I think they convicted her early on in the investigation and too narrowly focused their energy on proving that she did it. They conducted too few interviews, and did them in an ass-backward manner that would never fly in the States, and they disregarded evidence that didn't match their theory. The consensus, when I asked around about this case, was that a murder on a small island is bad for business. Especially if a local islander murdered a U.S. tourist. An American killing an American?" He shrugged his shoulders. "Not so much of a problem, and won't have an effect on tourism, as long as the case is closed quickly."

"Even if there were clearly things that pointed to Grace's innocence?"

Markus took another sip of scotch. "You know what prosecutors say around here? Any D.A. can convict a guilty man, but it takes a special D.A. to convict an innocent one."

"That's terrible."

"I'm not suggesting that was the mindset down there. But either way, Sid, there're some things about this case that can't be ignored. His blood in her room is one of them. Her prints on the boat oar that was used to kill him is another. That her best friend claims she was with Grace Sebold the night Julian Crist was killed is one piece to consider. But I'm sorry, Sid, the forensics trump someone's drunken recollection." He drained his scotch. "This friend, is she reliable?"

"She's a doctor," Sidney said without conviction.

"Plenty of doctors are liars. Do you trust her?"

Sidney thought back to her interview with Ellie Reiser. "I've got no reason not to."

"What's the timing? When did Grace's friend come to her room? Was it late at night, after the murder could have happened? After Grace could have cleaned the room?"

Sidney took a deep breath and shook her head. "I'm not sure. She stayed overnight, but I don't know what time she arrived. I'll have to pin down the timeline."

Her cell phone rang. "Sorry." She looked at the caller ID and saw a Raleigh, North Carolina, number. "Hold on a minute." She held the phone to her ear. "Sidney Ryan."

"Sidney? It's Livia Cutty."

"Dr. Cutty? Is everything okay?"

"Yeah, sorry to call so late."

"No problem. I'm still working."

"Me too. Actually couldn't sleep after I started looking into the Sebold case."

"Did you get a chance to look at Julian's autopsy?"

"I did, and I think we need to meet."

Sidney hesitated. "Find something?"

"I did. And I'm sure you'll want to see it."

"A discrepancy?"

"That's a polite word for it," Dr. Cutty said. "*Complete incompetence* is another."

"In what way?"

"The skull fracture."

"What about it?"

"There's no way it was caused by a boat oar."

CHAPTER 22

Thursday, June 15, 2017

Her plane touched down in Raleigh on Thursday, at 10:02 a.m., and a cab dropped her at the chief medical examiner's office just before 11:00 a.m. A nice young man led Sidney past a fenced-off room where the lights were low and a blue overhead projector threw images onto a screen while a doctor presented a case to a full room of his colleagues. A quick glance at the overhead's photo showed a naked body on a metal table. Sidney quickly pulled her gaze away from the snow-white, bloated body and hurried past the chain link and into the elevator. Her stomach dropped as the clunky elevator jerked and descended into the bowels of the morgue.

When the doors opened, the young man pointed. "Down the hall and to your left."

"Thanks," Sidney said as she and Derrick exited the elevator and walked the fluorescent-lit hallway. Peach tiles lined the walls and the smell of bleach and high-school chemistry lab filled the air. Her heels echoed as she walked, loud clanking that reverberated from the sterile tiles around them. She looked down at Derrick's feet and saw that he wore tennis shoes, quiet as a ninja.

"At least, they'll know we're coming," Derrick said. "May even raise some of the dead bodies down here."

Sidney gave him a sarcastic smile. "This place creeps me out."

"Really? I feel right at home."

They came to a set of boxed windows, the blinds of which were open to offer a voyeuristic view into the morgue. Twelve tables stood in symmetric rows of three. Shiny metal hoses hung from ceiling spigots over each table. Stainless-steel tubs lined the walls. Dr. Cutty stood with two other physicians around one of the tables. She was clearly in charge of whatever was happening, evidenced by the animated way in which she was organizing the scene. One of the doctors spotted Sidney and pointed at the window. Dr. Cutty turned and waved her in.

"Roll?" Derrick asked.

"Oh, yeah. This *has* to be good."

"Creepy as hell, anyway," Derrick said as he set the camera onto his shoulder, flicked his thumb, and adjusted the focus as he peered through the viewfinder. He followed Sidney into the morgue. He didn't need her direction. After three documentaries together, he knew what she wanted. He angled the camera so the back of her head took up the foreground and in the distance, over Sidney's shoulder, the three doctors, garbed in long coats and standing morbidly around an autopsy table, were blurred and ominous. As Sidney approached, their images hauntingly came into focus. It would make for a great intro shot, or even a "next time on *The Girl of Sugar Beach*" teaser.

"Sidney," Dr. Cutty said. "Good to see you."

"You too. Thanks for having me down."

"Of course." Dr. Cutty opened her arms. "Welcome to my office. It can be a little drab down here, and when it's empty, we get some echoing. Hope that doesn't hurt with your video."

"Derrick is a master. He'll edit everything down so it sounds perfect."

"These are Drs. Schultz and Tilly, the other pathology fellows here in Raleigh."

Handshakes all around as Sidney tried to ignore the autopsy tables on each side of them, and the white sheets that covered in lumpy fashion the bodies underneath.

"I told Dr. Schultz and Dr. Tilly about your request that I have a look at the Julian Crist autopsy. I asked for their help. All three of us reviewed the autopsy — the photos, the reports, the analysis, everything. We all came to the same conclusion."

"Which was?"

"Somebody screwed up."

Sidney slowly looked to the corner of the morgue where Derrick was filming. He gave a thumbs-up; he was getting it all.

"And you can prove this?"

"The autopsy report and photos are ten years old, but we've combed through them very carefully. Yes, we think we can show without doubt that the conclusions in the report are incorrect."

Sidney nodded slowly. Tomorrow night's airing would put her three episodes in, ratings were thin, and the audience was growing at a slower clip than anticipated. She needed an explosive installment. She needed an "aha moment" that caught viewers off guard, and made them talk about the documentary with friends and coworkers.

"Which conclusion?" Sidney asked.

"The one that suggested Julian Crist's skull fracture was caused by a boat oar. It was not."

"How were you able to determine this? And how can you prove it?"

"Here's the deal," Dr. Cutty said. "Our one-year pathology fellowship runs from July fifteenth last year to July fifteenth this year. That's a few days from now. So the three of us are all but finished with our training. We've written our boards, we've reached our autopsy numbers, and we've each accepted job offers. That means we're stuck here for two more weeks and we're bored as hell. The only thing we have left to complete is our end-of-year projects, which require each of us to conduct an experiment to prove or disprove a theory common to forensic pathology. We've all started researching our own projects, but, frankly, none of us has very good ideas. Typically, this end-of-training exercise is a way to kill the last week or two of fellowship and no one, including our chairman, takes it particularly seriously. But after you and I spoke, and we all had a look at the Julian Crist autopsy, the three of us figured we'd take a stab at changing that. We're going to conduct an experiment to show that it was impossible for the boat oar in question to have caused Julian Crist's skull fracture. In exchange, you agree not only to give it a prominent place in the documentary, but also to give each of us face time through interviews. Plus, list us as consultants in the credits."

Sidney lifted her chin. "Better than being published."

"We're already published."

Sidney shrugged her shoulders. "Agreed. Depending on what, exactly, you can show me. And what theory you're trying to prove or disprove."

"René Le Fort created classifications of skull fractures. We'll use his theories as our guide to refute the conclusion in Julian Crist's autopsy." Dr. Cutty lifted her hand to the autopsy table. "We did some experiments on our own to reproduce Julian's skull fracture. We'll do them again now, and we'll show you why that boat oar theory is complete nonsense."

CHAPTER 23

Thursday, June 15, 2017

Dr. Cutty pulled the white cloth from the first autopsy table to reveal a cadaver. Sidney had trouble making the connection between the rubbery, bleached thing on the table and a human being.

"I know," Dr. Cutty said. "Damian here has seen better days. But without a grant to conduct this experiment, we had to get cadavers from anyone willing to donate. Each of the fellows received one for our end-of-the-year experiments. To reproduce the results for you, we needed more. The medical school had two they agreed to part with. Damian is in the worst shape, but his skull is remarkably well preserved."

Dr. Cutty turned to the other table and whisked away the white sheet like a magician pulling a tablecloth free from a china-lined dining table. "This is Martha. Also, not in great shape anatomically, but, again, her skull is perfect for our purposes. We also have Synbone models if we need to run an exercise twice, because once we crush Damian and Martha's skulls . . . well, we can't really do it again."

"*Synbone?*"

"A polyurethane model of a skull. It reacts almost identically to the cranium, minus the vascular system, of course. But for the purpose of our experiment, we're interested only in the skull fracture. So we'll use the cadavers to reenact the assault, and then reproduce the results with Synbone models to confirm our findings. That'll be more high-tech, and we've got a wiz upstairs who can create computer models for you on what is happening with the skull during the impact. He'll show you the exact method by which bone fractures and the concussion wave radiates through the entire cranium and brain."

"Perfect," Sidney said.

"Which episode will this air on?" Dr. Schultz asked.

"Probably episode four, if I can cut it in time," Sidney said.

"With my fellowship, I haven't watched much television in the last year or so, but damn if I'm not hooked on your Grace Sebold special."

Sidney smiled. "Thanks."

"So the theory from Julian Crist's autopsy," Dr. Cutty said, "was that his skull fracture came as the result of blunt-force trauma. By definition, this type of injury is produced by low-velocity impact from a blunt, or dull, object. Or the low-velocity impact of a body against a blunt surface. So something that is nonjagged and not sharp, moving at a particular velocity that is considered low, struck the skull. In Julian Crist's case, the argument was made that a boat oar — specifically, a paddleboard oar — was used to strike him from behind."

Dr. Cutty leaned down on the other side of the autopsy table and produced a long, crusty-looking wooden oar.

"According to the autopsy report, this is the same brand and make of the oar in question."

Sidney cocked her head. "Where did you find it?"

"The office of the chief medical examiner has an extensive database from our tool analysis guys. We've got a guy who knows just about everything about pretty much any device ever used as a weapon. He pulled this oar up on the database and went hunting for one at Play It Again Sports shops around the state. Found this beauty the other day. Sawyer no longer manufactures these." Dr. Cutty held up the oar. "They're heavy and wooden. Over time, they became waterlogged and chipped. The newer ones are much lighter and made of composite plastic."

"Can I?" Sidney asked, holding out her hand.

"Sure."

Sidney took the oar, surprised by its weight and length. At least five pounds, and more than six feet. She lifted it over her shoulder to see what it would take to swing it. A surge of adrenaline filled her body as she thought of Grace Sebold doing the same.

"Tim," Dr. Cutty said to her colleague, pointing to the spot in front of her. Dr. Schultz walked from around the autopsy table and stood with his back to Dr. Cutty. "The theory," Dr. Cutty said, taking the oar from Sidney, "was that the perpetrator approached the victim from behind and swung the oar on an oblique plane."

She pantomimed the angle at which it was surmised in the autopsy report that the oar had struck Julian's skull. Sidney watched Dr. Cutty imitate the lethal blow and made a mental note to talk with Leslie Martin and see about creating an animated reenactment of the assault.

"Here's the problem with that theory," Dr. Cutty said. "First, the skull fracture was stellate in nature. That means it came from a single source of impact and then spread outward, like dropping a heavy object on a thin sheet of ice and watching the fissures spread through it. Now, no matter how you simulate the oar striking the skull, with either the flat side or the thin side" — Dr. Cutty placed the oar against Tim Schultz's head, first with the flat end pancaked against his skull, and then rotated as if to chop a tree with the slim side of the blade — "it is impossible for this oar to cause a stellate fracture in the pattern found on Julian Crist's skull."

"Impossible or unlikely?" Sidney asked.

"Impossible."

Sidney imagined the word *impossible* ringing out on episode four.

"How can you determine that?" Sidney asked.

"Because we've tried. Several times. And we'll try again today on Damian and Martha."

The other pathologist, Dr. Tilly, hoisted the first cadaver so it was bent at a ninety-degree angle from the waist as though Damian were sitting on the autopsy table. The leather skin cracked and oozed formalin as Dr. Tilly positioned it. With Dr. Schultz, she attached nylon straps to the chest and under the arms, which they secured to the corners of the autopsy table, where holes and fasteners were present, and then fastened the latches onto hanging braces that came from the ceiling. Apparently, sitting a dead body up in the morgue was a common practice.

"You'll want to stand over there," Dr. Cutty said to Derrick, who moved from the corner and positioned himself so that the back of the cadaver's head was visible through the viewfinder.

"Here are the photos from Julian's autopsy showing the skull fracture. Its epicenter is located in the posterior, superior aspect of the right parietal bone."

Sidney paged through the graphic photos depicting the top and back of Julian's skull. Several were taken with blood-soaked hair obscuring the details, then more after the head had been shaved, which more clearly showed the laceration. The last few photos had been taken after the scalp had been peeled away to reveal raw bone that brought clearly into view the caved-in area, which reminded Sidney of a broken china doll.

"I'm going to strike Damian's skull with

the flat end of the oar," Dr. Cutty said. "Then I'll do the same thing to Martha, but I'll use the sharp end of the oar blade. Now, of course, in this experiment we are creating postmortem fractures, which vary greatly from perimortem fractures. But we're not studying the blood pattern, skin lacerations, or the angles of the fractures. We are only analyzing the *pattern* of the fractures. The ones we produce on Damian will serve as excellent comparison to the fractures found on Julian Crist."

Dr. Cutty moved to the end of the autopsy table.

"Here goes."

Damian sat upright with his back facing her. Sidney glanced at Derrick, who offered another thumbs-up as he kept his right eye trained through the viewfinder. She stepped back a bit when Dr. Cutty raised the elongated oar over her right shoulder. In dramatic fashion, she brought the oar down hard into the cadaver's skull. A sickening thud mixed with the splintering of bone echoed off the walls of the autopsy suite. Damian jerked forward, but the nylon straps kept him upright and in place. Sidney felt an odd sadness for the cadaver, or the man he once was.

Resting the oar against the autopsy table,

Dr. Cutty slipped on latex gloves.

"The first thing you'll notice is that there's no breach to the scalp. No skin laceration. We did this experiment three other times on three other cadavers, plus multiple times on Synbone with pigskin covering, which is a close approximation to human skin," Dr. Cutty explained. "When using the flat side of the oar, we were never able to reproduce the scalp laceration that was found during Julian Crist's autopsy."

Dr. Cutty snaked a gloved finger under the surgically perforated flap of skin near the front of the cadaver's skull.

"Once we get past the absence of a laceration," Dr. Cutty said as she peeled the scalp and hair away from the skull, as if removing a mannequin's wig, "we can analyze the actual bone fracture."

There was not a drop of blood, Sidney noticed. Damian's vessels had long been dry. Dr. Tilly pulled a Canon camera from a nearby table and twisted the focus to snap several photographs of the bone damage.

"We'll make sure you get copies of these."

Sidney nodded as she moved closer to the table.

"This strike was with the broad end of the oar," Dr. Cutty said, holding Damian's skull in her hands. "The first thing you'll notice is that this type of trauma, blunt-force trauma, caused from a broad, flat object, didn't penetrate the skull. Fracture it? Yes. But actually *penetrate* the bone? No. Instead, as you see, it caused a nondepressed fracture that radiated away from the site, but which also stresses the suture lines and often times separates the skull along these margins — the sagittal suture on top of the skull, the coronal and lambdoid sutures in front and back. This wound is much different from the one documented in Julian's autopsy photos, where the skull is caved inward, or depressed, to a specific diameter and depth — three centimeters deep, seven centimeters wide, as measured by the St. Lucian pathologist — which is what defines a stellate fracture. We will repeat this many times on the Synbone model, with slow motion and still shots, to demonstrate that the flat end of the oar could not have caused Julian Crist's skull fracture." Dr. Cutty looked at Sidney. "So that leaves the edge of the oar."

Dr. Tilly and Dr. Schultz moved to the cadaver named Martha and positioned her with straps in a similar fashion as they had Damian until the body was sitting upright. When her cohorts were safely out of the way, Dr. Cutty approached again and lifted the oar, careful to rotate the handle so that the sharp edge of the blade was in the striking position. She lifted the oar over her right shoulder, Hank Aaron–style, and cracked it against Martha's head. The sound again reverberated in the corners of the morgue and gave Sidney a jolt. The autopsy suite was nothing but metal and tile, neither of which did much in the way of absorbing sound. Dr. Tilly again moved in to photograph the damage.

"You can see right away," Dr. Cutty said, "that using the blade side of the oar produced a scalp laceration. In future demonstrations, we'll use Synbone models and, with the help of our ballistics team and their contraptions, we'll vary the speed of the oar to the slowest velocity possible that will still produce a laceration *and* a skull fracture, just in case I swung harder than the assailant. But for our initial demonstration on the cadaver, you can see the scalp laceration that has been produced. So, if the oar was used to strike Julian, because of the laceration found, the blade of the paddle *had* to be the part of the oar that made contact with his head. So let's look at the fracture."

Dr. Cutty peeled away the scalp from a premade crowning incision.

"As you can see, a very different fracture

pattern as compared to Damian's, where the flat side of the paddle was used. This one is deeper, as the oar penetrated the bone and caused a depressed fracture. This is a classic stellate pattern, with multiple linear fractures radiating from the impact site. But the shape of this fracture is completely unlike the fracture caused by the flat side of the oar. It's longer, deeper, and more isolated since the source of the trauma — the edge of the oar — is much more compact than the broad side of the oar. And using the thin side of the oar, because the energy is so compacted, doesn't cause the separation of the suture lines."

Dr. Cutty went back to Julian Crist's autopsy photos, handing them to Sidney. In the pictures, Julian's scalp, too, had been husked away to reveal bare cranium.

"Even an untrained eye can see that neither of the fractures we've just produced, either from the flat paddle or the blade, match what was found on the back of Julian Crist's skull. And since we've determined that the flat side could not have caused the laceration, we have to assume the blade caused it. And this assumption can be easily dispelled by simply measuring the length of the fracture," Dr. Cutty said. "Remember, Julian's skull fracture was measured to be three centimeters deep and seven centimeters wide. No matter how many times we repeat this experiment, which we've done on four different cadavers, as well as multiple times on a Synbone model, the length of the fracture when using the blade of the paddle has never been less than four inches, or, ten centimeters." Dr. Cutty looked at Sidney as Derrick zoomed in on her face. "Bottom line? There is *no oar on this planet* that could possibly have caused Julian's skull fracture."

Sidney was silent as she stared at the ten-year-old photos from an autopsy that helped convict Grace Sebold.

She looked up from the photos. "If you can say for certain, in your medical opinion, that the paddleboard oar did *not* cause Julian's skull fracture, do you have an opinion on what did?"

Dr. Cutty shook her head. "Not on the actual object, but I can make a conclusion about that object. It was much smaller than a boat oar, and it was wrapped in organza."

"Organza?" Sidney asked.

"It's a type of nylon."

Dr. Cutty pulled Julian Crist's autopsy report from an empty table and flipped through it, then handed the earmarked page to Sidney. She ran her finger down to the middle paragraph. "The pathologist in St. Lucia documented that organza fibers were discovered within the scalp wound. No wood fragments, incidentally, which would be expected if a wooden oar had been used. Instead, nylon fragments."

Sidney blinked a few times. "So whoever struck Julian did so with an object wrapped in what? A nylon bag?"

"That's a much stronger conclusion than a wooden oar. Oh, yeah," Dr. Cutty said, picking up the paddle again. "Grace Sebold is listed as being five feet three inches tall, so to cause a fracture on this part of Julian's skull, who was listed as six-two, she would have had to grow a few inches or be standing on top of something in order to produce the angle of the fracture.

"And one more thing. Grace is documented to be left-handed." Dr. Cutty held the oar over her left shoulder. "Since Julian's skull fracture was on the right side of his head, no matter what she used as a weapon" — Dr. Cutty switched the oar to her right shoulder and made a show of reversing her hands so her right fist was now on top of her left — "Ms. Sebold is a helluva switch hitter."

CHAPTER 24

Friday, June 16, 2017

She flew from Raleigh to Hartsfield-Jackson Atlanta International Airport. Her return to New York had been open-ended, not knowing exactly what Dr. Cutty would reveal during her experiments. The conclusions, however, were a damning condemnation of the boat oar theory that had been used to convict Grace Sebold. Sidney sent Derrick home to New York to compile the footage they had recorded in Raleigh. Leslie would take the amassed recordings and trim the fat. By Monday, when Sidney planned to return, the hours of footage recorded during her time with Dr. Cutty and the ballistics team at the Office of the Chief Medical Examiner in North Carolina would be condensed to four hours of useable material. Sidney would then edit those hours down to the most important forty minutes, work with the writers to create her voice-over material, and cut episode four with the tech team in time to screen it to the network executives for their approval to air next Friday. If she were able to present Dr. Cutty's experiments with enough intrigue, it would be the most explosive installment of the season.

She touched down in Atlanta and rented a car, careful to use her personal card. Today's travel could not be expensed to the network. In fact, she wanted no one at work to know about her trips to Baldwin State Prison. Least of all Luke Barrington, who would hold her in contempt for the fact that her birth father, with whom Sidney had never had a meaningful relationship — besides during a brief window of her childhood — was serving a life sentence for murder.

She came to the now-familiar setting of low buildings strung out across the open land, contained by a tight perimeter of barbed wire and latticed chain link, a common theme no matter which jail Sidney visited. She spoke with the gate guard and waited while the fencing slowly parted and allowed her to pull into the complex. Prison visits were never fast, but Baldwin was longer than most. The screening was worse than any airport, and the waiting was on par with a bad layover. Eventually, an hour after she arrived, the guard called her name and led her past the thick door and into the visitation booths. There she took a seat and waited another fifteen minutes until her father appeared on the other side of the glass.

She did not know the man sitting across from her. Not well, at any rate. Memories of him came from when she was ten years old and her family life was still somewhat normal. Those still images and short clips of her family, just the three of them, were created before her father killed a man. Before her mother uprooted her from the Atlanta suburb, where every friend Sidney had ever made lived, and replanted her haphazardly in Sarasota, Florida. Sidney never created the same friendships in Sarasota that she had enjoyed her whole life in Atlanta, and the new life her mother attempted to forge in Florida was less *new* and mostly just *different.* Can life really be started over? Can you simply turn the page in the notebook of life that has recorded your history and start writing a fresh story? If so, Sidney and her mother did it incorrectly. They either wrote the wrong story, or an unoriginal new story, or one that didn't properly allow them to forget the pages that had come before. The failure was evidenced by the fact that Sidney sat waiting at a penitentiary to see her father more than two decades after he'd scribbled all over their original notebook — deep, crevice-producing gouges that ruined so much.

It wasn't until college that Sidney steered her life back on track. Even then, though, the identity of her murderous father, who was locked away in an Atlanta penitentiary, was a well-kept secret. None of her college friends knew about her father; and the further her life progressed from his conviction when she was ten years old and in fifth grade, the less she thought about him. Thirty-six now, Sidney had spent more than two-thirds of her life without her father being part of it. Only the arrival of an unexpected letter had sparked the idea of a reunion. In it, Neil Ryan made a simple request to his daughter: *Can I see you?*

She still struggled, even after three years of clandestine meetings, to view her father through anything other than the prism of a ten-year-old girl. It was how she remembered him. Ingrained in her mind was the image of her dad taking her to the deli after Sunday church service, and riding on his shoulders as they walked through the amusement park. With just the three of them, roller coasters always left an odd man out. Although Sidney dutifully divided her riding time between her parents, secretly she loved riding the coasters with her dad. She always felt safer with him. Now, as she stared through the glass at the man in an orange jumpsuit, no feelings of safety or comfort came from his presence. No feelings at all, really. Not anger or resentment. To Sidney, Neil Donald Ryan was a stranger much more than he was a father.

He picked up the phone and his voice rang in her head as Sidney pressed the receiver to her ear.

"Hey, kiddo."

"Hi, Dad."

"I watched last week. I've got most of the guys in here hooked on it. I'm real proud of you."

Sidney smiled. "Thanks."

She wondered if she should mention to the network suits that the inmates at Baldwin were fans of *The Girl of Sugar Beach.* She could use the ratings.

"I know you're real busy," he said. "But did you get the chance to look into the DNA?"

Sidney shook her head. "Not yet."

She gave her father credit. His original letter had requested to see her with no ulterior motive besides a reunion after more than twenty years. She had reluctantly visited, expecting him to ask if she could manage to free him the way she had freed so many others. It was a common plea in the letters she received from inmates. That she had, actually, only gotten three convictions overturned was immaterial to most felons she spoke with. The fact that she'd freed a single man was enough to draw the attention of convicts around the country. So, when Sidney visited Baldwin for the first time, she expected a similar reception. She didn't get it. Her father simply stared at her for most of the visit. He laughed a lot, too, shaking his head at the sight of his ten-year-old daughter who had blossomed into a beautiful woman with long brown hair, highlighted by faint streaks of auburn. Hazel eyes brightened with radial traces of ice blue. He couldn't, in fact, stop shaking his head during that first visit. It was two years, and nine visits later, before he breached the subject of his innocence.

"There are new techniques now," he had said. "That weren't available back when I was convicted. DNA analysis is much more specific and advanced these days. If I get you a sample of my DNA, then you could use it to show that it doesn't match any collected at the crime scene."

Sidney had changed the subject then, veering the conversation back to her mother. It was a common topic between them, and had been enough to distract him from pursuing things further. Then the letter arrived containing her father's fingernail clippings. Until Sidney had opened that small square of tissue that spilled ten perfect crescent moon fingernails onto her desk, she had been able to explain away her inaction. But since the potential source of DNA had arrived, it gnawed at her and prevented her from dismissing her father's pleas.

"Nail clippings are a viable source for DNA," her father said now. "I looked it up. And I put the tissue paper on my tongue, so a good lab should be able to draw a saliva sample as well."

The tissue and nail clippings sat in Sidney's desk drawer at home. They had spent the night next to her kitchen trash can, but Sidney had never gotten up the nerve to toss them in. Instead, she stowed the tissue and clippings in her desk and tried not to think about them.

She looked at her father through the glass now. "I haven't had them tested yet."

He shrugged. To most, Sidney figured, this would be discouraging. But she had found over the years that inmates, deprived of just about every luxury in life, possessed a great deal of patience. They never expected anything to happen quickly, and took news of delays in much the same fashion as finding the bathroom stall occupied. They simply took a breath and waited.

Too young at the time of the crime to understand fully what had happened, she had briefly researched her father's conviction in college. Accused of killing a man in the victim's home, he was sentenced to first-degree murder and was slated to spend his life in prison.

The single bullet fired came from a .22 automatic found at the scene. Neil Ryan's prints were recovered from the gun. It was a claim he vehemently denied, since, according to his attorney, he'd never held a gun in his life. Fingerprint experts grappled during trial about whether the prints were a definitive match to Neil Ryan's. Complicating matters was that another, overlying set of prints had also been pulled from the gun. The prosecution argued that the anonymous prints came from a young officer who had mistakenly, and against protocol, picked up the weapon when he arrived on the scene. But testing of the smeared prints could not definitively be matched to the officer. It was still claimed as a certain match by the prosecution's expert witness, refuted by the defense's own fingerprint guru, but not convincingly enough to keep Sidney's father out of jail.

When the fingerprint debate was over, the prosecution presented the blow, which would turn out to be of the knockout variety, that Neil Ryan was having an affair with the dead man's wife. Fingerprint arguments were quickly forgotten, and the idea of premeditation became a hot topic.

The jury settled on first-degree murder, agreeing with the prosecution's argument that Neil Ryan had gone to his lover's home with the intent to kill her husband, who had discovered the affair. Twenty-five years later, Sidney's father still sat in a prison cell without the possibility of parole. That he refused to admit to the crime, and showed no remorse for it, was a catching point for every parole board that reviewed his case. No board members had ever given a second thought to a man without remorse, or considered stamping Neil Ryan's case with anything other than *Denied.*

"You've been an exemplary prisoner," Sidney finally said, regaining eye contact through the glass partition. "If you would just take responsibility, you'd likely come up for parole."

"I didn't kill that man," he said. "Why on earth would I admit it?"

"Because it could get you out of here."

"It could also seal my fate. You know how many guys in here cop to things they didn't do because they think it'll get them outta here? Plenty. You know what happens to most of them? They still get denied. And then they can never take back what they told that board."

"Fine," Sidney said. "Don't admit to the crime, but show them some remorse for your involvement. If you hadn't been . . ." She almost said *cheating on Mom,* but it seemed so insignificant this many years later that she was embarrassed it still bothered her. "Sleeping with his wife, the idea of premeditation wouldn't have come up."

"I'm a lot of things. A terrible husband is one of them. But cheating on your spouse is not a crime, and it certainly doesn't prove I killed anyone. I'm not slicing my own throat in front of a parole board just to win their favor." Her father stared at her through the glass partition. "So, can you help me?"

What her father was asking was for Sidney to somehow pull that .22 out of a box buried somewhere in an Atlanta Federal Building's evidence room and prove that her father's DNA was not on the handle, or anywhere on the weapon, or at the crime scene. This, he was convinced, would be enough to get him a new trial. He'd done his homework, and the plan held some merit. Sidney had made some casual inquires in the last several months, but finding someone who still remembered the case from twenty-plus years ago was nearly impossible. And attempting to get anyone to pay attention to her request to pull evidence from so long ago had so far been fruitless.

"I'm working on it," she finally said.

Her father took a deep breath. "I guess that's all I can ask."

"Anyway," Sidney said, her way of letting on that she was ready to leave, "I just stopped on my way back to New York."

"Okay. We'll talk soon," he said.

Her father nodded and hung up the phone. He raised his hand and the guard was by his side a moment later, leading him back to his cell. Sidney sat for a while longer, staring through the glass at the empty chair a stranger had just vacated. Her imagination replaced him with her father from years ago. The man on whose shoulders she had loved to ride. Sidney was sure she owed the stranger nothing, but wondered if the other man deserved something.

In her car, colliding thoughts of her father and Grace Sebold ran through her mind. Since Dr. Cutty's revelations, Sidney had tried for the last day to find the arc of her story, imagining the best way to present the impossibility of the boat oar being the weapon used to cause Julian Crist's skull fracture and that, instead, some other instrument wrapped in nylon had been used to strike Julian Crist. It was an explosive argument that could have real consequences. It was backed by science, not some retroactive opinion offered by someone with thin credentials and labeled an expert, as Sidney had seen many other documentarians try to pull off. This development was legitimate, disproving a critical aspect used in Grace Sebold's conviction. It needed to be handled correctly.

Grace Sebold's problem, however, and what Sidney had wrestled with for the past twenty-four hours, was the same problem her father faced as he sat in jail. The unexplainable needed to be explained. If the documentary was going to suggest that another object was actually used to strike Julian, then the inconvenient facts of Julian's blood in her cottage, as well as on the blade of the oar, and Grace's fingerprints on the shaft, needed to be explained.

There were not many ways to rationalize those findings. There may not be any. But if one existed, Sidney knew where it rested, and she knew whom it needed to come from. Baldwin's chain-link fence slowly parted. Sidney turned the rental away from the prison and headed back to Hartsfield-Jackson Atlanta International Airport.

CHAPTER 25

Saturday, June 17, 2017

The Caribbean air was wet and thick as Sidney walked from the Hewanorra International Airport. A line of taxicabs waited for their turn to zip tourists around the island, the drivers eager to load suitcases into trunks and graciously accept tips from excited Americans and Brits overly gratuitous at the start of their vacations. Bringing these tourists back to the airport was never as fruitful as shuffling them to their resorts. Spirits were high and wallets loose at the dawn of their journey, quite the opposite by week's end.

So it was a strange expression the cabbie offered when he stepped from his car to find Sidney with nothing but a small rolling suitcase instead of stacks of luggage. That she was alone was another oddity. And her request, to be taken to the Bordelais Correctional Facility, was most peculiar of all.

But, the cabbie thought as he climbed behind the wheel, *a fare is a fare.*

It took forty minutes to reach Dennery, and it was the first time he'd dropped an American at the prison. The cab crested a hill and the clearing came into view, where the white rectangle buildings stood within a perimeter of fence. The driver pulled down, through the visitor's gate and into the parking lot.

"I'll be an hour. Hour and a half, at the most," the American woman asked. "I'll pay you to wait for me."

They settled on a fare. She offered half, delivering the American dollars over the seat. "I'll give you the other half when I get back, plus the toll back to the airport. Actually, Charlery's Inn. Do you know it?"

"Yeh, man. No problem."

The driver watched her walk to the prison entrance, where a guard waited for her. Once she was inside, he pulled the car into a parking spot, shut off the engine, and took a nap.

Her father and Marshall had visited three weeks earlier, so Grace was surprised to hear she had another visitor so soon. Usually, they came every three to four months. Sometimes it stretched to longer intervals, and she always recognized the annoyance in Marshall's eyes at the long span between visits. Despite Marshall's attempts to disguise it, Grace knew his condition was deteriorating. She noticed that his motor skills had diminished greatly in the last two years. The day he showed up in a wheelchair broke her heart. Marshall always complained to Grace that "they" wouldn't come any sooner, referring to their parents. Although Grace appreciated her brother's loyalty, and his desire to see her more often, she was no fool. Grace understood the cost, both in time and treasure, it took to travel to a foreign country to visit a daughter they loved, but whom they had determined they could no longer help. That Marshall simply didn't have the means or the ability to visit on his own was another source of his anger. His independent spirit, even after two decades of being reliant on his parents, had never died. The accident, that horrible part of their life, had taken so much from him, but it hadn't harmed his rebellious and sovereign mind-set.

With subtle headshakes and quick winks that went unnoticed by her parents, Grace always let Marshall know during their visits that she understood. If it were up to him, he'd come every weekend. And Grace truly believed that if Marshall had been a normally functioning adult with a middle-class job, he would come to St. Lucia every week or two to visit her. It broke Grace's heart that her parents, aging and tired after nearly twenty years of caring for their ailing son, had relied more and more lately on outside help for Marshall's care. Marshall hated the facility where they were planning to place him, something he made very clear in his letters to Grace.

Although he was unable to travel independently to St. Lucia, Marshall was free to communicate through written word. His letters had become one of Grace's greatest comforts over the years. They arrived like clockwork. At least twice a week, sometimes more, and Grace never grew tired of them. In those folded pages, Marshall kept her abreast of what was happening at home: His crumbling relationship with their parents. Their growing impatience with his *condition* — that was the word that the Sebolds used when discussing Marshall with doctors and therapists. From Marshall's visits over the years and from his letters, Grace knew that no one gave her younger brother enough credit. He'd never be the athlete he once was, and would never mentally be the same person he was before they climbed into the car on that fateful night, but Grace's brother was still one of the smartest people she knew. His intelligence was etched throughout his letters.

Despite the short span between visits, her stomach still fluttered with excitement to see him. She followed the guard into the visitation room and sat at the table. The guard closed the door and Grace waited in silence while the screening process took place outside. She looked up when the door opened moments later. Sidney Ryan walked into the room. Grace smiled.

"This is unexpected. I thought we were scheduled to talk on the phone this Tuesday."

"Hi, Grace," Sidney said as she sat in the chair opposite her. "Sorry to show up unannounced. This couldn't wait."

"What is it?"

"When I sat across from you last time, I told you I wasn't sure what I believed. Today I think I do. I met with a forensic pathologist back in the States who refuted the claim that the paddleboard oar caused Julian's head injury. And, although it's her opinion, she backed it up quite impressively with experimentation that I hope to base the next episode on."

"That's great," Grace said. "I mean . . ."

Grace's eyes became wet with tears. "Sorry," she said as she wiped her eyes and took a deep, calming breath. "It's been a long time since I've cried over any of this. But someone is listening to me. Finally someone is helping me. I knew that you'd find something if you looked." She reached across the table and squeezed Sidney's hand. "Thank you."

Sidney nodded. "Listen, Grace. This thing with the oar, it was really impressive what Dr. Cutty was able to show. It'll make an explosive episode. But I still need to disprove key aspects of your conviction."

Grace lifted her chin. "Okay."

"Julian's blood. It's a problem. It was discovered in the sink of your cottage bathroom."

Grace smiled. "So I've been told."

"I know you don't have access to the Internet, but for each site that supports you and tries to raise money for you, there's another site or message board that talks about how guilty you are. And a lot of what they talk about is the fact that Julian's blood was all over your room."

"I've seen the websites. Marshall sends me that stuff. Prints out all the Web pages and bundles them together so I can read them." Grace smiled. "Grisly Grace Sebold dripping with blood like Carrie White in Chamberlain, Maine. To the public, it was like popcorn — devoured kernel by kernel, while being fully entertained. To me, sitting in that courtroom and listening to it all during my trial, it was preposterous. And therein lies the problem with our — and by that I mean the world's — justice system. We are allowed to simply defend ourselves against absurd allegations, but the dirty little secret is that if the prosecution wants to convict someone badly enough, all they have to do is make the most farcical accusations they can think of, make many of them, and make them often enough to sway the jury. The blood was not found all over my room. It was found in the bathroom."

"Okay," Sidney said. "But the fact that *any* of Julian's blood was in your room is a sticking point for your critics."

"And for you?"

Sidney shrugged. "It . . . confuses me. And if it confuses me, it will confuse my audience. Julian's blood is a problem, Grace. His blood in the bathroom, his blood in the sink, and his blood on the oar. And another problem is the bleach that was used to hide it. So I can credibly show that the oar wasn't used to kill Julian, but I need you to help me with the rest."

"It wasn't bleach."

Sidney squinted her eyes.

"What they found in my room. It wasn't bleach."

Sidney raised her eyebrows. "What was it?"

"Alkyl dimethyl benzyl ammonium chloride," Grace said.

"What's that?" Sidney asked.

Grace leaned forward so her elbows rested on the table. "The active ingredient in Clorox wipes."

THE GIRL OF SUGAR BEACH
"The Razor Blade" Part of Episode 4
*Based on the interview with Grace Sebold

"Damn it!"

"What's the matter?" Grace asked.

She lay within a mess of white sheets in the king-sized four-poster bed that dominated the Sugar Beach cottage.

"I cut myself," Julian said from the bathroom.

"Why are you shaving? We're on vacation."

"Um, this is a problem. I'm bleeding like a sieve."

Grace untangled herself from the covers and climbed out of bed. The morning sun shone off the mahogany floor, promising a beautiful day of sunbathing.

"Let me see," she said as she walked into the bathroom. "Wow. What the hell did you do?"

Droplets of red blood freckled the white countertop and sink. Another impressive collection had formed on the tile floor. Red stained tissues were piled near the trash can.

"It's all the goddamn rum," Julian said. "My prothrombin time is probably five minutes."

"And you've been taking ibuprofen for your back. Your platelets are worthless." Grace looked at Julian in the mirror. They both started laughing.

"We're such nerds," he said.

"Here." Grace grabbed a washcloth from the wall and pressed it to Julian's chin. She kissed his lips. "Now go elevate it, or something."

"It's my chin. How am I supposed to elevate it?"

She looked at him with a snarky expression. "Just get out of the bathroom so I can clean this up. It's like a massacre in here."

Julian walked through the main room and opened the patio doors. He kept the washcloth pressed to his chin as he sat in the warm sun and stared at the Pitons. In the bathroom, Grace opened the cabinet under the sink and found a container of Clorox wipes. She pulled several from the dispenser and began cleaning the blood.

"It's like a slaughter," Grace said as she balanced on the paddleboard.

She dug the long oar into the water on the right side, and then lifted it across the board to do the same on the left.

Julian sat in front of her, his legs straight

and his heels hanging off the end of the board. "It's not going to clot. The alcohol and Advil will make it drip all day."

His chin was still oozing, and the bandage he'd received from the nurses' station was beyond saturated, now nothing but a red piece of adhesive on his chin.

"Getting your heart racing is not going to help any," Grace said. "But I can't get us back. The current is too strong."

"Are you serious? I'm weak from blood loss."

"Give me a break. Take me back to shore. I want a mojito."

Julian turned and looked up at Grace, who was standing on the paddleboard behind him. The sun was high in the sky, the silhouette of her head intermittently blocking its rays and casting a shadow over Julian. The oar rested on her shoulder, her fist gripped tightly around the shaft.

"Bleeding like a stuck pig," Julian said. "And my girlfriend can't get me back to dry land."

He gripped the edge of the board and leaned quickly to his right. Grace screamed as they both splashed into the ocean.

CHAPTER 26

Saturday, June 17, 2017

"Charlery's Inn. Yeh, man?" The cab driver asked.

"Change of plans. I've got to get to Victoria Hospital in Castries," Sidney said. She checked her watch. "But we have to hurry."

"Castries is a long way," he said.

"How long?"

"One hour. Fifty minutes if I drive fast."

"Get me there in thirty and I'll give you an extra fifty dollars."

"Yeh, man," he said, shifting the car into gear and racing out of Bordelais Correctional Facility.

They made it to Castries in just over thirty minutes. Sidney still rewarded him the bonus.

"This is my last stop," she said. "Then Charlery's. Wait for me?"

"No problem."

Sidney opened the back door and headed

to the front entrance of Victoria Hospital. At the reception desk, she asked for directions to the mortuary.

"Are you here to make an identification?" the woman asked.

"No. I'm here to speak with Dr. Mundi. I phoned him about an hour ago, and he said he'd be at the hospital until this evening."

The woman held up a finger, and spoke quickly on the phone. When she hung up, she looked at Sidney. "I'll take you."

They rode the elevator to the basement and Sidney followed the woman through the corridors. Besides that the hallways were darker, and the creep factor a bit higher, the St. Lucian mortuary wasn't much different from Dr. Cutty's.

"Down on your right," the woman said, pointing to the only open doorway at the end of the hall.

"Thank you," Sidney said.

She found Dr. Mundi behind his desk. A worn box, whose cardboard edges had been blunted by years of storage, was in front of him as he rummaged through it. He didn't notice her enter, so she cleared her throat.

The doctor looked up.

"Hi, I'm Sidney Ryan."

"Come in, come in," Dr. Mundi said.

Sidney sat in a chair in front of the desk.

"Sorry to call today, and then show up so quickly."

"No problem. I think it is here," Dr. Mundi said, digging into the box. "Yes, right here." The doctor pulled out a file folder and slowly turned the pages until he found what he needed.

"Yes," he said, raising his eyebrows. "I did note it. A one-point-nine–centimeter laceration on the victim's chin determined at the time of autopsy to be a typical shaving injury. These wounds are not difficult to identify, and are common autopsy findings. Usually on the face of male patients, the legs of females."

"Would you give me permission to record you while you explain that finding, and how you could determine that it was the result of a razor?"

The doctor looked up from his notes. "A twin-blade razor, I noted." He shrugged his shoulders. "Sure. I don't mind if you record."

Her phone battery was at 1 percent and she had no bars of service as the cabdriver shuttled her south through the mountains of St. Lucia and toward Vieux Fort. She hated being disconnected, but having spent the life of her phone capturing video of Dr.

Mundi's explanation of the laceration he had documented ten years ago on Julian Crist's chin, coupled with what Grace had told her earlier while she recorded their conversation, being cut off from the world was worth the footage. That the video was raw, recorded on a combination of her iPhone and a small handheld camcorder, was sure to add to the urgency of the episode she was imagining. She had stumbled across evidence overlooked during Grace's original trial and was now haphazardly recording her findings without the assistance of her camera crew. Coupled with the professional footage Derrick had shot of Dr. Cutty's demonstrations, Friday's episode had the potential to be a blockbuster.

When they finally reached Charlery's Inn, back near the airport, where she had met her driver earlier in the day, Sidney handed over the fare. He'd had a good day and never saw an island resort. She wheeled her small suitcase into her room and locked the door. After setting her phone to charge, she opened her laptop and booked a flight home for the next morning.

She found a Piton beer in the minibar and sat on the edge of the bed. Pastel hues of soft salmon and green covered the walls of the cheap hotel. Sidney took a long swallow of beer and picked up the hotel telephone, listening to the series of prompts until her call was finally patched through to New York.

"Hello," Leslie Martin said.

"It's me," Sidney said.

"Jesus, I thought your plane crashed. Where have you been?"

"I took a detour. I'm in St. Lucia."

"What? Why?"

"Because she didn't do it."

JURY DELIBERATION
DAY 2

"We need to discuss the blood evidence," Harold said from the head of the table.

"I don't believe her," the retired schoolteacher said almost before Harold was finished with his sentence. "How could that much blood be present in the room, yet she has no idea how it got there?"

"Well," Harold said in his calm, understanding voice. "That's not exactly what was argued in court. But again, this is a good start to the discussion. Let's reread the transcripts from her testimony and the cross-examination. We'll put the facts about the blood and the cleanup onto the chalkboard, like we did during our discussion of the murder weapon." Harold pointed to the green board behind them, covered now by white chalk dust after yesterday's spirited debate.

"And then," he said, "we'll

have a more accurate discussion about the blood, the body, and the cleanup."

■ ■ ■ ■

PART III
A RATINGS
JUGGERNAUT

■ ■ ■ ■

CHAPTER 27

Friday, June 23, 2017

A searing pain shot through his hip as he reached for the remote control. He turned up the volume and fumbled with his glasses before righting them on his face and staring at the flat screen that hung on the wall. A reporter's face filled the television as she offered a tutorial on skull fractures. The scene flashed to a pathologist dressed in scrubs as she explained on a skull model what was happening to the cadaver as they struck the back of the head with an oar. It was a chilling and engrossing sight that brought Gus back to his past, vicariously reliving through television the moments of his career when he spent time with medical examiners in the morgue.

He pressed a button on the guardrail and the bed hummed as it pushed him upright. A few deep breaths and the pain in his hip settled as he squinted at the television. He'd

requested a larger one weeks ago, even offered to purchase it himself, but "Nurse
Ratchet" ignored him.

"If we give *you* a bigger television, then
we'd have to give *everyone* a bigger television, Mr. Morelli," she had said in her
condescending voice.

"Then do it," he had responded. "Damn
things are practically free nowadays. And
I'm sure most poor folks in this place are
half blind. Don't you want them to be able
to see Alex Trebek's face each evening?"

His request went over about as well as
when he refused to use the bedpan just after
surgery. Now, weeks from the night he lost
his right leg — a difficult choice between
his lower limb and cancer — the pain was
more manageable, his health no longer on
the brink, and his attitude toward the staff,
although far from pleasant, was certainly
less hostile. Except for Nurse Ratchet. She
was a cruel woman the day he met her, and
would continue to be counted as such until
the day she died.

"What're you watching, Gus?"

The young physical therapist named Jason
walked into the room in his purple scrubs.
Out of every miserable person he'd encoun-
tered on this road to hell, Jason was a
standout. Young and vibrant, he appeared

to be, besides Riki the Friday-night nurse, the only one in this godforsaken place who enjoyed his job. And evidenced by his muscular biceps and forearms, Gus guessed that Jason pushed himself as hard in the weight room as he pushed his patients in therapy sessions. Handsome and charismatic, he reminded Gus of himself decades ago before the job and life and cancer had turned him bitter to the world.

Jason stood in stark contrast to the robots that strolled from room to room, jabbing needles and yanking catheters on their way to five o'clock. Gus Morelli had spent his fair share of time in prisons during his career, and these ladies would fit in just as well barking at inmates at the local penitentiary as they would screaming at the elderly patients here at Alcove Manor.

Most patients were here to rehabilitate from some catastrophic disease that had placed them at death's door. Many, Gus determined as he snooped through the hallways in his wheelchair, would be better off if someone had answered.

"Some documentary," Gus said.

"Here," Jason said. "Let me help you."

The young man pulled Gus forward in bed, rearranged the pillows behind his back so he sat more upright.

"Oh, Jesus. That feels better."

"Gotta keep pressure off the hip," Jason said. "Lean left and your incision will heal faster." He pulled bedsheets that had become tucked and trapped around Gus's leg and behind his back. "Did you get into a wrestling match?"

"I've been tossing and turning for an hour, trying to get myself free."

"Just call the nurses."

Gus smiled at him. "That'd be like little Anne Frank calling the Nazis to help her out of the attic."

Jason laughed. "That's pretty cold. Funny, but cold."

"At least you appreciate my humor. My charisma has been lost on the rest of the staff. Except the nice nurse that helps me Friday nights."

Jason shrugged. "I heard you called Ruth an icy bitch the other day. Not exactly the definition of charisma."

"Hell, I can't argue with you there. When I hear it like that, coming from you, I feel like a piece of shit for having said it. They manage to bring out my ugly side. I'm really not such an asshole."

"You lost your leg," Jason said. "You deserve to be a little bit of an asshole. Just pick your battles. Fighting with Ruth is pointless."

"I'm figuring that out. Have you seen this show?"

Jason turned to the television. "Oh, yeah. I'm hooked."

"What is it?"

"*The Girl of Sugar Beach.* A documentary about Grace Sebold."

"Who?"

"Grace Sebold. From when she killed her boyfriend down in the Caribbean."

Gus blinked at the screen as a still shot of Grace Sebold from medical school filled the television. The documentary cut to an interview of the girl, now a woman, slightly haggard with short-cropped hair, which was graying in random areas. Prison-issued, thick plastic glasses covered her eyes and reflected the overhead lights.

"It's addictive," Jason said. "It's a real-time documentary. The investigator is producing the episodes from week to week and then airing them. The audience is finding out what she discovers almost simultaneously as she discovers it. It's very popular with . . . younger people. And it looks like she might actually be innocent."

"What episode is this?"

"Four," Jason said as he typed information into Gus's chart. "I'm trying not to pay attention. It's on every television in this place. Mostly for the staff. I'm not sure the residents are keeping up with it."

"I thought you said you were watching it."

"I am. Gotta see what happens now. See if she did it or not."

Gus pointed at the screen. "You're missing it."

Jason smiled. "I'm DVR'ing it."

Gus lifted his chin, squinted at the young man.

"Recording it. I'll watch it tonight, so don't tell me what's going on."

"How can *I* do that?"

"Record it? You can't. No DVR in this place."

"How can I watch the first few episodes? Are they replaying them?"

"Replaying?"

"Yeah. Like a rerun."

"It a prime-time documentary, Gus. Not *I Dream of Jenny.*"

"It's *Jeannie,* you snot-nosed teenage punk."

"I'm thirty, but I'll take that as a compliment. No reruns, but you can stream the earlier episodes. Watch them whenever you want."

"What's that mean? *Stream?*"

"Watch 'em off the Internet."

"I don't have Internet here."

"Sure you do. Whole place has Wi-Fi."

"Can I do Wi-Fi through the TV?"

Jason smiled. "I thought you used to be a cop. Didn't you use computers?"

"I was a cop when you were in diapers. I finished my career as a detective, and I've never loved computers. I'm sixty-eight years old and don't plan to learn now."

"TV's don't have Wi-Fi, unless you have a smart TV. You don't. You need a computer to stream old episodes. Laptop or a tablet." Jason plugged more information into Gus's chart. "You still having trouble sleeping?"

"If by *still*, you mean for the last twenty years, then yes."

"Nurses can give you something to help you sleep."

"I'm sure they could. Probably cyanide." Gus looked back at the television. "Say her name again."

"Grace Sebold."

"Who was the guy she killed?"

Jason glanced at the screen, where he saw Grace Sebold sitting in a St. Lucian jail cell talking directly to the camera. "Julian Crist. Her boyfriend. You don't remember this story?"

"I do. My mind is just slow from all the

meds they're pumping through me."

Gus cocked his head as he stared at the television, brought his eyebrows together so they looked like wings of a diving hawk. It was something he did often, back in the day, to get his mind into the right mode for thinking. It took him a while longer now to get his brain churning than it used to when he was working and sharp and on his game. Despite the delay, his mind finally made the connection.

"Looks like she's innocent, though," the young man said. "That's what's all over the Internet. Everybody's talking about it. Tonight's episode is supposed to feature a medical examiner who ran some experiments that blew the forensics straight out of the water. People are starting to scream for her release."

"Son of a bitch," Gus whispered to himself.

CHAPTER 28

Graham Cromwell strolled into the conference room on Monday morning with a stack of papers in his hands. Half-spent coffee cups and pastry crumbs filled the long table, where morning sunlight slanted across the mahogany and the bright New York sky screamed of summer.

"Okay, people," Graham said. "Numbers are in and we officially have a hit on our hands!"

He tossed the packets into the middle of the table, and the herd of television personalities converged like a school of starving fish. Monday mornings were when the suits revealed the ratings from the week before, when numbers were discussed, when hierarchy was established. It was when each host discovered where he or she fared across all of American prime time and, more importantly, where they ranked within the network. Each of them wanted to beat their same-slot rival from competing networks, but bragging rights came from within the network.

"*The Girl of Sugar Beach* reached its highest audience yet with episode four. With a push from *Wake Up America* and Dante Campbell, who previewed the explosive forensic discovery, twelve million viewers tuned in Friday night. Sidney, you've got a ratings juggernaut. Congratulations!"

Sidney nodded and waved a thank-you as her colleagues applauded. Twelve million viewers was something special, and Sidney felt her stomach stir with anxiety. She'd seen other documentaries deliver in the middle and fizzle by the end. She wanted to make sure she didn't follow the same course, but one-upping Dr. Cutty's episode would be a tall task. Already, memes and GIFs had circulated since Friday's episode of Dr. Cutty's powerful swing of the boat oar to Damian the cadaver's skull. In one video, created by someone who clearly had too much time on his hands, side-by-side videos compared the swing of Dr. Cutty to Derek Jeter. Sidney had to admit they were eerily similar. The YouTube segment that featured Dr. Cutty's morgue experiment had already generated 3 million views.

As if Sidney's thoughts had been broadcast to the room, the applause quieted and the deep, practiced voice of Luke Barrington rang out from the head of the table.

"Grand audiences can mean grand falls."

Sidney kept the paper-thin smile. "Thanks for your confidence, Luke. You've had a grand audience for years. When should we tune in for your fall?"

"No time soon, I'm afraid."

"Actually," Graham said. "The projections are just the opposite. At least based on the website traffic. The first four episodes are being downloaded in huge numbers. *The Girl of Sugar Beach* is the most popular video streaming on iTunes."

"What does that mean?" Luke asked.

"Streaming is when people download videos from this thing called the Internet and watch them on something other than a television and outside of the eight o'clock time zone," Sidney said.

This brought a few chuckles.

"Cute," the Bear said. "What does it have to do with ratings? Nielsen ratings, which the network uses to determine advertising prices, are not based on *downloads*."

"Of course," Graham said. "Nielsen ratings are based on *actual* viewers who watch the broadcast during the time zone in which

307

it airs, and those who DVR the episode and watch it within twenty-four hours. So Sidney's downloads don't count toward her actual numbers, but the idea is that all those viewers who are discovering the documentary through word of mouth are racing to watch past episodes from our streaming platforms. Once they catch up, the assumption is that they will tune in to the Friday-night network broadcast. So we are all thrilled with twelve million viewers, but the projections are for that number to grow. Based on the downloads, projections of twenty million viewers tuning in to the Friday-night broadcast is a real possibility."

Graham shuffled some papers and then looked back at Luke Barrington.

"Any other questions?"

The Bear, for once, was silent.

"Okay," Graham continued. "*The Girl of Sugar Beach* was the big news from last week. Looking forward. Luke, this is your weekend. The Fourth of July is Tuesday, a week from tomorrow, and Part One of your four-part White House special debuts this Friday and runs through Monday, the eve of the Fourth. We expect a big audience, as usual. For the unveiling on Friday night, we've decided to air your special after *The Girl of Sugar Beach.*"

"After? I thought I was the lead-in?"

"Originally, you were. But with Sidney's audience as large as it is, the execs figured you could piggyback. Based on models, you're going to pull four to six million alone. If you draw a quarter of Sid's audience, your numbers will be huge. And she's doing well in the eighteen-to–thirty-four demo. Killing it, actually. So following *Sugar Beach* will help you with younger viewers."

Sidney thought briefly of commenting on the fact that the star of the network would be borrowing from her audience, but decided against it. So fragile was the Bear's ego that an outright blow in front of the Monday-morning crowd might send him into a tailspin. Instead, she badly suppressed a smile and caught a glance from Leslie Martin, who held down the same expression while flashing Sidney a quick wink.

CHAPTER 29

Tuesday, June 27, 2017

Janet Station was the U.S. Attorney for the Southern District of New York, appointed six years ago by the previous administration and a carryover now. She, like most left-overs, was waiting for the other shoe to drop and for the call to come that the new gang in Washington had decided on her replacement. But it had been several months and the turnover slowed, if not stopped altogether. So when the call from Washington had come the night before, she was surprised by the identity of the voice on the other end — the Assistant U.S. Attorney General — and more so by the request.

The call had sent her to midtown this morning, away from her office at 1 St. Andrew's Plaza in lower Manhattan. It was an unusual request, but only took a bit of digging after the phone call ended for Janet to understand Washington's concern.

Sidney Ryan's past three documentaries had all resulted in exonerations. It was, by any measure, an impressive string of success. Clemency took more muscle than any one filmmaker could manage on her own. Exonerations took the Innocence Project and attorneys and usually some politically connected individuals, who either had a relation with, or could apply pressure to, the district attorney's office that had originally indicted and prosecuted the subject. It took the discovery of new evidence, too, and usually some public outcry to gain a D.A.'s attention. When celebrities got involved, things usually turned ugly. And though most district attorneys basked in any media attention directed their way, certain forms of attentiveness — the negative kind that could ruin a career — was avoided at all cost.

It was never an easy decision for a D.A. to overturn a conviction, as this was typically an admission of incompetence. Some fast research the night before told Janet Station that the three individuals highlighted in Sidney Ryan's searing documentaries were pardoned, not by the D.A. or judge who had put them behind bars, but years later by a new prosecutor who filled the hole left by the retiring D.A. This new district attorney had less to lose from looking at a decades-old case and admitting that it was handled incorrectly by the previous administration.

These fights were hard and long, and no one came out clean on the other end. But Grace Sebold's case was different. Prosecuted and convicted by a foreign government, Grace had never returned to the United States after Julian Crist was killed. Sidney Ryan's documentary was chugging along, gaining a voice and an audience, and a hell of a lot of attention.

The conclusion being whispered around Washington? That a United States citizen had been wrongfully accused and imprisoned by a foreign government. The inevitable question that will be asked? Why had the government of the United States sat back and done nothing? The question and its implication was a runaway train Washington wanted to get in front of, and so the call had come to Janet Station to see how far along that train had gotten, and how fast it was running.

Her cell phone rang.

"Yeah?"

"She's in a booth in the back. Lady with her is Leslie Martin, a producer for the documentary."

"Got it," Janet said as she climbed out of the black Denali, which was parked across the street. She walked across West Forty-second Street and into the café. She spotted Sidney Ryan and walked directly over to the booth.

"Ms. Ryan?" Janet asked.

Sidney looked up. "Yes."

"Janet Station, U.S. Attorney for the Southern District of New York. Do you have a minute?"

Sidney looked at her producer, then back to Janet. "I guess, sure."

"May I?" Janet pointed to the booth.

"Of course," Sidney said.

Janet slid into the booth next to Leslie, across from Sidney.

"Sorry to intrude on your breakfast."

"This is Leslie Martin," Sidney said.

"Yes," Janet said. "One of the producers, correct?"

"That's right," Leslie said. "Is there a problem?"

"That's what I've come to find out."

A waitress approached. "Can I get you anything?"

"Coffee, please." Janet looked back at Sidney. "Your documentary is all the rave."

"You sound concerned."

"*Concerned* is a good word," Janet said.

"What are you concerned about?" Leslie asked.

313

"I remember the Grace Sebold case from back when it was in the news. Back then, it looked pretty cut-and-dry. I've refreshed myself since your documentary has become so popular. Some people in Washington are worried about the situation. That a U.S. citizen is sitting in a foreign jail for a crime she, perhaps, did not commit. The simple question is how much of what you've been airing is fact, and how much is pop-culture fiction?"

Sidney pushed a folder across the table. "Leslie and I were just reviewing everything. Here's all our research to this point."

Janet opened the folder and paged through the contents.

"I understand the skepticism," Sidney said. "With the current popularity of true-crime documentaries, there can be an undercurrent of sensationalism. But in this case, I think you'll see that our findings show a pattern of startling conclusions about how Grace Sebold's case was originally investigated by the St. Lucian government, as well as new evidence we've turned up that disproves one of the central conclusions about the case. Specifically, that the weapon suggested at trial as being used to kill Julian Crist, according to forensic experts here in the U.S., could not have caused the injuries found on the victim. This Friday's episode will tackle some of the other 'evidence' that was found in St. Lucia, including examining more closely the victim's blood in Grace's room and the so-called cleanup. It's all incorrect, mishandled, misconstrued, and possibly fraudulent."

Sidney pointed at the pages Janet was reading.

"Those are facts. Friday's episode will also be facts. No skepticism. No pop culture. Speculation does play a role, however. And it comes from the idea that tourism represents the main source of income for St. Lucia," Sidney said. "And in order to preserve this economic windfall, the detectives that ran the case succumbed to pressure of the St. Lucian government to find someone to blame, find them quickly, and put the future tourists at ease that St. Lucia was still a majestic and peaceful Caribbean island known for sunsets and beaches, not murder and mayhem."

Janet Station paged through the documents. After a moment of silence, she said, "Can you stall on any of this? Just until we have a chance to look into it more thoroughly?"

Sidney looked at Leslie, who shook her

head. "I'm afraid not," Leslie said. "The documentary is real-time. We're producing an episode each week. Whatever we learn, our audience learns."

"And we're under tight deadlines," Sidney said.

Janet Station smiled. "I was instructed to ask."

"It's not too late," Leslie said. "One of our citizens still needs our government's help. Has, in fact, begged for it for ten years."

"It will be in my report." She slid out of the booth and stood. "Have a good Fourth of July."

"You too," Sidney said.

Janet Station walked out of the café and to the waiting SUV. She climbed in the backseat and the Denali took off from the curb. She dialed her cell.

"Hello?"

"We've got a problem."

CHAPTER 30

Wednesday, June 28, 2017

"Here's the goal," Jason said. "I'm gonna lift your ass out of that wheelchair, and you're gonna use the rails to move said ass all the way to the other end. And you're going to put pressure on the goddamn prosthesis. Do you hear me? You've got to start putting weight on that side of your body."

"I could file a complaint about the way you speak to me," Gus said.

"Do it. And make sure you hand deliver it to Nurse Ratchet."

Gus cocked his head. "No thanks. I learned long ago, when I was still working, that if someone's got you by the balls, you shouldn't wiggle."

Jason smiled. "Good decision. No more stalling." He reached around Gus's waist and grabbed the belt harness. Gus put his hands on Jason's shoulders, and in a coordinated fashion, Jason pulled and Gus engaged the weakened muscles on his good leg, trying hard not to put too much pressure on his gimp right hip or the strange prosthetic device that connected his stump to the floor.

Gus groaned as he made it to his feet. "Son of a bitch."

"You okay?"

A quick nod and another grunt with gritted teeth. "It feels weird."

"But good to stand up, right?"

Gus was breathing heavily. "Yeah. But it also hurts like a son of a bitch."

"Grab the railings," Jason said.

Gus did so, gripping his hands around two parallel bars that ran out ahead of him and ended after ten feet. It could have been a football field. The rails would allow him to transfer as much of his body weight into his arms and shoulders as possible while he tried to walk for the first time since losing his leg. The rest of his weight would go onto his good leg; and when he felt brave enough, he was supposed to swing his gimp right leg and prosthetic forward and see what he could handle. The last time Jason got him onto the bars, Gus had given up without putting any weight onto his surgically altered leg.

"This far after surgery, you should be able

to make it ten paces on the bars."

"Haven't made it one yet," Gus said, out of breath.

"That's 'cause you quit last time."

"It hurts, you little shithead, that's why I quit. And it feels weird to step on that goddamn peg leg."

"You want to walk again, or get wheeled around for the rest of your life?"

"Walk."

"Then get going. And scream all you want, it wakes this place up and makes people scared of me. I like it."

Gus looked to the end of the bars. His weakened arms shook under the weight of his body.

"Jesus Christ. I used to be able to do thirty dips without a pause. Now I can barely keep myself upright."

"Because you've been sitting on your ass for a month. Now move, Gus!"

He took a deep breath, lifted his gimp leg in front of him, and released a guttural groan as he took his first step in several weeks.

An hour later, Gus was resting uncomfortably in his hospital bed. It wasn't technically a hospital, more like prison for the helpless and elderly, neither of which he considered himself.

"Here," Jason said as he entered the room and handed him a thin case.

"What's this?"

"My iPad."

Gus lifted the flap and pressed the button to display the home screen.

"What am I supposed to do with this?"

"Watch your show. *The Girl of Sugar Beach.* I downloaded every episode for you. You can binge watch over the Fourth. It's a long weekend, so I won't be around to torture you. This will keep you busy."

Jason tapped the screen a few times until the promo appeared: a close-up of Grace Sebold's face, with pale skin and gray-streaked hair, and the tagline *You Only Know the Other Side of the Story.*

"All you have to do is tap the screen and the episode plays. Tap it again to pause it. Go to the menu to find the next episode. Got it?"

Gus nodded. "Thanks. I owe you anything?"

"Keep working like you did today. That's good enough for me."

Jason typed for a moment on the keyboard near the foot of the bed, then closed Gus's electronic chart.

"See you next week?"

"Is that a question?" Gus said. "Where the hell do you think I'm going?"

Jason nodded. "See you next week. Let the nurses get you up this weekend. You've got to start using the prosthetic. I'll be back next Wednesday."

"Hope the pain is gone by then."

"Me too," Jason said. "But fear not, we'll find it again. Have a good Fourth of July."

Gus pointed to the window. "Good view of the fireworks from here?"

Jason offered a crooked smile. "Doubtful."

"Oh, well, there's always next year. Maybe I'll be up and around by then."

"Shit. I'll have you up and around next week. You'll be dancing by Labor Day."

When Jason was gone, Gus touched the screen. Eerie music filled his hospital room as the introduction to the documentary started.

"I'm Sidney Ryan," the narrator told him. "And this is *The Girl of Sugar Beach.*"

CHAPTER 31

Friday, June 30, 2017

The city started to empty on Thursday afternoon. Those who worked Friday cut out early, and by 2:00 p.m., only a select few business people walked the streets of New York. Everyone else had scampered to bus stations or train stations for their ride out of town. Cars had been packed up and driven from the city, leaving behind long streaks of bare curbs where normally a bumper-to-bumper chain of vehicles sat perpetually parked and vacant. Nothing emptied the city more thoroughly than the Fourth of July, which was the following Tuesday.

Roughly one hundred hours of freedom were in front of the citizens of New York. Most of them, anyway. Sidney worked at the network studios until 4:00 p.m. Friday, keeping a skeleton crew of staff in town over the long holiday weekend to finish the next installment of *The Girl of Sugar Beach.* It was the first time she stayed in the city over the Fourth of July holiday, and as she walked the deserted streets on Friday, she could barely believe she was in Manhattan. It was early evening, a time when the boulevards were normally choked with foot traffic and the streets lined with honking cabs and bike messengers weaving through traffic. Instead, she walked peacefully down empty sidewalks and enjoyed the evening sun. She pressed her cell phone to her ear as she walked.

"What did she say?" Graham asked through the phone.

"She just said Washington was concerned. I've been through this before with D.A.'s, they want to know what you have so they can decide what kind of press they're going to get. But this time I'm not an adversary, and a D.A. is not asking. A U.S. Attorney, appointed by the president, is poking around."

"What's the angle?" Graham asked.

"The U.S. government was not responsible for Grace Sebold going to jail. But they have a responsibility to help their citizens. It should only be in their best interest to help her if she's innocent. Janet Station wanted to know if I could delay any of the information that's coming about the blood and the so-called bleach cleanup. And about the prints on the oar and the blood on the blade, just until they had a chance to review everything."

"I hope you told her to piss off."

"Not quite, but I told her I had deadlines and there would be no delaying the documentary."

"Good. No delays. Your audience is ravenous. The latest test audience is pulling for Grace Sebold's innocence, polling at ninety percent. And the executive team met yesterday. They want the conclusion more displayed."

"Really? Is that what *the executives* want, Graham? And this whole time, I thought *I* was producing this documentary."

"You are. I'm just telling you what the higher-ups are looking at."

"You saw the outline I submitted. I'm going to show her innocence the best I can, Graham. There are always gray areas with these cases. But I'm going to paint it the best I can to be black and white. I thought I had their *full confidence,* according to Ray Sandberg."

"You do. They're just confirming the direction of the documentary. We've been through this, Sid. This is network television, not a freelance film. They like to maintain control and make sure they know what's coming."

She came to the Liberty, which typically could not be approached at 5:00 p.m. on a Friday evening. With the mass exodus, though, Sidney found it comfortably populated with only a few tables taken. The hostess seated her and Sidney ordered a $14 margarita and fish tacos.

"When you say *they,*" Sidney said, "you're talking about yourself. I hope you're aware that I know that."

There was a pause before Graham said, "I wish I'd have stayed in the city this weekend."

"Trust me," Sidney said, looking around the mostly-empty restaurant, "nothing's going on in the city."

"You're there," Graham said. "We could've spent some time together."

"Listen," Sidney said. "I'll make sure my documentary continues to show that Grace Sebold may, in fact, be innocent. As was the original goal of the series. As was laid out in the original pitch. As has been promoted by all the advertising, and by Dante Campbell herself. Now get off the phone and enjoy your weekend in the Hamptons, check off your little boxes for your rich buddies, and tell them we're all on the same page and that their precious little investment is going to turn out just fine."

"I believe that was the definition of changing the subject."

Silence.

"You've got the most-watched show in the country, Sid. I'm proud of you."

"Thanks, Graham."

"Luke's special starts tonight."

"Hence my blue-hair dinner at five o'clock. I want to get home to watch it. Have you seen any of it?"

"No. I missed the screening, but I heard it's good."

"I'm sure we'll hear about it next week. Enjoy the weekend, Graham."

She had two margaritas with her tacos, just enough to allow her mind to wander back to Graham's suggestion that he should have stayed in the city with her for the weekend. Sidney knew where that would have led, and she'd spent too much energy untangling herself from the mess to tie herself back up. Their six-month affair had ended more than a year ago. They had met at a cocktail party when Sidney was working on her second documentary and gaining a name for herself. She was an aspiring producer and Graham Cromwell was a powerful network executive. They each knew of the other's work, and conversation was easy. They casually dated for six months when Graham mentioned that Luke Barrington was looking for a producer. Sidney had just finished her second documentary and was considering her next project. Television had never been a consideration, but the exposure and experience of producing Luke Barrington's top-rated show was enough to convince her. When she signed her contract with the network, she had a talk with Graham. Sidney tried for a clean break, but those never work. Instead, a messier three months passed where they were on-again, off-again until Sidney ended things for good when she sensed whispers in the hallways at work. That Graham was her boss was the perfect reason not to get involved with him again. It was actually the perfect reason not to get involved with him in the first place, but that ship had sailed. All she could do now was right her course and not turn back.

She took her margarita buzz to the subway. She was comfortably on her couch in time to catch the opening of *The Girl of Sugar Beach*. She had always been her worst critic, but had to admit that with Leslie's editing and production, Geno Mack's writing, and the special effect team's magic, the opening was flawless. She watched the full hour, never once bored by the footage she had produced and put together. She made some mental notes about camera angles and lighting, noting that future scenes with the lovely Livia Cutty needed to be framed in grittier hues to bring out the haunting revelations the woman, who seemed to have been created to star in true-crime documentaries, brought to the screen. The closing music was perfect, the teaser promo for next week alluring, and when the credits rolled, Sidney allowed herself to feel proud.

Halfway through the project, with a building audience and a clear direction toward the finale, Sidney Ryan was finally feeling confident. The goal would be to show the possibility of Grace Sebold's innocence, to lay raw all the inconsistencies that helped convict her, and, in the end, show the woman Grace had become. Sidney would offer her own conclusions, but ultimately Grace's innocence would be left for the viewers to debate. She had an audience that rivaled *Making a Murderer* and that trumped *Serial*. The difference: Sidney believed she had an ending that would satisfy.

Sidney pulled her gaze from the television and looked down at the ratings spreadsheet from Monday morning's meeting: The Girl of Sugar Beach — *12.1M viewers/9.4 share.*

Luke Barrington's voice floated from the television, and his arrogant face filled the screen as his White House special began. Sidney hit the remote and the Bear's face disappeared. She mixed another margarita and headed to her bedroom, where she picked up the novel from her nightstand and pushed away the nagging truth that she was alone on a holiday weekend.

CHAPTER 32

Saturday, July 1, 2017

She slept in Saturday morning and enjoyed a near-empty subway car as she commuted to work through the vacant city. If Thursday was a purging of residents and Friday a slow trickle of those left behind, Saturday was the aftermath of Armageddon. A few stray cabs snuck quietly through the streets, and a police officer on horseback clicked along West Fortieth Street.

Sidney walked the twelve blocks from the subway instead of cabbing it, and enjoyed the wide-open streets and sidewalks. She grabbed two coffees from the Starbucks in the lobby and rode the elevator to the forty-fourth floor. Leslie was already on her computer cutting film that had been recorded the week before when Sidney visited Grace Sebold in St. Lucia.

"This footage is incredible," Leslie said with a pencil long ways between her teeth

330

and staring at the screen. Her hair was in a messy bun, she wore jeans and a wrinkled T-shirt, and thick plastic glasses sat on her face in lieu of contact lenses.

"Morning," Sidney said. "Here's your coffee. You look . . . casual."

"Did you shower?" Leslie asked.

"Foolishly."

"This place is a ghost town. Who are you trying to impress?"

"I forgot how empty it would be. What are you looking at?"

"Your footage from St. Lucia. You took it on the handheld, but it's great quality and we can do a lot with it. Plus, it looks . . ."

"Urgent."

"Exactly. This is going to make a great episode. Even what you shot on your iPhone looks great. I made it a little grittier, just the way you like it. Check it out."

Sidney sat down and looked at the computer screen.

Leslie had put together an animation of the crime scene as the St. Lucian detectives described it in the original report, coupling it with the ten-year-old footage taken by St. Lucian authorities. She touched the screen and a scene played out on the monitor. In it, a man stood near the edge of a bluff and a woman approached from behind. She raised a large boat oar and struck the back of his head. The footage was gritty and dark, with blue hues and grainy contrast.

"So this depicts the suggested way Julian Crist was struck. We found a couple of C-list actors to reenact the crime scene. But we also put together an animation that will show several variations. So, if we piggyback off of what we learned from Dr. Cutty's episode, we know Julian was six-two and Grace is five-three. The first animation shows that in order to create the skull fracture in the superior and posterior aspect of Julian's head, she would have had to swing the oar in an awkward overhead manner, like swinging an axe to chop wood."

"That's a nasty visual you just gave me."

"Sorry," Leslie said, hitting the touch screen. "This is the animation of the overhead swing."

They each watched the screen and the animated version of a short woman swinging a large oar, more than six feet in length, over her head to strike the back of a taller man's head.

"We can pair this next to Dr. Cutty's demonstration on the cadavers. As of today, there are over ten million views of her swing on YouTube, so let's ride that wave and show it again in Friday's episode."

"Agreed," Sidney said.

"Then we'll replay Dr. Cutty's explanation of why the oar in question could not have been the weapon used, and end the episode with footage of your trip to St. Lucia and the blowup of the proposed bloody room and bleach cleanup. But we'll leave it hanging there. We won't get into the full explanation of the blood and the bleach until episode seven. And reviewing all the footage you took in St. Lucia, we've easily got enough to cover two installments. That includes this coming Friday, episode six, and part of episode seven. Three episodes left after that to wrap everything up nice and tight."

"I love it," Sidney said. "What the hell time did you get here?"

"Early. I couldn't wait to get going on this. The city is empty and I'm feeling productive. I might work every Fourth of July weekend."

"I feel guilty for sleeping in."

"Please. You went to Raleigh to get the footage of Dr. Cutty, and to St. Lucia to follow up with Grace. I owed you some hours." Leslie took a sip of coffee. "Hear anything about ratings from last night?"

Sidney shook her head. "Not yet. All the suits are at their mansions on the beach, so they probably won't tell us until they get back. Did you watch Luke's special?"

"No," Leslie said. "I turned on the Yankees game after *Girl* ended, and I hate baseball. But I'm sure tons of old people couldn't wait to watch another old person talk about the history of the White House over a patriotic weekend. We don't want old people. Strike that. We want everyone, but our demo is under forty-five, and we're killing it. Eighteen to twenty-five? Our numbers are ridiculous, and once these episodes air" — Leslie pointed at the screen — "every one of them will be hooked until the end. Hell, I can hardly wait to see it and I'm putting it together."

"Okay," Sidney said. "I'm officially motivated. Move over, let's figure out the back half of episode six."

"Who knew it was so nice to work when everyone else is on vacation?"

"Yeah. If Luke Barrington could do his show from his house in the Hamptons for the rest of his career, I'd be a much happier person."

CHAPTER 33

Saturday, July 1, 2017

The members of the president's cabinet were not typically allowed to enjoy holiday weekends. Even if they managed to escape to a beach or lake house, their phones seldom stopped buzzing. The world, it seemed, didn't stop to remember American history. So it was that Bev Mangrove, the acting assistant attorney general, had the unenviable task of intruding on her boss's weekend. She'd taken an early-morning flight into Raleigh-Durham and was now snaking through mountain roads on her way to Summit Lake, North Carolina, where Cooper Schott had planned to spend the week in isolation, away from the politics of Washington, D.C., and isolated from the president and his staff and the problems of the country. Bev Mangrove was not happy to be intruding on Cooper and his wife, but the situation could not wait.

U.S. Attorney General Cooper Schott had a millennial name, despite being north of sixty. He'd spent his entire life correcting people who had called him *Mr. Cooper.* Now most of his friends had grandkids named Cooper. His parents were apparently ahead of the curve.

Bev pulled through the quaint downtown area of Summit Lake and found the turnoff for the long, serpentine driveway that led to the house on the hill, where her boss spent four weeks each year. The front door of the large Colonial opened as she pulled up, and Cooper Schott stood in the doorway, wearing jeans and a starched white shirt with French cuffs held tight by dazzling cuff links. Bev seldom saw him wearing anything but a suit, and she couldn't immediately tell if he looked more or less comfortable today.

"You made it!" Cooper Schott said as Bev opened her car door.

"It's beautiful up here," she said, climbing from the rental car and walking up the front steps. "I can see why you come here so often."

"Not often enough. Come on in," Cooper said, shaking her hand. "We'll head out back."

Bev followed her boss through the immaculate house, which was flooded with sunlight that spilled through the floor-to-ceiling windows and numerous French doors that lined the west side of the house, most of which were open to allow the lake breeze to stir through the home. Cooper walked onto a sprawling stone patio out back, the view from which captured the lake and the mountains in the distance. Bev sat opposite him at the patio table, protected from the sun by a large umbrella. A sweating pitcher of sweet tea stood on a serving dish, and Cooper poured two glasses. The man, Bev knew, had sworn off liquor years ago.

"So," Cooper said, "tell me what's on your mind."

"Grace Sebold."

Cooper took a sip of sweet tea and stared out at the lake. "The name rings a bell."

She knew it did more than that — the Sebold case had been on the Justice Department's radar for some time — but she was intruding on his vacation, so she played along.

"She was the U.S. med student who, in 2007, was convicted of killing her boyfriend while they were on spring break in St. Lucia."

"Yes," Cooper said, taking another sip. "I remember now."

Bev reached into her leather bag and removed several files. They were government files she had pulled from the State Department the day before.

"Are you aware of the documentary that is currently featuring her story?"

"I haven't watched anything but a Sooners game in many years."

"In that case, allow me to catch you up. Sidney Ryan is a producer and filmmaker. Her previous three documentaries were about small-time felons convicted of crimes, it turns out, they did not commit. Ryan's shtick is that she cherry-picks cases that are sent her way and finds the ones she believes are the most egregious examples of injustice. So far, she's batting a thousand. Two were in New York, one in Illinois. All three documentaries ended with the convictions overturned. She's becoming the most feared nonattorney for D.A.'s around the country, because she simply makes the prosecution look silly and, at times, dishonest in the way they reached a conviction."

"How does this case affect us?" Cooper asked. "The U.S. government, and the Justice Department specifically, had nothing to do with the conviction of the Sebold girl."

"No, we had nothing to do with the

conviction. But I sent Janet Station, from the Southern District of New York, to feel out Sidney Ryan and get an idea of where she plans to go with this documentary. If you look at what she's uncovered so far, and what she plans to produce in the coming weeks, it all points to the possibility that Grace Sebold is innocent. And if not innocent, it certainly appears that rules were bent to make sure she was found guiltier than she was."

"Bent by whom?"

"The St. Lucian government."

Cooper put his sweet tea down and pulled the files toward him. Bev spoke as he read.

"The documentary is wildly popular. Millions of people are watching it now, and millions more will be watching by the end. It's become a pop-culture phenomenon. And I understand that popular culture does not dictate our decisions, but our problem lies not in the fact that it is so popular, but in that the arc of the story will suggest that Sebold was wrongly convicted of a crime she did not commit and that a U.S. citizen has spent ten years imprisoned in a foreign country because of this conviction."

"And," Cooper said, "the U.S. government sat back and did nothing."

"Correct," Bev said.

339

"This will need to be investigated."

"I'm on it."

"The FBI will have to get involved."

"I've already made calls to the FBI, State Department, and to our U.S. ambassador to Barbados and the Eastern Caribbean."

Cooper lifted his chin slightly. "Who is?"

"Shelly Martindale. I looked her up."

Cooper ran a hand across his unshaven cheek. "I'll need to watch this documentary."

Bev reached into her bag and removed a DVD. "This includes all current episodes, including last night's. Ryan is producing them in real time. The next one airs Friday."

"How many hours?"

"Five, so far."

"Do you have somewhere to stay for the night?"

"Yes, sir. The Winchester Hotel in town. I have it booked for two nights."

"Can you be back in the morning?"

"Of course." Bev stood and fastened her bag over her shoulder, knowing the disc and files on the table had produced the effect she suspected they would. Her boss's vacation was over.

CHAPTER 34

Wednesday, July 5, 2017

Wednesday morning was groggy in New York, the fifth of July. The city began to fill late Monday evening and the streets were moderately crowded Wednesday morning with those who did not tack onto the long weekend. Busy but light, the traffic crept along with a smoother consistency than would be typical for the middle of the week. Tomorrow things would be back to normal.

Sidney watched from her network office as the thin crowds shuffled in unison along the sidewalks, and traffic shifted and halted at intersections. She had worked every day of the weekend, including the Fourth. She and Leslie had finished cutting and editing the sixth episode, her best yet, that contained the rehashing of the Dr. Cutty experiments that showed the impossibility of Julian Crist's injuries being caused by the paddleboard oar, the reenactment of the crime scene, and the teaser footage that introduced a more logical explanation for the blood found in Grace's Sugar Beach cottage. The episode ended with the suggestion that the so-called bleach cleanup of Grace's bathroom was a tortured hypothesis made by St. Lucian detectives that picked their suspect at the outset of their investigation and forced every finding during their search for answers to match that narrative.

Sidney and Leslie had created another explosive installment, and Sidney could hardly wait to screen it for the suits before the episode aired on Friday. She paced the conference room now. The holiday weekend could either help or hurt ratings. If enough people went out of town and forgot about *The Girl of Sugar Beach,* her ratings would slip. More than anything, Sidney was worried about how she fared against Luke Barrington's White House special.

The room filled slowly over fifteen minutes. Network executives, TV personalities, producers, and writers talked about where they spent the long weekend and when they got back in town. Graham Cromwell prepared the projector and tapped on his computer while everyone took their places at the table. Graham took a minute to prepare his presentation, then pointed to the only empty seat in the room.

"Sorry, we're just waiting for Luke," he said. "He's coming from the Hamptons and running a few minutes late."

"Maybe we should start without him," Sidney said.

"I thought about it," Graham said, "but his special aired this weekend and he wants to be here for the discussion."

"Then he should have come into the city last night, like everyone else."

"Settle down," Luke said in his deep, practiced voice as he strolled through the door. Not due on air until evening, he was ridiculously dressed in a long-sleeved golf sweater and short shorts, which bared his pale, liver-spotted legs. It was his routine to attend morning meetings and go through show prep before hitting the course at noon and returning in time to record his show. As the network's prime-time ratings king, only Luke Barrington was allowed such a schedule.

"I'm not even technically late." He looked at his watch. "I take that back, I'm one minute late. You'll all forgive me?" He lifted his Starbucks cup. "They had to brew it while I waited, otherwise I'd be drinking from the bottom of the barrel. You know what that's like," he said to Sidney. "Coffee grounds and bitterness."

Graham brought the screen to life, and several schematics appeared. It drew everyone's attention immediately away from Luke, who shuffled along the side of the table and found his seat. Graham covered the news segment ratings, down as they typically were during a holiday, but on par with other networks. He then reviewed the other prime-time programs, leaving Luke Barrington's White House special until the end.

"Okay, that leaves Luke and Sidney, whose specials are leading the way. Luke, great job. Friday's installment brought in two-point-six million total viewers, with a typical breakdown in demographics that we usually see with your audience."

There were no murmurs around the table. The silence was worse. Projected numbers had been 4 million total viewers.

"You gained on Saturday night, up three hundred thousand. Fell slightly on Sunday and then had a great ending on the eve of the Fourth. Monday-night numbers were just over three million. Huge success."

Luke lifted his chin to acknowledge Graham, but his eyes gave away his disappointment.

"Finally," Graham said. "*The Girl of Sugar*

Beach continues to surge. Episode five on Friday night played to the biggest audience yet. Fueled by word of mouth, and a cover piece in *Events* magazine, Friday's installment pulled in nineteen million total viewers. Demos are great, with all the keys met and exceeded. Eighteen to twenty-five is through the roof, which is driving ad revenues." Graham looked at Sidney. "We are heavily promoting the teaser over the next forty-eight hours, promising an explosive development that challenges the forensic and blood evidence key to the case ten years ago. Sidney and Leslie provided a rough cut and I screened it this morning. It's an amazing production and a blockbuster episode. Really, you two, it's the best you've done yet."

"Thank you," Sidney said. "Leslie's cutting the episodes, and she's doing an amazing job."

"Sidney's getting the footage, which makes my job easy," Leslie said.

"You make a good team. We all know you're putting in the hours and are fully committed to this project. Everyone is impressed and grateful for your effort."

The conference room broke out in applause. Sidney and Leslie acknowledged the support from their colleagues, and made sure to recognize their crew for all their hard work. Sidney looked down the table at Luke Barrington, who wore a paper-thin smile and never put his hands together.

CHAPTER 35

Wednesday, July 5, 2017

Jason walked into the room and stopped when he saw the empty bed. Then he noticed Gus in the bedside chair.

"You're up early," Jason said. "How'd you manage the chair?"

Gus grunted as he repositioned himself. "Nurse Ratchet."

Jason offered a confused look as he walked to the computer stand, opened Gus's chart, and reviewed what he'd missed over the long weekend. "Thought you two weren't talking."

"We're not. But we're pretty good at grunting at each other. I couldn't sleep and she got tired of me constantly ringing the nurses' station, so she helped me move at about three o'clock this morning. And by *helped me,* I mean she threw my ass in the chair while wearing gloves and trying not to catch cancer."

"Glad you guys are working things out. But three hours is too long to sit, big boy. So back to bed."

Gus shook his head. "I can't do the bed right now."

"Your other option is to stand for a while. Crutches or walker?"

"Walker," Gus said without hesitation. He could see it caught Jason off guard. Gus had refused the goddamn walker every other time it had been offered, because it meant he needed to use his prosthetic.

Jason slowly nodded his head. "Be right back."

A minute later, he returned with an ugly metal walker, the legs of which were capped with tennis balls to quiet the device from rattling against the linoleum floors of the rehab prison. It was a hideous-looking thing meant for the weak and the elderly. But the long holiday weekend had lit a fire. Since three in the morning, when he finished watching the fifth hour of the documentary about Grace Sebold, Gus had a desperate urge to get the hell out of this place. For the first time since retirement, when he handed over his badge and gun, he had something he needed to do. He had something to chase other than an afternoon whiskey buzz. Which, he had to admit, had been working just fine as a way to occupy his retirement until the pain started in his hip. The cancer diagnosis had promptly taken away his whiskey afternoons back then, and without too much of an introduction, it stole his leg a few weeks later.

The black abyss of depression had licked at his heels during those tough days of chemotherapy, when the poison nearly killed him, but had no effect on the tumor. More than once he'd considered allowing the despair to engulf him. Give in to the depression and the cancer and just let it all end. He had no kids, and his wife had passed more than twenty years ago, so no one would really miss him when he was gone. And when his options had been laid out in front of him, Gus decided that he had no desire to live the rest of his days with only one leg.

He still wasn't sure what had changed his mind, and he spent the last month wondering why the hell he had gone through with the procedure that had made his life worse than when his right leg was withered with cancer. Now his leg and the cancer were gone, and a strange phantom pain was present that shot down to toes that weren't there. Apathy had overcome him in the days after surgery, so thick and heavy that it smothered all ambition to walk, to heal, to live. But damn if he hadn't found inspiration in the most unusual place. A documentary.

His leg was gone, his badge retired, and his romance with whiskey would likely never be the same. But he had found over the weekend some unfinished business. It had never stopped gnawing at him, and if he were the self-reflective type, perhaps he would even admit that what he'd found over the Fourth of July weekend could explain the reason he had gone through with the surgery. Somewhere during the fifth hour of the Grace Sebold documentary, he decided that sitting in a goddamn hospital bed, feeling sorry for himself, was no way to chase down a woman who was guilty as sin.

CHAPTER 36

Thusday, July 6, 2017

On Thursday morning, two days after the Fourth of July holiday, a private jet landed in Castries, St. Lucia. Assistant U.S. Attorney General Bev Mangrove was the lowest-ranking member of the group that piled into the black SUV. Those that outranked her included her boss, Cooper Schott, whose vacation she had ruined a few days before, the director of the FBI, and the head of the State Department. A half-dozen staff members squeezed into a trailing vehicle. They rode mostly in silence, occasionally mentioning the beauty of the island and the lush tropics of the rain forest that surrounded them. But the lure of relaxation that the Caribbean typically offered was nowhere in the vehicle. There was serious work to be done.

Thirty minutes later, they pulled up to the Government House on the northern edge of Morne Fortuné, a hill that overlooks the southern Castries. The building was the personal residence of the governor-general, a location where official business was rarely conducted. An exception was made today. An assistant greeted them when they arrived and led them into the building. Waiting for the U.S. entourage and seated around the living room were the prime minister, the governor-general, and the Honorable Francis Bryan, judge of St. Lucia's Supreme Court. Greetings and handshakes were exchanged, and everyone took their seats. Present in the hilltop home in the eastern Caribbean were the men and women who ran the Justice Department in their respective countries. They had a great deal to discuss, much to bargain, and wide authority from the few people more powerful than them to get this issue resolved.

CHAPTER 37

Monday, July 10, 2017

Four days after the summit in St. Lucia, Sidney sat in front of her computer and edited the clips Leslie had strung together for episode seven. The previous Friday, episode six showed again, in dramatic fashion, how Julian Crist's skull may have been fractured from something other than a boat oar. Several theories about alternative murder weapons were produced, and they all contrasted sharply with the paddleboard oar that was used to convict Grace Sebold. The theories offered all hinged on the fact that microscopic amounts of organza fibers, a type of nylon, had been discovered in the skull fracture. The suggestion was that a household object might have been wrapped in a nylon bag or sock and used to strike Julian while he was high on the Soufriere Bluff.

The episode drew a startling 20 million

viewers who took to the Internet to share their own theories as to what the object could be, and what revelation episode seven would lay bare regarding the blood and the cleanup. The documentary was the biggest television event of the summer. The Internet, Facebook, and Twitter were abuzz with shouts of Grace Sebold's innocence.

Some part of Sidney felt bad for Julian Crist's family, which believed for years that his murderer was behind bars. The documentary could provide no satisfying conclusion for the Crist family: Either Grace was innocent, and the tragedy of their son's death had ruined yet another life, or she was as guilty now as she was ten years ago, and a commercial documentary was bringing doubt into what they believed was an open-and-shut case. Either way, Sidney knew it was an ugly time for the Crist family. The media was on a constant push to interview Julian's parents and get their opinions.

The success of the documentary had elevated Sidney's modest celebrity to movie star ranks. Everyone in America knew her name, and every family member or friend with a loved one in jail seemed to be sending her letters and packages begging for her help. Her desk was cluttered with manila envelopes stuffed with court documents and affidavits and witness lists. Proof, each letter claimed, of innocence.

Graham walked into her cluttered office. "The execs want to meet next week."

Sidney continued to stare at her computer. "Why? Numbers are good. What could they possibly want to complain about?"

"Your numbers are exactly what they want to discuss. They want another documentary for next summer. Same format. They're putting together an offer and want to discuss it with you next week."

Sidney laughed and looked at Graham. "I'm not even done with this one. Nor am I sure how exactly it will end. I've got four episodes left to produce."

"It shows their confidence in you."

"Can't they just enjoy all the money *Girl* is putting in their pockets before they start worrying about how to make more?"

"There's going to be money on the table for you, too, Sid. It's a nice offer, trust me. And I haven't even seen all the details."

Sidney didn't respond. She'd spent her career on paper-thin budgets, making films that sometimes were never picked up. Only in the last few years had she found some success. And though she never imagined television would be the place she'd find steady work, the success of the documentary and the doors that were opening for her were something she would eventually have to address. As soon, that was, as she had a free moment to consider her future beyond each Friday-night episode.

"Next week, okay?" Graham said.

"Graham," Sidney said, swiveling her seat around to face him, "I'm barely making my weekly deadlines. You understand this, right? You all sit in your corner offices up there and the draft episodes just magically appear each Wednesday. But in order to get those finished, my staff and I are working around the clock. This format is great for the viewers, but a death wish for me. Let's see what happens when we wrap this up. Let's see what I can put together and how I end the Grace Sebold story before we start talking about next summer."

Graham smiled. "Oh, they're anxious to see that as well. We'll discuss it next week, okay?"

Sidney shook her head. "Fine. But I swear to God, if I'm behind schedule, I'm canceling. I've got to get this footage cut for the final edits and do the voice-overs so you all can approve the draft before it goes to production."

"You're doing a hell of a job," Graham

said before he left her office.

Sidney went back to her computer. Her phone buzzed a minute later. She saw the strange set of numbers and knew it was Grace Sebold calling collect from Bordelais. She clicked on the recording device so the conversation could be captured to use potentially, as many of their previous discussions had been, in the documentary.

"Yes?" Sidney started, knowing she would not be speaking with a live person. The recording took over.

You have a collect call from . . .

"Grace. Sebold." Grace's voice was short and direct as she pronounced her first and last name in a stoic monotone.

. . . an inmate at the Bordelais Correctional Facility in Dennery, St. Lucia.

Sidney pressed 1 to accept the call.

"Hello?"

"Hi," Grace said in an urgent tone foreign to her usual detached demeanor. "Did you know about this?"

"About what?" Sidney asked.

"My correctional officer, who I meet with once a month, just told me the prime minister is looking into my case. He said they're considering a pardon or a retrial or an acquittal based on new evidence that was presented to him."

Sidney pressed her phone harder to her ear. "When was this?"

"Yesterday. This was the first time I could get to the phone. What's going on?"

"I'm not sure. I don't know anything about it, but I'll make some calls. I met with a U.S. Attorney here in New York. She ambushed me at breakfast last week and asked a bunch of questions about the documentary. Did your corrections officer tell you what's next?"

"No. I got the impression he is not happy about it."

"Oh, I'm sure none of the people who were involved in your conviction are pleased right about now. It makes them look bad."

Two minutes, a recorded voice said through the line.

"I've gotta go," Grace said. "Will you call my parents? Tell them what's happening."

"Of course."

"I'll try to call tomorrow if they let me."

"I'll make some phone calls and see what I can find out. But, Grace, no matter what happens from here, this is good news."

There was a long pause. Sidney heard muted crying. Finally Grace's voice came back over the line.

"Thank you."

CHAPTER 38

Tuesday, July 11, 2017

The proceedings were planned purposefully and expeditiously in order to avoid a circus of media that would converge on the small island of St. Lucia and bring more attention to the fact that the government was admitting they'd imprisoned a woman for a crime she did not commit. Grace's call had set things rolling the day before, and when word leaked about a hastily scheduled hearing set for the following morning, the network execs knew they couldn't miss footage of Grace Sebold being marched back into court. They splurged to charter a plane for Sidney and her crew, which departed at 11:30 p.m. Monday and flew through the night to land in Castries just before 4:00 a.m. They managed two hours of sleep before setting up shop in the courtroom. Sidney and Leslie, as well as Derrick and his camera crew, were the only media presence visible in the near-empty courtroom.

At 9:00 a.m., the Honorable Francis Bryan took his place behind the raised bench. He brought the court to order; and from a side door, Grace Sebold was led into the courtroom by two armed guards. She wore a blue jumpsuit, and her glasses were slightly crooked, as if she'd fallen asleep wearing them and had arrived straight from her bed. Her hair looked disheveled. Sidney had the impression that since Grace's phone call, less than twenty-four hours ago, things had moved quickly for her. The St. Lucian government was doing their best to clean their hands of the situation.

Grace scanned the thin crowd, looking, Sidney was certain, for her parents and her brother. She settled on the only familiar face that was present: Sidney's. Sidney lifted her hand in a small wave and smiled. Grace's eyes displayed shock and confusion, still unsure exactly what was transpiring. She took a spot next to the court-appointed counsel while the high court came to order. The Honorable Judge Bryan spoke.

"Mademoiselle Sebold, are you of right mind this morning and properly represented by counsel?"

"Yes, sir," Grace said in a muted tone. She didn't mention the fact that her actual lawyer, Scott Simpson, was in fact not present to represent her, but instead the man who stood beside her was the St. Lucian attorney who had so badly fumbled her case years ago.

Derrick captured the courthouse scene. Two other cameramen recorded from different angles to catch Grace, the judge, and Sidney.

"Under St. Lucian statute," the Honorable Judge Bryan continued, "in accordance with the Eastern Caribbean Supreme Court, as well as the Judicial Committee of the Privy Council, and in light of new evidence provided to the court by the government of the United States, and reviewed by the St. Lucian authorities and this high court, it is within my right and is my final decision, along with the prime minister and the governor-general, to reverse the ruling on June 29, 2007, of murder in the first degree. All previous and formal charges, as of this day, 11th of July, 2017, are annulled and removed, and you, Grace Janice Sebold, are hereby granted clemency and exoneration of formerly charged crimes."

Despite the thin attendance, murmurs filled the court. The Honorable Bryan did not bother to silence the crowd. Instead, he offered a quick apology to Grace Sebold, directed the guards, and banged his gavel. He was up and gone through a rear door, having spent less than five minutes on the bench.

Grace looked back to Sidney; tears ran down the inmate's cheeks as the guards pulled her toward the exit as her counsel whispered in her ear. The entourage of constables ushered her through the side door from where she had emerged; a mere seven minutes after the court was brought to order, Grace Sebold was exonerated.

The proceedings had moved so swiftly that Grace's parents were absent when their daughter was released from prison. Their flight was scheduled to land that night, and without a soul to welcome Grace when she was released, Sidney found herself late in the afternoon waiting next to a taxi in the parking lot of the Bordelais Correctional Facility when its gates opened. Clanking chain link rattled and whined in protest, but finally parted to grant the thirty-six-year-old prisoner, who had spent more than a quarter of her life within its walls, her freedom.

Along with a handful of local press, and a one-man camera crew from *The Voice* and *The Star* — two of St. Lucia's largest media outlets — Derrick rested the camera on his shoulder and captured the gates parting and Grace Sebold's face as she walked into the warm, sticky Caribbean air and looked up at the sky, as if she hadn't seen it in years. She had, though, Sidney's voice would eventually narrate to the audience, in the prison yard and through the dirty windows of the mess hall. But today was the first time in more than ten years that she was seeing it as a free woman.

CHAPTER 39

Tuesday, July 11, 2017

When formal word of Grace Sebold's exoneration leaked, the Internet went wild. The biggest real-time documentary in television history got bigger, despite the fact that what was sure to be featured in the final episode had just been spoiled. The final installments started writing themselves in Sidney's mind as the taxi pulled from the Bordelais Correctional Facility and onto the main road.

Without a credit card or a dollar to her name, besides the St. Lucian currency she was issued just before she was released, Grace Sebold was as helpless as a newborn when she walked from prison.

"Thank you," Grace said. "I don't know where to go. My counselor said they'd pay for a taxi, and I got the impression they just wanted me out of the prison as fast as possible."

"It's no problem."

"Not just for picking me up, though. For everything."

Sidney nodded. "You're welcome."

The taxi clicked into a higher gear as the driver merged onto the highway.

"Listen, Grace. There's a reason things happened so fast. The St. Lucian authorities wanted you out of their hair before the press started to swarm. The documentary has become very popular back home, and the Internet is already buzzing about your release. They wanted you out of their courts before the cameras were raging and journalists were shouting questions. It looks bad for them, for the St. Lucian government. A large portion of their economy depends on tourism and they want badly to avoid being painted as a tropical island that unjustly imprisons vacationers. They want you out of their country as fast as possible. In time, they'll hope that America and the United Kingdom and every other country whose citizens vacation on their tiny island will forget that St. Lucia once wrongly convicted you."

Grace nodded. She stared out the window of the van, lost suddenly in the lush rain forest that blurred past.

"You'll soon be the most sought-after interview in the United States," Sidney continued. "Later today, journalists will arrive in St. Lucia and start looking for you. I'm sure they know when your parents' plane is landing. As soon as your parents step foot off that plane, there will be cameras in their faces and journalists asking for their reaction to your exoneration."

Grace didn't answer. Her freedom, Sidney believed, had overwhelmed her.

"I reserved a room for you at a hotel near the airport. I used an alias, so if we get you there quickly, I think you'll be okay until you get to the airport tomorrow."

Grace continued to stare out the window.

"Grace, are you listening to me? You need to get ready for a media storm, and you should start thinking of ways to avoid it."

"I want to go to Sugar Beach," Grace finally said.

"Not a good idea."

"I have to." She looked away from the window for the first time and locked eyes with Sidney. "I have to see it again."

Captured by the camera that rested on Derrick's shoulder as he sat in the backseat of the van, Grace's words would ring out in a future episode. Millions of viewers would watch the back of her head, her hair prematurely graying and in a prison-issued crop, as the taxi snaked through the mountains of

St. Lucia en route to Sugar Beach, where her ordeal had started ten years before. The viewers would be given a voyeuristic glimpse as the girl convicted of a crime she did not commit climbed from the taxi forty minutes after her release from jail and stared down at Sugar Beach and the mountainous Piton from which the man she loved had been pushed.

She was a free woman the last time she laid eyes on the Pitons, young and in love. It was evening now, and the sun was starting its descent. With Bordelais situated on the eastern side of the island, this was the first time in a decade that Grace Sebold would watch the sunset. During her ten-year nightmare, only the beginning of each day was visible, never the end.

Today, Sidney would tell the viewers in a dramatic voice-over, Grace Sebold was ten years older, free at last, and with a life unrecognizable from when she last stood and watched a sunset at Sugar Beach. The only thing that remained unchanged was that she still very much loved Julian Crist.

CHAPTER 40

Thursday, July 13, 2017

Newly motivated, Gus made fast work of the parallel bars over the past week. The ten steps required to conquer them from end to end were now accomplished with almost no pauses. His grunting and swearing came from choice rather than reaction. The walker was like a strange friend he came to rely on, even if he still detested it. He was able to shuffle down the hallways, and although he couldn't make the full loop around the floor — which required four turns and nearly two hundred steps — Gus made it his goal to complete the trek by the end of the week. If someone had told him a year before that sitting on a toilet and walking without assistance would be considered gifts from God, he'd have thought they were certifiable.

He sat in his bedside chair with the breakfast cart pulled in front of him and a steaming cup of coffee resting next to badly poached eggs and burnt toast. He ignored the food and indulged in the aroma of hazelnut. Drinking coffee and reading the paper had been one of the joys of life, and for the first time in many weeks, he was beginning to notice such subtle benefits of being alive. He scanned the front-page stories and then lifted the paper to see the stories below the fold. He stopped when his gaze fell to the headline:

WOMAN CONVICTED OF MURDER
EXONERATED
Grace Sebold freed after ten years in a Caribbean jail

He quickly unfolded the paper and read the article. Grace Sebold, made famous once more by the current documentary *The Girl of Sugar Beach,* was exonerated after new evidence surfaced that put into question the forensics used to convict her.

Jason strolled into his room as Gus finished the article.

"Hello, there. Ready for therapy?"

"No," Gus said. "I need a favor."

"What's up?"

He scribbled onto a yellow notepad and ripped off the page, handing it to Jason. "I

369

need you to make a run for me. Pick something up."

Jason held the sticky note in his hand.

"What is it?"

"An address. I was hoping to get there myself, but I can't walk out of here yet, and I'm short on time."

"Where is this? Your house?"

"Not my house. Listen, kid, I haven't asked for much while I've been in this place. I've pretty much followed the rules. Your rules, anyway. The goddam nurses are another story. I've got no one else to turn to for this, and, frankly, I wouldn't trust anyone but you. It's important — otherwise I wouldn't put you out. Will you help me?"

Jason looked down at the newspaper and saw the headline about Grace Sebold's exoneration. He held up the sticky note and slowly nodded.

"Tell me what you need."

CHAPTER 41

Monday, July 17, 2017

The press, with news vans and camera crews, had been camped outside the Sebold residence since news broke of Grace's exoneration. They gathered the morning Grace made her appearance at the courthouse in St. Lucia and shouted questions at Gretchen and Glenn Sebold as they left for the airport. The crowd of reporters grew throughout the day and into the next as they anxiously awaited Grace's return, hoping to capture images of the girl from Sugar Beach. They were hoping, despite such things seldom happening, that Grace would return home and stand proudly on the front lawn and field questions while cameras popped and live feeds streamed.

Instead, a neighbor tipped off Gretchen Sebold about the mob of reporters that had grown out of control, and suggested they avoid bringing Grace home just yet. The neighbor then phoned the police to tell them about the public nuisance of vans and trucks parked illegally in the quiet neighborhood, and the group of reporters that was loitering in the streets and stomping down the grass of the common areas. Soon the police arrived and set up barriers to keep the journalists sequestered in one corner of the neighborhood, their news trucks forced to park on the main road thirty yards away.

Despite their vigilance, which lasted through the weekend, Grace Sebold never showed.

Ellie Reiser's apartment was located at Windsor Tower in Tudor City, a short walk from the hospital. Many beat reporters, Sidney knew, were waiting lazily at the Sebold residence in Fayetteville, hoping for a sound bite. Most had no ambition to perform real journalism, and certainly not of the investigative manner. So when Sidney recommended that Grace ask her old friend Ellie for a place to stay until the media attention died down, the Sebolds thought it was a grand idea. Grace would stay anonymous at Ellie Reiser's Manhattan high-rise, at least until an ambitious reporter decided to get to work and do some digging. Of course, their work had been done for them.

One of the first episodes of *The Girl of Sugar Beach* featured Ellie Reiser and her close relationship with Grace Sebold. Had any of the beat reporters been paying attention, they'd know Ellie was a practicing physician at Bellevue Hospital in Manhattan; and with Grace a no-show in Fayetteville for the past few days, Dr. Reiser's apartment would be a good place to look. But Sidney was betting none knew even this much. Grace was safe for a while.

On Monday evening after work, Sidney and Derrick rode the elevator to the twenty-sixth floor and found the corner apartment. She knocked and Ellie Reiser opened the door with a smile a moment later.

"Hi, Sidney. Come on in."

Derrick stayed anonymous behind his camera. Ellie Reiser barely noticed his presence.

As soon as Sidney passed the entrance threshold, she heard the boisterous conversation of a family giddy to be reunited after so many years apart. Sidney followed Ellie through the entrance foyer and into the sleek, modern living room, with tall windows that offered a beautiful view of the New York skyline, which Derrick captured as he settled into the corner. The small group turned when she entered. Grace came over and wrapped her arms around Sidney. They hadn't seen each other since Sidney dropped Grace at the small St. Lucian hotel near the airport a few days before.

Sidney had been in this position before — three other times, in fact — on the receiving end of praise and gratitude when the wrongly accused was finally reunited with his or her family. Scores of people participated in and were responsible for exonerations — and in Grace's case, elite officials inside the United States government did more for Grace than Sidney could ever have managed on her own — but still, Sidney was the one who received the recognition.

Grace took Sidney's hand and led her into the room. "You all know Sidney Ryan."

Despite having interviewed nearly everyone present, Grace made formal introductions. The only ones Sidney had not met were the couple that stood in the back of the group.

"Sidney," Grace said, pulling the man forward by his hand. The woman with him carried a stoic look as she followed him. "This is Daniel and Charlotte Greaves, old and dear friends."

Sidney recognized the names. Daniel and Charlotte's wedding had brought the group to Sugar Beach so many years before. Sidney also knew that Daniel, along with Ellie, were the only friends registered in the Bordelais Correctional Facility books as having visited Grace during her incarceration.

Sidney shook Daniel's hand. "Nice to meet you. It always inspires me to meet the people who stick by their friends in tough times."

She reached for Charlotte's hand. The woman offered a limp shake and curt smile.

"Through tough times, and for many years," Grace said, putting her head on Daniel's shoulder and patting his chest. "He's my Superman." Grace stared at Daniel for a moment before turning her attention to Charlotte.

Sensing the awkwardness, Grace pulled Charlotte forward.

"Sidney," Grace said, "check out Charlotte's shoes. She's always had the best taste in shoes. Ungodly, hideously expensive shoes. But always beautiful. And nothing has changed in all these years."

Sidney looked down at Charlotte's Giuseppe Zanotti shoes. She nodded. "Beautiful shoes," she said to fill the silence.

Mercifully, Grace pointed toward another person in the room. "And this," Grace said, "is my brother, Marshall."

Grace walked next to the wheelchair and placed her hand on her brother's shoulder. "Marshall, this is Sidney."

"Good to see you again, Marshall," Sidney said.

"Thank you," he said, offering a hand twisted by atrophy, "for bringing her home."

Sidney took his hand and smiled. "You're welcome. I'm glad you'll have time together now."

"I'll teach her how to play chess again," Marshall said.

Grace smiled. "Ellie has a summer home in Lake Placid. She's offered it to us for as long as we need it. We're thinking of heading there if the media doesn't die down in a few days." She glanced at Marshall. "I bought him a new chessboard as a bribe to get him to come with me."

"Sounds like a nice vacation," Sidney said. "And one that's much needed."

Ellie came over and draped her arm over Grace's shoulder.

"It's nice of you to offer your home," Sidney said.

"Of course," Ellie said. "They know they can stay here as long as they want. Or the lake house. I don't get to use the house in Lake Placid as much as I'd like. It's terrible that it sits empty. My apartment here is secluded, but no one will find them out at the lake."

Grace smiled and looked at her friend. "Thank you."

Sidney watched the two friends embrace and sensed something strange from their body language. Maybe it was that Ellie stood so tall over Grace, who looked up into her friend's eyes like a helpless child staring at a parent. Maybe it was the aura of regret that Sidney felt between them. An unspoken acknowledgment that suggested Grace, too, should be a successful surgeon. To look at the two friends now, once brought together by their similarities, it was impossible to notice much now besides the things that separated them, which today, Sidney knew, was much more than inches.

Dr. Ellie Reiser, in her designer blouse and perfect-fitting jeans, standing in her chic Manhattan apartment and offering the use of her summer home, was the picture of success. Grace, in her too-large clothing that sagged from her shoulders, skin and hair neglected for a decade, looking up at her old friend and without a dollar to her name, was the polar opposite.

"What am I missing?" Daniel came over to where Grace and Ellie were hugging.

Grace pulled Daniel in to create a three-person hug. After a moment, Grace's parents joined the group that huddled around Marshall's wheelchair. Sidney noticed Charlotte, standing off to the side. The stoic look of indifference never left her face as she slowly approached the group and leaned in with a light hand on her husband's shoulder.

Grace broke out of the group and wiped her eyes.

"Gone for ten years, and there's not much left when you get back."

Ellie put her arm around Grace again. "Stop talking like that. You are loved by many people."

Grace wiped her cheeks again with the backs of her hands, a quick swipe meant to erase the vulnerability she had known to suppress for the past ten years of incarceration. But here, with people who loved her, she allowed it for just a moment.

"Maybe that was true one day," Grace said. "But today, these are the people left in my life. And I'm so happy to have you."

Ten years of bottled-up emotions — fear and regret and anger — suddenly flooded from Grace Sebold as she sobbed. After an initial attempt at stifling it, she eventually gave in with no effort to disguise it. Ellie and Daniel hugged her again, and her parents rushed to comfort her. Charlotte patted her on the back. Marshall seemed lost to the circumstances, still studying the new chessboard in his lap.

Sidney took a quick glance to the corner of the room, where Derrick stood with his camera on his shoulder. She knew Grace's homecoming would play well in one of the concluding episodes, and secure the audience's sympathy for the girl America had once hated.

CHAPTER 42

Monday, July 17, 2017

Jason pulled his car off the highway and onto the exit ramp. He'd plugged the address Gus had given him into the GPS, which told him that his destination was on the left in one-point-three miles. A light drizzle fell and the lights of New York collected in a matrix of yellow and red starbursts on his windshield until his wipers swept them away and allowed the halos to begin forming anew. He squinted through the mist until the billboard sign, illuminated by two bright spotlights that also highlighted the falling rain, told him he had arrived at Red's Self-Storage.

He pulled his compact Toyota Corolla onto the gravel lane, which led into the facility. There were endless rows of single-story storage sheds, with garage door openings in the front and large numbers on top of each unit. He wound down three lanes, avoiding potholes, until he found number 67. A yellow incandescent light glowed above every third unit. Gus's number 67 was not one of the lucky ones. Jason angled his car so the headlights fell onto the closed garage door.

He climbed from the driver's seat with an eerie feeling of isolation and bemusement as to what the hell he was doing in the Bronx during a rainstorm about to open the storage unit of one of his patients. He walked to the shed and held the paper so the headlights allowed him to read the code, which he punched into the keypad on the side of the building. He pressed *enter* and the garage door rattled open. The headlights tunneled through the rain and brightened the small ten-by-ten space. It was filled with storage boxes — the sort with hand slots on each side for easy carrying — and which were capped with cardboard tops. They looked to be meticulously organized; and, indeed, once Jason started searching, he realized the boxes were organized by year.

He checked the note Gus had given him again, and glanced from stack to stack until he saw boxes marked *1999*. There were four of them. Jason pulled the top off the first. File folders lined the inside of the box, packed tight with no room to spare. He pulled one loose and opened it. The top of the first page was stamped with a Wilmington Police Department seal. Jason riffled through the report, some portions typed neatly and others written in all-caps block letters of a man trying hard to make his thoughts legible. Jason leafed through a few pages and then glanced at the bottom of the report and saw the scribbled signature. The hurried scratch of the name was indecipherable, but typed underneath was *Detective Gustavo Morelli.*

Jason stood bathed in the glow of the headlights as the rain came down harder now, pelting the metal roof of the storage facility.

"Damn, Gus," he said aloud. "I thought you were retired."

A few minutes later, he backed his car to the opening of the storage unit, opened the trunk, and loaded all four boxes from 1999.

CHAPTER 43

Tuesday, July 18, 2017

Traversing the hallways was an accomplishment, but still carried the weight of embarrassment. The corridors were tackled only after a nurse set him up with his walker and got him started like a child bicycling for the first time without training wheels. *Look at him go!* Gus could almost hear the nurse yell that when she let go of the tennis-ball coated walker as he took off shuffling the linoleum runways. But he swallowed his pride and kept his ass moving.

Navigating the room, too, was becoming something he could handle. Thanks to Jason's drill-sergeant-style physical-therapy sessions, Gus could manage his way into and out of bed all on his own. He had become proficient at attaching his prosthesis and was able to hobble around his room on crutches, no longer at the staff's mercy when he needed to take a leak. It was a healthy milestone both for him and for the nurses he was driving to the brink of insanity.

Tonight he waited until the rehab prison was dark and quiet. Until the hallways outside his room were soft with night lighting. He knew he had two or three unfettered hours now that the overnight nurse had left his room. He no longer needed the hourly medicine checks, the repositioning, or the drainage of his tubes and catheters. His hard work had earned him three hours of freedom each night, and he planned to take advantage of them.

Slowly he shifted on the bed until his leg hung from the side and his stump floated in the air. He attached the prosthesis. He hadn't quite conquered the proper technique, and the pain of the maneuver was shocking. When it passed, he eased off the bed, took hold of his walker, and hobbled to the closet. Inside were the four boxes Jason had brought from the storage unit the night before. It had taken all the patience he had left in him to wait until now, 3:00 a.m., to retrieve them.

It took twenty minutes to drag the boxes to the bedside chair but, finally, retired Detective Gustavo Morelli sat with his files stacked around him. For a moment, he felt like his old self. He opened the first box, plucked a folder from within, and spread the contents across the overbed table. The pain in his hip, from the last thirty minutes of effort, faded. He hadn't felt this alive in years.

The files were marked 1999. It had been so long, he hadn't been sure of the name. But over the Fourth of July weekend when he binge watched the Grace Sebold documentary on Jason's iPad, it had come to him. Now the file of Henry Anderson was in front of him. He ran his index finger under the name: *Henry Anderson.*

The boy was eighteen years old when he died. Gus, who finished his career with the New York Police Department's Detective Bureau, had been a senior detective out in the sticks of Wilmington, New York, back in 1999 and was called to investigate the boy's death, which occurred on Whiteface Mountain. A few minutes of paging through the reports was all it took to transport Gus across the years. The memories flooded back to him. Two hours into reviewing the file, the rising sun brought dawn through his hospital window and slanted a bright streak across his table. By then, Gus remembered vividly the boy named Henry Anderson, as if Gus were still working the case.

As if it hadn't been put to rest nearly twenty years before, but instead were alive and active and exhaling hot breaths of air that fogged the prism of his mind the way all his homicides used to do.

He slipped the pages back into the boxes. He didn't have the energy to stow them in the closet, but knew Jason would be the first person to arrive this morning. He climbed back into bed and removed his prosthesis. Then he pulled the table over to him. He clicked his pen to life and touched it to the blank page. The heading was easy:

Dear Ms. Ryan,
I believe you've made a great error . . .

CHAPTER 44

Tuesday, July 18, 2017
Sidney spent the day on Long Island shooting scenes with Grace for the final episodes. Grace had a few destinations in mind that she told Sidney she had dreamed about in Bordelais. One of them was the Montauk Point Lighthouse at the far tip of Long Island. Derrick shot footage of Grace climbing the tower and looking out across the water. Sidney, watching Grace stand at the top of the lighthouse, propped on her tiptoes while holding the railing, and with the breeze splaying her sweater behind her like a cape, considered that the scene exemplified the very definition of *freedom* and might make for the perfect ending to episode ten.

Finished filming for the day, Sidney crossed the East River at 6:00 p.m., Tuesday, in bumper-to-bumper traffic through the Midtown Tunnel on her way into the city. It was past seven when she dropped the fare over the front seat. A muggy summer night, Sidney immediately missed the cool air-conditioning of the taxi as she walked along East Forty-second Street on the way to Mc-Fadden's Saloon.

In jeans and a tank top, her skin glowed with a subtle layer of perspiration by the time she entered the restaurant. The air-conditioned interior gave her a chill when she walked in, quickly turning her skin to goose bumps. She spotted Graham Cromwell across the bar and he raised his hand to wave. He slid off the stool as she approached, and Sidney was surprised when he kissed her on the cheek. An overtly private man, Graham had never shown any form of public affection during their brief relationship. What might have transpired between them was a mystery, one that lately Sidney sensed Graham was interested in solving. During times of pure honesty, Sidney admitted to herself that she wondered, too. But there weren't many success stories that started by sleeping with your boss, and as a fiercely independent woman, Sidney refused to give anyone a reason to call her success something it was not.

It had been more than a year now since the two had been intimate, and Sidney's longings had finally faded like an old scar, just a faint splotch of pink remaining where once a wide wound had been. Nowadays their relationship was such that they usually managed at least one lunch during the week, or coffee in the mornings. Sometimes they met for drinks in the evening. Work was always the topic, but it was nice to get away from the stuffiness of the office.

"Hi," Graham said.

Sidney smiled. "What's gotten into you?"

"Relax. I'm happy to see you outside the office."

"Things have been crazy for the last week or so."

"How'd it go?"

"Today? I don't know. I got some good footage and sound bites from her. But her reunion last night? Probably the saddest thing I've ever seen," Sidney said. "She's almost forty years old and she has no one in her life."

Graham sat back onto his stool. "But she's out of jail, so you can hang your hat on that."

Sidney took the stool next to him. "It's so goddamn unfair. She was a young girl on her way to a surgical residency and a promising career. Then, in an effort to put a notch on his belt and settle a terrible crime, some tropical-beach ranger pinned a murder conviction around her neck and ruined her life."

"Sid, you've done this before. Without you, she'd still be sitting in jail. What's worse? To be free and starting over, or to be incarcerated? Because those are the only two options."

"She didn't do it, Graham."

"Which is why she's free today."

"How does she get the last ten years back?"

"She doesn't." Graham lifted his hand when the bartender passed by. "She's going to need something. Quickly."

"Casamigos on the rocks," Sidney said.

"I thought you were a tequila drinker."

"I am. It's George Clooney's brand."

"George Clooney makes tequila?"

Sidney looked at Graham in the dim light of the tavern. "How old *are* you?"

The bartender delivered her drink. Sidney squeezed a lime over the top and took a sip.

"She doesn't get the years back, Sid," Graham said after a moment of silence. "But she gets the next ten years. And the ten after that. And it's all because of your work."

"You know the worst part? Her best friend, one of the only people who stayed in touch with her, is a successful doctor."

"Why is that a bad thing? Isn't her friend helping her out?"

"She is. But years ago, they went to medical school at the same time. Now Grace's friend is set up in this crazy apartment at Windsor Tower. She's got a bustling private practice and her whole damn life set up pretty as can be. The entire time I was with Grace the other night, I could see it in her eyes. She was imagining her own life if things had not gone to hell."

"Why has this gotten you so wound up? You've done this three other times and it's never bothered you like this."

Sidney spun her drink as the ice formed beaded condensation that rolled down onto the mahogany bar. "I don't know. It's just a travesty. You know my desk is filled with letters begging for help, each writer claiming to have been wrongly convicted? I know they can't all be correct, but how many of them are?"

She stared at her tequila and thought of her trips to Baldwin State Prison.

"I don't mean to be insensitive," Graham said after a moment of silence. "But who the hell cares? Currently you sure shouldn't. You've got the biggest story in the country sitting in your lap. You've got the most-watched documentary in television history on your shoulders. Twenty-two million people tuned in last Friday. That's bigger than *The Jinx*. Bigger than *Making a Murderer*. And you've got three episodes left to produce. That's where your focus should be, not on a bunch of envelopes sitting on your desk from a bunch of deadbeats hoping to get lucky. You're not a crusader, Sid. You're a filmmaker. And you're on a helluva run. Don't get sidetracked with sentimentality. You want to help all the wrongfully convicted? Well," Graham said, picking up his drink, "you can't, because sadly there are too many for one person to tackle. That's what the Innocence Project is for, and all the other organizations that fight on behalf of the wrongly convicted. You want to help someone else when you're done with *The Girl of Sugar Beach*? Good. The network wants that as well. You want the details now, or you want to be surprised when you come in tomorrow?"

"I don't really care about the next one, Graham."

"I think you'll change your mind when you see the details."

Sidney shook her head. "I doubt it."

Graham tipped his scotch back and emptied his glass. "You want to mourn for Grace Sebold? Fine. She'll never be a doctor like her friend. That's too bad. But she's likely to get a truckload of money when she sues the St. Lucian government, so financially she'll do just fine. She won't get those years back, but that's why it's a story. That's why it's the biggest documentary we've ever seen. So worry and fret all you want, but do it after you finish this documentary."

Sidney took a sip of Casamigos and stared into the mirror behind the bar, her image intermittently blocked by a score of liquor bottles.

"Spoken like a true suit," she said.

"You'll excuse my concern. I put my reputation on the line to get this project green-lit."

"I'd say you're doing pretty well on that bet."

"And I want to make sure it pays off for both of us. Where are you with Friday's episode?"

Sidney continued to stare into the mirror. "I'm meeting with Leslie early tomorrow to make the final cuts. I'll have it to production by noon."

Sidney took another sip of her drink and wondered how this casual meeting had gone to crap so quickly.

"You hungry?" Graham finally asked.

She shook her head.

"Christ, Sid. Please don't steal defeat from the jaws of victory." Graham stood and dropped two twenties next to his empty scotch and walked out of the bar. She watched him leave, following his image through the myriad liquor bottles in the mirror. When he was gone, she finished her drink and ordered another.

She was halfway through her second tequila when a man took a seat on the stool next to her. She looked down the bar at the several open spots where he could have chosen to sit. Before Sidney could contemplate whether he was going to offer to buy her a drink or whether this guy simply had no appreciation for personal space, he turned to her.

"Are you Sidney Ryan?"

"Depends on who wants to know."

"I do."

"Do you have a name?"

"Jason."

"What paper do you work for, Jason?"

"I'm not a reporter. I just need to give you this." He pulled a white envelope from the back pocket of his jeans and slid it across the bar.

"Let me guess," Sidney said. "A relative is in jail for a crime he didn't commit."

"Nope," Jason said as he stood up. "But

before you get too much further in your documentary, you better read that. Have a good night."

It was the second time in ten minutes that a man had promptly walked away from her. This time, Sidney turned from the bar to watch him exit through the front door and into the summer night. When the stranger was gone, she twisted her stool back to the bar and looked at the envelope he had left. She picked it up, slid her finger under the flap, and pulled out the single page. She looked around the bar before she read it, as if some great secret might be revealed within. It was written in a man's abrupt penmanship.

Dear Ms. Ryan,
   I believe you've made a great error with Grace Sebold. Please look up the name Henry Anderson, a boy who died in 1999. I believe you will find the circumstances of his death very interesting.

Sincerely,
Ret. Det. Gustavo Morelli

Sidney read the letter again. She looked around the bar to see if anyone was watching. Conversations happened all around, and no one paid attention to her. She brought her phone to life and typed *Henry Anderson* into the browser. There were many Henrys in the world with the last name Anderson, so she refined her search with *1999* and *boy killed.*

An article came to the top of the browser: BOY'S DEATH IN TRAGIC MOUNTAIN FALL RULED ACCIDENTAL.

Sidney skimmed the article, her eyes stopping halfway through when she spotted the name. Henry Anderson was a high-school senior when he fell to his death while hiking a mountain trail, apparently getting too close to the edge of a bluff and tragically falling. The cause of death, determined by the medical examiner's autopsy, was due to a head trauma from the fall — a large fracture in the back of Henry's skull. He was on vacation at the time of the accident with his girlfriend's family.

The girlfriend's name . . .

Grace Sebold.

"If we move past the murder weapon, which I believe from day one's debate we all agree is a damning piece of evidence that cannot be refuted, no matter how many times we go over the arguments of the defense — and if we agree to stick only with the facts that we know about the blood that was discovered in the room, then today we should talk about motive," Harold said.

"The judge explained that motive is important because it will help prove or disprove premeditation. So I'd like to open the floor to debate. If we agree that she did it, and *how* she did it, can we now hash out *why* she did it?"

"Why?" the retired teacher said. "Because she had done it before."

Harold held up his hands in a calm show of protest. "That's speculation. The prosecution created a clever slogan in their closing arguments. But the defense objected to this reference of past wrong-doings, and the judge sustained the objection. We were instructed to disregard that comment, and the entire line of questioning that had to do with past misconduct. The judge was very clear that we should consider only the facts presented to us during *this* hearing. One victim, one trial, nothing else from the past should come into play."

"How can it not influence us? She killed other people!"

■ ■ ■ ■

PART IV
THE OTHER SIDE

■ ■ ■ ■

CHAPTER 45

Wednesday, July 19, 2017

Wednesday morning Sidney pulled into the lot of Alcove Manor, a rehabilitation center. Her grandmother died in a place like this, and Sidney had been leery of them ever since. Today she had no choice but to make a visit. Her cell phone rang just as she parked her car.

"Hello?"

"Sid, where the hell are you?" Leslie asked.

"I meant to call you. Something's come up. I won't be in until later."

"When? The draft of episode eight is due today and we're not even close on the edits. Graham has already been down this morning asking about it. He said you promised he'd have it by noon. Production is having a fit."

"How close are we?"

"On the edits? Not close. I need your input."

"You'll have to stall. I can't get there until later today."

"Where the hell are you?"

"I'm in the city, but I've got to take care of something. I'll call you later."

"We're going to miss the deadline."

"It'll be the first one we missed. They'll forgive us. We've got the biggest audience on television and we should start acting like it. Call you in a bit."

Sidney ended the call. It was just past 9:00 a.m. when she walked through the front entrance of Alcove Manor. She headed for the reception desk, where a young woman sat paging through a magazine.

"Hi," Sidney said as she approached. "I'm visiting."

"Sign in, please," the girl said. She pointed to a log for Sidney to print her name, and removed a visitor badge from a sheet of labels.

"I'm not sure of the room number," Sidney said. "This is my first visit."

The girl handed Sidney the badge. "What's the name?"

"Gustavo Morelli."

The girl typed the name into the computer. "Two thirty-two," she said. "Take the elevator to the second level. It'll be to your left."

Sidney attached the visitors badge to her lapel and rode the elevator to the second floor. When the doors opened a few minutes later, she walked onto the floor of the rehab facility, which shone with unnatural fluorescence and smelled from ammonia. Nurses in rose-red scrubs pushed carts down hallways and sat around computers at the station that occupied the middle of the unit. Two physicians in long white coats scribbled orders while they stood at the counter of the nurses' station. Sidney walked to room 232 and peered inside. She saw a hospital bed lumpy with an occupant's feet under the covers. She entered to find the man propped up in bed eating breakfast and reading the newspaper.

"Detective Morelli?" she asked.

The man looked up, folded his paper, and placed it on the table in front of him, covering his half-eaten breakfast. "That was fast," he said.

"You know how to get someone's attention."

"Sorry I sent the kid the way I did. My goal was to track you down myself, but I couldn't make that happen fast enough."

He pointed to the crumpled mess of

blankets that covered his lower body.

"Sit down," he said. "We've got a lot to discuss."

"The brass were convinced it was an accident," Gus said. "The kid fell off a mountain ridge while he was hiking, end of story. When the pathologist finished his report and determined the cause of death to be internal bleeding from the trauma of the fall, that was the end of it."

"But not for you."

"I had my doubts back then. I saw a group of high-school kids that were covering for each other. Something sinister happened to Henry Anderson, and at least a few of those kids knew what it was."

"What stirred your suspicion?" Sidney asked.

"You conduct enough interviews during your tenure and you learn to pick up a vibe. During the Henry Anderson case, I picked up a bad one. But it was me against the world on that case. I was at the start of my detective career, I didn't have a ton of clout, and I had to choose my battles. I was stuck out in the sticks, and I wanted into the city. Bottom line — I was in no position to make waves. But those doubts about the Henry Anderson case never left me. Then the

Sebold girl was brought to trial eight years later for the death of another boyfriend. I fought with my superiors to convince them that she was involved with Henry's death, even went over their heads when they told me to forget about Henry Anderson. Nearly lost my job for insubordination. When Grace Sebold was convicted, I was supposed to be satisfied with the fact that she'd spend her life in jail."

Gus shifted in bed.

"I never was satisfied, though. And my suspicions never died. Since I started watching your documentary, they've been rekindled."

Sidney nodded her head. "For what it's worth, you've got me thinking as well."

"Listen, I'm a detective. I used to be, anyway. We do a lot of our work on instinct and hunch. But we also do a lot on straightforward common sense, and here's some for you. If a girl's boyfriend dies by falling off a mountain bluff once, it's a sad case of bad luck. If that same girl has *two* boyfriends fall off a mountain in the same lifetime" — Gus looked at her — "that ain't luck — bad or otherwise. That's suspicious."

Sidney took a deep breath. In one, articulate sentence from Gus Morelli, she felt her blockbuster documentary falling to pieces.

"You remember the Henry Anderson case well?" Sidney asked.

"No. It was almost twenty years ago." Gus pointed to the closet. "But I pulled my old files from that case and read through them. Your girl was hiding something when I interviewed her. I'm certain about that, and I noted it way back when."

"Grace?"

Gus nodded. "I brought my suspicions to my superior when the case was getting shuffled off as an accident. The problem was that I could never figure out what, exactly, she was hiding. The autopsy report came back indicating the manner of death was accidental, and that put an end to my official investigation."

"But not your suspicion."

"No, that never went away. I had other cases throughout my career that did the same thing to me — where the facts didn't add up, but I couldn't get to the bottom of it. Each one bothered me and nagged me, caused me to lose sleep and maybe lean on the whiskey a bit too much. But then another case came along and stole my time and attention and I had no choice but to move on. There were a few cases over the years I couldn't let go of. To make myself feel better, I took the ones that bothered me most and copied everything — every evidence report, every autopsy report, every interview. Boxed them up and shoved them in a storage unit in the Bronx."

"Why?"

"Because it helped me let go. I convinced myself that if I stashed everything about those cases away, then someday I'd come back to them and figure out what I missed. I've got a few from Wilmington, a bunch more from NYPD."

"How are you doing so far?"

"The Henry Anderson case is the first one I've come back to," Gus said. "I've seen that kid so many times in my dreams and in my thoughts. I never forgot about him. About the case and about the details? Yeah. But never about *him*. Then I found myself laid up in this godforsaken place and I came across your documentary about Grace Sebold. Two boyfriends fall off a cliff? I wasn't buying it during her trial in 2007, and I'm not buying it now. And when I saw the episode where the forensic expert showed how his skull fracture could not have come from a boat oar? That episode reminded me a lot of Henry Anderson. Henry's skull fracture was unique. I remember sitting in on the autopsy. The pathologist noted it and showed it to me during the exam. It was ruled, ultimately, to be the result of his fall down the mountain. But when I watched your documentary" — Gus stared at Sidney — "that's your link."

"What link?" Sidney asked.

"The one between Henry Anderson and Julian Crist."

Gus leaned forward and patted the bed where his leg should be.

"I'm a sixty-eight year old man who just lost his leg to cancer."

Sidney saw the blankets flat and empty on his right side. The hollowness of the space sent a flutter through her.

"I know people will think I'm making these claims to stay relevant, or to find some piece of myself that I'm not sure exists anymore. And trust me when I tell you that folks will call me crazy for what I'm about to say, but I've been called worse. It's only logical to conclude that both of these young men's deaths are connected. And I've got a hunch that the same tool used to strike Julian Crist was also used to strike Henry Anderson. And I'd wager a shot of Johnnie Walker that Grace Sebold was holding it."

CHAPTER 46

Wednesday, July 19, 2017

Grace Sebold sat at the kitchen table across
from her brother. It was Wednesday morning. She'd been a free woman for eight days.
From his wheelchair, Marshall scrutinized
the chessboard in front of him. Grace had
just taken his bishop in a devastating move,
and she watched now for how he would
react. She was beginning to remember her
younger brother's strategy and game play
from years ago. His ability to tackle every-
day activities varied widely since the accident. Some days he seemed like his old
self; on others, he was a stranger, lost and
confused in a world he did not understand.

It was during the bad days, Grace was
remembering, that Marshall was the most
difficult to handle. A tumultuous circle of
aggravation could develop suddenly from
something as benign as forgetting that he
was not allowed to drive. The loss of this

privilege was nothing new. Since the accident, and the traumatic brain injury, seizures had plagued him, and the risk of suffering one while driving a car was too great to climb behind the wheel. So on good days, when Marshall was feeling like his old self and wanting independence, telling him that he could not drive was a trigger that sent him into a rage. Depression was a major factor in his life and something, Grace was learning since her return, her parents were badly mismanaging.

But somehow, back then and still today, playing chess put Marshall's mind in a state of ease, where he was calm and happy. In front of a chessboard, a level of focus and concentration came over him that transformed Marshall Sebold, if not entirely back to the person he once was, as near as Grace had ever seen him come. It was his only oasis from a world he had lost control of years ago.

She and Marshall had played chess every day since her return from Bordelais. Grace had yet to beat him. She fought hard, and occasionally the game could last for hours. Sometimes Grace felt like she was strolling to victory, only to see that Marshall had cleverly lured her into a trap, her queen falling first as an early indication that she had taken the bait, her king following shortly behind. Their connection, once fierce, was one of the greatest things she missed about her brother, who had such a difficult time communicating in this world. But in the world of chess — where speaking was unnecessary, where people of different cultures and languages could play one another as simply as brother and sister — in this world, her brother was free. She missed him greatly.

Grace moved her gaze to the tall windows that lined Ellie's high-rise apartment, while Marshall considered his next move. She stared out over Manhattan: at the streets and the traffic and the lights changing from red to green, at the commuters shifting on the sidewalks below like colonies of ants. She considered that what was happening today was the same thing that had happened every day of her incarceration.

She studied the skyline, framed by the blue sky and horizontal clouds brightened by the early sun. Today's view was in stark contrast to a few days ago when palm trees bent by the constant push of ocean breeze were her only escape from the monotony of Bordelais Correctional Facility. Palm trees are a universal image of relaxation and vacation, but years of staring at them from the prison yard had jaded Grace to them. Grace Sebold was a free woman, and she planned to never lay eyes on them again.

"Check," Marshall said, sliding his rook into position and capturing Grace's bishop.

"What?" Grace pulled her gaze from the window back to the board. "How? You totally set me up."

Marshall smiled.

"You wanted me to take your bishop."

"And you did," Marshall said. "It left you vulnerable."

"You didn't play at all while I was gone?"

Marshall shook his head. "Just sometimes. But only online. Not with them."

Them. Her parents. In all his letters over the years, Marshall had never written the words *Mom and Dad* when referring to their parents. Grace wanted to ask how he could stay so competitive without playing regularly for ten years, but she already knew the answer. His mind worked differently than most. There was something about her brother's brain that clicked on and off. Grace had been aware of it since the accident. She had always enjoyed the times her brother was *on*, when his conscious thoughts settled in the undamaged portion of his brain, where the old Marshall could still be found. These moments only happened during chess games, which explained why they had played so much over the last week.

"Why don't we play on my old chessboard?" Marshall asked.

"I told you why."

"I brought it here so we could play. I didn't know you had bought me this new board."

"Don't you like the new one?"

"I do, but my old set is . . ." He picked up one of the new pieces. They were mass-produced pine, not handcrafted porcelain. "The pieces are more elaborate, that's all."

Grace paused for a moment. "I don't think there's any way to fix this, Marshall."

He made brief eye contact. "There's not." He pointed to her rook. "But you can make two moves before checkmate."

Grace stared at her brother for a moment longer, then took her king and laid it on its side. "I think I'll concede this one, and look to get even tomorrow."

Grace's king rolled slightly until it came to rest.

"You're going to have to deal with Daniel," Marshall said.

Grace looked at her brother. "Daniel is a dear friend, that's all. And one of the few who kept in touch with me over the years."

"And why do you suppose that is?"

When Grace offered no response, Marshall gave his own.

"Because he's still in love with you. Just like this one here." He pointed toward the hallway where the bedrooms were located. "She's another problem you're going to have to figure out."

"Okay, Marshall. Let's not get into this right now."

"If not now, when? After she's allowed you to take over her tranquil house on Lake Placid? After you owe her everything?"

Grace swiped her fallen pieces into her hand and dumped them into the chess case. "Game's over, Marshall. We'll play again tomorrow."

"Charlotte is still upset about you and Daniel."

"Marshall!"

"You didn't see her the other day at your homecoming. I'm tired of everyone thinking I'm a damaged buffoon unaware of the things that go on around me. I was watching her, Grace. She cringed every time Daniel touched you. I don't want her to be a problem for you."

"It was a long time ago, Marshall. I can't change the past. And if Charlotte can't get over it, then I'm not the one to help her."

"Perhaps Daniel should help her get past

it. She's his wife. He should have helped her get over it years ago."

"Marshall, I'm tired today. We'll play again tomorrow. Okay? I've had enough for now."

"Charlotte was a raging lunatic when she found out about you and Daniel. Are you forgetting the fight you two had at Sugar Beach?"

"I'm not forgetting, Marshall. I'm choosing not to dwell on it." Grace stood.

"You better hope she chooses the same thing."

Marshall stared at her a moment longer, then turned his attention to his new chess set, lining the pieces in careful order before closing the chessboard on itself and sliding it into the case as he wheeled his chair away.

"No," Grace said. "You can walk. No more chair when you're around me."

And just like that, her brother was gone. The fierce mind and coherent conversation Marshall had displayed during their chess game was like steam on a fresh cup of coffee, present for only a short time. When the game was over, Marshall's attention span and comprehension evaporated, as if it had never been there at all. As soon as the chess set was packed away, her brother retreated to the ravaged part of his brain and was lost to the world.

Grace stared into his lost eyes and saw some hint of understanding. If he wanted to avoid the full-care facility their parents were considering, he needed to help himself. Finally Marshall pushed himself upright, and shuffled his orthopedic shoes in a staggered gait toward the guest bedroom, his chess set still hanging from his shoulder.

With Marshall in his bedroom, Grace found herself alone. It was one of the rare moments in the last week when she could claim such a thing. Ellie was at work and her parents had gone to the hotel. She was surprised to find she enjoyed the solitude. The last ten years had been spent in isolation. Twenty hours of every day spent in her prison cell. She got to know herself well in that time. For many years, she longed to be back with her family and friends; but now that she was here, she craved the privacy she had wanted so badly to escape. Her years in medical school, and the many books she'd read in prison, told her this was merely a habitual response to a new environment. It was normal to retreat to the solace of isolation because it was all she had known for the last many years. In time, it would pass. But today she craved the solitude. Marshall's comments had stirred fear in her

416

gut, something only a free woman would feel. At Bordelais, her future was invisible, so she never sensed the worry that was hidden in the spent years of her life.

She walked to her bedroom and closed the door. From the top drawer of her dresser, she pulled out her love lock, which held Julian's name below her own. She held the heavy, vintage lock in her palm and stared at their names. A strange sense of loss had found her in the past week. The ghost of Julian Crist, a bizarrely comforting presence during her incarceration — and a thing that Grace hated and blamed during various spans in the last decade — was softening only to the man she once loved.

She placed the lock on the desk and opened Ellie's laptop. With no Internet access during her time in jail, suddenly all the information she had ever wanted was at her fingertips. Facebook was still a new medium when Grace went to prison, and she hadn't been an active user. But she understood the website's ability to track people down. She logged into Ellie's profile and typed *Allison Harbor* into the search area. Grace scrolled through a few profiles before she found her. Julian's ex was now a pediatrician in New Jersey, married with two kids, and with a hyphenated last name. She was different from what Grace remembered. Heavier and less attractive than the image Grace had kept in her mind during her time in prison. A nauseous feeling stirred in her stomach at the thought that this plain-looking woman had nearly stolen Julian from her. Grace spent thirty minutes looking at pictures of Allison Harbor and her family. Then, she logged out of Ellie's Facebook account, and pulled up the Internet search engine.

She typed *Julian Crist* into the browser and was inundated with thousands of options. The first few pages of results pertained to *The Girl of Sugar Beach.* Grace read through them, but she was more interested in the stories from just after Julian was killed, before Sidney Ryan's documentary had brought him back from the dead. Arrested two days after Julian's death, Grace had never gotten the chance to read many details about the case — only what her negligent defense team presented to her and the articles Marshall had sent.

She searched the Internet for nearly an hour without pause, sucking up the information like she was reading a riveting novel. She found no stories that made the connection. She turned finally from the computer and walked to the bedroom door, quietly engaging the lock. Knowing Ellie would soon be home, Grace hurried back to the computer. The antique love lock sat on the desk. She stared again at Julian's name, knowing that another had once taken his place. Her fingers moved over the keyboard as she typed the name into the search engine: *H-E-N-R-Y A-N-D-E-R-S-O-N.*

CHAPTER 47

Wednesday, July 19, 2017

This morning's escapades would be on her own dime. Sidney didn't dare expense any of it to *The Girl of Sugar Beach* budget. The documentary was a cash cow pulling in millions in advertising revenue, and Graham and the rest of the lot wouldn't bat an eyelash if Sidney told them she needed to fly back to St. Lucia for some last-minute footage, let alone expense some mileage and a lunch meeting. Dollars, however, were not what concerned her. Sidney wanted to keep the suits in the dark about the recent developments. The less they knew about Henry Anderson, the better. At least until she understood what, exactly, it all meant.

She stood in the lobby of Alcove Manor Rehabilitation Center, having just finished hearing Gus Morelli's story and his startling theory of how Julian Crist and Henry Anderson might be connected. She held the phone to her ear and listened to the voice mail.

"Sid, production was down asking for the cuts for episode eight again, which obviously aren't ready because you haven't been in the studio for two days. The shit is hitting the fan! Graham Cromwell's having a heart attack, and our entire staff is hiding in their offices to avoid him. Where the hell are you? Call me back. Or better yet, get in here."

Sidney tapped her phone and ended the voice mail. In her mind's eye, she could see Leslie at her desk, biting her nails and running a hand through her hair. Sidney knew she should call, but lying had never been her strong suit. And she was particularly bad at fabricating stories to her friends. Within a minute of starting the discussion, Leslie would know the documentary that had America on the edge of its seat was about to crash and burn in spectacular fashion. And once Leslie knew this, corporate would know it, because the only person worse than Sidney at lying was Leslie Martin.

Standing in the lobby, Sidney punched the numbers into her phone. It was the third time this morning she had called the number. This time, a woman answered.

"Hello?"

"Mrs. Anderson?"

"Yes?"

"My name is Sidney Ryan. I wanted to ask you a few questions about your son."

"David?"

"No, ma'am." Sidney hesitated. "This is regarding Henry."

There was a long pause.

"Henry passed away years ago, Ms. Ryan."

"I know that. It's the reason I'm calling."

Betty Anderson lived in Saratoga Springs, New York, a three-hour drive from Manhattan. Sidney arrived just after two o'clock. A pleasant neighborhood with tree-lined streets — red maple and sycamore — Sidney found the home easily. She rang the doorbell and a moment later Henry Anderson's mother answered. Frail and gaunt, Betty Anderson looked older than her sixty-seven years. Cloud-white hair was cut short, framing a face that sagged with wrinkles. Heavy, hooded lids nearly shut her eyes, and only the constant effort of her pinched forehead kept the world visible.

"Mrs. Anderson? I'm Sidney Ryan."

"You came all the way from the city?"

"Yes, ma'am."

"Is this about your television show?"

"It is."

Betty Anderson pushed open the front door. "Come on in."

Sidney walked into the foyer and followed Betty into a living room, where they each sat, Betty on the edge of a love seat and Sidney adjacent to her on a side chair.

"David, my older boy, told me about the documentary."

Sidney nodded. "Have you watched it?"

"No, dear. I don't watch too much television."

"But your son has seen it?"

She nodded. "He told me about it. That it had to do with Grace and what happened to her."

"How about Mr. Anderson? Has he seen it?"

"Hank senior passed a few years ago."

"I'm sorry," Sidney said.

"Cirrhosis. He drank too much. Had an awful time of it the last many years. He never quite got past Henry's death. We divorced many years ago, not long after Henry died. Common thing, we learned. Divorce after a child's death. He took to drinking and never came back around."

"I know Henry's death was many years ago, but I was hoping to ask some questions about it."

Betty nodded.

"Henry died during a vacation, is that correct?"

"Yes. We all went to the mountains for a long weekend."

"Who did that include?"

"Several families. Our kids were all in high school together, and most of us had been friends for years."

"The Sebolds?"

"Yes, Gretchen and Glenn were there. Of course, Grace and Marshall as well. The Reiser family."

"Ellie Reiser?"

"Yes. There was quite a crowd. Maybe six or seven families from the neighborhood. I'm afraid I can't remember them all."

"Can you tell me about the day Henry died?"

"Well," Betty started. "The kids were out on a hike. The plan was for everyone to meet back at the resort in the evening, and we would all go to dinner. It was Sunday night, with everyone planning to leave the following day. Henry . . . never showed up that night. At first, Hank and I assumed he was simply running late. But as evening pushed on, we asked around and no one had seen him since the hike that afternoon. We started to search for him. His friends joined in. It wasn't until eight o'clock that evening, as it was getting dark, that we finally phoned the police. About an hour later, we found Henry in a shallow ravine below the trail where he had been hiking."

"I'm very sorry."

Betty nodded.

"Was Henry dating Grace Sebold around the time he died?"

"Yes. They were quite serious. I mean, as serious as teenagers can be. Grace was Henry's first love. We really loved Grace, so Hank and I had hoped they might be the rare high-school sweetheart story that made it last."

Betty smiled as she reminisced. The upward push of her cheeks caused her slivered eyes to close. "It was long ago, but I still remember being happy that my son had found someone who made him feel special. Grace and Henry had planned to attend Syracuse University together."

Sidney's mind flashed back to the many photos of Julian Crist she had seen during the creation of her documentary. A sick feeling sat in her gut when she considered what had happened to both of the young men who had loved Grace Sebold.

"Did you keep in touch with the Sebolds after Henry's death?"

Betty Anderson shook her head. "No. Sadly, we lost touch with many of our friends after Henry passed. Hank started drinking and we had marital problems, so it was easy to melt away."

"Are you familiar with what happened to Grace Sebold?"

"Yes. I know she was convicted of murder. I always thought the circumstances didn't fit the girl I knew. I'm glad to hear after so many years that she is finally home with her family."

"The circumstances surrounding Grace Sebold's conviction . . . ," Sidney said. "You remember them, don't you?"

"Yes."

Sidney was silent for a moment as she waited for Mrs. Anderson to elaborate. When she did not, Sidney spoke. "A young man named Julian Crist was killed while in St. Lucia on spring break. The circumstances of Julian Crist's death are, frankly, startlingly similar to your son's."

"So I've been told."

Sidney placed her elbows on her knees and leaned closer to Henry Anderson's mother. "Grace and Julian were dating when he was killed. They were finishing medical school at the time, and preparing to start a residency program together. Like your son, Julian Crist fell to his death from a mountain bluff."

Betty was already shaking her head. "Henry's death was an accident. A tragic accident that took my son at a horribly young age."

"Do you remember Gus Morelli?"

Betty attempted to raise her sagging eyelids as her voice took on a controversial tone. "He was one of the detectives involved in Henry's case. And he came to me during Grace's trial with the same theory I think you're trying to present now."

Sidney took a deep breath. "Back in 1999, Detective Morelli believed that there may be more to Henry's death. That, perhaps, it wasn't an accident."

"Henry fell off that bluff. I wish it hadn't happened, Ms. Ryan. I've offered so many times to take his place. My boy is gone and I hope to see him again someday. But I'm not going to try to bring him back to life by turning him into some pop-culture star to help your television program."

Sidney pursed her lips and nodded her head. She didn't mention that turning Henry into a star was the furthest thing from her mind, or that her *television program* was likely as dead as the two boys who once loved Grace Sebold.

"I understand," Sidney finally said.

Betty Anderson's grief, even all these years later, was still palpable. If she didn't want to hear that her son had possibly been killed, then Sidney guessed her audience, who was salivating for the episode that showed Grace Sebold's exoneration and release from jail, did not, either. Graham Cromwell and Ray Sandberg certainly would not be interested in pursuing anything that might disrupt the smooth sail they saw for the final three episodes.

The question Sidney weighed as she sat in Henry Anderson's old house was whether fame and fortune were enough for her, or if the truth was the only thing that mattered.

CHAPTER 48

Wednesday, July 19, 2017
The New York Office of the Chief Medical Examiner was located on East Twenty-sixth Street. Sidney made it back to the city just before seven, agitated from the gridlock and with a sore right hip from navigating stop-and-go traffic. She was led to the third floor, where Dr. Livia Cutty sat behind her new desk and typed on her keyboard.

"Hey," Livia said when Sidney appeared at her door, "you made it."

"Traffic. Sorry, I'm late. And sorry to call on you during your first week in New York," Sidney said.

"It's perfect timing. I don't officially start until August first. They buffered me a couple of weeks to get settled and find my way around. I can't take a formal case until then, and I'm bored as hell. I was happy you called. Sit down. I'll show you what I found."

In 1999, Henry Anderson's body had gone to the Adirondack Medical Center Morgue in Essex County, New York, for autopsy. Since receiving Sidney's call early this morning, Dr. Cutty had made some calls to Essex County and tapped into the New York State database to bring herself up to date with the old case.

"Back in 1999," Livia said, "there were no electronic medical records, so everything I pulled on the Anderson case is on file. This is what I was able to track down on short notice." She pushed a manila file folder across her desk.

Sidney spun the folder around and opened the cover. The first page was a summary from the scene investigators who arrived at the site where the Anderson boy's body had been found. Sidney skimmed the findings while Livia summarized.

"The Anderson boy was an eighteen-year-old high-school senior visiting Whiteface Lodge with his family for the Memorial Day weekend. He went missing after a group of teenagers, sixteen in all, went on a hike to High Falls Gorge, where they all ate lunch. That evening, Henry Anderson never came back to the resort. Police were called and a search was started. A couple of the boy's friends" — Livia looked down at her notes

— "Charlotte Brooks and Daniel Greaves, eventually found Henry's body just after eight in the evening."

Sidney looked up from the report when she heard the names. "Where are you getting these specific details?"

Livia pointed to the page in front of her. "I'm reading the detective's notes. A copy was in the file. Is something wrong?"

"Charlotte Brooks and Daniel Greaves were Grace's friends who got married at Sugar Beach."

"In St. Lucia?" Livia asked.

Sidney nodded. She again saw her blockbuster documentary, set to air the final three episodes that showed the unearthed blood evidence and the debunked cleanup that helped exonerate Grace Sebold, as well as her triumphant return home, falling to pieces as some larger conspiracy swirled in her thoughts.

"What can you tell me about Henry Anderson's autopsy?"

Livia pushed crime scene photos across the desk.

Sidney looked at the awkward angles of the young man's limbs as he lay on a dust-covered slab of granite, with shrubs partially covering his face. A dark circle of blood spread along the stone on which his body

431

lay, haloing his head like a cherry sunrise. His eyes were half opened, like he was stuck between sleep and consciousness.

"He was estimated to have fallen fifty feet," Livia said. "The scene investigators were able to track the marks in the side of the mountain where he likely made contact on the way down. Detectives were able to match his shoeprints to the edge of the bluff just above where his body was found. There were many other shoeprints. It was a popular trail and the only hiking route that offered access to the mountaintop café."

Sidney turned another page to find the autopsy report and photos. She quickly tucked the images of Henry's naked body splayed on the metal autopsy table underneath the report so they were out of sight.

"With such a long fall," Livia continued, "interrupted intermittently by impact on the mountain face, there was quite a bit of internal organ damage. The cause of death was determined to be exsanguination due to aortic dissection, meaning the main blood vessel attached to the heart dislodged on impact and he bled to death internally."

Livia pulled pages that she had kept off to the side. "I know you were interested in the Anderson boy's skull fracture. Here's what I found."

Livia slid autopsy photos of Henry Anderson's bare skull across the table.

"There were several fractures noted." Livia pointed to the photo. "Including a large stellate fracture on the posterior right parietal bone."

Sidney shook her head again. "Just like Julian Crist," she said.

Livia nodded. "Not only in the type and location — they both were depressed stellate fractures to the back, right side of the head." Livia slid another page of the report across the desk. "But I also compared the measurements of the fracture taken from Julian Crist's autopsy to the ones taken from Henry Anderson's."

"And?" Sidney asked.

"They are close to identical."

Sidney looked at Livia without blinking. "How close?"

"This is a photo from what you provided of Julian Crist's case." Livia slid another image toward Sidney so that it was next to the photo of Henry's skull.

To Sidney's untrained eyes, each of the young men's shattered craniums looked the same. In fact, if Livia switched the pictures around, Sidney would have difficulty determining whose skull she was looking at.

"The measurements from Henry Anderson's skull fracture were documented to be two and a half centimeters deep, and seven centimeters long. Nearly identical to what was documented in Julian Crist's autopsy."

Sidney ran a hand through her hair. "Jesus Christ."

"There's more," Livia said. "The scalp lacerations are also similar, if not identical."

Livia again arranged the photos from each autopsy next to each other for comparison. Sidney remembered Julian's laceration reminding her of a split in a leather sofa. Henry Anderson's looked the same.

"The measurements of the two lacerations are also the same," Livia said as she sat back in her chair. "I'm not much for conspiracy theories, but if I were a betting woman, I'd say there's a damn good chance these two injuries were caused by the same weapon."

Sidney also sat back away from the photos that were spread across the desk, folded her arms in front of her. "Yeah, well, an old detective already offered that theory. And wagered a shot of whiskey that the same person was swinging that weapon."

Livia shrugged. "I discovered one other thing that you'll find interesting," Livia said.

Sidney leaned forward. "What else?"

"Trace amounts of organza fibers were

detected in Henry Anderson's scalp wound."

CHAPTER 49

Wednesday, July 19, 2017

She'd not eaten all day. Her whirlwind journey had taken her from Alcove Manor and her discussion with Gus Morelli early this morning, to Betty Anderson's home in Sarasota Springs, to Livia Cutty's office. It was 9:00 p.m. when she grabbed a taco from a street cart. Sidney ate while she walked. She promised to keep Detective Morelli abreast of any developments, and after a ten-minute walk, she found herself again in the lobby of Alcove Manor. She checked in at the front desk and found her way back to room 232, where her day had started.

Gus was sitting in the bedside chair, more put together tonight than he had been when he lay in his bed this morning. Sidney took a quick glance at the prosthetic leg that hung from his right hip and bent at the knee to reach the floor.

She knocked from the doorway. "Sorry. Is it too late?"

Gus waved her in. "I didn't expect you back today."

"I promised I'd show you what I had on Julian Crist. And with the day I've had," Sidney said, "I could use another set of eyes."

Sid pulled a thick file folder from her purse. It was the same information on Julian Crist that she had given to Livia Cutty weeks ago when the doctor agreed to help with the documentary. The file felt more sinister now than it had then, when Sidney hoped to find enough evidence hidden in the pages to free Grace Sebold. She placed it on his bedside table.

"That'll be my middle-of-the-night reading," Gus said. "Here," he held out his hand. "I've been sitting too long. I've gotta walk. Do you mind?"

"Of course not," Sidney said, hurrying to his side and helping him stand.

"Got the cancer bug," Gus said. "It was me or my leg. For some reason, I chose me. I'm still getting used to this goddamn thing, but you should have seen me a month ago."

With Sidney holding his hand, Gus took three impressive steps to his walker.

"I know it's hard to imagine," he said.

"But what you just witnessed is as close to a miracle as I've ever seen on this earth. Mind if we take a stroll?"

"No. That's fine."

Sidney kept pace next to him as he shuffled down the hallways with the aid of his walker.

"I do better with a single crutch, but I need to learn to rely on this peg leg. And my armpit is so damn sore, I can't stand the thought of crutches."

"It looks like you're doing just fine," Sidney said.

"I'm out of here in two more weeks. That's my goal." Gus lowered his voice. "I can't take it any longer with these old people in here. And the nurses have had enough of me. It's time I suck it up and get back to my life."

They made it to the end of the hallway and turned to conquer the next stretch of linoleum.

"So let's hear it. You're back so soon not just to give me the kid's information. What did you find?"

Sidney shook her head. "I'm starting to worry that I'm going to owe you that shot of whiskey."

They made a full loop around the unit. His

first, Gus told her, while Sidney explained what she'd learned from Betty Anderson and Livia Cutty. She helped him into bed and watched as he removed his prosthesis.

"It's starting to feel better with the damn thing on than off," Gus said. "I feel naked."

"Maybe that's a good thing," Sidney said.

"I suppose so. Pull the table over, I want to take a look at what you brought me."

Sidney wheeled the table close so that it rested above his bed. Gus went to work, paging through the file. In just a few minutes, he was lost in the details. Sidney let him work, taking a seat in the bedside chair and checking her voice mail. It was filled with urgent messages from Leslie and Graham. Then Graham's final message was disturbingly calm as he explained the deadline for Friday's episode had been missed and the network was taking steps to announce the eighth installment of *The Girl of Sugar Beach* would not air as scheduled.

An hour later, Gus finally spoke.

"Take a look at this," he said, pointing at a page from the file.

Sidney killed her phone and slipped it into the back pocket of her jeans. She leaned over the bed to see what Gus was pointing at.

"These are photos of the Crist boy's clothes, taken by the M.E. in St. Lucia."

Depicted in the photo was Julian's shirt. It had been stretched out on a staging table for photography. The collar was stained red.

"The blood?" Sidney asked.

"No," Gus said, pointing to the bottom of the shirt.

Sidney squinted. On the back of the shirt was a dirt mark in a horseshoe pattern. The smudge was faint and cut off by the bottom of the shirt.

"It says the body was in the ocean all night. I bet this stain was diluted by the salt water."

Sidney remembered her trip to Sugar Beach when she climbed to Soufriere Bluff and stared down at Pitons Bay, where Julian's body had been discovered by two kayakers on their anniversary. It seemed like a lifetime ago that she'd made that initial trip to St. Lucia. So much had happened to her career since she asked the island to tell her its story. Part of her wished she'd never listened.

"Here." Gus removed his reading glasses and hovered them over the photo to act as a magnifying glass.

Sidney peered through them at the enlarged image that captured the mark on the back of Julian's shirt.

"I don't know," she said. "What is it? A shoeprint?"

"Half a shoeprint," Gus said.

He paged through the file until he found the photo of Julian's shorts. They were also drawn out across the staging table. He pointed to an area on the back of the shorts. The blemish on the seat of the shorts was even fainter than the one on the shirt. Gus folded the pictures so the bottom of the shirt aligned with the shorts. The two smudges came together to form a nearly invisible, full shoeprint.

"I'll be damned," Sidney said.

"I'd love to know whose foot produced this."

Sidney leaned closer to get a better look.

"Me too."

It was past 10:00 p.m. when Sidney and Gus packed up the Julian Crist file, which they had spread across the table and around the bed. Gus still had some contacts inside the New York Police Department, and offered to have them take a look at the print on Julian Crist's shirt and shorts. His guys, Gus promised, could confirm that it was indeed a shoeprint, and also run an analysis on the make of the shoe if they were able to get details from the tread.

"I don't want to put you out," Sidney said.

"Are you kidding me?" Gus said. "I haven't felt this alive in years. The last couple of hours were the first time I actually forgot that they took my leg. Please," he said, "let me help."

Sidney nodded her head. "Thanks. Let me know what you find."

"I'll make some calls first thing tomorrow." Gus packed the last of the Crist file. "What's this?" he asked, holding up an envelope.

"Oh," Sidney said, taking her father's letter from him. Inside were the fingernail clippings he had sent months ago for DNA analysis. Sidney had nearly forgotten about them. "It has to do with another case."

"Anything interesting?"

Sidney smiled. "It's a long story."

"I barely sleep at night," Gus said. "I could use a good story to pass the hours."

"Maybe another time. This is a story best told over a couple of proper drinks."

"Now you're just teasing me. I haven't had a drop in months, and this far removed I'm not sure I can go back to the hard stuff. How about we compromise with coffee? I'll buy."

Sidney got the feeling he didn't want to

be alone. The hallways had darkened, and the floor was quiet. "I saw a coffee machine down the hall."

"Now you're talking," Gus said.

She returned a few minutes later with two steaming cups, and sat back down in the bedside chair.

"You really want to hear this story?" Sidney asked, holding up her father's letter.

"No doubt," Gus said.

"Stop me when it gets too bizarre."

"I was a Homicide detective for twenty years. You won't be able to shock me."

As the rehab facility shut down for the night, Sidney sat next to a stranger and for the first time in her life told the story of her father's conviction.

CHAPTER 50

Thursday, July 20, 2017

Early Thursday morning, with her voice
mail filled with messages and unanswered
texts blinking on her phone, Sidney emerged
from the elevator to find her office floor
empty, too early yet for staff to be present.
She walked in and sat behind her desk, immediately assaulted by a barrage of yellow
sticky notes pasted to her computer, her
desk, her phone, and any flat surface available.

Where are you?
Are you alive?
Corporate needs edits today!
Left you several messages, I'm pissed!

They were all written in Leslie's familiar
handwriting.

"Shit," Sidney said to herself. She spun
her chair toward the window to look out
over the city, grabbed her phone from her
purse, and dialed Leslie's number. She

pressed the phone to her ear and heard a chiming ringtone behind her. When she swiveled back around, Leslie stood in the office doorway, holding the ringing phone up for Sidney to see.

"Oh," Leslie said in an exaggerated tone, looking at Sidney's name on the phone. "It's my friend and coproducer calling. Since we're under a shit storm of a deadline and I know she's calling about said shit storm, I think I'll let it go to voice mail."

Sidney ended the call with a quick finger tap. The chiming stopped.

"I'm sorry, Les."

"And then," Leslie said, "when I see that she left a message, plus a thousand texts, I think I'll ignore them all."

"Got it. I'm a bitch."

"And you're selfish. The suits threw a fit yesterday when we missed the deadline. And since none of them could get ahold of you, they took it out on me."

"Yep. They left me a few messages, too. None were very pleasant, if that helps at all."

"It doesn't." Leslie walked into the office and stood in front of the desk. "What the hell, Sid?"

Sidney shook her head. "Look, I'm sorry I was gone yesterday, but we've got a major problem. Or, I don't know, possibly a major problem."

"Yeah. Production needed cuts for episode eight yesterday, and we didn't deliver them. We have nothing decent to give them, and even if we did, there's not enough time to pull an episode together by tomorrow night. So, yeah, I'd say we have a major problem."

"Well," Sidney considered this, "then we've got more than one problem, but mine's bigger than yours."

Leslie crossed her arms over her chest. "What's going on?"

Sidney stared at her producing partner for a moment as yesterday's events spun through her mind.

"I think Grace killed Julian Crist."

Chapter 51

Thursday, July 20, 2017

"Good," Graham said as he entered Sidney's office. "You're here."

"Graham, before you start —"

"Nope," Graham said in a calm voice. "Not before I start, not after I start. I'll talk, you'll listen. You too," he said to Leslie. "You are an employee of this network. I'm your boss. When I call you regarding a deadline, you *call me back.* Not the next day, not a week later. We have millions of dollars tied up in a project that you're producing. None of your staff knew where you were yesterday. No one had answers to why the deadline was being missed. This is not some shit show for Netflix. This is a prime-time production for a major television network. You follow our rules, or we cut you loose. We don't have renegades here. You want to act like some free-spirited filmmaker? Go back to the Internet. The edits were due to production yesterday for Friday's episode. Where are they?"

"Graham."

"Sidney. Are the edits ready?"

"No."

"Why not?"

"Something's come up."

"Did someone in your immediate family die?"

"No."

He pointed his index finger at her like he was throwing a dart. "You signed a contract to produce ten episodes this summer. One episode per week. You outlined that format, you pitched that format, we bought that format. We all understood it would require long hours and tight deadlines, and you promised you could handle it. We took a chance on you, and now we have one of the biggest audiences in television history prepared to tune in tomorrow night for an episode we're not going to air! What the hell, Sid?"

His tie was crooked and the sleeves of his suit jacket had crept up his forearms during his rant.

"Leslie and I were just discussing our options, and we both agree we need a filler episode for tomorrow night."

"Filler?"

"A recap," Sidney said. "A summary episode of what's taken place so far. It's the perfect time for it. It'll help reluctant viewers who don't want to commit to streaming seven hours of television. A recap episode will bring everyone up to date and prime them for the final episodes. Ray Sandberg should love this idea. More viewers mean more money to stuff into his already-fat wallet. And instead of ten episodes, he gets eleven."

"I don't understand your contempt for the success of your own documentary. Yes, the network is making money. But so are you. At least, you stand to, if you don't crap all over this thing. And you're positioned to make much more money when Sandberg offers you a contract to produce another documentary for next summer, which he had planned to do, but hell if that's going to happen now. And at the moment, I don't know that I'm fully behind the idea of rehiring you for another go-round."

"Let's not overreact, Graham. I missed a deadline."

"I'm not concerned with your career today. What's most pressing is that I need an episode for tomorrow night."

Sidney took a deep breath. It had always been a challenge to balance her personal relationship with Graham and the reality of the professional hierarchy at the network. She wanted to call him *an asshole* for screaming at her like a lunatic, and for walking so abruptly out of the bar a couple of nights ago. And she would have done exactly that, had this encounter occurred anywhere but her office, with Leslie as an eyewitness and with the door wide open. Sidney was sure her entire staff was standing on tiptoes just outside her office, craning their necks to hear every syllable. Instead of calling him names, Sidney decided to bluff with the straightest face she could manage.

"Leslie and I will cut the recap episode today. We don't have to shoot anything new besides narrative from me, maybe have the sound guys record some voice-over. All the footage will come from previous episodes. We'll do it this morning and have it to production by this afternoon. I'll work with them all day, and I won't leave until the episode is polished."

"And next week?"

"It'll be an original episode."

Graham ran his hand through his hair, pulled on his cuffs to bring his suit into order. "I'm meeting with Sandberg now. I'll let him know about the recap and that I think it's a good idea."

Sidney felt like he wanted to say something more to her, softer, she imagined, than the tone he had taken to this point. But whatever she saw in his eyes or heard in his voice, all she got was a subtle nod before he turned and walked out of her office.

When he was gone, Leslie opened her palms. "Why didn't you tell him?"

"That the girl I just had exonerated is guilty as sin? A few reasons. One, Sandberg would lose his mind. Two, I'd be fired, which would mean you'd get fired. Three, I wouldn't be able to finish this thing the way I want to end it. And four, I'm not sure about a damn thing yet."

"So what's the plan?"

"I don't know. But I've got a week to figure it out."

CHAPTER 52

Thursday, July 20, 2017

She worked in the production studio without breaks alongside the sound engineers, writers, and the graphic techs. At 3:00 p.m., as instructed, she turned in the cuts for the recap episode. Graham Cromwell and Ray Sandberg quickly voiced their displeasures with her work and delivered a long list of changes. Sidney and Leslie slogged through them until 8:00 p.m. Production waited unhappily as the summer sun set on a Thursday night and darkness covered the city. By nine, they had the final cut of the summary episode, green-lit by the network heads and cued for Friday night's broadcast. Sidney felt no relief. The clock had reset and had begun ticking again. She had less than one week before the next episode was due, and she had no idea what the content would be.

She left the office and dismissed her craving for a Casamigos. Grace Sebold, still stashed away in Ellie Reiser's high-rise, was her next stop. It was a confrontation she had avoided thinking about all day, but one she could put off no longer. She took a cab to Tudor City and found Windsor Tower. Sidney gave her name and waited while the doorman called upstairs. When he gave her the okay, Sidney slid into the elevator just before the doors closed. Grace was waiting in the hallway when the car arrived.

"Hi," Grace said.

Grace looked better than Sidney had ever seen her. Her prematurely graying hair was fashionably styled, a stark change from the matted-down prison do that Sidney had known from her visits to St. Lucia. Allowed to pamper herself with products other than prison-issued bar soap and foam shampoo, including assistance from a layer of foundation and blush that hid the pallor of her skin, the transformation was remarkable.

"Wow. You look . . . Is it cliché to say *beautiful*?"

Grace smiled. "I don't care if it's cliché, it's the first time someone's called me that in years. I actually feel like a *person* again. Come in."

Sidney walked into the apartment. The long windows were filled with the lights of

New York City.

"No Derrick?" Grace asked.

"No. We'll get more footage later. Maybe next week. I need to talk with you about something that's come up."

"Sure. Whatever you need. Ellie's not home from work yet. She was called in for a delivery."

"Who is it?" came a voice from the other room.

Sidney recognized the slightly slurred speech of Marshall Sebold.

"It's Sidney," Grace said. "He's been more" — Grace wobbled her head back and forth as she chose a word — "outgoing since I've been home. My parents tell me, anyway. They said he had coiled into himself the last few years, but now he's talking more. It's a good thing, but with guests he can be a little overwhelming."

"Marshall and I have met before," Sidney said. "Even before the other night. I spoke with him when I interviewed your parents originally. We actually played a game of chess."

Grace smiled. "Of course, you did. He can sucker anyone into a game. He's such a con man."

They walked into the large living room, decorated with contemporary furniture and modern art. Everything was at sharp-right angles. *Ellie Reiser,* Sidney thought again, *is doing well for herself.*

"Marshall," Grace said. "You remember Sidney, don't you?"

Marshall sank into his wheelchair and looked down at his lap, his curled wrists and atrophied fingers slinking between his knees.

Sidney smiled. "Hi, Marshall."

"Do you want to play chess?" Marshall asked, his voice muffled as he spoke into his chest.

"Sidney didn't come to play chess, Marshall."

"Just one game. Like before," Marshall said.

Grace looked at Sidney and smiled. "Sorry. He's a little stir-crazy locked away up here with me. As soon as we're done shooting whatever remaining scenes you need, Marshall and I are thinking of heading up to Ellie's lake house for a change of scenery. It'll be good for both of us."

"Probably a good idea."

"Will you play?" Marshall asked again.

Sidney shrugged. "I'll have a game, Marshall. You'll remember that I'm not very good."

"You're a saint," Grace said. She looked

at Marshall. "One game. A fast one."

Marshall took his hands from his lap and placed them on the wheels of his chair to roll himself into the den, where his chess set waited. As he passed Grace, she stuck her foot out and stopped the wheelchair's progress.

"But only if you walk," she said.

Marshall looked up from his chair, took his hands from the wheels, and placed them back into his lap, his chin falling again to his chest.

"Nope," Grace said. "That works on Mom, not on me. You either walk to the den and sit on the couch, or Sidney doesn't play with you."

Sidney stood quietly as she watched the interaction between the siblings, catching both an aura of friendship and the maternal nature of an older sister who likely had been the only person, besides his parents, that Marshall could rely upon.

"Do you want to play or not?" Grace asked.

Finally Marshall pushed himself up from his wheelchair and walked to the den in only a slightly altered gait, his orthotic shoes clapping as he marched. As soon as he sat on the couch and began to assemble the chess set, his curled wrists and stiff fingers magically unfolded as he gripped the pieces to place them on the board. The transformation in stature, Sidney noted, was remarkable. She remembered something similar from weeks before at the Sebolds' home.

"He can do a lot on his own," Grace said. "But he has to be pushed. The TBI, the brain injury, has led to progressive muscular dystrophy. If he doesn't use his muscles, he'll lose them. He never used to be this bad. It nearly broke my heart the first time I saw him in a wheelchair when he visited me at Bordelais. I was shocked to get home and see that it had progressed so much. My damn parents haven't been making him help himself for years. Without motivation, he'll just sit in that chair and let his body atrophy to the point of brittleness. He doesn't know any better. He can't help himself unless he's reminded. Now that I'm around, he's reminded often. More than he likes. I think he's getting tired of me."

"I doubt that," Sidney said.

"Chess is his only interest. When he plays chess, his physical ailments disappear. His muscles loosen and he can use his hands and fingers just as well as you or me. His speech improves and the slur disappears. The doctors explain it as tapping into a small portion of his brain that he can't access any other way than through the analytics of chess. When he utilizes this part of his mind, it supersedes his physical limitations. Essentially, when he's playing chess, he's his old self. Even though he doesn't notice the change — at least, he's never mentioned it — I think it's why he likes playing so much."

"That's amazing," Sidney said, watching Marshall sit and move as if he had no physical ailment. "He walks really well."

"It was worse just after I got home. It's better now in just a few days since I've been pushing him. I remember the doctors telling us, you know, before I went away, that with physical therapy he could reasonably walk for many years, well into his thirties. Maybe even his forties, before he was confined permanently to a wheelchair. I just have to stay on him. My parents . . . I love them, but Marshall has been a lot to handle. He'll need more help than I can give him, but my parents were ready to shuffle him off to a full-care facility. He's not ready for that, and neither am I. As soon as things settle down with the media, I hope to move back home and take better care of him until I can get a place of my own."

Sidney blinked as she stared at Grace. Seeing her with Marshall made this visit harder than it was already going to be. "You're a good sister."

"I'll make coffee. Go play chess, then we'll talk. What's going on, by the way? Any problems?"

Sidney hesitated before she answered. "I'm not sure yet."

Grace gave a quizzical expression. She nodded toward the kitchen. "We'll talk when you're done." She squeezed Sidney's wrist. "Thank you for playing with him, and for treating him like . . . an equal."

Grace headed to the kitchen, and Sidney turned to the den, where Marshall was organizing the pieces on his new chessboard, the one his sister had purchased for him on her return home after ten years in jail. She walked into the den and sat down across from him.

"I like the new chess set," Sidney said.

Marshall offered an indifferent look. "It's not as nice as my old one."

Sidney remembered the Lladró porcelain set from weeks before when she played chess in Marshall's bedroom. The intricate medieval pieces replaced now with traditional wooden figures. The cheap, composite plastic chess case she looked at today seemed quite a leap from the elaborate, pinewood cases that held the competing black and white Lladró pieces.

"Why did Grace buy you a new one? Your old chess set was beautiful."

"She doesn't like to play on the old one. It brings back bad memories for her, so she asked me to put it away. For as long as she was gone, I did. I only took it down once, when you and I played."

"Why does it bring back bad memories for her?"

Marshall shrugged. "Just reminds her of her old life. She wants a new life now. I don't blame her. Like this chess set, I think she's hoping her new life will be simpler than her old one. Black or white?" Marshall asked.

Sidney looked down at the pieces. "White."

He pushed the stray pieces from his previous game with Grace over to Sidney. She arranged them in order.

"You open," Marshall said.

Sidney moved her pawn forward.

Marshall quickly advanced his own pawn, immediately opposite.

"Why do you like chess so much?" Sidney asked.

Marshall shrugged. "I don't know."

"No idea?"

"I guess it's because I used to play football, and chess is a way to compete."

"Your mom tells me that you were quite a star in high school."

Marshall stayed quiet.

"You still miss it? Football?"

He shrugged again. "I don't watch it. I've never been able to watch an NFL or college game. It just makes me think of . . . what might have been."

"Chess brings out that competitive edge. Is that why you never lose?"

"I lose," Marshall said. "I just don't like it when I do."

Sidney looked toward the kitchen. Grace was out of sight. Sidney heard the faucet running as Grace filled the coffee pot. She looked back to Marshall.

"When we talked last time," Sidney said, "when you and I played chess at your house, you told me that you knew a lot about Grace's friends."

"Yeah," Marshall said, staring at the chessboard.

"That you listened a lot, and that people underestimated your awareness."

"I remember."

Sidney hesitated just a moment. "What can you tell me about Henry Anderson?"

The mention of Grace's high school boyfriend caused Marshall to look up from

461

the chess pieces. He made eye contact just briefly before returning his gaze to the board.

"What do you want to know?"

Sidney paused again. "I want to know how the same thing could happen to two different people who loved your sister."

A long stretch of silence followed, while Marshall scrutinized the chessboard, before he spoke.

"You know, it's funny. I was thinking about the last time we played chess, too," he finally said, looking up from the board. "You told me that everyone involved in my accident likely had regrets about it. That Ellie, especially, must carry remorse for that night. You remember telling me that?"

"I do," Sidney said. "Are you still angry at Ellie because of the accident?"

Marshall shook his head. "I was never mad at Ellie."

"No?"

"No," Marshall said. "She wasn't driving."

Sidney sat back. She sensed something happening between them, stayed silent.

"Grace insisted on driving," he said. "Ellie offered, but Grace got behind the wheel, anyway. Ellie knew the consequences for Grace. Her best friend drunk and in a bad car accident. Neither of them was injured, so before the police arrived, they switched places and Ellie climbed behind the wheel. The other driver, the U-Haul guy, had been drinking. The blame fell on him, which was perfect for Ellie and Grace. It took them both off the hook. For me" — Marshall looked back down at the board — "it didn't really matter."

Another moment of silence fell between them.

"What does that have to do with Henry Anderson?" Sidney asked.

"I was mad at Grace for a long time. She got away with it, and I was stuck the way I am. Bad back then, worse today. Worse still, in the future. But my anger at Grace didn't last. The two of us? We have a connection that no one else understands."

"Because you saved her? When you donated your bone marrow?"

"Yeah, that's part of it. But lots of people donate marrow. After the accident, I realized that I needed her to help me when my body fails. Grace knew it, too. I couldn't stay angry with her for long. And I was relieved when she came home."

"Still, Marshall, how does Henry Anderson play into all of this?"

"Now that Grace is back, I refuse to lose her again. I've kept their secret long enough."

"Ellie and Grace's secret? About the accident?"

"And all the other secrets that group has hidden and buried."

Sidney glanced toward the kitchen, then back to Marshall. "What other secrets?"

Marshall cocked his head as he analyzed the board in front of him and contemplated his next move.

"Marshall, what other secrets?"

"You figured out that Daniel and Ellie were the only friends who stayed in contact with Grace. You have to know by now that they are both in love with her. It must be obvious to you."

Sidney blinked a few times. Leaned forward slightly. "In love with Grace?"

"It's sad. Even today, all these years later." Marshall moved his rook.

"You mean they *love* Grace. They're not *in* love with Grace."

"No," Marshall said, finally looking into Sidney's eyes. "I said it right the first time."

Sidney waited without speaking as Marshall leaned over, opened the desk drawer, and pulled out a cloth bag. It contained Grace's love lock, which Marshall held up.

"You know she kept this the whole time my sister was gone?"

"Who?"

"Ellie. She kept it hidden away after Grace went to prison. It was important that no one found it after Sugar Beach. She probably pretended it belonged to her, and tried to ignore what it really represented. I was surprised she actually handed it over when Grace was allowed a few personal items in jail. They both hate this love lock. Daniel and Ellie. They each wanted their own name under Grace's."

He dropped it back into the long cloth bag and handed it to Sidney, who slipped the large, antique love lock into her hand with a strange feeling of foreboding in her gut.

"Ellie or Daniel hated the names on that lock."

Sidney looked down at the lock. It was as big as her palm. Heavy and old, a two-pronged key extended from the locking mechanism at the bottom. Etched onto the surface were two names: *Grace & Julian.*

It was just as Sidney remembered from the first time Grace showed her the lock at the Bordelais Correctional Facility.

"They hate names?" Sidney said. "Grace and Julian?"

"Julian and Henry," Marshall said, analyzing the chessboard again.

"Henry's name is not on this lock, Marshall."

"Not anymore. It used to be. Underneath."

Sidney looked more closely at the lock and noticed the scuffs in the surface where Julian's name was located. Sidney imagined Henry's name scrawled there originally, scratched over and erased some years later to produce a clean slate for Julian's title. The weight in her stomach grew heavier.

"That lock has been a dangerous thing over the years," Marshall said. "It's caused a lot of pain. But I'm done keeping secrets." He shook his head. "My loyalty is waning. I know everyone underestimates me. Assumes I'm unaware of the things that go on around me. But I'm not going to let the same thing happen again. I warned Grace that I wouldn't."

"Warned Grace about what?" Sidney asked.

"You've obviously looked into Henry Anderson's case. I know what you must be thinking. Grace will never tell you the truth. She's too loyal. I don't want my sister tried again for a crime she didn't commit."

Marshall tapped the chessboard with his finger.

"Your move," he said. "Make it a good one."

Sidney looked around the den, and then glanced toward the kitchen one last time. She heard the coffeepot gurgling and Grace clinking the mugs as she pulled them from the cabinet. Sidney slipped the love lock back into the mesh satchel. As she did, she felt its smooth, rounded edge. Her mind flashed to the side-by-side photos of Julian and Henry's skull fractures that Livia Cutty had shown her the day before. The vein in Sidney's neck pulsed more rapidly. Her breathing became shallow and inefficient.

She mindlessly moved chess pieces for another sixteen minutes until Marshall announced checkmate.

CHAPTER 53

Friday, July 21, 2017

On Friday morning, Sidney stood outside the New York Office of the Chief Medical Examiner. She paced for a few minutes while she waited. The sun was just up, casting the city in a lavender radiance as it peeked over Brooklyn and slid its reflection along the East River. Derrick leaned against the building's façade, his back against the brick and his Ikegami camera on the sidewalk next to him.

Livia Cutty appeared from around the corner, offered a quick good morning, keyed the front door, and all three headed inside. Ten minutes later, they were in the basement morgue.

"I wish I could get my hands on another cadaver," Livia said. "But they're not easy to come by. We only scored the two in Raleigh because we used them for the end-of-the-year project. If you give me a week, I might be able to pull some strings."

Sidney shook her head. "I don't have a week."

"Then the Synbone and pigskin will have to do," Livia said. "As you saw during the original experiments, they are remarkably similar to human bone and skin. This wouldn't hold up in a courtroom, but for what you're after, it'll be just fine." Livia lifted her chin to Sidney. "Let's have a look."

Derrick was already filming when Sidney pulled Grace Sebold's love lock from her purse. She'd placed it there last night after her chess game with Marshall and before claiming a headache to avoid having the conversation she had originally planned with Grace. It had been an abrupt and awkward departure, but with her mind processing so many things at once, Sidney could think of no more graceful way to get out of the apartment. She had called Livia on the way home and arranged this morning's meeting.

She handed the mesh satchel to Livia, who poured the lock into her hand.

"Well," Livia said, "it's heavy enough. And the edges are smooth and round."

"Do you think it could cause Henry or Julian's skull fracture?" Sidney asked.

"Let's find out."

Dr. Cutty got down to business. Next to the morgue table was a Synbone replica of a human skull. Sidney remembered the polyurethane imitation that closely resembled human bone from when Cutty and her cohorts used them in Raleigh, along with cadavers, to disprove the boat oar theory. Livia draped the back of the skull model with pigskin, which contained an adhesive interface that tightly gripped the synthetic skull. She set the model on a pole and adjusted its height to six feet two inches to match Julian Crist.

Livia dropped the lock back into the satchel and cinched the strings together. Then she grasped the top of the sack in her fist like she was swinging a sock filled with lead, which she was. She stepped behind the skull on the pole, took an aggressive kickboxing stance, raised the satchel and love lock over her right shoulder, and finally brought it down hard onto the synthetic bone.

The sound of impact was less sickening than when Livia had struck Damian the cadaver, but it still sent a shock wave through Sidney.

"Let's see the damage," Livia said.

She handed the love lock to Sidney and pulled the Synbone cranium off the pole.

Like husking a coconut, she peeled away the pigskin to reveal the bare polyurethane beneath. Livia noticed immediately that the synthetic material was splintered with a dramatic depression fracture, which made her pulse quicken. She waved Sidney over, and together they viewed the damage while comparing it to the enlarged photos from Julian and Henry's autopsies.

Livia used a measuring device to determine the depth of the break in the Synbone, as well as the length and width. She took the measurements silently, and then looked at Sidney. The YouTube video of Livia's cadaver experiment had gone viral, with close to 20 million views. Dr. Cutty's stock had risen in the circle of forensic medicine, and her celebrity had spawned interview requests and invitations to author chapters in forthcoming pathology textbooks. She had received a score of calls from defense attorneys around the country (and one in the U.K.) inviting her to consult (lucratively) on their cases. She was readying to start her first job after fellowship at the prestigious New York Office of the Chief Medical Examiner, and by all accounts, Dr. Cutty needed no more enhancements to her profile. Yet, the scene in front of her was certain to bring it.

"Same depth," Livia said. "About three centimeters. This could vary, obviously, on how hard the lock was swung. But the length and width of the fractures are a spot-on match. At least similar enough to argue that they were produced by the love lock."

Sidney ran a hand through her hair and looked briefly at Derrick, who hadn't taken his eye away from the viewfinder.

"Let's run a fiber analysis on that satchel," Livia said. "See if it's made from organza nylon."

CHAPTER 54

Friday, July 21, 2017

It was Friday evening, just about the time the season recap episode of *The Girl of Sugar Beach* was airing, when Sidney shut down her computer. She had just strung together the footage Derrick had taken this morning in Livia Cutty's morgue. What, exactly, she was planning to do with it was not yet clear. Graham had stormed into her office earlier in the day to show her the latest test audience numbers, which indicated that 95 percent of viewers would be satisfied with Grace Sebold's exoneration, which was scheduled to be shown in the final portion of episode ten. Graham also revealed the proposed outlines the executive team had created that detailed the content for episodes eight and nine. Sidney listened to Graham's pitch with the type of deaf concentration of someone with more pressing matters on her mind.

When he left, she had spent the rest of the afternoon buried in Julian Crist's file, reading and re-reading the information, until she found what she was looking for. She remembered Don Markus, the detective she had interviewed early in the documentary, having mentioned the document. It was buried in the reams of information that came from the St. Lucian Police Force, but after a page-by-page search, she'd located it. The find sent her mind off on a tangent until she put together its potential use. Now, at nearly 8:00 p.m., at the end of a whirlwind week, black circles grew darker under her eyes and a fluttering twitch took to her left eyelid. The pressure of what she had discovered, and the anxiety of being on the brink of proving it, had exhausted her and she still needed to make one more stop tonight. Without warning, the deep, practiced voice of Luke Barrington filled her office. It was sure to add to her stress level.

"I hear you're causing quite a fuss for the brass around this place," Luke said.

Sidney grabbed the thumb drive that contained her edits from the past two hours and dropped it in her purse, which she hung over her shoulder.

"I was just leaving, Luke. Do you need

anything, or are you just here to give me grief?"

"I'm here to tell you I'm proud of you."

She was collecting the pages from Julian Crist's file and preparing to walk past him without offering eye contact, but his sentence stopped her. She stood upright behind her desk and stared at him.

"I'm not much for humility," Luke said, "so take this for what it's worth. You've got them running scared, I hope you know that."

"Who?"

"The suits. They consider you a loose cannon, but they also know you're a talented producer. They hate you for not conforming to their way of doing things, but they love you for creating a show that twenty-plus million people are watching each week, and on which advertisers are fighting for space. For executives at a major network, you scare the hell out of them. You make them money, but you're unpredictable."

"And what? They sent you to rein me in?"

"Yes. They talked with me about it. I told them I'd talk with you."

"Luke, I missed a deadline. It's not the end of the world, and in the grand scheme —"

"Don't do it their way," Luke said, cutting her off.

"What?"

"Do it *your* way. Shit, Sidney, if I could start my career over and take a path that more closely represented my interests, I'd do it in a second. Instead, here I sit. I'm a ratings whore. I live by my ratings, and eventually I'll die by them. I've painted myself into such a tight corner that I don't even get to choose my stories anymore. I have to stick with the masses. They tell me what to feature, and I do it. If I run something that's not a ratings giant, I'm a failure. Don't set your career on the same course."

"Why are you telling me this?"

"Because I know what you're after. And I compare it to what I chased my entire career. I was after fame and fortune. You're after the truth. What I could never figure out until watching you over the last few months is that you don't have to chase one or the other. But you've got to start off looking for the truth, not the other way around."

A slight smile came to Sidney's face. "I'm not sure Ray Sandberg would appreciate the advice you're giving me."

Luke smiled also. "Fuck 'em." He turned to leave. "Can't wait to see the final episodes. But do them your way."

For the first time since knowing him, when Luke Barrington left her, there was no cavernous ringing in her ears.

Although it was a dump of an episode, created because new findings had caused her to question how she wanted to proceed with the documentary, Sidney refused to produce substandard work. She and Leslie made sure the episode was a well-constructed and entertaining retelling of the previous seven installments that summarized the details of Julian Crist's death and Grace Sebold's incarceration, the holes that existed in her conviction, the mistakes in judgment and procedure made by the St. Lucian Police Force, and an explanation for the evidence against Grace Sebold.

Anyone interested in jumping into the documentary now had an opportunity to get caught up in sixty minutes. Her problem was where she went from here. She knew, in light of recent developments, that Graham's outline for the final three episodes was garbage. The way the executives wanted the documentary to end — nice and neat, with a big red bow tied to Grace Sebold's exoneration — was not going to happen. Once Henry Anderson's death was revealed, all hell would break loose. And if she moved forward with her theory about the love lock and who had swung it, there was no chance of wrapping things up in three weeks.

She hailed a cab and paid the fare twenty minutes later when the driver pulled to the front of the Alcove Manor. She checked in at the front desk, stuck her name tag onto her blouse, and rode the elevator. She found Gus Morelli sitting in his bedside chair watching the recap episode. He pulled his gaze from the television when she walked in, then pointed to the screen.

"What the hell is this?"

"A summary episode."

"I just cringe watched the whole season, I don't need a recap."

"*Binge* watched. And I missed a deadline, thanks to your letter. This is what you get."

Gus muted the television. "What did you find?"

"The skull fractures are the same," Sidney said.

He narrowed his eyes. "How do you know for sure?"

"The M.E. compared Henry's skull fractures from autopsy to Julian Crist's. They're nearly identical."

"Son of a bitch," Gus said.

"And," Sidney said, "I think I found the murder weapon."

Gus shook his head like it was too much, then waved his hand. "Help me up. I've gotta walk while you tell me this story."

A few minutes later, Sidney walked next to Gus as he shuffled down the hallway, his walker sliding over the linoleum as he limped on his prosthesis. She told the story of the last twenty-four hours, her aborted attempt to confront Grace Sebold, her cryptic chess match with Marshall, the love lock, and her visit to Dr. Cutty's morgue this morning.

"That's a helluva find," Gus said.

"Now the question is, what do I do with it? I've got to talk to Mrs. Anderson again to let her know what we found and to see what she wants to do about it. Then I've got to talk to the police."

Gus shook his head. "Reopening a twenty-year-old case is never tops on their list. They weren't keen on it when I tried after eight years. But with enough evidence and pressure, like you might be able to bring, they won't be able to ignore it. The other issue is that she just got out of jail."

"Grace?"

"Yes. She was exonerated by a foreign government, and I'd have to check the books to make sure, but I don't think St. Lucia has a law against double jeopardy. So it's possible that she could be retried for the same crime down there. Plus a new trial for Henry Anderson here in the U.S."

"Unless it wasn't her," Sidney said.

Gus stopped shuffling and looked at her.

Sidney shook her head. "You talked about instinct before. That you sometimes relied on it when you were working. Well, my instincts are telling me that it wasn't Grace."

"Then who was it?"

"I don't know. One of her friends. Ellie Reiser."

"Where does this theory come from?"

"Something Marshall Sebold told me. I get this feeling he knows more than anyone has given him credit for. I also get the feeling that whole group from Sugar Beach has secrets. That they're covering for each other. The same group that was in Sugar Beach was also at Whiteface Mountain when Henry Anderson died."

"Wild theories might make great television," Gus said. "But police hate them."

"What if we had more than a theory?" Sidney asked as they rounded the corner and continued along the hallway back toward Gus's room.

"Such as?"

"Have you made any progress on the shoe-print you found on Julian's shirt?"

Gus shook his head. "I made some calls today. I've got an old friend looking into it for me. Probably hear back in a day or two."

"If you dig into Julian's file, which I did for most of the afternoon today, you'll see that the St. Lucian Police Force took samples of all the shoeprints they found on the bluff. They also confiscated many shoes from the guests at Sugar Beach, including everyone in the wedding party, to see if they matched. When they found a hit on Grace's shoe, they stopped there. But that document was still in the file. It contained a list of everyone's shoes. Type of tread, size, and the corresponding make and manufacturer. A detective friend of mine helped me out with one of the early episodes. He brought this document to my attention. What I need to do is get an ID on the type of shoe that caused the print you found on Julian's shirt and shorts, and then cross-reference it to see if it matches any of the prints logged by the St. Lucian Police Force. If we get a match . . ."

"Then you've got some proof and not just a theory. What if it comes back as the Sebold girl's shoe?"

"Then I owe you that shot of Johnnie Walker. But I'm worried that we're going to find it belongs to someone else."

"And if it does match her friend?" Gus asked.

"Then we go to the police. At that point, this thing will have gotten bigger than the biggest documentary in television history."

They made it back to Gus's room. He took a few steps without the aid of the walker and sat on the edge of the bed.

"In case I can somehow salvage this thing," Sidney said. "Are you interested in appearing in my documentary? I'd love to show my audience the letter you sent that started me along this road, and introduce them to the man who for twenty years never let the memory of Henry Anderson fade."

Gus looked at the television. Dr. Cutty was staring into the camera, as if speaking directly to him, explaining her findings from when she had conducted her experiment weeks before on the cadavers. Slowly Gus nodded.

"I think I'd be okay with that."

"Excellent. I'll be in touch. I'll bring my crew for the interview. When your guy gets back to you about the print, let me know."

"Thanks," Gus said. The edges of his lips turned up slightly.

Sidney noticed and lifted her chin. She had never seen the man smile during the hours she had spent with him. "Excited about your television debut?"

"No," Gus said. "I don't give a crap about being on television. But it feels good to feel like a cop again."

CHAPTER 55

Saturday, July 22, 2017

Derrick stood in Central Park with his equipment bag on the ground next to him and his backpack strapped over his shoulders. He'd done a lot for this documentary in the last few months: traveling to St. Lucia, late-night shoots with seedy detectives, filming dead bodies being knocked around in a morgue. He was, as the reckless players liked to say at his card games, all in. So when Sidney called him late last night and asked for a favor on Saturday afternoon, he never considered saying no.

He spotted Grace when she entered the park. She wore big aviator sunglasses, which hid her eyes, and an NYU hat pulled low over her head. She was a quasi-celebrity and still keeping a low profile. Unlike their shoot at the Montauk Point Lighthouse, which was remote and isolated and allowed Grace Sebold some freedom, Central Park was congested on Saturday afternoon. The disguise was necessary. But the park had been one of her favorite spots, and she wanted to do the interview there.

Derrick waved when Grace was closer and they moved to a secluded bench under a maple tree.

"Where's Sidney?" Grace asked.

Derrick smiled and delivered the favor he promised. "She's running late. She'll be here in a bit."

He pointed toward Belvedere Castle. "Let's get some stills by the castle and at the Ramble before it gets too crowded. Sidney will be here by the time we're done."

Grace nodded, pulled the cap lower on her head, and followed Derrick as they walked through Central Park.

CHAPTER 56

Saturday, July 22, 2017

Sidney rode the elevator in Windsor Tower and exited on Ellie Reiser's floor. She knocked on the apartment door and waited until Marshall answered.

"She's not here," he said when he opened the door in his wheelchair.

"I know," Sidney said. "I came to talk with you."

Marshall backed his wheelchair up, turned around, and headed into the living room. Sidney walked into the apartment and closed the door. She followed Marshall into the main room, where she saw his chess set arranged on the table. He rolled his chair up to it and looked at her.

"You beat me pretty easily the other night," Sidney said. "I don't think I'm much of a challenge for you."

"That game wasn't about winning or losing," Marshall said as he wheeled himself to the chessboard.

"I need to ask you some questions, Marshall. About what you told me the other night."

Sidney wanted to speak with Marshall without Grace being present. Derrick had taken care of Grace; and Sidney knew that to get Marshall in the right frame of mind, she'd have to do it over a game of chess. She sat across the coffee table from him. The metamorphosis took shape again as Sidney watched his wrists unfurl and his sclerotic posture loosen when Marshall took hold of the chess pieces and arranged them across the board.

As she sat down, Sidney noticed one of the pinewood cases and recognized it immediately. She saw the edge of the second pinewood case inside the white cloth bag that rested next to the chessboard. "This is your old chess set," she said.

Marshall nodded as he continued to arrange the cheap, wooden pieces on the board in front of him. "I brought it with me when we came here. It was before I knew Grace had bought me this new set."

"Why is it out? I thought you said it brought back bad memories for Grace."

"Grace isn't here," Marshall said. "I might use it today."

Once the board was complete, Marshall opened by advancing a pawn. Sidney did the same.

"I wanted to talk with you, Marshall, about what you told me the other night."

"Okay," he said, moving another pawn.

"And about what happened at Sugar Beach."

"I figured you would," he said. "You probably also want to know more about Henry Anderson." He regarded the board in front of him. "It's probably why you're here and Grace is somewhere else, thinking she's going to meet you. Ellie's at work, as I'm sure you know."

The openness of the discussion paused her arm as she reached for a chess piece. "I'm trying to make sense of it all," Sidney said. "And yes, I wanted to speak with you alone. You told me that you're used to people underestimating you. I'm not like most people. I know you can help me. And I think that if you help me, you'll help your sister, too."

"Probably." He pointed at the board. "Your move."

Sidney advanced a pawn.

Marshall picked up his own pawn. "In the tiny world of chess, have you ever wondered how crappy it is to be a pawn?"

Sidney's lips came together and her forehead wrinkled. "No, I can't say I've ever considered that line of thought."

"Their only role is sacrifice and diversion."

Marshall placed the pawn back onto the board, advanced it forward.

"Your move."

Sidney allowed the dodge to pass in silence. Marshall was growing nervous, and Sidney knew she'd have to push him.

Sidney picked up her knight. "Will you help me, Marshall? Tell me what you know? Because I think you know a great deal about Grace and her friends."

He stayed silent and stared at the board.

"I think you know the truth, Marshall. And I think it's finally time for you to share it."

"I know that if you think Grace killed them, you'd be wrong. And if you make a big deal about Henry in the documentary, the public will convict her, like they did last time. She can't handle it again, and I won't sit quietly this time while she is tried for Henry and retried for Julian. I did that once before."

"I don't think Grace killed them. I came here today to find out if I'm correct about who did." Sidney put her knight down.

"Marshall, help me. Tell me what you know, and I promise we'll do the right thing. You and Grace and me. Together, we'll make this right."

Marshall pointed to the credenza, which stood in front of the window. "It's in there. She actually showed it to Grace last night."

Sidney slowly turned her gaze toward the credenza and spotted a thick, hard-covered book. She walked over and looked down at it, a high-school yearbook from 1999.

"This?" Sidney asked.

"Bring it here. I'll show you."

She carried the yearbook over and handed it to Marshall, who flipped through the pages with only slight difficulty. He placed it down when he reached his desired location. Sidney looked at the page covered by photos of girls in chemistry lab, safety goggles on their faces and short white lab coats. She recognized Grace and Ellie in a photo on the bottom left of the page. A message in dark Sharpie marker was scrawled across the photo: *Ellie & Grace, nothing will separate us!*

"She searched for the love lock last night," Marshall said. "I could only laugh at her stupidity."

"Was Ellie responsible for Henry and Julian?" Sidney asked. "Did she have something to do with their deaths, Marshall?"

The yearbook lay open on the coffee table next to the chessboard. Marshall reached for a chess piece, but Sidney put her hand softly on his. He looked up at her.

"Tell me what you know, Marshall," Sidney said. "Tell me about Ellie. Don't keep your secret any longer."

An awkward moment of silence followed while Marshall stared at her.

"You have to give me Grace's lock back. She'd be upset if she knew I gave it to you. She'll be upset no matter what, but I don't see what else I can do now."

Sidney slowly nodded. She reached into her purse and removed Grace's love lock, placing it, and the satchel that held it, on the open yearbook.

"She's always had a strange affection for Grace. She took the blame for my accident in order to protect Grace, and she carried that burden all this time. She told Julian about Grace and Daniel's past hoping it would keep Grace and Julian apart. When that didn't work . . ."

Marshall pointed at the items on the coffee table. Sidney looked at the love lock, the open yearbook. She saw again Marshall's old chess set just as her phone rang.

Marshall moved his gaze back to the game

491

and scrutinized the board while Sidney dug her phone from her purse.

"Hello?" Sidney said, holding the phone to her ear.

"Hey, it's me."

"Gus?"

"Yeah. My guy just called with an ID on that print."

Sidney waited.

"I think I got it wrong," Gus said. "The lab guys took a look. It was hard to ID because the print was so faint and the kid's shirt was folded. Half the print was on the shirt, with the other half on the shorts, and the picture isn't great. Anyway, it came back as a man's size thirteen. So, unless our girl has some monster feet, I think *I'll* be buying *you* that shot."

"Size thirteen?" Sidney said.

"Yeah. Definitely not a woman's shoe," Gus said. "I know you were talking about the Sebold girl's other friend. The Greaves kid. Daniel? You'll have to see if it matches. Was he on the list you found?"

"Yes," Sidney said, remembering Daniel's name marked on the list from the St. Lucian Police Department's file. Sidney looked at the open yearbook. The picture of Grace and Ellie stared back at her. "That's not the news I was expecting."

"My guy mentioned something else," Gus said. "The print came from a Pro-Line orthotic shoe. Pro-Line makes this type of specialty shoe for people with gait problems. My guy's still working on the specs, but he thinks he narrowed it down to a specialty shoe for someone with neuropathy in their feet, or some other neurological problem that causes a degradation in gross motor skills and makes walking difficult. That make any sense to you?"

CHAPTER 57

Saturday, July 22, 2017

After thirty minutes in Central Park, Grace figured it out. Derrick was a bad actor and a worse liar, and as soon as the plan dawned on Grace, she pushed herself off the railing of Belvedere Castle and ran toward Tudor City. Being alone with Marshall was a terrible idea, especially if Sidney had pieced together Grace's past and was looking to confirm things by extracting information from him.

Grace ran out of the mouth of the park, hat pulled low and sunglasses hiding her face. Somewhere along the journey, her hat blew off or was knocked off when she sideswiped a fellow pedestrian. Grace never hesitated as the hat spiraled on the sidewalk. She kept a frantic pace toward Windsor Tower.

Henry Anderson had been her first mistake. Falling in love so soon after the accident was a miscalculation, considering Marshall's fits of rage. Grace and her parents were shocked when they first saw the wrath in Marshall's eyes when he became angry that first year after the accident. They'd quickly learned that this behavior was common in TBI patients, and it took many months to understand how to manage Marshall's anger. But Grace was young, and the love she felt for Henry Anderson was real and not easily ignored. She should have predicted how Marshall would respond. But despite the metamorphosis in mood and temperament that Marshall went through in the months after the accident, anticipating that her younger brother was capable of murder was impossible. At the time, Grace did not fully understand the "new" Marshall that was evolving. She had no idea that his damaged brain had changed him so completely. And she was clueless to how helpless Marshall was when these dark fits of rage came over him.

Back then, she didn't understand how far Marshall would go to ensure that Grace stayed by his side as the chronic and progressive damage from his trauma stole his independence. Things came clearly into focus, however, the night of Henry's death when Marshall entered their hotel room at

Whiteface Mountain and asked to have a game of chess. Then, while they played on the Lladró chess set she had given him after the accident, Marshall calmly confessed that he not only knew where Henry's body was located, but how it had gotten there.

"I'm going to be helpless, Grace. I can already feel it in my hands and feet. The damage to my brain will eventually leave me withered and destitute. I heard the doctor tell Mom and Dad what to expect. You're the only one who will take care of me. You and I are connected, Grace. Since we were kids. It's always been you and me. We have to keep it that way."

As Grace ran now down the subway stairs, she remembered Marshall's confession. She remembered her revelation from that night as well. She was no longer talking to her brother, but instead some damaged version of him. A stranger she had created with her bad decisions that fateful night when she climbed behind the wheel of their car. It was Grace who had decided to leave the party that night. It was Grace who had insisted on driving, despite Marshall's pleas that he take the wheel. It was Grace's decision to ignore the most logical solution of allowing Ellie to handle the responsibility.

As Grace slipped into the subway car just

as the doors were closing, she remembered again that game of chess when Marshall confessed to what he'd done to Henry. She remembered the corner of one of the pine-wood chess cases, which was stained pink from Henry's blood having soaked through the nylon bag Marshall always carried his chess set in. She remembered her promise, too. Her promise of silence. Her promise to allow Henry's death forever to be considered an accident, as police had defined it. She remembered her pledge of loyalty to Marshall, and her commitment that she would forever be by his side as his condition worsened. She remembered their mutual understanding of their existence: Grace would not be here without Marshall, and Marshall without Grace. She was alive because Marshall had saved her. Marshall was alive because Grace needed to be saved. Even if their parents would not admit as much, Grace and Marshall knew the truth. Their sibling bond was stronger than anything else. It would persevere — even through the death of the boy she loved. Grace would give up her dream of delivering babies in order to understand the neurological condition that plagued her brother.

The subway car bounced and swayed.

Grace checked her watch. Without the cover of her hat, she noticed the stares from passengers around her, which fell onto her unhidden face. They all pretended to read their phones, a device Grace had not yet acquired since her release, while they stole quick glances at her. She kept the sunglasses in place and ignored the gawking. Instead, her attention shifted to Daniel Greaves. She had felt herself falling for him when they found themselves together that summer. Grace knew her budding relationship with Daniel would likely cost her friendship with Charlotte, but she could not deny the feelings that were developing. That is, until a cool conversation with Marshall, when he mentioned that Daniel was stealing her the same way Henry had stolen her years before. To protect him, Grace had abruptly ended things with Daniel. He never accepted Grace's explanation that he should be with Charlotte, or that Grace's friendship with Charlotte was worth too much to ruin it.

By the time she met Julian in medical school, Grace felt that she had a better handle on understanding Marshall's condition. The years of different medications had finally been refined. His mood swings occurred less frequently, his temperament calmed. There had been, over the years, a growing independence as she and Marshall were separated while she was away, first at college and later at medical school. Marshall, Grace believed, had adapted to his condition and had accepted his limitations and his future prospects. The medications were working, and his physical therapy was keeping him away from a wheelchair and maintaining his individuality.

The first time she introduced Marshall to Julian was at Sugar Beach. It was a few days later — on that ill-fated night in March of 2007, when Marshall stood at the door of her cottage covered in blood and with his Lladró chess set hanging in the nylon bag from his fist — when Grace realized how badly she had miscalculated her brother's progress. She was saddened, not just that the man she loved was gone, but also that the brother she once knew was gone as well. Marshall was replaced now by this weeping person in front of her, a person incapable of controlling himself. A person she had created. She knew she would protect him, even though it would cost her dearly.

Today, with her newfound freedom, she was happy to dedicate her life to helping Marshall exist. And she had told him as much when she returned home from Bordelais, a long conversation had over their first game of chess in more than a decade. But now, Grace worried for Sidney. The elaborate plan to get Grace out of the apartment could only mean that Sidney wanted to be alone with Marshall. It explained Sidney's hastened departure the other night, when she had come to discuss a pressing issue but never got to it, instead departing quickly after her chess match with Marshall.

Grace's fear was that Sidney was now attempting to extract information about Henry Anderson and Julian Crist out of the very person from whom she should hide every detail of her discovery.

The subway mercifully slowed. Grace snaked through the doors as soon as they cracked open, and raced up the steps toward Windsor Tower.

CHAPTER 58

Saturday, July 22, 2017

Sidney blinked her eyes as she held the phone to her ear. She looked down at Marshall's feet as he sat in his wheelchair, still contemplating the chessboard and his next move. She saw thick-soled, black high-top shoes with heavy Velcro straps that provided stability to his wobbly ankles.

"You still there?" Gus asked through the phone.

Sidney tried to bring her breathing under control. Her eyes darted from Marshall's ugly orthotic shoes, to the open yearbook next to him, and the love lock on top of it. She looked at Marshall's old chess set resting next to their current game board. One of the pinewood cases was positioned halfway into its storage bag — a sheer material with a cinch string at the mouth, which she knew immediately was made from organza fabric. She looked at the corner of the compact Lladró chess case, noticed the smooth titanium elbow that covered the pinewood. She thought back to Livia Cutty's description of the shape of the weapon that likely caused Julian and Henry's skull fractures. Any of the case's four rounded edges would be a perfect match.

Grace asked me to put my chess set away because it brings back bad memories for her.

In an instant, it came together, and Sidney understood how badly she had gotten it all wrong. Her gaze finally moved to Marshall, who was still staring down at the chess pieces, analyzing his next move.

Without warning, Marshall looked up from the chessboard and made eye contact with her. Sidney wanted to leave calmly, to point casually to her phone and let him know she needed privacy. She'd be just a minute in the hallway. She'd done a similar thing hundreds of times. But during the second in which she hesitated, Sidney saw the hint of recognition in his eyes. Her face, she realized, told Marshall Sebold everything she didn't want him to know.

The phone dropped from her hand as Sidney stood quickly, the chair screeching across the hardwood and toppling backward. She turned toward the door, noticing from the corner of her eye that Marshall, too, was hurrying to stand from his wheel-chair. She managed only two steps before she felt it. A synapse that radiated through the neurons of her central nervous system, producing a jolt that coursed over her body. It started in the back of her head, a quick shock that stalled time and made her limbs heavy. Her legs noodled as she tried to lift them for another step. The hardwood floor rose up to fill her vision before the world went black.

The apartment door burst open and Grace ran into the living room. Marshall stood over Sidney's body, his old Lladró chess case and the nylon bag that had held it for the past ten years, hanging from his clinched right fist.

"No, Marshall," Grace whispered.

"She knew. She was talking with the detective from Whiteface. *Gus.* I heard her say his name. She knew everything."

They both looked down at her body. A syrupy puddle of dark red blood was creep-ing from underneath her and spreading across Ellie Reiser's hardwood floor.

"What do we do?" Marshall asked. He looked down at his old chess set hanging from his right hand, the strings of the satchel that held it wrapped tightly around his fist. He looked up at Grace next, as if he were surprised to see it in his hands. There was blood on the mesh pouch. He held it out for Grace to take.

"Help me, Grace."

She looked down at the body and the blood; then she looked up into her brother's eyes.

"You're going to listen to me very carefully," Grace said. "And you're going to do everything I tell you."

She took the nylon bag that contained the Lladró chess set. It wasn't the first time Grace Sebold's brother stood in front of her, covered in blood and asking for guidance.

Gros Piton
March 29, 2007

The blood was a problem.

He'd swung his chess set so aggressively that it split Julian's scalp, the gash spitting blood in a fast splatter across his face and shirt. It covered his hands and arms. His aggression was a manifestation of his anger. Julian acted like she belonged to him, looking at Marshall with pity and sorrow for the life that might have been. Marshall had an image of the way his life should be, and also the way it likely would proceed from here. He couldn't

504

change the past, but he would make sure his future got no worse. He knew what was coming. He could feel it in his tightening muscles and his defiant neurons. His fine motor skills were already failing. His ability to walk would soon leave him. His speech too. His aptitude for clear thought had succumbed to intermittent bouts of cloudiness. The combination of his ailments would come together in a perfect storm that would require more help than his parents could offer. Marshall believed the one who was responsible for his condition should be the one who stood up to assist. Running off with Julian Crist could not happen, the same way Henry Anderson was not allowed to take a bigger role in Grace's life.

Marshall needed Grace. He needed her now, and he'd rely on her more in the future. During their last "life management" meeting with his therapist, Marshall's parents had discussed in-home care. Basically, a stranger coming into the home at some point in his future to bathe him, change his clothes, and help him get to the toilet. Marshall was managing these things on his own now, but his therapist preferred presenting future events so Marshall had time to "process" the change that was coming. She had flipped open a brochure for a full-time facility, where those with traumatic brain injury and other chronic, debilitating conditions eventually "gathered." The therapist presented it like an opportunity, something to look forward to. His parents and the therapist had only gotten that far in their discussion of his future because Grace had been gone at medical school and had not been around to protest. Being in New York for residency would be a benefit, as she would be closer to him. But the idea that she would spend that time with Julian ate at him. Like Henry Anderson, Julian could not be allowed into Grace's life.

Marshall knew Julian's death would be a shock, but Marshall and Grace shared the secret of Henry Anderson. He knew she'd absorb this secret as well. They existed, Marshall and Grace, because of each other. They would endure together. It was the only way.

The spray of blood startled him and froze him. The blunder made his mind wander. He began to analyze his mistake and look for a solution, even before his current task was complete. He saw Julian stagger to his feet. Without thinking, he lifted his foot, kicked him forward, and watched him stumble to the edge of the bluff and over the side. The chance that this would be considered an accident, like the last time, was close to zero, given the blood that covered the granite bluff. It was a terrible error.

He made it back to the base of Gros Piton, breathing heavily. When he wiped his brow, the back of his hand came back smeared in red. He could only imagine a picture of himself, speckled in blood and sweat, with his chess set hanging from his shoulder as he ran through the resort. He waited in the shadows of Gros Piton while the purple glow of the setting sun spilled from the horizon and poured onto the white sand of Sugar Beach. A tuk-tuk was not an option, so the long trek back to the cottage would be on foot. His silhouette cut across the corner of the beach, unnoticed by those watching the sunset, as he headed into the foothills of the resort.

He was staying in a two-bedroom villa with his parents, and that, too, was not an option. Instead, he veered to the right when he made it up the steep incline. The door was locked when he tried the handle, and he worried that Grace had already left to meet Julian. He knocked loudly. When Grace answered, he simply handed her the bag that held his chess set.

"I need your help."

■ ■ ■ ■

PART V
ON THE ROAD
AGAIN

■ ■ ■ ■

Harold stood next to the chalkboard. His hands were covered in
a white, dusty coat of chalk. On
the board was a detailed summary
of the three previous days of
deliberation. He had taken the
morning to review meticulously
their discussion from each day,
making sure each juror was on
the same page and that there was
no confusion about the facts
presented during the long trial.

"It's now three o'clock on day
four. I think we've had a very
careful, and sometimes spirited,
discussion about the case. I
know I've learned a great deal
from listening to each of your
opinions, and I hope my own
views have helped shape our
decision. When we sat down four
days ago, we took an initial
vote that had us nearly split in
half. Today, after a careful
review of the facts, and unless
there are objections, I propose
we take our second vote to see

where we stand as a group. To complete this process, we all know we must come to a unanimous decision. Are there any objections to conducting an open vote again now?"

There were not.

"Okay," Harold said, taking a seat at the head of the table. "I'll need a show of hands. First I'll ask who believes she is guilty. Then I'll ask who believes she is *not* guilty. Are we clear?"

All twelve agreed they were.

CHAPTER 59

Thursday, September 13, 2018

The courtroom was standing room only. Each pew was packed, shoulder-to-shoulder. The front pews held family and friends. Those of the victim on one side; those of the accused on the other. The rest of the crowd was made of eager spectators that considered a spot in the courtroom more coveted than World Series tickets. Those standing in the back of the court were media; they not only clogged the rear walkway, but they also spilled out into the hallway. Those not lucky enough to gain access stood outside on the courthouse steps.

Local news stations and every cable news program had cut into regularly scheduled programming to bring the world the verdict live as it happened. After four days of sequestered deliberation, news had broken that the jury was back with a decision. Attorneys had been summoned, the judge was in chambers, the defendant was en route, and the jury members were being shuffled into the courthouse from their deliberation room. The participants had taken some time to assemble, which gave cable news a gratuitous hour to rehash the last three months of drama. Legal analysts, after witnessing closing arguments, had predicted the verdict would come immediately, perhaps after only a few hours of deliberation. But as the days passed, the experts predicted a hung jury. They all took to the airwaves now to offer new predictions. It was being called the trial of the young century, rivaling even the theatrics of the O.J. Simpson trial of the '90s.

The famed line "If it doesn't fit, you must acquit" from the Simpson defense team had been replaced this century by the prosecution's claim "If she did it in her past, it won't be her last."

At 5:06 p.m., Judge Clarence Carter rapped his gavel to bring the court to order. The crowded courtroom quieted as the judge prepared his notes. Only the hum of the fans that had been brought in to help cool the room was audible.

The judge gave the typical overview of how to conduct one's self in a court of law, and warned that immediate removal by bailiffs would be ordered if anyone veered from this conduct.

"Mr. Foreman," he finally said. "Have you come to a unanimous decision?"

"We have, Your Honor."

A bailiff took the verdict from Harold Anthony and delivered it to the judge.

"Will the defendant please rise?"

Sitting at the defendant's table in one of her designer dresses that no longer hugged her body the way they used to, now baggy and loose from weight loss, was Ellie Reiser. It had been fourteen months since Sidney Ryan's body was discovered poorly hidden in her apartment, a year since she was arrested for the murder, and three months since she first sat behind the defendant's table. She'd been released from her position at the hospital, and had spent her life's savings on her defense team. She stood.

"Dr. Reiser, will you please face the jury?"

Ellie turned with a somber expression and faced her peers.

The judge turned to Harold Anthony.

"Mr. Foreman?"

Harold stood and read from his card. *"Superior court of New York, in the matter of the people of New York versus Ellie Margaret Reiser . . . We, the jury, in the above entitled*

action, find the defendant, Ellie Margaret Rei-
ser, guilty of the crime of murder in the first
degree of Sidney Ryan."

The courtroom exploded with cheers and sobs, applause and moans. The judge rapped his gavel again. The crowd refused to quiet. Ellie put her hand over her gaunt cheeks and sank back down into her seat.

Amid the commotion, a man stood from the back pew and limped gingerly out of the courtroom on his prosthetic, until he was past the crowd of media people and in the hallway.

Chapter 60

Sunday, September 16, 2018

He hadn't been on the road for months. A steep learning curve came from driving with his left leg, but he felt there was nothing he could not conquer after ridding himself of the goddamn walker. And what better way to teach his left leg the nuances of pedal work than a fourteen-hour road trip? Now, out of the city and on the open road, with the windows down and the breeze strong in his face, he felt damn good.

Gus took the drive in two days. Four shifts of three hours, give or take. It had been more than a year since he had bid adieu to the folks at Alcove Manor. During the grand ceremony of his departure, he even managed to hug Nurse Ratchet on the way out — both smiling, but with looks that told another story. He had considered telling her to piss off, just a quiet whisper in her ear as she hugged him. He was sure a similar sentiment was on the tip of her tongue. Instead, when he had made it home, he lifted his prosthetic leg onto his coffee table, popped a beer, and turned on the Yankees game. Between innings, he picked up the phone and ordered flowers for each nurse to whom he had been a complete asshole. It wasn't much, but it was the best he could do.

He made the final three-hour stretch of his journey without issue. He had resisted the urge during the past two days to push his driving time much past three hours. He still worked once a week with Jason, who had warned about sitting for too long, and Gus had learned over the last year to listen to what the kid had to say. It was Jason who had originally gotten his ass up and walking, and without that kid, Gus might still be lying in the rehab prison, relieving himself into a plastic jug.

He found the hotel, checked in at the front desk, and politely turned down the young man's offer to help with his bag. His limp was visible, but less prominent than three months back. He had undergone his final fitting a month earlier when Jason completed the laser-scanning technique that allowed for the final design of his prosthesis, and Gus was still getting to know his new leg. He had turned down the "runner's option," which would produce a robotic-type extension from his hip that would allow for more versatile mobility.

"You'll be a literal Robocop," Jason had told him.

But Gus was no longer a cop, and agility hadn't been his strong suit when he had two functioning legs, so he saw no reason to attempt to achieve it with one. He chose the more practical solution of a carbon-fiber hip socket and 3R60 knee, which allowed him to walk with an almost normal gait that would improve with time and experience. The Ottobock Triton foot, as opposed to the Robocop futuristic boomerang, was designed to allow him to wear a shoe that, when wearing pants, made him look like any other sixty-nine-year-old man. It had been more than a year since he lost his leg, and he was doing better than anyone had predicted.

In his hotel room, he sat on the edge of the bed and removed his prosthesis. He rubbed his stump to relieve the pain, which still came from time to time. He sat back on the bed with his shoulders against the headboard, opened his fast-food burger, popped a beer, and pulled the file folder from his bag.

After an hour, he set the file aside, turned off the lights, and went to sleep.

CHAPTER 61

Monday, September 17, 2018

He left the hotel at nine o'clock the following morning and made the thirty-minute drive into Atlanta. He found the police department headquarters on Peachtree Street and pulled into the parking lot. He flashed his retired detective badge at the gate attendant, who saw gold and waved him through without scrutiny. Gus found a parking spot, refusing to use the handicapped spot in the front row, and walked to the entrance.

"Gus Morelli!"

Gus smiled as he managed the steps up to the front entrance. "Johnny Mack," he said when he reached the landing. They shook hands like the old friends they were.

"That a rental I saw you in?"

"They don't rent rusty '92 Beamers. I drove down. I needed to get out of the city and on the road again."

"Yeah?" John said. "The long ride's got you limping pretty good."

"Yeah," Gus said. "Fourteen hours did a number on my back."

"Come on in, pal. I'll get you a coffee and show you what I found."

Gus did his best to keep up with his old friend as John McMahon led him through the Criminal Investigation Unit. The guts of the Atlanta detectives' department didn't look much different from New York's, where Gus had spent the last decade of his career. After twenty minutes of touring, Gus finally sat down in front of John's desk.

"So," John said, pulling two boxes from the floor and placing them on his desk, "this case you asked me about is more than twenty-five years old. Had a hell of a time pulling the boxes, but here they are."

"How much trouble will it be for me to have a look?"

John shrugged. "I'm nine months away from retirement. No one is expecting me to follow any rules. And letting an old colleague look at an ancient cold case isn't going to raise any eyebrows."

"Thanks, John. I'm just gonna have a look to get myself up to speed on the details."

"Of course. Can I get you anything other

than coffee?"

"Yeah," Gus said. "You know some lab guys who could help me out?"

"Maybe. What do you need?"

Gus pulled an envelope from his pocket and carefully removed the tissue that was inside. He gently unfolded the corners to reveal the fingernail clippings.

"I need someone to run DNA analysis on these, and then compare them to what was found at the crime scene in here." Gus pointed to the box.

"I knew you were onto something when you called," John said. He looked down at the clippings. "I could probably find a tech that could do it. But it ain't cheap."

"Don't worry about the cost. I'll cover everything."

"Someone cashing in on a favor you owe them?" John asked.

"No," Gus said. "I'm just making good on a promise."

CHAPTER 62

Friday, September 21, 2018

His Atlanta road trip lasted nearly a week. Two days after his return, Gus bellied up to the bar at Jim Brady's, a favorite Irish pub in Tribeca. Paul, the proprietor, was an old friend. They caught up over a pint of Guinness, calling each other *Mick* and *Guinea* more times than anyone around them cared to hear. They toasted to Gus kicking cancer's ass.

"Let's hope it doesn't come back for another round," Gus said with a frosted lip. "I've only got one leg left to kick with."

"Well, my friend," Paul said. "I hope you're finally able to enjoy your retirement."

"Nah," Gus said. "This whole fiasco over the last year has shown me that I'm not the retiring type."

"You're not going back to the force, are you?"

Gus laughed. "I'm sixty-nine, with one

leg. No police force is taking me back. And I'm not interested."

Gus reached into his pocket and pulled out his wallet, opened it up to show Paul the license inside. It wasn't quite as powerful as pulling out his badge, but it still felt good.

Paul leaned over the bar. "Private investigator?"

"Passed the state examination last month," Gus said.

"What the hell is an over-the-hill, retired detective going to investigate?"

"A few cases from back in the day. They're calling me out of retirement."

Paul lifted his pint. "Maybe you'll stop in more often, like the old days."

Gus toasted his friend again. "Maybe."

Paul left to tend to other customers. Gus sipped his beer and ate a burger as he read the paper. He turned down the young bartender's offer to refill his pint, and waited for the lunch crowd to thin before he pulled the file folder from his bag. It felt just like the old days, sipping a pint and digging for clues. He was no longer a cop, and his retired detective's badge combined with his new P.I. license would only get him so many perks compared to the real thing. But he was also no longer on the clock, and he could choose what he spent his time on. He'd fulfill his promise to Sidney to look into her father's conviction. And he had plans to revisit the storage facility in the Bronx and dig through those old files that still haunted him. He was sixty-nine, he still had time. But before he dusted off cases from the past, there was another that was much more pressing.

He spent an hour at the bar reading through the file. When he finished, he looked up at the television. Airing was a replay of the final episode of *The Girl of Sugar Beach.* A year after taking America by storm, the documentary was being rerun in prime time, and replayed constantly during the day on the network's cable affiliate, to correspond with Ellie Reiser's trial, which had just wrapped. In the wake of Sidney's death the previous year, the final three episodes were watched by tens of millions of viewers. The final installment, which showed Sidney welcoming Grace Sebold as she walked through the gates of the Bordelais Correctional Facility in St. Lucia, and concluded with a shot of Grace Sebold standing on the Montauk Point Lighthouse as a free woman, arms outstretched, sweater like a cape in the breeze, had generated an audience of more than 60 million. The monstrous ratings were topped only by the recent trial that was connected to the documentary. Ellie Reiser's verdict, aired live on every network late on a Thursday evening, had been watched by more than 150 million people, matching the numbers produced when O.J. Simpson was found not guilty more than twenty years before.

Gus kept his eyes on the television until the shot of Grace Sebold atop the lighthouse faded and the words appeared on the screen: *In Loving Memory of Sidney Ryan.*

Gus motioned to the bartender.

"Give me two shots of whiskey, then close my tab."

"Jameson?"

"Johnnie Walker," Gus said.

The bartender returned a minute later.

"Need another beer with these?" the kid asked as he set the brimming shots in front of Gus.

"No thanks. Just some privacy."

The kid nodded and headed to the other end of the bar. Gus packed up his file and folded his newspaper. He stared at the mirror behind the bar, locked eyes with himself. Before cancer had found him, it was whiskey that had taken hold of his life. It hadn't been easy to admit, but the truth has a funny way of catching up to you when you spend six weeks in a hospital bed. He had decided his new life would come without the brown stuff, and he had done well over the last year to stay away from it. But a bet was a bet, and today there was no way around it.

He'd been close on his theory all those months ago. Close, but not quite right. And the circus trial that had taken place over the past few weeks had done little to convince him that the world was any closer to the truth about what had happened to the two boys who had loved Grace Sebold. But with so many unanswered questions, he knew one thing for sure. He was wrong about what he'd written to Sidney months ago. Grace Sebold didn't kill Henry Anderson. He was quite certain she didn't kill Julian Crist, either.

He took his eyes from the mirror and looked down at the two shots of whiskey. He picked one up, brought it close to his lips.

"Cheers, kid," he whispered before he tipped it back and swallowed it down. He stood from the stool and took a moment to right himself on his prosthesis; then he placed his empty shot glass next to the other. He stared down at the bar, afternoon sun spilled through the front entrance and slanted across the mahogany. He looked at the two shot glasses — one full, one empty — tapped his fist twice against the railing and limped out.

As he pushed through the front door and into the afternoon sun, his cell phone rang. Gus pulled it out of his pocket and looked at the display: *Dr. Livia Cutty.* He'd been expecting her call.

Gus placed the phone to his ear as he hobbled down the street.

"Hey, Doc," he said. "You got those results for me?"

CHAPTER 63

Friday, September 21, 2018

He took the 1 train from Jim Brady's to Brooklyn. He still had some contacts at the Metropolitan Detention Center, and had called ahead to make arrangements. Gus was on no visitor log, so an old friend pulled some strings and didn't ask questions. It was a popular request, and the gesture did not go unnoticed. It would cost him a case of scotch, but was well worth it.

When Gus walked up the subway stairs at Twenty-fifth Street in Greenwood Heights, the sun was still bright and hot. He took the five blocks with confidence, stopping only once to give his stump a rest. When he made it to the front of the detention center, he stood tall and did his best to hide his limp. His friend met him at the entrance, Gus pretended not to notice the subtle glance at his prosthetic leg, and they both entered the prison. His friend cut through the red tape Gus would otherwise have had to endure. Within ten minutes, he was sitting in a private visitation room made up of four chairs and a table. He was dressed casually in slacks and an oxford button-down shirt. His bag rested on the table and a snapshot of himself, seated with his hands folded as he waited, made the woman's first sentence logical when she entered the room.

"I don't need another lawyer," Ellie Reiser said. "Mine are crappy enough."

"Good. 'Cause I'm not a lawyer."

Ellie sat across from him. She was wearing standard prison orange.

"Who are you, then?"

"I'm an old friend of Sidney Ryan's," Gus said. "I'm also a detective. Used to be. I'm retired now, but I was working with Sidney when she died."

Gus ran his tongue along the inside of his cheek.

"I actually think I was talking with her on the phone when she was killed."

Ellie shook her head. "I had nothing to do with her death."

"I watched your trial. The whole circus," Gus said. "I was one of the regulars that showed up every day in court and sat in the back row." He pulled the file from his bag, opened the folder, and placed it in front of him.

"Let me summarize the prosecution's argument against you. Sidney goes to your apartment. She discovers that, due to some irrational jealousy issues you have about Grace Sebold, you killed not only Julian Crist in St. Lucia, but also Henry Anderson years before. The only two boys who ever loved her. When Sidney confronts you with her suspicion that Grace Sebold's love lock, which had for years been in your possession, was wrapped in a nylon bag and used to strike and kill both victims, you engaged in a confrontation with her. Ultimately you did what you do best. You used the love lock to strike Sidney and kill her. 'If she did it in the past, it won't be her last.' Do I have the argument correct?"

"My attorney told me not to speak to anyone who showed up unannounced."

"You might change your mind when you hear what I have to tell you."

Gus looked back to the file.

"Then there's the evidence," he said. "And it's overwhelming. The blood in your high-rise, which you poorly tried to clean up, the body hidden in the bathtub, the love lock stashed away in your drawer. The nylon bag that held it covered in blood. I could go

532

on, but I think a body, blood, and murder weapon are sufficient. It certainly was for the jury that convicted you."

Ellie continued to stare at him. Tears welled in her eyes as she shook her head and looked away. "I know how it looks. And if you were Sidney's friend, I know what you must think about me. The entire world despises me, and I have no idea how any of this happened to her."

"Listen, I'm old, grouchy, and bored," Gus said. "I'm also angry."

He closed the file and held it up.

"Here's my problem with all of this." He reached over and took Ellie's hand, gave her a gentle squeeze. When she felt the gesture, she looked up to meet his eyes, seeing the enemy she thought was sitting in front of her morph suddenly into an ally.

Gus offered a subtle smile.

"I don't believe it."

ABOUT THE AUTHOR

USA Today bestselling author **Charlie Donlea** was born and raised in Chicago. He now lives in the suburbs with his wife and two young children. Readers can find him online at charliedonlea.com.